CW00794175

WICKED BOND

(The Wicked Horse Series)

By
Sawyer Bennett

All Rights Reserved.

Copyright © 2016 by Sawyer Bennett

Published by Big Dog Books

This book is a work of fiction. Names, characters, places, and incidents either are products of the author's imagination or are used fictitiously. Any resemblance to actual events, locales or persons, living or dead, is entirely coincidental.

No part of this book can be reproduced in any form or by electronic or mechanical means including information storage and retrieval systems, without the express written permission of the author. The only exception is by a reviewer who may quote short excerpts in a review.

ISBN: 978-1-940883-49-6

Find Sawyer on the web!
www.sawyerbennett.com
www.twitter.com/bennettbooks
www.facebook.com/bennettbooks

Table of Contents

Prologue
Bridger

I WALK INTO my cabin that sits on Double J property, completely exhausted. We had a packed house at The Silo, so I stayed until the last customer left. When there are a whole lot of people doing freaky fucking, the hormones and pheromones that circulate can make them crazy.

As it turns out, I had to break up a fight between two girls over some dude's huge, pierced dick, as well as stop a whipping session that got out of hand because the fucker wielding the whip had no clue what he was doing. He drew unnecessary blood on a woman who wasn't prepared to handle that level of pain. Although she was fully consenting, and it was, in fact, her idea to let her "date" try some new kink on her, I knew she was going to be in a world of hurt if I let it go on. The dude was pissed and threatened to pull his membership. I grabbed him by the back of the neck, dragged his sorry ass out of The Silo, and told him his membership was revoked before I slammed the door in his face. The fucker had the balls to beat on the door. When he wouldn't stop, I opened it up, stepped out, and kicked his ass. It wasn't much of a fight as two punches—one to his jaw and then one to his right kidney—had him down moaning like a bitch and I'm sure he'll be pissing blood tomorrow. I had one of the male bartenders take him home with strict instructions to impart to him he'd get more of the same if he came back on the property again.

Then I went back in and fucked the girl he was whipping because she was all worked up despite his lousy job. Fucked her right in the same room her blood was first drawn with The Silo crowd watching. I did it dispassionately. Although, I did get her off too. I put her on her hands and knees, and, ignoring the people pressing their faces in on the glass, I banged out an effective orgasm. I really don't care for public sex, but it won't stop me if the mood strikes.

As per usual, the minute I felt my balls pull up with the need for release, I pulled out of her, whipped the condom off, and shot all over her back. I gave her a sharp slap on the ass at the same time, dragged my thumb through the wetness on her back, and then shoved it up her ass. She went off like a firecracker again, and my job was done. I left her on the floor panting as I tucked my dick back in and walked out.

So yeah… exhausted and more so than normal. It's been getting harder and harder to maintain my role as head of The Silo, and I'm not sure if it's because I've been doing it on my own for almost six months now since Woolf left or if I'm just losing the taste for all the kink. There was a time in my life that this shit was the only thing that kept me sane and grounded, but I'm finding I'm actually developing a bit of an intolerance for it. It's why I spend so much time holed up in my office at The Wicked Horse, depending on some of my most trusted Fantasy Makers to make sure things run smoothly.

Sadly, the people I can depend on are dropping like flies. First, Woolf exited the business when he got involved with Callie Hayes but I don't begrudge my best friend happiness at all. I'm still happy for him to this day, although I do miss him as we see each other very infrequently now. Then Cain fell for Sloane, Rand for Cat, and just recently, Logan gave it all up for Auralie. While these guys will always love to mix kink in their fucking, they're also the type who give up the days of debauchery once they commit to a woman. It's not unheard of for monogamous couples to frequent The Silo, but while those couples do indeed have an amazing amount of trust to lead this lifestyle, I've always known there's something missing from their relationship that leads them here.

Woolf, Cain, Rand, and Logan?

They have everything they could possibly want waiting in bed for them at home, so yeah… their days in The Silo are over, and it's just me left.

Sighing, I head into the kitchen and pull a beer from the fridge. I twist the cap off and lob it into the garbage can before taking my first pull. It goes down nicely, and before I can even take a second sip, I'm craving another beer already. It appears I'm well on my way to getting shitfaced, but after the crap I had to handle tonight, I deserve it.

I head into the living room, sit down on my leather recliner, and put my beer down on the table beside it. After I take off my boots—cowboy tonight, although on any other day, it could be biker boots—I kick the recliner back. I pick up my beer from the table as well as the necklace that lays there so I can examine it.

It's silver and tarnished with age with a simple lobster clasp that was broken years ago and never repaired. On the blackened chain rests a silver men's wedding ring that doesn't come off as I ended up tying the ends of the thin chain into a knot. I hold the ring up, which is also changing color with the passage of time, and I let memories take me over.

I don't want them to take me over, but they do anyway.

They do every fucking time I look at this necklace and ring, and I look at it frequently.

Flat on my back, tied up. Wrists to headboard, but my legs are loose and lying flat on the dirty, stained mattress. I let myself be tied, but I'm not here willingly. I'm here through no choice of my own.

She rides my cock slowly, hands to my chest, using it for leverage to slide up and down my shaft. The needle marks on her arm are like bright beacons, and I focus on them so I don't have to look at that fucking necklace and ring swaying back and forth as she fucks me.

"Feels good, doesn't it, baby?" she murmurs in a raspy voice thick with lust, but not drugs. She's always sober when she wants to fuck because she doesn't want the sensation of what she does to me dulled. She'll shoot up as soon as we're done.

I grunt in unwanted acknowledgment because as much as I hate this fucking bitch, my cock will give her what she wants.

I concentrate on the feelings… wet slide of flesh, my balls tingling with the need for release—not because I want it or crave it, but only because I want this done and this skank to get off me.

"Give it to me," she moans, moving on me faster. "Come inside me, Bridger, love. Give it to me."

I grit my teeth. Her words are foul, grating on my ears, even as they do their job and force my orgasm closer. I want it and I hate it. I'll hate myself even worse once I give it up.

"Mmmmm," she taunts me. "Maybe one day, I'll even let you knock me up. We'd make a beautiful baby together, wouldn't we?"

She recognizes her mistake right away as my eyes go blank and every bit of hated lust I'm feeling starts to slide away. My dick even starts to deflate, so she backpedals quickly. By that, I mean she reaches out and viciously twists my nipples. They're already reddened from the belt she used on me before she climbed aboard. The pain fires through me and gives her the intended results, my cock going rock solid again inside her well-used pussy.

She bounces harder and faster, and then she taunts me further by grabbing the ring swaying from the necklace in one hand and bringing it to her lips. Pushing it into her mouth, she sucks on it as she looks down at me in triumph before she spits it back out and pants, "You're so fucking good, baby. I'll never get tired of this cock, you know."

I'm on the edge and she knows it, so she propels me along by reaching a hand back and giving a vicious squeeze to my balls. They shrink and harden as the pain drives through me. With utter silence, I unload inside of her. I do it silently because it's the one way I can show this bitch that my body might react to her—and only because it's been brainwashed to do so—but that's the only acknowledgment she gets.

She watches me with interest as the orgasm ripples through me, and then she comes to a complete rest with my spent cock inside of her. She climbs off, not having achieved her own orgasm, but I'm not sure she's even capable of it. I've never seen it, and she doesn't fuck me to get off. She fucks me because she's a sick bitch who likes the power and control.

With a calm that shows just how whacked she is in the head, she undoes the ropes around my wrists and releases my bondage. She looks down at me with that smug look of superiority tinged with madness before bending over and placing a light kiss on the tip of my nose. It's an endearing kiss and I suspect, in her own fucked-up world, she's doing this to show she loves me.

The thought causes my flesh to crawl and fury to wash through me.

She gives me a condescending pat on my chest and starts to scoot off the bed. Before I can even reason with myself what I'm doing, my hand flies out and catches her around the back of her neck. Her eyes flare wide for a brief moment, sizzling with both anger and lust that I'd dare make such a move.

My other hand strikes, grabbing the necklace and tearing it from her body, the weak clasp easily shredding.

"Bridger," she shrieks, making a grab for the necklace.

I roll swiftly, using my grasp on her neck to flip her over me and down onto the mattress, where I throw a leg over her wasted body and straddle her.

"Get off me," she yells, and the fear in her eyes motivates me.

Motivates me to take my life back.

My hands wrap around her neck, the silver necklace wound through my fingers and the ring—my dad's ring—coming to rest at the hollow in her throat. I squeeze and for a brief moment, her eyes flash with lust.

This motivates me as well.

I squeeze harder. Moving my thumbs to rest over her windpipe, I press them down.

The lust turns to fear instantaneously, and fuck my soul to hell… that motivates me further.

I tighten my hands and I start to choke the ever-loving shit out of her. I watch, fascinated, as she gasps, her hands now scratching and clawing at my hands, her legs kicking underneath me frantically. She tries to buck me off, but the lack of oxygen and the fact she's weak of body makes her attempts futile. Her face turns a beautiful shade of crimson… not nearly as red as the belt marks on my chest, but enough to satisfy me.

It starts to turn purple, and her eyes bulge as they leak copious amounts of tears. I watch as a blood vessel blooms and bursts in her right eye, and that fascinates me too.

Leaning down, I hover my mouth right over hers, which is opening and closing like a gasping fish, and I whisper to her, "I'm. Done. With. You."

Her eyes are blank, mostly because she's oxygen deprived, and I'm not sure she even understands me. I make my point by releasing my hands from around her neck, taking only a moment to enjoy the red marks there that I know will turn purple as well, and roll off the bed. She immediately starts coughing and gasping, sucking in precious air. I bend down to the floor, pick my clothes up, and walk out of the bedroom.

I get dressed in the hallway, shoving the necklace and ring in my jeans pocket. I grab my wallet off the food-stained kitchen counter and make my way through the living room, where drunk and drugged-out people lay scattered all around, a few of them fucking on the filthy carpet.

I open the door and walk right out of my stepmom's house.

I'm just fifteen years old, but I'm never coming back.

A loud banging on my front door jolts me out of the memory, and for a moment, I'm confused as to what the sound is. But it comes again, louder this time.

Boom, boom, boom.

I kick my legs down, putting the recliner back in an upright position. After placing my beer and the necklace on the table, I stalk across my living room as the pounding reverberates through the house.

Without bothering to look to see who's outside, I throw the door open and glare at the intruder, only to have my jaw drop wide open.

Kyle Sommerville stands there, holding something cradled in his arms.

A woman.

An unconscious woman by the looks of it.

"What the fuck?" I say in astonishment, but then Kyle is barreling past me and causing me to step backward so he can make an entrance. I shut the door and turn to watch him walk over to my couch. He lays the woman down with incredible care.

"Jesus fucking Christ, Kyle," I growl at him, my eyes cutting down to the package he just deposited.

He spins on me, his face grim. "I need your help."

I stomp over to the couch and look down at the woman. Her eyes are closed, face pale with dark lashes fanning bruised skin underneath. Her brown hair is dirty and matted with what looks like blood, and there's dirt streaked all over her face. Her clothes are filthy as well.

"Who the fuck is that?" I ask as I point down to the woman.

"Listen to me," Kyle says urgently as he steps into me. "I am sorry for fucking involving you, but I had no choice. She is in serious fucking danger, and I need you to hide her for a bit."

"Are you out of your goddamn mind—?"

"Bridger," he shouts. "I'm not fucking around on this. She has one foot in the grave if you don't take her in."

"You cannot leave her here," I shout back at him. I have no clue what this crazy son of a bitch biker has gotten himself into, and I want no part of it. "Take her to the police or something."

"I am the goddamn police," Kyle snarls at me in frustration, and I take two unsteady steps backward.

"What?" I ask in bewilderment.

Kyle takes a deep breath, scrubs his hands through his long, blond hair, and says, "I'm ATF, and I've been deep undercover with Mayhem's Mission for over three years now. I've been investigating illegal firearms, drugs, and a sex-slave ring they're running through all the clubs throughout the Midwest over to the West Coast."

I can't even comprehend what he's telling me. This is Kyle Sommerville, badass biker who is yeah… a friend… but not a good one. I know him marginally, and never once did I ever get a whiff that he's law enforcement. I can't even begin to process because I've seen this fucker do shit that's highly illegal. I've watched him snort coke and clean what I'm sure were stolen guns. I've watched him fuck club pussy in the nastiest of ways, and I watched him cut a guy up at a party once just because he seemed to feel like it.

"I don't believe you," I say uncertainly.

"Why?" he mutters. "Because I'm really good at my undercover job? When you immerse yourself in this shit, Bridger, you go all in. You have to do the dirty with the people you get in bed with or else they won't fucking buy the cover."

That makes sense.

Sort of.

But shit… I thought that stuff only happened in the movies.

My eyes cut back down to the woman. I must believe some of what he says because I ask, "She part of the sex-slave trade?"

He shakes his head. "No, she's part of something bigger, and I need you to keep her hidden."

"Why me?" I ask with narrowed eyes.

"Because if I didn't get her out of there tonight, she was going to be dead by morning," he says ominously. "And I am not ready for this bust to go down. I've got three fucking years invested in this operation, and I've done stuff that has destroyed my soul. I've given up my life to bring these fuckers down, and I cannot let it be ruined. I have to see it through. But I couldn't let her die, either, so I'm begging you… just keep her safe until this is over."

"How long?" I ask, completely disbelieving I'm even considering this lunacy.

"I don't know. Weeks?"

"What's wrong with her?" My eyes cut down to the frail woman lying unconscious on my couch.

Kyle's body shifts and his head inclines, so I know he's looking down at her too.

"Everything, man," he whispers almost fearfully. "Everything's fucking wrong with her."

Chapter 1
Bridger

*E*VERYTHING'S FUCKING WRONG *with her.*

Kyle's words are still buzzing in my head as I look down at the unconscious woman.

He's only been gone a few minutes, but already I'm overwhelmed with the enormity of what he's laid upon me.

My first reaction is that this doesn't sound right. Kyle coming in here and dumping this on me, claiming he's undercover ATF. I feel like I'm being set up for something, but maybe that's just paranoia kicking in. Still, it's just too goddamn hard for me to accept that Kyle Sommerville is anything but a thug who rides with Mayhem's Mission.

Don't get me wrong… his criminal proclivities never bothered me. I don't judge, and I sure as shit don't get messed up in it. Keep that shit away from me and as long as you can do that, I can hang and party with the best of them. And I've partied with Kyle on several occasions, no doubt, which is why it doesn't make sense he'd come to me to conceal this woman. We don't know each other all that great because sharing booze doesn't necessarily lend itself to strong bonds of friendship. As such, he has no idea if I'll keep this woman safe or turn her over to Zeke. Shit, I've spent more time with the club president, Zeke, and his old lady, Kayla, doing all kinds of nasties with them, than I have with Kyle. How in the fuck does he not think I wouldn't have more loyalty to Zeke?

Not that I do.

I can't stand that son of a bitch actually. He's a thug times ten and rules that club with more than an iron fist. If the money he pays me weren't so fucking awesome, I would never do the kink he hires me for. Sadly, though, selling my services for money is what I know best. It's where my fundamental value as a human resides, so I'm not likely to turn my nose up at it.

The ironic thing is I don't need the money. I make plenty just off The Wicked Horse and The Silo. But it's not the same. A dollar earned for an orgasm I can dole out is far more valuable to my fucked-up sense of self than money earned otherwise. While I don't allow my Fantasy Makers to earn money for sexual services, I don't have the same qualms when it comes to me accepting it, and that's because I don't get off on what I do. It truly is just a job. There's no real pleasure in it for me, but it is important to me on a level no one could ever under-stand. Being the one controlling the whip and doling out the pain, while being revered for doing so to such an extent that I'm given true value for my abilities…

It's necessary for me to survive.

The woman on the couch hasn't moved, but I can

tell by the steady rise and fall of her chest that she's still breathing. And it looks strong too, which means there's no need for me to feel for a pulse. Still, the blood matted in her hair concerns me, and I'm afraid there may be other things wrong with her that I can't see. Maybe wounds under her filthy clothes or inside her mind… which I'm kind of thinking might be the case.

Everything's fucking wrong with her.

"Christ," I mutter to no one, as she can't hear me.

Pulling my phone out of my pocket, I flip through until I find Logan's number and tap the screen.

He answers with a, "Yo, dude?"

My eyes cut down to the woman, and I mutter another almost silent curse before I say, "I need you to come to my house. I've got sort of an emergency I need help with."

Logan doesn't question me but simply says, "I'm on my way. Assume you want me alone?"

"Yeah," I say, my eyes still pinned to the unwelcome visitor on my couch. Logan disconnects immediately without even a goodbye. It's best Auralie stays out of this, although Logan will probably tell her about it anyway. Those two practically have one step on the altar even though it's been a little less than a month since she's come back to live here with Logan. But when Logan finally decided to live in the real world, he jumped into the deep end with both feet and gave himself fully to Auralie.

About two weeks ago, Logan stopped by my office at

The Wicked Horse, almost timidly knocking on my door in the middle of the day. He came in when I called out the door was open, and by the look on his face, I knew immediately he wanted to unburden.

Turns out, the reason Logan was running from his demons was about as legitimate as I'd ever heard. Ranks right up there with my reasons, but Logan has more general fortitude than I do apparently because he decided to confront them rather than cherish them the way I do. He sat in my office for over an hour and told me all about his life in Chicago where he was a successful surgeon. My chest squeezed with pain for my friend when he told me his daughter died while under his care and the incredibly torturous guilt he'd been living under.

Why he told me these things, he never revealed, but I suspect it's because I had made a casual reference to my own demons to him once. I'd given him sage advice and told him that you can't outrun them because they're inside of you. He turned it back on me and wanted to know if I'd gotten rid of my own, but nah… they're still there, very much fluid and alive within me.

Like I told Logan… I'm keeping those fuckers around as a reminder to me of all the shit I've endured and what I'll never go through again. What I didn't specifically reveal to him was the importance of their reminder; it never lets me forget that love is for idiots and trust is for fools. Staying strong behind an iron wall of protection is far healthier to my sanity than opening up to the unknown. There isn't much that frightens me in this world, but not knowing what's around the corner causes me heart-pounding anxiety. It's exactly why this mess of a woman on my couch is wigging me out a bit. It's destroying my carefully ordered world.

While I wait for Logan to arrive, I walk back to my master bathroom, which is where I keep my first aid kit. It doesn't have much other than antiseptic and bandaging supplies, but I'm guessing it's going to be needed. I mull over what Kyle told me during his very brief visit, and it clearly wasn't enough for me to be able to wrap my head around whether or not I can trust him.

After he revealed he was undercover and then went all cryptic on me by telling me this woman had one foot in the grave, I pressed him for details because fuck if I was going to keep a half dead person in my house without a little bit more from him.

"Dude," I'd said in frustration. "You've got to give me more of an explanation. I do not want to get tangled up in something illegal with Mayhem's Mission."

Kyle shook his head. "I wouldn't ask that of you. She's got nothing to do with any of the illegal stuff."

I took that as solid verification she wasn't part of the sex-slave ring he'd mentioned. My fate was sealed when Kyle added on, "She's an innocent in all of this. Got caught up in that shitty world. It was going to cost her life if I didn't get her out."

"How would it cost her life?" I pressed, because I needed more still.

Kyle started walking toward my front door, apparently assuming I was on board with this woman staying with me. I was not, and I wouldn't hesitate to dump her at the police station door if he didn't satisfy my curiosity.

"Kyle," I barked as he grabbed for the door. "I need to know the trouble she's in before I agree to this."

His shoulders slumped. When he turned to me, it looked like he'd aged twenty years. "She's Zeke's property, and Kayla isn't quite on board with that. Zeke's on a run and for the past four days, Kayla's been torturing her. She wouldn't last another day."

"Torturing her?" I grit out in stunned disbelief. Not disbelief that Kayla could torture someone because that chick is seriously twisted, but that she'd bring it to the point of murder.

Kyle's eyes slide to the woman on my couch, and then back to me before whispering with such pain that it makes my ears feel like they're bleeding. "I've watched some sick shit happen over the three years I've been deep. I've watched people die. I've let people die while I watched. Just couldn't do it again. I had to get her out. I'm begging you to just keep her safe for a bit until I can get things finalized for the ATF to take this club down."

Jesus Christ.

I know all about being unprotected and alone, completely at someone's mercy. I know all about helplessness, sadistically delivered pain, and the hopelessness that comes with forced isolation and antipathy. Fuck me good and hard, that touched me deeply, although Kyle would never understand the power her plight had over me.

"Fine," I said as I exhaled a long breath. "Just… fine. I'll keep her."

Kyle merely nodded, then he was gone, and it appeared I was on my own with trying to figure out what the fuck to do next.

I carry the first aid kit back into the living room, seeing the woman is still laying in the same position, but I pause a moment to watch to make sure she's breathing. I don't get any closer to her, and I'm not sure why other than the possibility that she might stop breathing scares the fuck out of me.

Placing the kit on the coffee table, I sit back down in my recliner, but I don't lounge. Rather, I sit on the edge, feet planted solidly on the floor, and I sip at my beer as I watch the woman slumber in her unconsciousness. I wait for Logan to arrive, which he does not fifteen minutes after I hung up the phone with him.

His knock on the door is soft, as if he knows this whole encounter is covert. My socked feet padding across the floor are equally furtive, which is ridiculous really. I swing the door open and step to the side, my head nodding toward the couch.

Logan walks in, but then immediately halts when he sees the woman lying there.

"Who's that?" he mutters.

"No clue," I tell him honestly as I shut the door. "And I can't tell you the details of how she came to be here, but she's in danger and has been roughed up."

I purposely don't use the word torture, because I don't want to freak Logan out any more than necessary.

Logan veers off into my kitchen. While he told me the day he stopped by my office that he was never practicing medicine again, I can tell it's not going to stop him from helping me. "Let me wash my hands first," he says by way of explanation.

I wait in the living room for him, pacing back and forth nervously, my eyes cutting from the woman to my feet as they traverse the hardwood flooring made of reclaimed lumber.

When Logan returns, he rolls up his shirtsleeves before taking a seat on the coffee table by the couch so he can get a good look at her. "How long has she been unconscious?"

"Not sure. She was like that when he brought her here."

"Which was when?" he asks as he leans forward and takes a closer look at the dried blood on her head.

"About two minutes before I called you," I verify.

Logan nods and says, "I need a flashlight."

Turning from him, I walk over to the large entertainment unit against the wall and pull a flashlight from the drawer. I have them all over the house in case the power goes out. After giving it to Logan, I watch as he uses his thumb and forefinger to open one of the woman's eyes and shines the flashlight in it briefly, then does it to the other eye. She doesn't move a muscle or react in any way, which doesn't surprise me. I'd been observing her carefully since Kyle walked in my door with her, and she was truly unconscious.

After handing the flashlight back to me, Logan carefully prods at the bloody and matted hair on her head. He takes her pulse and seems satisfied. "I don't think this head wound is serious. Her pupils are reacting fine."

"So what's wrong with her?" I ask.

He turns to me and shrugs. "I'm going to have to give her a thorough examination, but Bridger... there's only so much I can do. I have no equipment. Hell, I can't even listen to her heart or lungs without a stethoscope. No clue what her blood pressure is. I'm sort of hamstrung here."

"I understand," I say gratefully. "Let's figure out what's wrong with her if you can, and then I can decide what to do."

Logan nods and turns back to the woman. I hover beside him, ready to help if he needs it, but otherwise not having a fucking clue as to how badly my life just got turned upside down.

Chapter 2
Maggie

LOW VOICES—MEN, I think—talking quietly. It hurts my head even though they're not that loud, and I fight the pull my body has to wake up. I don't want to hear what they're saying because I'm pretty sure they might be discussing something like the best way to get rid of my body. I don't want to wake up, because my body has clearly found solace in the state of unconsciousness. I've had plenty of experience with that the last few days, my body so overwhelmed with pain and my mind so overwhelmed with hopelessness, that I'm ready to give up.

Bright light flares, causes everything to go white before turning black again.

I lecture myself to relinquish hold of my increasing consciousness, and feel myself floating back under.

Bright light again, and oh… that hurts so much.

Even when it's gone, my brain seems to twist in agony before being left with pulses of electric pain.

The voices don't necessarily get louder, but I understand them a bit more clearly. I hate my body and its clear failure for self-preservation.

...don't think this head wound is serious...

...what's wrong...

...have to give her a thorough examination...

...then I can decide what to do...

A sharp pain jolts from the top of my head, down through my brain, and seems to sizzle down my spine. My eyes fly open, unable to ignore the sensation, and my hands go flying to push whatever it is away from me.

"Don't," I rasp out, my voice so shredded from hours of screaming that it's barely audible. Or is that because my eardrums are busted from the blows I repetitively took to my head?

The pain diminishes and I blink against the light now assaulting my eyes. It's not overly burning and I sense I'm in a dimly lit room, but coming out of utter blackness, it still hurts all the same. I try to focus, blinking again several times before I see a man start to take shape before me.

Dark hair, olive skin, full beard.

My brain is working better than I expected because I can immediately tell by the worry in his eyes and the state of his clothing that he's not Mayhem's Mission. No twinkle of appreciation for my pain. No tattoos. No stale beer smell. A button-down blue chambray shirt that no motorcycle gang member would ever be caught dead in.

"Who are you?" I ask tentatively, my vocal chords throbbing from the effort as I try to sit up on the couch. More pain throbs, not only from my head but also seemingly from everywhere on my body. I wince, grit my teeth, but still manage to pull myself up and push myself as far away from this guy as possible. He looks "nice," but I don't know him. The only thing that prevents me from getting any further away are the back cushions of a couch I'm apparently lying on.

The man smiles at me in understanding, but I don't trust that look one bit. There's no way he could ever understand the depth of my fear at this point.

He turns his head to the right and looks upward slightly. I follow his gaze, my eyes coming to rest on a terribly large man glaring down at me with his arms crossed over his chest. I shrink back further into the cushions because of the loathsome look on his face. That movement is not lost on either man. The big guy's facial features smooth out a bit, and I see a hint of guilt in his eyes for scaring me.

My eyes skitter back to the other guy, and he holds his palms out in the universal gesture of "calm down, we're not going to hurt you". It doesn't ease my anxiety at all, because I can't remember the last time I've been around someone who didn't want to hurt me.

"A friend brought you here," the bearded guy says reassuringly.

"I don't have any friends," I deny in the raspy voice that doesn't hurt quite as bad the more I'm using it. Now, more than ever, I'm distrusting everything about my circumstances.

"Kyle Sommerville," the big guy provides. His voice is deep, but it sounds like it's filled with smooth stone gravel at the same time. It has a rumbling sort of effect that causes shivers of—fear, maybe—to ghost across my skin.

Now Kyle Sommerville is absolutely a name that instills genuine terror, and the fact he brought me here means these men most definitely cannot be trusted. My body energizes, filling with adrenaline that spikes hard and makes me slightly dizzy. But the great thing about adrenaline is that it also masks pain, and in a surprise move that has both men rearing backward, I fly off the couch in a desperate attempt to escape. My eyes immediately land on the front door across the living room, and my feet hit the floor with a frenzied burst of near hysteria to get away.

The door races toward me… or am I racing toward it?

Doesn't matter, because I'm so damn close.

Almost there.

Just as my fingers brush the knob, large arms band around me from behind, pulling me away and back into the hard, muscular body of who I inherently know is the large man who called Kyle Sommerville my friend.

Pain bursts and blooms all over my body, the shot of numbing adrenaline quickly expended.

"Stop," I shriek against the agony in my back, ribs, arms, hips, and legs. I try to twist free, but the pain peaks so severely my head starts spinning and bile rises in my throat.

The arms immediately release me the minute the

word 'stop' leaves my lips, and I fall unceremoniously, my knees jarring solidly on the wooden floor. I ignore that pain because it's nothing compared to the electrical shocks that seem to be firing from every nerve ending. My hands come to the floor to support my weight and my back involuntarily arches upward as I gag reflexively against the firestorm of torment my body is feeling once again.

"Jesus," I hear the big guy growl from above me. I feel his fingertips delicately pulling at the bottom of my shirt that's ridden up a bit on my back. "Look at her."

I scramble away from him, fear of his touch—any touch—propelling me forward. My hand slips out from under me and my body twists toward the floor, the muscles and skin around my ribs screaming in protest. Nausea starts to rise again, but mercifully, darkness starts to seep in from the periphery of my vision.

And I go under, once again in a protective measure to escape the misery.

WHEN I START to wake up again, I immediately feel something is different.

First, I'm in a bed. I know this because the sensation of soft sheets and pillowy support under my head versus hard concrete under my back feels like heaven. In fact, I can't remember anything ever feeling this nice before.

I also feel warm.

And I don't feel pain.

I hesitantly open my eyes. The room is dimly lit from what appears to be a lamp to my right, although I'm afraid to turn my head to look at it. I fear the pain that might come from such a small maneuver.

"First thing you need to understand is that you are safe and no one is going to hurt you again." The voice is deep, lower and softer than I'd heard it before.

Still, I'm scared and can't help but jolt with awareness as I turn my head toward him. The first thing I notice, because how could I not notice when pain has been a part of my daily—no wait, hourly—existence, is that while I feel a dull throb in my head and from the multitude of bruises all over me, it's actually manageable. I take a deep breath and focus in on the large man, waiting to see what he says next.

"I get by your reaction last night that Kyle Sommerville is no friend of yours," he says tentatively. "So I need to tell you this so you can at least relax and know you're safe."

My eyes clear up a bit and I note the man is sitting on a chair beside the bed, leaning forward with his elbows on his knees. His face, while grim, is also gentle. He's actually quite handsome, something I hadn't noticed earlier, but that's not something I give a shit about. Who cares if he has beautiful brown hair that's untamed and longish as well as eyes the color of warm amber? I certainly don't.

But the fact those stunning eyes are gentle causes me to stay still.

For the moment.

"Kyle is not a friend of mine," the man says carefully. "He brought you to me and told me you were in danger."

"He wouldn't help me," I whisper.

The man nods in understanding. "He's a cop—ATF. He's been undercover for three years."

I shake my head. I don't buy it. Kyle's a sadistic son of a bitch. He egged Kayla on when she tortured me.

"I promise," the man assures me, as clearly doubt is written all over my face. "He got you out because he was afraid Kayla would kill you."

A tremor runs through my body because that is an absolute truth. She would have killed me for sure, and I know this because she told me she was going to.

After she finished making me suffer.

"Who are you?" I ask hesitantly. While I don't trust this big brute as far as I can throw him, I need to understand why I'm here if I'm going to escape. I need to know everything about my captor.

"My name is Bridger," he says in a voice like a low rumble of thunder that is oddly comforting right now. "I promise I'm not going to hurt you, and I'm not going to let anyone else hurt you."

That means nothing to me. Trust is earned, not handed out like candy. His few words of reassurance bounce right off, and my mind starts figuring out how quickly I can get away from him. If I can get my battered body out of this bed, that is. I tentatively dig my elbows into the mattress, trying to raise my upper body a bit to scoot up further onto the pillows below my head.

My body aches with the movement, but I'm stunned it's not the excruciating level I'd been accustomed to. This confuses me, so it's my next question. "Why don't I hurt the way I was a little bit ago?"

The man—Bridger—doesn't move a muscle, and I understand immediately he's trying to be unassuming. "I had a doctor friend come and tend to you. He treated your injuries while you were unconscious."

"The man who was just here?" I ask curiously.

Bridger shakes his head. "First, he wasn't just here. That was almost twenty-four hours ago."

I gasp as I realize I've lost almost a day with no recollection, and yet… it's probably the best twenty-four hours I've had in years.

"And no," he continues. "That was my friend, Logan, who has some medical training, but he couldn't handle what was wrong with you. I had to call another friend in for a favor."

"A favor?" I ask, now suddenly wary again.

"Yes. A favor," he says, and there's no mistaking the distaste in his tone. "He bound your ribs and cleaned the wound on your head. Although it was too late to put stitches in it, he did stitch up some cuts you had on your stomach. And he gave you a shot of a painkiller. I've got some more pills he left. You had some about six hours ago, but I'm assuming you don't remember that as they're pretty heavy duty."

No wonder I felt fairly good. I was doped up, but again… was thankful for the reprieve. Perhaps I was actually in good enough shape I could get out of here now.

I start to sit up from the bed as I say, "Well… Bridger… I do appreciate your help, but I've probably imposed on you enough—"

"Lay down," he orders me, and because the effort of trying to lift myself up is fairly draining, his words and command have me immediately sinking back down again as my head swims with dizziness. "Those were some fairly heavy narcotics he gave you. You're not going anywhere for a while."

"But… I need to go," I mumble, the effort of just that small maneuver having seemingly exhausted me. My eyes feel heavy.

"No, you don't," Bridger says softly, and I'm surprised by the gentleness of his tone. It's almost as if the gravel in his vocal chords were replaced by velvet. "You're going to stay here until you're healed, then we'll figure out the best way to keep you safe."

I can't help it. I don't want to trust a thing he says, but I feel the weight of injury, stress, and exhaustion pressing down upon me. I haven't slept more than brief snatches of time here and there for the past four days— last twenty-four hours excluded, of course. My eyes start to lower, my body demanding I give in to the drugs and the need for rest.

Before I fall back under, I find the strength to look at

him for a moment and ask, "Bridger… what's your last name?"

"Payne," he says simply.

Ironic, I think, just before I close my eyes and give in to my fatigue.

Chapter 3

Bridger

SCOOPING THE SCRAMBLED eggs from the pan, I transfer them to the plate next to the bacon I'd nuked in the microwave before turning to the toaster and pulling out two pieces of blackened bread. I curse at my ineptitude when it comes to the simple act of making toast, throwing them in the sink where I'll jam them down the garbage disposal later.

Pulling two more pieces of bread from the bag, I put them in the toaster, adjust the timer to a lower setting, and try again. While that's in process, I reach across the counter and pick up the bottle of hydrocodone, shaking two pills from it. I then do the same with the antibiotics. It's time for my mystery guest to wake up, so I can feed and medicate her again.

I saw the bruises, welts, and cuts all over her body from the top of her head to her calves, and I know she's going to need the strength from the food and the numbing effect from the narcotics. It's going to take her a few days before she'll be able to move around without these precious drugs.

Logan and I were utterly sickened the night before

last when we got a peek at her back. We were both stunned when she tried to bolt out of my house, faster than I could have ever imagined anyone in her condition moving. I reacted on instinct, lunging at her and grabbing her from behind in a bear hold.

But the moment she shrieked at me to 'stop,' I immediately recognized the sound of pain in her voice, not panic, and I dropped her like a hot potato. When she fell to the ground and her shirt climbed up a bit, I had to swallow hard against the bile that was forming after seeing the black, blue, purple, and green that covered her exposed skin. Kyle had said she was tortured, but he clearly wasn't conveying to me the brutality of what happened to the woman whose name I don't even know, who is now sleeping in my bed.

After she passed out, Logan helped me get her to my room. We unceremoniously stripped her down, taking advantage of her unconsciousness so we wouldn't hurt her while she was examined. Logan dispassionately cleaned her up as best he could with a warm, wet cloth and antiseptic. Both of us made sounds of disgust low in our throat as we took in the bruises that covered most of her body, and Logan managed to clean some of the blood off her for a better look. But bruises were only part of it as Kayla apparently took a knife to parts of the woman's body. Mostly shallow cuts that coagulated and crusted over on their own, but one to the middle of her abdomen that was still open and oozing with blood, so it appeared to be fairly fresh.

It was patently clear to me without Logan saying a word that this was beyond his capabilities. Well, maybe not beyond his capabilities, but it was beyond his reach. He didn't have a license and he had no access to the necessary supplies he'd need, not to mention the clear fact that this woman needed medication for recovery.

As such, I had no choice but to call someone else to help. I weighed the option briefly, remembering Kyle's words of warning over the secret nature of his operation, but figured he'd want her to get the help needed. It justified the call to one of The Silo's patrons, Jared Crossgrave. He's a doctor who practices general medicine in Jackson and has been a member of The Silo since we first opened.

When he arrived, I sent Logan on his way.

I then impressed upon him the secrecy I'd require before I asked him for his help and revealed to him the woman in my bed. He promised complete confidentiality, but as I'd told the woman last night, he wanted a favor in return.

After he patched her injuries, then shot her up with something to kill the pain and ensure she'd rest for several hours, Jared asked for his favor.

A hard ass fucking, but I wasn't surprised. The guy is as gay as they come, but in conservative, rural Wyoming, it's not something he feels he can reveal to the public. So he keeps his oblivious wife happy with fancy cars and jewelry, and he's managed to fuck her at least on two occasions as he's got two kids, but outside of that... he gets his gay rocks off in The Silo.

I don't begrudge him this. In fact, I'm pleased he has The Silo to turn to. It's one of the reasons Woolf and I opened it, so we could provide a haven for people to express their sexual desires. For closet homosexuals, it's probably more important to them than just people into generalized kink. Jared comes in a few times a week, happily sucking dick and getting his ass pounded as he prefers bottom. Because I know his dirty, dark secret he's afraid to reveal to the world, I knew I could call him and be guaranteed relative security in obtaining his help.

As I said, I'm not surprised he wanted me to fuck him. He's made no secret of his attraction to me, and he has subtly inquired to others how he could catch my notice. He'd learned relatively quickly that I don't give my notice to anyone in The Silo unless they had a penchant for some hardcore BDSM and only then, I'll hand it out without taking anything in return but cash. Jared might like his sex a little rough, but he's not into the type of pain I would normally hand out.

So Jared treated the mystery woman and after handed me two prescriptions written in my name for a painkiller and antibiotics, because he thought the open wound on her stomach looked a little irritated, he primly asked if he could collect his favor immediately.

I didn't care one way or the other and gave him a careless shrug before leading him into one of the spare bedrooms. Because I know Jared is generally submissive and finds thrill in being controlled, I grabbed him by his hair, pushed him to his knees, and made him suck my dick for a few minutes just to get me hard.

I did this all with almost robotic precision, putting on a show for this man as much as I would if I was caning someone inside The Silo. I know how important it is to someone like Jared to feel as if I were as into him as he was into me.

But the truth is that I wasn't into him at all. Nope… not into guys, preferring warm, wet pussy, but that doesn't mean I won't fuck ass, male or female. I'll do anything with my cock really, as I see it as nothing more than a tool I can use for personal gain. Not talking about orgasmic gain, although that certainly happens when I let it, but rather as a way to meet my needs, whether they are sexual or not. In this case, I needed a doctor's services on the sly. He wanted my dick.

So he gagged and choked on my cock as I fucked his mouth for a bit, because I knew that's exactly the way he wanted it, then I fucked his ass. I lubed up good, and I pounded him hard, just the way I've watched him take it time and again in The Silo.

My mind wandered as I serviced him, worried about what to do with the woman in my room. I'd become adept at multitasking, able to fuck my way to an orgasm without much thought. My cock knows what to do and my body reacts because that's what it's been trained to do. I could probably engage in a focused chess match as I was ploughing someone, able to stealthily checkmate my opponent while getting my rocks off. That's just how good I am at compartmentalizing my sex away from the rest of me.

So Jared squealed like a little girl as I tunneled in and out of his ass, all the while his hand worked his own little cock feverishly. It ended satisfactorily to him as he shot his load all over my guest comforter with a moan of relief—which I made a mental note to throw away and buy another—and I pulled out before I came, snapped the condom off, and shot my spunk all over the back of his legs as I wasn't paying attention to my aim.

As I orgasmed, I had a very brief moment of respite. As with every time I come, it's not necessarily pleasurable and it's never earth shattering. Rather, it's more like a purging of a sickness and there's a second… maybe two… where I'm numb to everything. It's the paralysis of all my senses that I enjoy, giving me relief from my existence even if it's over all too quickly. Probably why I fuck so much, always seeking to extend that moment of oblivion.

Whatever shot Jared gave the woman, she was out of it for almost twenty-four hours. Didn't mean she slept that whole time, and I'm sure she has no recollection, but I helped her get out of bed and to the bathroom twice during the night and once the next day. She mumbled her thanks and once called me Aunt Gayle, but then she slipped back into heavy slumber when I put her back to bed.

The reason I knew she needed to go to the bathroom was because I sat by her bed that entire time. I was terrified to leave her—sure she'd wake up at some point completely lucid and ready to bolt. But she didn't, except for that brief conversation we had where I think I was successful in reassuring her she was safe, and then she was out again.

I'm pretty sure she's sleeping so hard, not because of the shot Jared gave her, because that would have worn off a while ago, but because she was utterly exhausted both in body and in mind. I would like to think that she accepted my assurances of safety and was able to let her body fall into a restful sleep that would help to heal her.

But now it's time for her to get up, and the two pieces of toast popping up brings me back to task. I pull them out, relieved they are lightly browned, and spread some butter, followed by some raspberry jam, on them. No clue if the woman will like it but if she doesn't, she doesn't have to eat it.

I take the plate along with cutlery and a glass of orange juice back to my bedroom. I put her in there because I wanted her to have the bathroom close by if she needed it, and also because I felt she deserved a nice bed after all she'd been through. Why that matters to me, I can't figure out, but when I saw her injuries, something within me committed to helping this woman.

Just like I'm almost powerless not to equate pain and pleasure together, as well as harboring an extreme desensitization to sex because of my upbringing, I'm also equally as powerless to turn my back on someone who's been abused.

The moment I turn from the hall into the master bedroom, I'm immediately relieved to see she's awake and sitting up in the bed. She's wearing one of my t-shirts, which swallows her up, and the blankets are pulled up around her lap.

"Brought you some breakfast," I say as I walk in toward her, and I note with a measure of satisfaction that there's less wariness in her eyes than I've seen before.

"I heard you banging around out there," she says softly, but there's no humor in her voice. In fact, it's quite flat.

"You must be starved," I tell her as I sit the plate down on her lap and place the juice on the bedside table, along with the medicine. "And there's some more pain medicine as well as antibiotics to take after you finish."

Her eyes slide to the pills, and then back to the plate before she gingerly picks up the fork I placed on top of the food with the handle hanging off the side. "Thank you."

"How do you feel?" I ask as I take the chair beside her bed. While I want her to eat, I also want more answers.

She gives a shrug and scoops up a forkful of eggs. Before she puts them in her mouth, she says, "Maggie."

"Excuse me?" I ask, confused by her answer.

"My name's Maggie. Thought you'd want to know." She places the eggs in her mouth and chews as she stares at me.

"Maggie what?" And I feel a little shitty for not having asked that first.

She swallows and murmurs, "Waylon. Magdalene Waylon, but my friends call me Maggie."

Interesting she lumps me into the friend category, but I know deep down she doesn't mean it. She may not have that wariness in her eyes and she may be accepting my food, but I can tell she's still holding herself out as an island amidst a sea of sharks just waiting for one to take a bite out of her.

And because I know a little something about abuse and how to deal with it, I start off with more reassurances. "Just want to remind you about our short talk last night. You're safe here. No one knows you're here outside of my friend Logan and the doctor who treated you last night, but they won't tell a soul."

"And Kyle," she says, fear edging through her quiet tone.

"He helped you," I remind her.

She doesn't argue, just picks at the bacon, removing a tiny portion and putting it in her mouth. It's a sweet mouth, actually… now that my focus is drawn there. She has full lips, and I got a peek of straight, white teeth when they parted. Yeah… I know most guys look at lips and think of blow jobs, but I look at them and think of biting. So lips are interesting because they hide the teeth that can cause sweet pain, and I love a soft, generous pair that peel back just before the teeth behind sink into skin.

My cock twitches at the thought, but I banish it. This woman is off limits, and besides, she's not all that attractive.

Well, that's not exactly true. I can't really tell as she's still covered in a lot of dirt and some blood Logan didn't get off, not to mention black and blue all over. But her hair is long and wavy, a pretty shade of brown that has hints of caramel and rust within. And her eyes… very nice… a soft, summer green. Body is definitely to my liking, and by that, I mean she's soft and curved with a figure I think most women think makes them "fat," but I find the soft swell of a woman's belly and an ass I can sink my fingers into hot as fuck. I suspect this has to do with the fact I was abused by a stepmom who was nothing but a skinny sack of bones, and so my attraction is for the exact opposite of that.

But whatever.

I shake my head and tell her, "I need you to tell me what's going on so I can figure out the best way to keep you safe. Kyle didn't say much other than you were being tortured by Kayla and that he had to get you out of there."

"You trust he's with law enforcement?" she counters, not answering my questions.

I'm honest with her. "I'm not sure. I don't know him all that well."

"You know Kayla though," she guesses. "I could hear the familiarity in your tone."

Christ, did I know Kayla. I'd whipped and caned her before. Did lots of kinky shit while her husband watched. Still, I'm careful when I answer. "I know both

Kayla and Zeke, but I am not friends with them. I don't owe them any loyalties."

Except I kind of do. Zeke turned over one of his men who'd attacked my friend Cat to the police, and in return, I'd promised to put on some "shows" for his club with the bevy of free and loose pussy there. Not sure when I'd have to fulfill that obligation. If I'm lucky, Zeke won't call to collect before Kyle can bring the club down.

Assuming Kyle is telling the truth.

"Can I finish eating, and then perhaps get a shower first?" Maggie suggests tentatively. "Then I'll tell you everything."

I have no clue if she's playing me. She could crawl out my bathroom window for all I know, but I really can't keep her prisoner here.

So I place my hands on my thighs and push up from the chair as I say, "Sure. You can rummage through my drawers. I have some sweatpants and stuff in there. Take whatever clean stuff you want, and we'll get your clothes washed after. I'll be waiting in the kitchen."

I don't wait for her to answer, and I figure she'll either come in there after she gets cleaned up or she'll sneak out and run. I find I'm probably okay with either choice she makes.

Chapter 4
Maggie

THE EGGS, BACON, and toast fortified me. The shower made me feel nearly human again. There was a brief moment where I considered declining Bridger's hospitality and just leaving, but I really had no clue where to go. I had no money, which meant no food, transportation, or shelter. I had no friends. I had no family I could call upon, save for one, and no way was I dragging her into this.

So I decided my best course was to stay here and recuperate. Hopefully, along with regaining my strength, I'll come up with some idea on how to save myself first, and then Belle after.

I was sore as hell when I got out of bed, the effects of whatever shot I was given having faded long away. But I popped the pills Bridger left by the bed without even once considering they could be dangerous, because that's what happens when you run out of options and you're too tired to think about self-preservation. I figured if the worst that happened was I overdosed on some bad drug, at least Belle would be safe and well cared for.

As it turned out, the pills dulled the pain again even

though they made me a little foggy. The shower also helped loosen my sore and abused muscles, as well as cleaned the dirt and blood from my body. I carefully washed my hair three times with some manly smelling shampoo Bridger had, not feeling guilty at all to be wasteful, and being overly watchful of the scabbed-over cut on the top. It had been days since I'd been clean. I felt I could have scrubbed myself ten times over and still wouldn't be able to get rid of the complete stench of the Mayhem's Mission compound.

The shower took a long time, but it took even longer for me to comb the snarls out of my long hair. Not only were there knots galore because it had been so filthy and neglected, but Bridger also didn't have any conditioner—must be a man thing—and I ended up yanking a good amount out of my head by the time it was all said and done. The good news was the cut appeared to be knitted together enough it didn't bleed again.

Almost an hour after my breakfast and cleansing, I pull on a pair of workout shorts I found in Bridger's drawer. They're huge, and I have to roll the waistband several times so they'll stay up. I then pull out a black t-shirt with a logo on the back that says "The Wicked Horse." The words are in neon blue. I pull the cotton tee over my head without putting my filthy, sweat-stained bra back on. This bothers me a bit because I'm quite large chested, but the t-shirt is massive and swallows me up, so I don't think Bridger will notice my puppies swinging free. Besides, I'm assuming he's seen them already since I was already wearing one of his shirts.

He's an interesting man—this Bridger Payne—and I've figured out a few things. The furniture in his bedroom is heavy and masculine. The comforter is navy blue with taupe sheets. The drawers of his dresser are filled with only men's clothing without a scrap of girlie stuff in the bathroom. This tells me he's single and does not have a woman stay over at his house.

His bedroom and bathroom are immaculate. Everything is picked up and orderly. Even his clothes are folded with almost military precision. This tells me he's disciplined.

Finally, the night I was brought to his house, I'm pretty sure I heard him having sex with another man. While my mind was cloudy from the medicine, I have what I believe is a solid memory of a male—maybe the doctor, or maybe the man he called his friend Logan—crying out, "Fuck my ass harder, Bridger." This was accompanied by moans and squeals that, while they sounded girlish, were clearly from a man. Definitely not Bridger because his voice is much deeper, and you can tell by looking at him that he'd never squeal or moan. No, he'd be the type who would curse and grunt if something felt good to him. But I know I heard those words.

Fuck my ass harder, Bridger.

So yes… pretty sure Bridger had sex that night, so that tells me he's gay, which also explains the lack of anything female in his house. This makes him interesting because he most certainly doesn't look and act gay, but it really means nothing to me. I don't care what he is as long as he helps me out like he promised, and I've decided to accept his help. While I don't necessarily trust his words, his actions are speaking to me. He's gotten me medical attention and fed me. He's clearly protecting me as Kayla, Kyle, or any other club member hasn't shown up to drag me back to hell. So I've decided that my best course of action is to grudgingly accept his help and hope to God he follows through with his promises to keep me safe.

It's the best course of action.

It's my only one at this point.

Gathering my empty plate and glass, I head out of his bedroom and down the hall, which leads me into a living room with an open kitchen just beyond. Bridger sits at a square table set in a nook off to the side, his eyes pinned on me as I walk toward him.

With a nod of his head toward the sink, he says, "Just lay those in there. I'll get them later."

I round the large kitchen island done in distressed gray wood with black granite tops and place the items in the sink. The kitchen is gorgeous, also immaculately kept except for my now-dirty dish and glass, and reeks of money. My eyes glance back to the large living room I'd walked through. It's filled with high-end leather furniture, an expensive-looking entertainment unit, and a TV more massive than any I'd ever seen before. While his house isn't overly large, the appointments are luxurious.

"Let's talk." That gravelly voice floats across the kitchen to me, and the hair stands up on the back of my neck. It's so deep and masculine. I'm having a hard time reconciling that I suspect he's gay.

Turning back toward him, I keep my eyes lowered as I walk across the tile flooring to the table, taking a chair opposite of where he sits.

"Feel better after that shower?" he asks gruffly.

I slowly raise my head to look at him. "Yeah," I murmur, my throat not feeling nearly as shredded. I think it might have to do with the fact I haven't used my voice much the past two days. "Thanks."

He nods and cuts to the chase. "So what's the deal? Why was Kayla torturing you?"

"Because Zeke wants me." I tell him the simple truth. I've decided to give it to him because seriously… what do I have to lose at this point?

A flash of irritation crosses his face. "Try again. Zeke wants and fucks other women in the club, but Kayla's not the jealous type. She's his old lady and at the top of the food chain."

"Not true," I mutter, and he blinks at me in surprise. "I'm at the top of the food chain, and Kayla's one rung below me."

"Explain," he says calmly. "Because what I know about Zeke, pussy is pussy to him."

I wince, because that's so crude even if it's utterly accurate. But I've been listening to crass men for a very long time, and I'm not easily offended. But the truth is, while I was in the shower, I did a lot of hard thinking about what I should disclose to Bridger. My initial fears of this man and my current situation have been somewhat alleviated. While my base instinct is not to trust him, especially since Kyle is the one who brought me here, I finally decided I had to give a little. I deduced this by reasoning it would have made no sense for Kyle to bring me to a man who would just turn me back over to Zeke. It served no purpose. In fact, it would have angered Zeke if Kyle or anyone had dared remove me from the compound, regardless of what Kayla was doing to me.

So I decided I had absolutely nothing to lose at this point by disclosing the truth as to what had happened to me. The worst-case scenario is I'd end up right back where I was if Bridger didn't want me here. The best-case scenario is I could stay safe until I had a good game plan.

"That's true," I tell Bridger simply. "Zeke doesn't care what he fucks, but the difference between Kayla and me is that her ovaries are dead and shriveled, and she can't give him what he really wants."

"What's that?" he asks cautiously, but he knows what I'm saying.

"A child," I provide with a direct stare.

"And you can?" he asks dubiously.

"I already have," I murmur, my eyes misting up as I think of Belle's sweet face and her baby fine hair that's blonde but will turn my color, I'm sure of it. She looks exactly like me when I was a baby and has nothing of

Zeke inside of her.

I am also sure of that.

Bridger jolts from my proclamation. "You had his baby?"

"I did, and I have her hidden away from him," I say with my chin raised high. "And he's never finding her."

I also decided to be truthful about this, because again, nothing to lose and Belle is not a secret. If Bridger is really friends with Zeke and intends to give me back to him, he'd already know about Belle.

I can see as comprehension dawns fully within his eyes, which are actually a shade darker right now… almost the color of a copper penny. They are really quite beautiful. He stands from the table and walks over to the refrigerator. Opening it, he pulls out a bottle of water and holds it up to me. I nod and he reaches back in, pulls another bottle out, and comes back to the table. Setting one of the bottles before me, he opens the other and takes a long pull from it. Rather than sit back down at the table, he walks back to the island and takes one of the stools done in dark gray wood and wrought iron.

"Start from the beginning and tell me everything," he commands. It's not said in a superior, domineering way, but rather with frank curiosity tinged with worry over my circumstances.

I open the bottle of water he brought me and take a few sips, loving the soothing coolness against my raw throat. After setting it back down, I take a deep breath and tell him my story.

"I left home about ten years ago." I start from the beginning as he instructed me. "Nice family, upper middle class. But I was a rebellious kid and thought I knew more than my parents did. Set off at eighteen to see the world and never looked back."

"Where did you go?" he asks.

"Everywhere and nowhere," I reply. "My parents are from Cheyenne, and I'd lived in Wyoming my entire life. Headed west but never made it past Idaho. My grand adventures got sidetracked because I fell in with the wrong crowd. Worked odd jobs, partied, did drugs. Became a complete failure in life… at least that's how my parents saw it."

"How did you meet Zeke?" he prods. Apparently, he doesn't need the details of my vagabond years.

"I drifted back this way, hoping to find some steady work in the area. Met Zeke in a biker bar. He got me drunk and fucked me. The rest is history."

"How long ago was that?" he asks.

I shrug. "About three years ago. He moved me out to the Mission compound, which was great by me. I didn't have a job, hardly any money, and was one step away from living on the streets."

"You became a club whore?" Bridger asks, his voice tight with tension.

"No," I tell him with brutal honesty. "I became Zeke's whore. No one was allowed to touch me."

"And how did Kayla respond to that?"

Another shrug. "Like you said, she's not a jealous

woman. She knows and accepts Zeke fucks around. We avoided each other and just sort of existed in that same space together. Of course, she lived with Zeke out of the compound, so I didn't really see her unless there was a party she came to. Zeke visited me at the compound when he wanted."

Bridger's lips flatten out in a look of distaste, and it makes me feel dirty. I mean… I am dirty. I let myself become a kept whore, but for some odd reason, I don't want Bridger to view me that way. He's the first man to show me a measure of kindness in well over a decade, and that alone makes me respect him somewhat.

"You became pregnant?" he asks, keeping the story flowing.

"Condom broke," I tell him in a voice roughened with emotion. "It was the moment my life changed for both the better and the worst."

"Boy or girl and how old?" he asks, cutting even quicker to the chase.

"Girl," I tell him. "Her name's Belle, and she just turned two a few months ago."

"Where is she?"

"That I will never tell you," I say fiercely. This is where I draw the line and keep the most important truth to myself. "She's safe and far away from Zeke."

"You ran with her?" he guesses.

"Yeah," I say bitterly. "I ran just after she turned two. I got her to safety. After that, I ran in the opposite direction of Belle, knowing he'd eventually find me."

"And when was that?"

"About a week ago," I murmur. "Found me in Nebraska and dragged me back. Kept me locked up at the compound and tried to force me to tell him where Belle was."

Bridger utters a low curse. "What did he do to you?"

"Beat me," I say in a matter-of-fact tone. "Thought he could beat the information out of me, but that fucker underestimated my resolve. I'll die before I give Belle up to him."

Bridger nods, and I see a healthy dose of respect in his gaze. He takes another sip of water. After he swallows, he says in a gentle voice, "I'm going to play devil's advocate here for a moment, but Zeke's her father. Doesn't he have a right to see her?"

Rage fills every fiber of my being that he would even dare to suggest such a thing. But still, I keep my voice as level as possible. "How well do you know Zeke?"

"Not well at all," he admits. "Been around him a handful of times."

"Well, that should have been plenty for you to get he's a mean son of a bitch. Runs that club as if he's Hitler and uses that same mentality on everyone around him, even his baby daughter. He's rotten to the core, and that sick bastard has no fondness or love for Belle. She's his property, and that's all he cares about."

I'm not sure what it is about that last statement, but Bridger's entire body goes tight and his eyes flame with something akin to hatred. His voice doesn't rise, but there's no hiding the thunder of repressed anger. "Why exactly did you run? You stayed there for a few years after she was born."

Shame overwhelms me because he's forcing me very close to considering the question I've asked myself over and over again in the past few months. It's not the same exact question he just asked, but it's close enough.

Why didn't I run sooner?

"You have to understand," I whisper in response to what he just asked. "I didn't think Belle was in any real danger at first. I mean... most of the time, Zeke ignored us both. Sometimes, he'd yell at me to keep her quiet if she was crying, but we were usually left alone. I cared for her, stayed in my room for the most part, and we sort of flew under the radar."

"What happened?" he prods.

As Belle grew, started to walk, and became insanely curious about the world around her, I had a harder time keeping her in the solitary confinement of our room at the compound. I'd carefully take her outside when I knew Zeke was out and about to let her play in the fresh air. We were pretty much ignored, which was good.

Until the time when Belle wasn't ignored.

"There was a stray dog that hung around the compound that had puppies," I tell him with my eyes once again lowered to the table and my voice sounding oddly detached. "Belle liked to play with them. It was the highlight of her day to be able to go outside to be around them. One day, Zeke came out into the yard area where

Belle was playing. He was drunk, which always made him meaner. I tried to pick up Belle and get her inside before he noticed us, but she's two years old and she did what most toddlers would do. She pitched a fit and started crying, wanting to stay with the puppies."

Bile starts to rise in my throat so it chokes my words down. I take another sip of water and hesitantly slide my gaze over to Bridger's. His face appears impassive, but his eyes are simmering with anger. Yet his voice is surprisingly encouraging when he says, "Go on."

I give a slight cough to clear my throat and press forward. "Her cries got Zeke's attention, and he came our way. She was struggling to get out of my hold to get to the puppies… you know… in full-blown tantrum mode. Zeke yelled at her to 'shut the fuck up'. That just made her scream louder. So he reached down, grabbed one of the puppies by the scruff, and held it up for her to see. I'll never forget the way he taunted his daughter. He shook the puppy and told her, 'I'll give you something to cry about,' and then he punted the puppy like a football. Poor thing didn't stand a chance against those heavy biker boots. He was dead before he hit the ground."

My body shudders as I say those last words, my mind immediately turning to Belle's reaction. "She went limp in my arms, her mouth hanging open as her tear-filled eyes watched the limp puppy lying on the ground several feet away. I'll never forget the tiny little moan that slid past those precious baby lips, then her mouth clamped shut and she didn't utter another sound. Not for five days."

"Jesus fucking Christ," Bridger grits out as he pushes off the stool. I involuntarily shrink backward, thinking his anger for the situation is aimed at me.

Because let's face it… it's my fault Belle was in that environment. I should have run the minute I found out I was pregnant. I knew Zeke, and I knew he wasn't father material. I knew… *something* like that would happen one day.

"I'm a terrible mother," I say as he advances on me. I admit my failure to him, having no clue what he's going to do to me, but by the murderous expression on his face, I know it's going to hurt.

Bridger stalks right to me but rather than raising his hand to strike me, or pulling me from my chair to throw me out of the safety of his house, he drops to his knees by my chair and puts a large hand around the back of my neck, forcing me to turn to look at him. "You are not a terrible mother. You took your child and ran. You protected her."

"Not at first," I argue, my mind refusing to believe his words.

"You did what you had to do, and you did what was right when it truly mattered."

I don't respond, but I don't drop my gaze from his either. I study him critically to see if he's just blowing smoke up my ass or if he truly believes those words. He stares right back at me, and I can see from deep within those orbs the color of molten cognac that he knows a little something of what I've been through. In that moment, I realize I was right to trust him with this information.

With a soft squeeze to my neck, Bridger releases me and stands up, but he doesn't move away. Looking down at me, he asks gravely, "You don't have to tell me details, but are you sure Belle's safe where she's at?"

I give a tentative nod. "I think so."

"Well, at least that gives us some time to decide what the best thing to do is," Bridger says almost absently as he turns from me and reaches for his bottle of water. "For right now, I imagine the only person looking for you is Kayla, but when Zeke returns, he's going to put all his resources into finding you again."

I nod, because I know that's true. "Then I should probably leave."

"You're not going anywhere," he says gruffly. "You're going to stay here and recover. It will be the last thing Zeke would ever think… that you'd stay in this area."

His words warm me… fill me with a small measure of hope, but I have to remember the reality of the situation. "Bridger… if he finds out you're helping me, he'll…"

I can't even say it.

"I know," he says resolutely. "But fuck if I'm going to let him get his hands on you or Belle."

And by the tone in his voice and the blazing determination in his eyes, I know he's making me a promise he intends to keep.

Chapter 5
Bridger

T HE ORGASM IS just beyond my reach, taunting me with its special brand of relief. It's not something I really want, but it's definitely something I need. Opening my eyes, I look down at the blonde head bobbing vigorously over my cock. I can't see her face, but I can feel the warmth of her mouth as she takes me in deep and sucks hard.

Carina. One of my bartenders.

She gives good head, minimal gag reflex.

I should be busting an easy nut, but my body's not cooperating. Oh, my cock's hard enough and it feels good, but I can't seem to get the job finished.

For the first time in… well, forever… I'm being side-tracked by worries, and it's impeding on my ability to blow a hard load.

Fucking Maggie.

Goddamn gorgeous woman with a shit life and an even shittier future at this point, camped back at my house and completely lost in this world. I don't want her problems to be my problems, but, for the life of me, I can't seem to shake them free. I'm obsessing about her healing, keeping her safe from Zeke, and wondering how in the hell I can help protect her daughter when I don't even know where she is. I've taken on her worries because I know how hard it is to break free from a terrible situation. I know what it's like to have no good options. Most importantly, I understand the overwhelming guilt that gets directed toward yourself for not doing it sooner once you finally do get free.

Almost as if you enjoyed the abuse you were receiving.

And Christ... the abuse she took. Maggie probably doesn't understand it, but when I realized all that shit she took... beatings and torture, but she never broke down and gave Belle up? Well, that right there had me respecting the shit out of her.

Carina changes tactics, concentrating on just the head of my dick and jacking the base with her hand. Yup... that feels good too, and I try to concentrate on that feeling so I can get it done.

Involuntarily, I start to imagine warm, brown hair instead of blonde, with streaks the color of a dark caramel running through. It's the first thing I noticed about Maggie when she came out of the shower three days ago and I saw her clean for the first time. Her hair was stunning, even still damp, but it dried while we talked. The colors broke through then, and I couldn't stop checking her out.

A tingling starts in my balls. This gives me relief the end is in sight and my dick isn't broken. Apparently, just the thought of Maggie's hair does it for me. I wonder what would happen if I imagined those full lips pulled back and her teeth grazing against my cock…

"Pull off," I mutter to Carina as an orgasm starts to build from deep within. Thoughts of Maggie sucking my cock become vivid. In my imagination, she looks up at me with fern-colored eyes filled with lust as her teeth scrape over the head of my cock.

Carina doesn't listen, apparently wanting to show me that her amazing skills include an aptitude for swallowing, and she tries to suck me in deeper.

I wonder if Maggie could deep throat me?

"Fuck," I mutter as a violent tremor runs up my spine. I grab Carina's hair, pulling her off me just as I start to erupt. Not a single drop lands on her tongue, thank fuck, but instead hits the side of her face as I push her away from me with a low groan of half-hearted release.

"For fuck's sake, Bridger," Carina complains as she sits back on her haunches and wipes my jizz off her face with the back of her hand. "I was willing to swallow."

"Yeah, well, I wasn't," I growl at her as I push out of my desk chair and tuck my softening dick back in my jeans. That was utterly lackluster. The three seconds of pleasure seems almost wasteful, the only redeeming part of the whole experience was imagining Maggie on her knees before me.

Christ, I have got to get control over this shit. I've got no business even thinking those thoughts.

I don't look back at Carina as she starts to push off the floor, but I do gentle my voice somewhat. "Go ahead and get back to work. There'll be a little bonus in your paycheck."

She snorts in response but in moments, I hear her walk out the door and pull it shut behind her. Carina likes pretty clothes and designer handbags, and gladly sucks my dick while we both pretend the extra money I add to her regular paycheck isn't a form of prostitution. It sort of compromises my morals, but those are so tattered to begin with, I don't obsess about it much.

I look back to my desk. There's no denying I've got plenty of work I could do. I have to look over account reconciliations and sign off on inventory orders, but truth be told, I'd rather head back to my house and see what Maggie's doing.

There's a brief moment of indecision before I think, *Fuck it.*

Grabbing my keys off my desk, I head out of my office and call it an early night.

I FIND MAGGIE on her usual perch, on my big leather couch, sitting on one end with her feet curled up underneath her. I don't need to look at the television to know she's watching *The Walking Dead*. I know it by the way she has a soft blanket covering her body with the edges pulled protectively up to her neck as she stares at the screen with wide, tension-filled eyes.

"Thought you were too scared to watch that by your-self," I say as I close the front door and lock it. I toss my car keys on the small table sitting to the side of the door.

She doesn't take her eyes off the TV but says, "I can't help it. I'm addicted."

A lot and not much has happened in the past three days since Maggie came out of her drug-induced stupor and told me about her predicament. She's slept a lot, and that's good. It's the best thing for her healing, and I can tell she's moving around more easily now and taking less pain meds.

She's quiet for the most part, trying to be unobtru-sive in my house because she doesn't want to be a burden on me. I'm sure she'd be fascinated to know that I don't find *her* to be a burden, but I am worried about the situation as a whole. Instead, I find Maggie to be a calming sort of roommate. She's considerate and keeps her stuff picked up, which includes a ton of new clothes that I went out and bought for her despite her protest. I merely pointed out to her that she couldn't live in her one outfit. It had bloodstains that wouldn't come out.

I also told her I didn't mind getting her the clothes, although I'll admit my thoughts ran on the lewd side as I was picking out her panties and bras in silk and lace rather than practical cotton.

Maggie's cleaned my house, although I've asked her not to because I don't expect it, and I know she has to still be in some pain. She ignores me though, and when I get home from work, my house is sparkling and she's got dinner cooked. I don't argue against dinner though as she's a much better cook than I am. In the evenings, I found myself coming home early from The Wicked Horse, and we'd end up watching TV together. She told me that first night when I introduced her to *The Walking Dead* that she hadn't seen a movie or television program in well over three years as there wasn't a TV in her room at the compound. The most she'd seen had been some bad porn Zeke would play before he fucked her—a fact I would have rather not known about, but Maggie doesn't hold anything back. It's as if once she told me the truth of her past, she wasn't going to hide the brutal details from me.

"Did you eat dinner?" she asks as she pulls the remote control out from underneath the blanket and points it at the TV, pausing it.

"Yeah," I mutter as I walk around the coffee table and sit in my recliner. "Grabbed something at the club."

I told Maggie I owned The Wicked Horse, but I obviously left out the part about me owning a secret sex club attached to it. There's no way she's ready to hear about The Silo and everything it entails.

I haven't seen Maggie all day, having left early this morning before she awoke. I'd moved her into the guest room—not the one I'd fucked Jared in as I hadn't been able to replace the comforter—and she'd been asleep when I'd left this morning to go help Woolf out on the ranch. I'd been wanting to get back on a horse and ride range for a while, something I find myself deeply desiring the more time I spend in my office as I'm a true outdoorsman more than I am a businessman.

My eyes quickly roam over her, and I observe, "You look better. Feel okay?"

I ask her this each night before we watch TV together. She smiles, like she always does, and nods. "Yeah… I feel a lot better each day. I didn't even take any pain medication today."

"You should take it," I admonish gently.

She shakes her head. "No, seriously… I'm feeling much better. The bruises are fading, and I'm sleeping a lot. I really don't hurt very much."

"But you still hurt," I point out.

"Not enough for those pain meds," she counters with a pointed look. "I don't like the way they make me feel, and besides… Jared said I didn't have to take them if I didn't want to."

I grimace. Fucking Jared.

He came to check on Maggie yesterday at my request. He proclaimed her to be healing very well, which was fantastic news.

But when I walked him to my front door, he turned to me with expectant eyes. I shut that shit down quickly. "I thank you for what you've done and I owed you, but I also paid you. Got it?"

He hesitated only a moment before nodding at me with a look of sadness. He started to turn away but stopped when I said, "Jared."

Once his eyes connected to mine, I made sure he understood the situation. "You do not tell a soul about Maggie, you hear?"

He nodded again. While I'm pretty sure he'd never say a word, I reiterated. "You've got secrets that I protect too. Quid pro quo, right?"

"Of course," he assured me. "Quid pro quo."

Maggie pushes the blanket off her and it draws my attention, snapping me back to the present. She stands up from the couch, and I have to clamp my teeth down hard to keep my mouth from falling open. She's wearing a t-shirt and a pair of workout pants that I bought her. In hindsight, they might be a tad too small. They look painted onto her. I take notice of how luscious that ass of hers really is and that her tits are huge, which is something I can't appreciate when she's wearing my t-shirts. I swallow hard and turn my head toward the TV screen.

"I'm going to make some tea and then take a bath," she says softly. "Want some?"

No, it's definitely not tea that I want. Bath sounds interesting, but she's clearly not inviting me.

"No, thanks," I tell her with a pasted smile on my face. She smiles back hesitantly and turns toward the kitchen. I unabashedly stare at her swaying ass as she walks away. When her body is hidden by the kitchen island, I push up from my recliner and make my usual rounds that I implemented the day Kyle dumped Maggie on me. I walk through the house and check all the doors and windows to ensure they're locked. After, I set the security alarm, and then check my stash of guns.

It's Wyoming and as a native son, I have guns. Lots and lots of them.

I use them mainly to hunt and target shoot, but now I've got them set up strategically around the house in case I were to need them for... oh, say... Zeke finding out I've got Maggie and coming after her. Got a shotgun under the couch, a pistol in one of the kitchen drawers, another taped under my bed, and a fourth shotgun in the middle guest room mounted just behind the door. I asked Maggie if she knew how to use a gun, and she shook her head with a look of extreme fear in her eyes. I assured her I'd find some time to teach her, but she looked positively sick at the thought so I let it go for the time being.

Maggie did ask me an interesting question on the heels of that though. "Do you think I should just go to the police right now? Tell them Zeke kidnapped me, beat me, and that Kayla tortured me?"

I had to give that some serious thought, but ultimately, I didn't think it was a good idea. First, he'd probably be arrested and let out on bail, then Maggie would be in more danger than she was right this moment. Also, I didn't want to do anything to screw up Kyle. He asked for some time, and, as long as Maggie was safely hidden, we could afford to give it to him.

As I'm walking down the hallway to head back into the living room, I hear the sound of running water from the guest bathroom as I pass by it. The door's closed and light seeps out from the crack below. I can tell by the sound that she's filling the bathtub up, and I sigh with frustration that I want the woman who sits on the other side of that door. But that's certainly not cool, particularly when I've told her she's safe here and being with me would not be safe.

I'm slightly startled when my phone buzzes in my back pocket. I pull it out and see it's Cal Carson, a friend of mine from New York.

I walk back toward my bedroom for some privacy as I answer, "Hey, man. What's up?"

"Just got off the phone with Logan and Auralie, giving them an update. Thought I'd do the same for you."

I enter my bedroom and shut the door behind me. A few weeks ago, Cal helped out Auralie and her father by arranging legal protection for them. He facilitated a deal with a federal prosecutor to help bring down Magnus Albright, a fucking skeevy son of a bitch who was using Auralie to run a con in The Silo. He was peddling her as a virgin to the highest bidder, and she had no choice but to do his bidding or Magnus would kill her father. It was a bad situation, and my buddy Logan got caught up in it, but all's well now. At least, I think it is.

"Everything okay?" I ask hesitantly, and I hope to fuck it is. I've got enough worries at the moment.

"It's all good," Cal assures me. "Magnus is still in jail and can't afford bail. The prosecutor wants to know if you're interested in pressing charges since you're sort of a victim too as the owner of The Silo."

"No way," I say without needing to think on it.

While I'm in no way ashamed of my business, I don't want it paraded out there in public. "Besides... I'm sure they got more than enough to put him away for a long time."

"That they do," Cal says with a laugh. But then he gives a cough and says, "Listen... Macy and I want to take a little trip. Figured we'd finally accept your invite to come visit The Silo. That still good?"

I smile as I pace my bedroom floor, because I know without a doubt that Cal and Macy will love The Silo. In fact, I'd first met them in New York when Woolf and I were visiting a sex club there called Voyeur. We visited several around the country as we were making plans to open The Silo, getting ideas and taking the best of them to create our own vision. While Woolf and I didn't participate with Cal and Macy, we certainly watched each other do some kinky ass shit. After that, we all went out for drinks together. It started a solid friendship based upon a mutual appreciation of the more debauched pleasures in life.

Cal had openly admitted he'd had a hard time with the concept of a sex club and didn't like his first experience there. But since then, he's indulged Macy. After his third scotch, he even more openly admitted that once he gave his heart to her fully, there wasn't anything he wouldn't do for her. And if that included indulging in her sexual whims, he would happily do so. He also admitted, after the fourth drink, that once you love someone, the worries and insecurities seem to melt away, and it makes the kinky fucking that much better.

Woolf howled with laughter at that, but Macy merely smiled at him with eyes shimmering with love.

It was nice.

They're nice.

"Sure," I tell him. "Love to have you. Just shoot me a text when you'll arrive. I'll book a hotel room for you at The Wort, and you'll have VIP access the entire time to The Silo."

"Excellent," Cal says jovially. "Macy's been hounding me for months, but I've been so fucking busy with work. But it's a good time for us to slip away and have some relaxation and fun."

"Look forward to seeing you," I tell him, but my mind starts slipping away and focusing back on Maggie. I can't put off this talk. "Listen buddy… I've got to get going. Text me details, okay?"

"Sure thing," Cal responds. He disconnects the call after a quick, "Later."

Taking a deep breath, I look at my bedroom door, knowing Maggie's on the other side and just down a short hallway. As soon as she finishes her bath, it's time we talked.

More accurately, it's time she learned about The Silo and what I do for a living. I have no choice but to disclose it to her now.

I look back to my phone, tap on the "text" icon, and pull up my messages.

The one on top with the bolded name "Zeke" seems

to pulse like neon. I'd received it a few hours ago. It's what precipitated me to have Carina suck my cock to try to work off some of the tension it immediately caused.

Be back in town tomorrow. Be at compound at 11pm. I want a show.

Yeah.

It's time Maggie knew about what I did for a living and how that connects me to her abuser.

Chapter 6

Maggie

I KNOW I shouldn't be doing this, but I can't help myself. Bridger looked damn good when he came home a bit ago. He was too damn nice when he asked me how I was doing, the worry evident in his eyes. He's been an amazing host these last few days, but more than that, he's given me sanctuary. For the first time in years, I feel safe.

And the overwhelming gratefulness I feel for him is now starting to screw with my mind. I'd thought he was beyond handsome the first time I'd seen him, although my fear was too great then for me to appreciate it. But the more I get to know him, and the more time we spend in each other's presence, he's become more than just a gorgeous man to me. I've become attracted to him in a way I have no business being. He's gay, for God's sake. Here I am, lusting after a man who could never feel that way about me, and even shittier, has done nothing but be kind and generous to me.

And I feel terrible for it.

Sometimes, he'll be talking to me and all I can think about is having sex with him. This embarrasses me so much, because I'm not one who thinks about sex like that. It's not ever been about my pleasure.

Not ever.

It's been a commodity I use, and it's gotten me places. Not good places, granted, but it's provided me with what I've needed to survive.

But Bridger… he makes me think of sex in a completely different way. Not as a tool or even a burden, but in a way that makes me think it can be sensual, decadent, and mutually satisfying. A foreign concept for sure, but I still fantasize about it anyway, even though I know he's interested in men and not women.

It just fucks with my head, that I could be attracted to someone who would never have an interest in me. A man who's completely untouchable. Perhaps that makes him even sexier to my way of thinking. Add on the fact he's become a hero to me in a few short days by taking me in and keeping me safe and I'm completely romanticizing him in my mind.

Just like right now as I sink down into the tub just far enough that the warm water laps over my breasts but doesn't touch the Bose headphones Bridger told me I could use to listen to music. He gave them to me a few days ago when I asked him if he had a stereo I could put on while I cleaned. He said he didn't and disappeared into his bedroom, but he came back with an iPod and the headphones that I've used religiously since then.

Bridger has excellent taste in music. I choose one of my favorite songs, "Let's Make Love" by Faith Hill and

Tim McGraw, closing my eyes as the music fills my ears. I immediately start to relax, which is testament to the fact that over the last few days, I've given into the security and comfort Bridger and his home have offered to me. It's the safest I've been in a long time, and only because I don't have to look over my shoulder or worry about being tortured to death by Kayla. While I miss Belle so much my chest continually aches, I know she's safe and in the best place she can be right now.

As the warm water soothes me and Faith and Tim sing about the sexiest of times, I think of Bridger because I can't help but do so. He's physically perfect to my way of thinking, his looks more masculine and rugged than any Wyoming cowboy has a right to be. One morning, I found him in the kitchen in just a pair of sweatpants. I stared like an idiot at his torso, which was rippled with muscle and adorned by a flock of blackbirds flying up his rib cage.

But truth be told, it's Bridger's eyes that do it for me. Golden brown, sometimes even glowing with a hint of orange like a Wyoming sunset. On more than one occasion, they have been filled with a fierce protectiveness when he talks about keeping me safe from Zeke. Call it hero worship or whatever, but it struck me deep and true and sparked some vivid fantasies that make me want to turn him hetero.

Like right now.

I wonder if Bridger would be gentle or rough. I've had gentle a few times, but it was mediocre at best.

Mostly, I've had rough. Thankfully, it was over fast. Somehow though, I think Bridger might be both and that causes my hand to slip unbidden in between my legs as I think about how hard he must have been fucking Jared that night based on the sounds of pleasure I heard. And I've deduced it was Jared because when he came to check on me, I definitely noticed some gay mannerisms, although I could be wrong as I don't remember much about Logan at all.

A shudder works its way up my spine, and I imagine what his mouth would feel like against mine or his hands on my breasts. An ache develops between my legs. As my fingers gently touch my clit, I fantasize that it's Bridger's tongue there.

My hips jerk as I press my fingers down, and a long moan slips out of my mouth. I'm immediately mortified because it was loud. I know it was loud because I could hear it over the music in my ears.

My eyes slowly open, my heart pounding with fear that Bridger might have heard me, but movement from my periphery startles me. I bolt upright in the tub as I realize Bridger is leaning into the bathroom, the door partly open. His eyes are burning as they stare at me. I rip the headphones off and toss them to the floor while stammering, "What are you doing?"

I can feel my face burning hot from embarrassment. As an afterthought, I bring my hands up to cover my breasts as I slouch back down in the water.

Bridger's eyes never waver from mine, but his voice is

thickened when he says, "I was knocking on the door, but you didn't answer. I was worried."

"Well, I'm fine," I huff out as I lean my head back against the tub, wishing I'd just melt into the water and never have to deal with him again. I can't believe he caught me masturbating, and I seriously just want to die from the mortification.

"I didn't mean to disturb you," he says carefully, but I close my eyes, refusing to look at him. "I'll let you… um… finish."

"I'm finished," I blurt out, reaching for the towel I'd put on top of the toilet tank beside the bathtub.

"Take your time," he insists, and my face flames hotter. I still refuse to look at him, but then he says, "When you're done, we need to talk."

His voice sounds so ominous that all thoughts of embarrassment flee. "Is it about Zeke?"

"Sort of," is all he says, and then he steps backward and pulls the door shut.

I scramble out of the tub, my heart racing. I do a half-assed job of drying off, putting on clean underwear and another pair of yoga pants Bridger bought me. He doesn't know much about women's fashion, but I really don't care, as I'm not going out in public. I pull on another t-shirt, foregoing my bra in my haste to find out what he knows, and almost bust my ass as I slip on a wet spot on the floor as I try to bolt out of the bathroom.

I take a deep breath as I half walk, half jog to the living room where I find Bridger sitting in his recliner, but he's perched on the edge of the seat with his elbows to his knees. He nods at the couch. I take my usual position at the end, facing him with my legs crossed Indian-style.

Before he can say anything though, I try to diffuse my embarrassment and I'm sure his as well. "I'm really sorry that you saw me…"

Bridger holds his hand up to stop me. "You don't have to apologize."

"But I do," I insist.

"Maggie," Bridger says with an admonishing look. "What you were doing is natural and trust me… it was no hardship watching a beautiful woman pleasure herself."

My jaw drops open over his words, which are dripping… yes, absolutely *dripping* with appreciation, even though his face remains impassive.

"But you're gay… aren't you?" I blurt out.

Bridger blinks at me with a look of stunned disbelief. For a moment, I think perhaps he's deep in the closet and doesn't want anyone to know, which makes me feel even more wretched. Then his lips peel back and he lets out a deep laugh, his eyes crinkling with jolly amusement.

"Aren't you?" I insist.

"Darlin'," Bridger says as he chuckles. "I am the farthest thing from gay that there is."

"But… I heard you that night… with Jared. At least, I think it was Jared…"

Bridger stops laughing and his jaw hardens slightly.

He stares at me a moment, almost as if trying to figure out the best way to drop bad news, and this has me tensing up all over.

His voice is rough… not with embarrassment, but maybe with disgust when he says, "You heard me fucking Jared, who is gay. It's what he wanted in payment for treating you."

My jaw drops again. "You fucked a man to pay him for treating me?"

"Do it again if faced with the same decision," he says gruffly. "It was a fair trade."

"A trade," I ask in disbelief. "You fucked a man even though you're not gay so he'd give me medical treatment?"

" 'Bout sums it up," he says dryly.

I'm so confused and deeply saddened for some reason as I struggle to understand. "So you're bisexual then?"

Bridger pushes off the recliner with a grunt of dissatisfaction, takes two steps, and sits next to me on the couch before turning his body to face me. His hand reaches out, grips me by my jaw, and he leans in before saying in a low voice. "Hear me, Maggie. I'm not gay. I'm not bisexual. I'm turned on by women and not men, but it doesn't mean I haven't fucked men in my past, and probably will again in my future if it serves my needs."

"But… but… I hate that you did something like that for me. That you had to do something terrible…"

Bridger's fingers squeeze my jaw. "It wasn't terrible,

Mags."

Mags.

He called me Mags.

My best friend in middle school used to call me that, and I'd always loved that endearment. "It wasn't terrible?"

He shakes his head and shrugs. "I got off. I mean, fucking is fucking, you know?"

"No," I whisper. "I don't know."

Because I don't. It's hard for me to get off with a man, mainly because no one has ever cared about my pleasure before.

Bridger's hand pulls back. He brings it to his own head where he rakes his fingers through brown locks that look in desperate need of a trim. Yet, I hope he leaves it just as it is. With a sigh, he says, "I need to tell you some stuff about me."

"Oh-kay," I say cautiously, the tone of his voice putting me on edge.

"I own a sex club called The Silo," he says, and I wasn't prepared for that at all. Of all the things I thought he might say, that would not have been near the top of any list.

"I thought you owned a nightclub," I mutter.

"I do, as well as a sex club. My life… my career… it's about sex. It's always been about sex for… well, as long as I can remember. And I've taken that and turned it into something good, not only for me, but also for other people who want a safe place to act out their dirtiest fantasies without fear of judgment or recrimination."

I just stare at him, oddly repulsed and fascinated. With horror, I realize… also slightly turned on now that I know he's not gay but still fucked a man so that I'd have medical care. And damn… now I wished I'd seen that rather than just heard it because the thought of Bridger…

I shake my head, trying to clear my thoughts. "Why are you telling me this… that you own a sex club? It has nothing to do with me."

"It does," he says as his eyes cut downward to his lap briefly. It's an action I recognize… shame. "It's how I know Zeke."

"What?" I gasp.

His eyes snap back up to mine, and they're filled with resolution. "I was introduced to Zeke by a mutual acquaintance, and I was subsequently invited to some parties out at the compound. I went a few times… met Kyle and got to know some of the other guys as well. I performed some services… for Zeke and Kayla."

"Services?" I ask, my throat tightening up with apprehension.

"BDSM," he says. "Zeke had me do things to Kayla while he watched."

"What kind of things?" I rasp out, not wanting to know but needing to desperately. He's talking about things of a sexual nature and while he's maintained to me all along he's not friends with Zeke, I'm sorry… but sex is personal and I'm starting to feel my spider senses tingle with fear.

Bridger's eyes hold mine captive. "Kayla gets off on pain. So I give it to her. Usually with a whip, sometimes with a cane. I'd hurt her until she came, and then Zeke would fuck her."

"Did you—" I start to say, but my voice cracks. I clear my throat, start again. "Did you fuck her?"

"Never," he says forcefully. "Not once."

"Zeke?"

"No, Maggie." Bridger growls with frustration and launches off the couch. He steps past the coffee table, heading toward the door where he peels the blinds back and peeks outside. I'm not sure what he expects to see, but he quickly turns back to me. "You don't understand… I don't get off on handing out the pain. Not in a sexual way. They pay me money to deliver it, and I accept it. It's what I do, that's all."

"It's what you do?" I inquire stupidly, because I'm more confused than ever now.

"I have to do it," Bridger says quietly. "It's who I am."

I shake my head, look down briefly at my hands clasped in my lap, and then back up to him. "I don't understand."

"Join the club," he mutters as he walks back toward me. Rather than taking the couch, he sits down on the coffee table and reaches out. His hands cover and engulf mine, holding them protectively. "I owe Zeke a favor. He's summoned me out to the club tomorrow night."

"To service Kayla?" I ask with quiet dejection as my eyes fall down to his hands covering mine.

"I don't think so," he says softly. That makes me look back up, because I hear relief in his voice. "He gave up one of his club members a while back who attacked a friend of mine. Turned him over to the police. That's the favor I owe him. In the past, he told me he wants me to come out and put on a show for the other members with some of the club girls."

I nod, but I still don't understand. I mean... I get what Bridger is saying and I'm clear on what he's done in the past. I guess what I don't understand is if he still intends to protect me or not. So I ask the question I'm dreading the answer to. "So... are you going to turn me over to him?"

"For fuck's sake, Maggie," Bridger practically barks at me, his hands tightening on mine almost painfully. "Didn't I tell you I'd protect you?"

His eyes flash with fury, and there's no doubt he's pissed over my lack of faith in him.

"I'm sorry... I just... you threw me for a loop, Bridger. And what am I supposed to think? Doing sexual... um... things to someone... for someone... well, that's sort of a personal relationship. You also owe Zeke a favor. Why not turn me over to him and collect on your favor?"

"Because I'm telling you I wouldn't ever do that," he growls at me. "I will protect you."

God, can I believe him?

I want to believe him so much because I don't want to give up this safety I've been feeling. I don't want to lose the hope I've started to foster that I'll get Belle back as soon as Kyle takes Zeke down.

I'm not ready to give up… Bridger?

I mean, damn it… he caught me masturbating to fantasies of him, advised me he wasn't gay, which seem to make the fantasies okay now, and then proceeded to tell me he whips Kayla while Zeke watches. I'm appalled and turned on all at the same time.

I'm so fucking confused. "I'm sorry. I'm just a bit stressed over everything."

Some of the heat dies down in his eyes, but he still looks at me with chastisement. "I've got to go tomorrow night so I don't arouse suspicion, but I'm hoping I can use it as an opportunity to talk to Kyle… see what's happening. I'm hoping to get some information at the very least that will clue us in on what we need to do next."

I look at him directly in the eye, and I see determination to help me. I can see it sitting there with stubborn refusal to accept anything less than my absolute protection, and God help me… it makes me want to kiss him.

"Tomorrow night…when I go to the compound," Bridger says, his thumb now stroking the back of my hand. "I'm going to have a friend come stay with you."

"Do you think that's necessary?" I ask with worry.

"Probably not," he assures me. "But in the very off chance Zeke knows you're here and he's doing this to lead me away, I want someone looking over you and willing to protect you in my absence."

I nod, because what else can I do but accept this? I don't want to die, and I sure as hell don't want to go back to the compound with Zeke.

Then Bridger surprises the shit out of me when he leans forward and gives me a quick kiss on my forehead. His lips are warm and dry… soft and gentle. It's a sweet move on his part, but it's sexy to me.

Bridger pulls away and stands up, refusing to look at me as he turns toward the hallway. "I'm headed to bed."

I don't want him to go. I want him to stay and continue to talk to me. I want him to kiss me again, this time on my mouth, maybe my breasts, and then on my—

"Bridger?" I call out to him, wincing internally at the desperate tone in my voice. It reeks of a pitiful need I have but that I really have no business asking him to fill.

He stops but doesn't turn back to me, his head bowed downward. "Don't."

"But—"

"We can't," he says firmly, still refusing to look me in the eye while he denies me.

And without another word, he disappears from sight.

Chapter 7
Bridger

I ENTER THE front door of the main building of the compound, assaulted by loud music, smoke, and the cacophony of drunk bikers partying. It's the last place on this earth I want to be, but it has to be done.

Woolf came over to stay with Maggie at my house tonight while I do my thing. I told him about her when I was at his ranch the day before, not because I thought I'd need his help to watch over her, but because I didn't keep many secrets from Woolf and I trusted his wisdom. I thought I had a good handle on the situation, but I wanted to know if he would see things different than I was.

Not surprisingly, he felt I was doing the right thing and volunteered to help in any way he could. One way he suggested was going to Kyle's sister, Andrea. I'd met her briefly when Woolf's brother, Tenn, got married on the ranch. Tenn knows Kyle, probably better than I do as he had Kyle do some work on his bike. They once rode cross-country together as Kyle wanted to visit Andrea, who lived in the Outer Banks of North Carolina. Andrea used to be an FBI agent. Woolf surmised that maybe

Andrea knew about Kyle's undercover operation and could help us get word to the ATF about Maggie and Belle. Maybe they could even put Maggie in protective custody until Kyle could finish his bust, but I really didn't like that idea because I didn't want Maggie to leave.

Which is fucking stupid because I owe her nothing. I shouldn't be overly concerned with her protection if it can be gotten from a better source.

Still, I declined Woolf's offer by reasoning there was a chance Andrea didn't know about Kyle's undercover work and that it was something he should tell her and not us. He seemed to buy it and agreed. Turning down his offer certainly had nothing to do with the fact I liked Maggie in my house more and more every day.

The main building of the compound houses a large room on the first floor that has a built-in bar, several pool tables, and various pieces of furniture for members to sit on. The second floor houses bedrooms for club members to sleep or fuck in, and I know this because that's where Zeke had me perform with Kayla before.

Hitching the strap of my tool bag higher over my shoulder, I wind my way in and out of the partiers. Big, burly men with sweat-stained shirts, worn leather cuts, and reeking of booze and pot. Trashy-looking women in miniscule clothing and garish makeup holding on to said sweaty men in an effort to perhaps elevate from club whore to old lady. Other women, slightly less trashy looking, stand in small pockets talking to each other, without the need to command the bikers' attention. Those are the old ladies who've already captured the interests they wanted.

I nod at a few of the members I recognize, pushing my way to the bar. I surreptitiously sweep my gaze around, looking mainly for Kyle but also keeping a lookout for Zeke. I'm handed a beer from a woman behind the bar whose face is pockmarked and teeth rotted from meth, and take a sip before turning around to peruse the situation.

My gaze first lands on Kayla, standing with a few other old ladies near one of the pool tables with a cue stick in her hand. Even across the room, I can see the vicious bruise she's sporting around her right eye and cheekbone, and there's no doubt in my mind Zeke handed that out to her. If I had to put money on it, I'd bet he was not happy to have returned and found Maggie missing. He probably took it out on her. Not the first time I'd seen bruises on her. Hell, I'd put bruises on her at his direction.

Sweeping my eyes past her, I see Kyle walking in from the door that leads out back where I know the party will be raging around a huge bonfire. He looks at me, our eyes connecting for just a moment, and then he looks right past me. I watch as he walks over to a woman sitting on a low-slung couch that is probably stained heavy from beer and cum. He reaches down to grab her hand and then leads her up the staircase to the second floor. His message is clear. To everyone else in the room who may have watched, he's going to fuck this woman. To me, his immediate brush-off said he didn't want to talk to me. I have to assume he doesn't want to risk anything at this time.

A hand claps me on the shoulder, and I turn to see Zeke standing there. He's an average-built man standing at about five-ten or so, which has me looking down at him as I top him by several inches. Not too muscular but not skinny either. I'd guess he's in his late forties, early fifties, but it's hard to tell. His face is haggard and his dark, braided ponytail is streaked with silver, as is his beard. I've always thought his eyes were ice cold despite being a warm brown, and the thing that makes him somewhat intimidating is that they are filled with intelligence. He doesn't rule just with brute force, but he does so using his brain, which makes him a formidable opponent even though I could probably whip his ass with one arm tied behind my back.

"Right on time," he says gruffly, and then turns from me as he puts his forefinger and thumb in his mouth, giving a shrill whistle that's heard by everyone above the music. They all turn to the sound, but Zeke's eyes are pinned to a woman across the room who is sitting on a biker's lap. His hand is massaging her breast. She makes eye contact with Zeke, and he jerks his head for her to come to him.

Everyone else goes back to partying. When the woman comes to stand before Zeke, I feel the salaciousness vibrating off her. Her eyes are filled with a pathetic need to be recognized by Zeke.

"What's up, baby?" she purrs, stepping into Zeke and putting her hand on his crotch to rub him.

Zeke tilts his head to me. "This is Bridger. I want you to do whatever he tells you to do."

My skin tightens with unease. "Need her full consent," I tell Zeke pointedly, and we engage in a bit of a staring war. He wants to prove his dick is big enough to order a woman to let me whip her and that she'll do it with a smile on her face. But I don't back down, refusing to break eye contact or move until I have her full consent.

Zeke finally turns to the woman and says, "Bridger is going to put on a show with you for the boys. It will probably involve a whip. Most definitely is going to hurt. He might fuck you or have one of the boys fuck you. Could be in any hole you got. Could be multiple guys. Now do me a fucking favor... tell him you consent."

The woman turns to me. I note with a measure of relief that her eyes are clear and she appears lucid. She smiles at me. I'm surprised that it's a pretty smile with straight, even teeth that tells me she had braces in the past. "Darlin'... I'll take anything you throw at me. Make it hurt good."

"I'll give you a safe word—" I start to say, but she shakes her head in denial.

"I don't need a safe word," she says, sliding a brave look toward Zeke, who she's clearly trying to impress.

"You'll have one or I walk out of here," I growl at

them both, and Zeke laughs.

"Fine," she huffs, looking extremely disappointed I won't let her shine in front of Zeke. "What's my word?"

"Let's go with 'stop'," I tell her with an incline of my head. "It works universally."

"But that's so ordinary," she huffs.

"And yet, it works just fine," I point out and take her by the elbow. "Just don't say it unless you mean it."

I NEVER DID find out her name, but the woman Zeke thrust upon me to do a show is a true champ in every sense of the word. Even now, she continues to take it even though my part is long done. I didn't do anything all that unusual. Well, at least not unusual for me, but by the hormones and lust permeating this place right now, I'm guessing most here have never seen the likes.

I used a cue stick as a spreader bar, tying her ankles securely toward the ends so she was splayed open. I then bent her over the end of one of the pool tables, tied her wrists together with rope, and secured them to the legs at the opposite end. She couldn't move and she couldn't escape, the only thing saving her from my flogger was the word 'stop'.

She used many words as I landed blows against her tan skin, but 'stop' was never one of them. We drew a crowd all tightly packed in a circle around the pool table three men deep, the women all seeming to melt away who either didn't want to watch or were too jealous over the attention the girl was getting. I especially noticed that Kayla walked outside as I was tying the woman up. Not five minutes into my performance, one guy crawled onto the pool table and made her suck his dick. It was comical watching him trying to get his pants down enough, while figuring out how to get his dick within reach of her mouth since she was stretched flat against the felted surface with no wiggle room. Even funnier was watching his head knocking against the pool table light as he contorted his body into a painful-looking position.

But apparently not too painful as she made him come in like a nanosecond.

Then it was a free-for-all, and she was getting fucked in every hole just like Zeke promised her. Guy after guy came up behind her, most not even worrying about condoms, and pounded her pussy or ass. The truly adventurous tried to get their dicks sucked while battling with the pool table light.

The woman moaned the entire time. When her mouth was free for a few moments, she would encourage other guys to step forward. She clearly liked being gang banged, and while normally that thing is a turn on to me in the right circumstances, it just wasn't tonight. I suspect in part because I kept thinking about Maggie and all she'd endured from this hellhole, and also in part because these assholes are nasty. It isn't about eroticism or sexual freedom to them. It's about busting a quick, raunchy nut while your buddies egg you on in between belches of cheap beer. Thank God Zeke didn't demand I partake in the sex because I'm not sure I could have gotten it up.

Zeke was the first guy to fuck her, and I wasn't surprised he used a condom. Kayla's his old lady, and I'm sure he's not about to bring some crotch crud home to her. He started with the woman's pussy, which I have to say was glistening so she was clearly turned on. Like a true gentlemen, he managed to spit on the end of his dick before he fucked her ass. Next guy gallantly came in her ass sans condom, so the lube situation there was taken care of.

Yeah... the woman is enjoying it, but there's no doubt she's going to be walking funny tomorrow. I don't feel compelled to stick around now that my part is over, and because I saw Zeke walk outside after he was done, I look around the room for Kyle. A jolt of surprise runs through me when I lock eyes on him. He jerks his head toward the front door of the compound.

Without hesitation, I grab my tool bag and walk that way, sensing Kyle on my heels. When we clear the door and step out into the crisp air, Kyle immediately addresses the two bikers who are standing guard. They're young recruits and probably have to do all the shit work.

"You guys want to go inside and jump in on a little gang-bang action, there's a juicy cunt all tied up and spread over a pool table for you," he says to the men. I wince over his crudity, making me wonder if this is the true Kyle talking or undercover Kyle. He pulls out a joint from the breast pocket of his leather cut and lights it.

"I'll watch the door for you."

Both men's eyes simmer with lust, and they give nods of appreciation as they push past us to head inside. When the door closes, Kyle steps in closer to me so he can talk in a low voice. "That will give us a few minutes of privacy. How's Maggie?"

"She's fine," I tell him. "Healing nicely."

"Good," he says on a genuine exhale of relief. Any doubt I might have had that Kyle is truly batting for the good guys is dispelled.

"How long before you bring Zeke down?"

He shrugs, not in a careless way, but in a clueless way. "Waiting for confirmation from my handler with the ATF, but I can't communicate with him regularly. I've got a meet set up with him later this week, but we were just waiting for this last run. They're going to tell me when so I can be ready to assist."

I nod. "And what happened when Zeke came back yesterday and found Maggie missing?"

"Not happy," he said, his voice dropping even lower and sounding more urgent. "He put all available members, even from other chapters, on the hunt."

"Looking for Maggie or Belle?" I ask.

Kyle gives a small jerk of surprise, and I'm betting he didn't think Maggie would share the full story with me. "Mostly for Maggie, but he's getting desperate. He might start looking at her family. Is Belle safe?"

"Supposedly," I admit with frustration. "She hasn't shared with me where she is."

"Look," Kyle says softly. "I'm fairly confident Zeke has no clue I'm the one who got Maggie out of here. I was pretty rough on her, and even acted as if I enjoyed what Kayla was doing to her, and I made sure I was vocal about it so others wouldn't suspect me. But Zeke is fucking smart and suspicious by nature, so trust me... he knows someone in this compound got her out. So this is the last time we talk, okay?"

"Fine," I say in agreement, but I impress upon him something very important. "But I can't keep her hidden away forever. She deserves a life, and frankly... I deserve my life back too. If this doesn't go down soon, I've got to be able to do something."

"Don't do it unless it's an absolute emergency," Kyle warns me. "My handler is Joseph Kizner; he's originally out of Chicago, but he's been here for the last three years posing as a used car salesman over in Driggs. But do not contact him unless you think you or Maggie are in immediate peril. Understand?"

"Got it," I say just as the front door to the compound opens.

Kyle smoothly puts the joint to his mouth and takes a deep hit, holds the smoke in, and passes the blunt to me. He turns casually as he exhales. We see Kayla standing there looking at us with pure suspicion on her face.

"What are you two doing?" she asks.

I take a hit off the joint, but not as deep as Kyle. I hate this shit and the way it makes me feel. As I blow it out, Kyle says, "Bridger had some good weed he wanted to share with me, so I gave the guys on door duty a chance to get in on that sweet little gang bang Zeke arranged."

Kayla's face pinches with anger, and I can tell he mentioned the gang bang to rile her up. She tries to school her features into impassivity as she turns to me. "Can I have a hit?"

"Sure," I say as I hand her the joint. She takes three successive drags, burning half of it down into her greedy lungs as we watch her.

When she exhales, she passes the joint to Kyle but asks me. "When can Zeke and I expect you for a private show?"

"Few weeks," I answer tersely, but I add on, "I've got some traveling to do."

"I'm thinking Zeke might want it sooner," she challenges me.

"Well, that's something Zeke will have to get over," I tell her smoothly, but there's a hard edge to my voice. I don't want her to ever think that she or Zeke have a hold on me. My debt to him for helping to identify Cat's attacker is paid in full as of tonight.

"We'll see," is all she says, but there's no denying the silky taunt in her tone.

Kyle hands the joint back to me, but I shake my head. "You guys finish that up. I've got to head over to the Wicked Horse and check in."

He shrugs, puts it to his mouth, and sucks in a drag.

"Later, dude," he says on an exhale. "Good show too."

"Later," I say as I turn toward my car, which I had parked across a small gravel parking area that runs the length of the compound.

Kayla doesn't say a word, but I don't care. My mind is already turned to Maggie and the renewed danger she's facing now that Zeke is back and on the hunt.

Chapter 8
Maggie

THE FRONT DOOR to Bridger's house opens, and he walks in as the clock is getting ready to strike one AM. He looks exhausted and the lingering flicker of disgust in his eyes tells me he did not enjoy his work tonight.

Woolf pushes out of the recliner he'd been sitting on and walks to Bridger, who remains by the door with it still open, a clear indication Woolf can leave. He's a nice guy... Woolf, but he wasn't overly talkative. I tried to get him to tell me more about Bridger and the sex club, because Bridger admitted to me this morning Woolf was his best friend and had started it with him.

I still can't believe Bridger has a sex club. My mind ran away last night as I tossed and turned in bed, trying to imagine what all could possibly go on in such a place. And did Bridger partake? Was he with a different woman every night?

And what about the BDSM? I don't know much about it... had a few tie me up, a few others spank me, but Bridger talked about whips last night and I sort of got the impression it's not something you take casually or lightly. While I don't mind a hot palm on my ass because it makes things interesting, I can't even imagine handling the type of pain a whip would cause.

I also can't imagine Bridger being the one to hand out that pain. Everything I've come to learn about him the last few days has led me to believe he's a kind man. He's provided me with a safe home to live in and promised to protect me. It's almost inconceivable to me that he would whip a woman.

And he told me last night, *It's what I do. I have to do it.*

What does that even mean?

Woolf and Bridger only talk for a few minutes in lowered voices while I hold my usual place on the couch sitting cross-legged. I nervously fiddle with the hem of my t-shirt, which has become almost my standard uniform, along with yoga pants. Finally, Woolf turns his head to me and says, "Later, Maggie. Nice meeting you."

"You too," I say softly as he walks out the door. Bridger closes it and locks it before setting the security alarm that protects us at night along with his guns.

When he turns around, he walks immediately to the couch, taking a seat beside me. He sinks back into the cushion, rests his head there, and sighs as he stares up at the ceiling.

"Rough night?" I ask hesitantly.

"For the woman I worked over… yeah… it was a rough night." His statement is pointed. Clearly, it was just another day on the job for him, but it still makes my stomach curdle to think that Bridger hurt someone tonight. And because my imagination has always run rampant, and I am envisioning all kinds of awful things, I push at him to tell me more as I'm sure it can't be worse than what I'm already imagining, and if it's better, I'll have peace of mind.

"What did you do to her?" I whisper, wishing my voice were stronger and more demanding so he wouldn't think to dismiss my need to know.

He turns his head to look at me, still resting on the back cushion. "You really want to know?"

"I can't envision you hurting someone," I murmur in bewilderment. "I can't reconcile that with the man I know."

"You don't know me, Maggie," Bridger says gruffly. It's an unkind statement. His eyes are hardened, and it's meant to put me off.

"I know you took in a total stranger, had sex with a man to get me medical treatment, and then nursed me back to health. You've provided me a safe environment while I healed, and you're putting yourself in danger by hiding me. I think I know a little about you."

Bridger's eyes warm slightly, turning from dark bronze to golden whiskey. "How much do you know about BDSM?"

"Not much."

"Well, the people who participate in and like it... they get off on pain. It's sexually gratifying to them. So yes, while I provide that pain, it's because they want it and pay for it. I'm good at what I do, and I provide people with something they desperately crave. It's as simple as that."

"And the woman tonight?" I ask, because I can tell tonight was a bit different. The way he sits on the couch, looking totally defeated, tells me tonight wasn't ordinary for him.

Bridger sighs, turns his face away, and stares back up at the ceiling. "I have no clue what her experience was, but she took what I handed out like a champ. Never used her safe word and orgasmed a few times. I think she enjoyed it."

"Enjoyed what?" I press him, now not really understanding why I want the details. I think perhaps I'm fascinated by the concept that Bridger can make a woman orgasm but takes nothing for himself.

At least, I don't think he took anything for himself.

Bridger mutters a curse. Pushing up from his reclined position, he turns to me, slinging an arm over the back of the couch. His look is dismissive of my last question and that's verified when he says, "We need to have a serious talk about you and Belle."

"What about?" I ask carefully, my heart now pounding that he's mentioned Belle. He's not asked me about her once since I told him of her existence and refusal to disclose where she is.

"Zeke has all the Mayhem's Mission chapters out looking for you," Bridger says, and I go slightly dizzy at the implication. Not only is that a lot of fucking muscle going into this hunt for me, but it means he's pouring some serious dedication in retrieving his property. I know Zeke, and I know that means he will not quit until he has his hands on me.

Before I can even think of a response, Bridger adds on, "Kyle thinks he might go after your family... to figure out where you might have stashed Belle."

"Oh my God," I moan as I push off the couch blindly, fear making me dizzy. "I've got to warn them. I've got to get Belle."

Bridger's hand shoots out, latches on to my forearm, and pulls me back down to the couch. I immediately go berserk, thinking he means to deny me my right as a mother to protect my child.

I try to launch back off, crying out, "Let me go," as I slap at his hand on me.

"Just calm down," he growls. That only infuriates me more. I twist viciously against him and launch a bare-footed kick at his shin that only manages to send pain streaking through my bones.

Bridger wraps his arms around me and pulls me down onto his lap. I squirm and wiggle, trying to get free.

"Mags," he says roughly into my ear, tightening his hold. "Calm down. I'm going to help you get Belle."

I immediately go still, his words penetrating my fear. I twist my neck to look at him as he shifts me sideways onto his lap. "You will?"

"Yeah," he says earnestly. "If Zeke is going to do

that, and assuming she's with someone your family knows, I think it's best to move her."

"Then let's go," I say as I try to push up again, but he holds me in place.

"Tomorrow," he says softly. "Well, later today since it's already tomorrow, but we need sleep. And Kyle's not even sure Zeke is going to do that; it's just a worry he has, but right now, no move has been made that way."

"We should—" I start to say, but he cuts me off with another squeeze of his arms.

"And I need to get a few things worked out," he continues on. "We'll take Woolf's SUV in case someone is watching me."

"Do you think someone is?" I ask with panic.

"No," he responds quickly and with a reassuring rumble. "I don't. But let's just be very safe about it, okay?"

"So we'll go get Belle tomorrow?" I ask to make sure I understand.

Bridger nods. "She close by?"

"In Idaho… with a great aunt," I admit.

"Then we'll go get her tomorrow. After that, I think we should come back here," he says confidently.

"Back here? Near Zeke? We should run," I argue.

"Mags," he says softly, another squeeze from his arms, and my heart trips madly as he uses that nickname for me. "It's the last place he'll expect. He'll expect you to run, and it will spread him thin looking for you. We keep you hidden until Kyle takes the club down, which hopefully will be very soon. I can keep you safe here until then."

His reasoning makes sense, but I'm still terrified to bring Belle so close to Zeke. It's one thing if he gets his hands on me again, because after what I survived with Kayla, I know he'll never get me to break and reveal her whereabouts. The big question is—do I trust Bridger and that he can keep us safe?

The answer comes to me clearly and swiftly.

I trust this man with my life, but more importantly... I trust Belle's with him.

"My family," I point out. "They need warned."

"No sense in waking them up. You can call them in a few hours," Bridger says. He finally releases his hold on me, which makes me feel oddly naked and alone. I don't make a move off his lap, hoping for a reconnection.

We stare at each other, but I still make no move to leave my perch. His head tilts at me curiously. "What's wrong?"

I drop my gaze briefly to my lap, take note of my legs draped sideways over him, and think about the fact I'm sitting right on his...

"Thank you," I blurt out as I look back up at him. "I don't know why you're doing this for me."

He doesn't respond, just stares at me.

"I mean... why *are* you doing this for me?" I press him.

His eyes flick back and forth between mine for a moment before he answers. "I know a little something about being desperate for help. I had someone help me once, and it's time for me to pay it forward."

It's not what I expected him to say. In fact, Bridger is so mysterious sometimes I figured he'd just play off his being a Good Samaritan. But his words are so sincere and full of gratitude, I'm a bit taken aback. In fact, I can tell by the tone of his voice that whatever his desperate times were, they were awful and his savior had a huge impact on his life.

I knew there was something elusive I couldn't quite put my finger on that factored into my attraction to Bridger beside his obvious good looks and sexiness or the mere fact he saved me from certain death. But now I know it's because we share a past that includes something horrific that molded us into the people we are today.

"What happened?" I whisper as I place my hand on his chest, right over his heart. I feel two steady thumps before the beat picks up and it starts to gallop away.

"Nothing I want to talk about," he says, and there is no mistaking the coolness in his voice. He reaches up, takes my hand in his, and pulls it away from his body, then he starts to move to dislodge me from his lap.

A desperate need to hold onto whatever fragile connection we have fuels me, because for some insane reason, I simply have to know what exactly Bridger Payne is made of.

"Wait," I blurt out, my free hand shooting to his chest where I grab onto his t-shirt in a tight clutch.

He stills, doesn't release his hold on me, and gives

me a slight pause so I can continue. "You never answered my other question," I say in a lame attempt to keep this conversation going since he doesn't want to talk about his past.

"What other question?" he grits out.

"The woman tonight," I whisper, relaxing my grip on his shirt and flattening my palm back over his chest. "What did you do to her?"

I brace, expecting him to dislodge me from his lap, but I don't get what I expect. In fact, I get something quite different in the form of an erection starting to grow under my butt.

Bridger's eyes flicker with heat, his eyelids going to half-mast, and the corners of his mouth curving upward in a sensual smile. "Why… does that type of stuff turn you on?"

His voice is taunting, and I realize even though he's getting extremely hard underneath me, he's annoyed with my question and is trying to shame me for it. He's daring me to give up this quest for information, and I have no doubt if I press him, what he'll share may not be pretty at all.

But I'm desperate to understand this man who has cloaked me in his protection. "Maybe," I answer truthfully. "But I don't know because I can't envision it."

His eyes gleam with what one could consider malice, and I know he's going to give me the cold, hard facts about his kinky life. I also inherently know he's doing this to push me away, thinking I'll be disgusted.

I brace yet again when he says, "I stripped the woman naked and tied her down to a pool table with her legs spread wide. I then took a flogger and whipped her with it, not enough to draw blood but enough to leave some pretty nasty welts."

Bridger pauses and studies my reaction, and I can see he's disappointed I'm not scrambling away from him. His eyes go a shade colder, and he growls, "She was so turned on by what I did to her that her pussy was dripping."

Oh, God… his voice sounds so sensual that I can feel an ache start to form between my legs, even as the common sense within me knows this is him merely trying to turn me off rather than on.

"Then I let all the men fuck her," Bridger murmurs, and I feel his cock actually jump underneath me. I have to control myself not to squirm on his lap. "They all lined up and fucked her mouth, her pussy, and her ass until she was raw and filled with loads of cum and covered with their sweat and spilled beer."

I swallow hard and feel a tiny wave of nausea as I envision the scene. It disgusts me to think of that happening, and I'd seen other lewd shit happen at the compound during my years there, so I don't doubt what he's telling me is true. But at the same time, I'm turned on by the erotic sensuality of Bridger's voice and the thick shaft pushing against my butt, as it's clear he finds some beauty and appreciation in the scenario he's laying out to me.

Almost as if he can sense my warring thoughts, he leans his face in close to mine and murmurs, "Turn you on, Mags? Or does it thoroughly disgust you what I do?"

Both, I want to answer him, but I'm sidetracked by the swirl of colors in his eyes that tells me he might be torn too. Golden yellow competing with burned copper, which clues me in that he's just as conflicted. I'm further sidetracked by the feel of his breath on my face and his lips so damn close to mine.

Without thinking to answer him, and without acknowledging he's pulling my emotions in a hundred different directions, I merely lean into him and place my mouth on his. I immediately feel his entire body stiffen in shock before his hands come to my shoulders to push me away.

And I almost let him too… push me away, that is, but I also immediately feel his erection swell bigger and harder than I would have thought possible underneath of me.

So I press my lips against his and open my mouth, forcing his to open in turn, and letting my tongue dart in for a slow swipe against his. A growl rooted deep in his chest rumbles. I think it's in approval, but then his hands tighten on my shoulders and he does, in fact, push me back so our mouths break apart.

I stare at him in confusion, because I know he's turned on and I know he wants me. But it doesn't fit in with the chill in his gaze and his unwillingness to kiss me.

"That stuff turns you on?" he asks coldly.

I'm losing the connection and I can see him retreating, so I tell him the only truth I'm sure about right now. "*You* turn me on."

Bridger stares at me, his eyes going from glacial to muddy confusion.

"What do you want from me?" he practically croaks, and there's no denying the tinge of fear in his eyes.

My heart plummets that I make this man scared because I was pretty sure he feared nothing. I want to cry because he's petrified that I want him and for the life of me, I can't imagine what happened to Bridger to make him fear a woman wanting him.

"I want to kiss you again," I say breathlessly, wanting to push past his fears and have him give me something back in return. Something that lets me know I'm not the only one imagining this spark that's pulsing between us.

Bridger's body seems to lock tight, and he glares at me like I'm a complete annoyance. But then… his eyes drop down to my lips and he lets out an almost wistful sigh.

I hold my breath, waiting to see what he does.

Chapter 9
Bridger

GODDAMN HER.

Goddamn her for kissing me and making my dick hard and telling me she's turned on.

Goddamn her summer eyes and luscious ass pressing on my erection; those sweet fucking lips that felt so good on mine I was on the verge of a major freak-out; and finally, goddamn myself for not pushing her off me and ending this catastrophe in the making.

Push her off, Bridger. Just push her off, man, and put her out of your mind. You do not need this dangerous complication in your life.

Goddamn her.

My eyes stay pinned on her mouth and her words rattle around in my brain, taunting me. *I want to kiss you again.*

My own lips fucking tingle from the brief touch she gave me moments ago, and my balls actually ache with the need to come. I think about that blow job Carina gave me last night and how long it took me to get relief, and I know without a doubt that if Maggie just barely whispered her lips against my dick, I'd fucking blow like an unruly volcano.

I almost resolve in my mind to push her off my lap, then she does the unthinkable and nervously licks her lips. So now they're not only soft, but they're also shimmering… fucking begging me to have at them.

"Bridger," Maggie whispers and my gaze slides up to meet hers. Expectation, hope, and desire swirl within those fern-green irises and the ache moves from my balls to the middle of my chest.

Goddamn her.

My body is not my own to command because rather than pushing her away, I use my grip on her shoulders to pull her to me, crushing my mouth down onto hers. Maggie's sweet moan strokes over my tongue, and I'm pretty sure I've never tasted anything as good in my entire life. I bet her pussy is even sweeter, and that makes me feel something I've never felt in my entire life.

From a mere kiss, a low groan starts in the bottom of my chest as a shudder of desire shoots up my spine, and then tears free from my throat to explode in her mouth. The sound is guttural and tormented. It shames me because it clearly speaks to the depth of need I have for her right now, and I've never needed someone before.

Never.

But it doesn't shame me enough to push her away and end the kiss.

How can I when it feels this damn good?

I sure as hell have fucked a lot of women in my life, but I've never been much of a kisser. Never been much of a face-to-face kind of guy now that I think about it, preferring to stare at a woman's back while I fuck her or the top of her head while being blown. Rather look anywhere than in a woman's eyes because they'll inevitably morph into hers, and I'll read triumph and power in them even if that's not really what I'm seeing.

I'm not sure what makes this different from any other woman I've been with, but for the first time, I get a pure thrill from the simple intimacy of kissing. It's as erotic to me as if I were to pull her onto my face and have her ride my tongue. Her sweet, soft lips and tiny moans, and the way her tongue tentatively swipes at mine but otherwise prefers to let me have my way with her mouth. Even her hands that are now both clutching onto my t-shirt as she twists in my lap makes this kiss seem like the best thing that's ever happened to me.

Which is fucking ridiculous.

I should stop it.

So I kiss her deeper, one hand slipping behind her neck to hold her in place so she'll never go away.

Fuck... fuck, fuck, fuck. I'm so fucking fucked.

Maggie squirms some more, starting to pant. My cock turns so hard it starts to hurt as the backs of her legs and ass rub all over me. I bring a hand down to her thigh and grip her tightly, trying to hold her still, but that does nothing more than cause her to moan in protest. It's like torture to me that she needs something, and, apparently, I'm the one to give it to her.

Ripping my mouth away from hers, I pull my head

back so I can look her in the eye and tell her this cannot go any further. I am not going to fuck her, because if her kiss is this dangerous and has the power to cause me to lose all sense of myself, then what the fuck will her pussy do?

Except her eyes are shut tight, brow furrowed in consternation. She gives a rumble of protest and slowly opens her eyes, which are fogged over with lust. It takes her a moment to focus on me, but when she does, her eyebrows draw in even closer with confusion. "Bridger? Why did you stop?"

"We can't do this—"

"Yes," she exclaims, her hands moving from my t-shirt to slide behind my neck where she holds me tight. Tilting her head to the side, she presses her lips to corner of my jaw before whispering, "We *can* do this. Please don't stop. I'm begging you not to stop."

"Mags," I whisper consolingly, because the emotion and need in her voice slays me.

She tilts her head back so she can look at me. With a swiftness I didn't think was possible, she grabs one of my hands and shoves it in between her legs, spreading them so my palm presses right against her core.

Heat sears my skin and I groan again… and what the fuck is up with the God-awful sounds of need that are popping out of me? I'm simply out of fucking control, and I hate it.

"Please, Bridger," she whispers plaintively, and rather than sound annoying and whiny, it appeals to some deep-seated need within me to give this woman everything she craves.

"Goddamn you," I mutter and rather than push her away, which would be the best thing for my self-preservation, I roll us until she's on her back and I'm on top of her. Her legs part willingly and my cock comes to rest right over her pussy. She gasps, rolls her hips, and starts to writhe in an attempt to create friction between us.

I hiss... another fucking God-awful sound I apparently can't help but make when I'm touching Maggie, and because that felt too goddamn good and I have no intention of fucking her, I shift us to our sides so we're facing each other on the couch.

Maggie mews like an abandoned kitten and tries to scoot closer to me, her hips flexing inward for contact.

"Not going to fuck you, Mags," I tell her harshly. She goes still, her eyes flaring wide with surprise, and focuses on me intently. She opens her mouth to argue, but I beat her to the punch by shoving my hand between her legs and giving her pussy a rough squeeze.

She cries out in almost pained pleasure, hips twisting and seeking more from me. She's so fucking turned on and rabid for me that I almost feel dizzy from wonder. No woman has ever responded to me like this, but granted... I've never kissed a woman the way I kissed Maggie.

"Not going to fuck you," I reiterate as I slide my hand to the waistband of the stretchy-type pants she's wearing that fucking fit like a glove and make me hard whenever she's wearing them. "But I am going to take care of you."

"What?" she says, her voice sound slightly slurred from lust and confusion.

I don't answer. Instead, I show her, sliding my hand down the front of her pants, past her lace panties that I bought her, and right through the cleft of her pussy where my middle finger grazes over her clit on the way to the wetness I'll find just beyond.

"Oooooohhh," Maggie cries out, her back arching hard, which causes her to press against my hand, making it so easy to sink my finger into her.

And goddamn traitorous body of mine, another fucking groan rips out of me as I feel the tight, wet heat surrounding me. I have a moment where my mind actually sort of blanks, and the overwhelming need to rip her clothes off and bury my cock deep inside her makes me go dizzy with confusion. In this moment, I've never wanted to fuck someone so bad in my life.

Blinking a few times, I try to clear my head. I focus in on Maggie's delicate neck that's bare and exposed as her head is thrown back and pressed hard into the cushion. Mouth parted, she's panting like she just ran a marathon. Her eyes are squeezed shut tightly, and her teeth are pressed down into her lower lip.

The expression is as clear as day that she's dying for me to make her come.

I'm dying to give it to her.

Leaning my head down, I press my lips to the middle of her throat as I start to pump my finger in and out of her slowly. Maggie makes a strangled sound that has my lips curling into a smile as I graze them to the side and move lower until I'm just above her collarbone.

Lifting my mouth briefly from her skin, I ask her, "Want to come, Mags?"

"Y-e-e-e-s-s-s," she stammers, and then screams when I pull my finger out of her pussy and start to circle it around her clit.

So goddamn responsive.

Goddamn her.

I give her an openmouthed kiss at the side of her throat near the base, and then I suck against her tender skin while I alternate between finger fucking her and stroking her clit. I suck against her neck like a goddamn vampire, but not with the need to draw her blood. More with the insane need to mark her in some way.

Maggie starts thrashing, hips moving so violently against me that she's doing most of the work and riding my fingers. I lift my mouth from her skin and look down at her face again. Eyes are still shut tight, but now she's biting down on her knuckle in an effort to not scream.

It's sexy and fucking adorable and just... goddamn her.

I push my middle finger back in her, feel her reflexively tighten around me, and then pull it out. I shove two back in and she grunts... which shouldn't be, but it's fucking adorable too.

Pull both of those out, put three together, and push them inside, feeling the stretch of her tender skin and wondering what that would feel like against my cock, which is now in utter agony. I fuck her with those fingers, knowing the fullness feels good because she writhes and thrashes harder as she moans.

"So close," Maggie pants, her hand falling away from her mouth but her eyes staying closed. "So close. Please, Bridger."

God, I want her to come, and I want her to say my name again when she does. I'm immediately disgusted with myself for wanting something so… so… ultimately useless to me.

So as I pull my fingers from her tightness to circle back around her clit, I lean forward and kiss her hard, my teeth knocking against hers in a desperate attempt to distract her from saying my name when she comes and keeping me protected from this foolishness.

My tongue overwhelms and captivates her mouth, so when I flick my thumb against her clit and she starts to break apart on me, any word that could possibly resemble my name gets swallowed down my throat as she cries out. Maggie bucks against my hand as she starts to shake from the force of her orgasm. I work her clit through the downfall, gently circling the edges until she comes all the way back, all the while kissing her in a more leisurely but no less dominating fashion.

When she finally stills under me, I lift my mouth from hers and pull my hand from her pants. Maggie's eyes flutter open, immediately capturing mine, and she gives me a tremulous smile.

Raising a hand, she places it against my chest and whispers, "Let's go to your room."

My cock jerks in agreement and my chest aches, but I shake my head, pushing up and rolling over her to get off the couch.

I don't look back at her as I walk to the door. "You need to get some sleep. We've got a big day ahead of us."

"Bridger?" she calls to me, clearly perplexed and hurt.

I don't turn around, knowing that will hurt her even more, but I do issue a gruff, "I'll be back later."

"Bridger?" she calls again, this time in desperation. The tiny quaver in her voice causes my chest to squeeze with brutal force.

I ignore her and walk out the door, shutting it behind me. Without thinking, I trot down my porch steps and get in my Corvette, cranking it up and doing a quick turn around on my double concrete driveway so I can head down the long, paved road that leads back out to the main highway.

My hands grip the steering wheel tight as I think about Maggie calling my name, and the way she thrashed like a hellcat just from my fingers and fuck… I can smell her on my goddamn fingers and my cock starts hurting again. It's still hard as a rock and with a growl of frustration, I slam on my brakes and come to a screeching halt. After slamming the gearshift into neutral and pulling up violently on the emergency brake, my hands immediately work at my jeans to get the fly open.

Then my cock is out and in my hand. I'm stroking hard with pure agony that it's not Maggie's hand on me but with relief I can make this pain go away pretty quickly. I jack myself viciously, twisting hard at the top and when I close my eyes, I remember how wet Maggie was and the way she begged me to make her come. My balls draw up tight and start to tingle, and with three more pumps of my hand, I'm barking out a hoarse cry of release as I shoot my wad all over the steering wheel of my car.

Fuck, that felt good. Way better than the blow job Carina gave me, but not as good as it would have been to fuck Maggie. Poor, abused, and frightened Maggie. Dropped on my doorstep and wiggling her way into my worries. Beautiful Maggie with the curvy body, tight pussy, and a mouth that was made for kissing.

I look around my car helplessly for something to clean the steering wheel and myself, seeing nothing in sight. I watch the pearly cum sliding down over the Chevy symbol, and I feel utterly defeated.

Because for the first time in my life, I want something I can't have, and I can't have it because I don't deserve it.

Chapter 10
Maggie

M Y FINGER ABSENTLY strokes over the reddish-purple mark on the side of my throat. It's too high for my sweatshirt to hide it, but it's low enough a turtleneck would do the job. Sadly, I don't have one.

When I saw Bridger this morning, having sleepily stumbled out of my room at six AM when he woke me up, I was cognizant enough to see his eyes immediately drop to the mark on my neck. I may have been imagining it, but I swear I saw a look of triumph in his eyes. Which is weird, because Bridger clearly doesn't want me. Not the way I clearly want him, and my face heats up with embarrassment as I think about the way he made me lose utter control in his arms before turning around and walking out on me.

I struggle to suppress a tiny snort that wants to come out. Despite this strange and enigmatic man who I don't think I'll ever be able to figure out, I find it comical he left a bruise on me. A hickey really, and it doesn't hurt at all, but it is vivid. It's funny to me because as my other bruises left by Kayla are fading, he puts a practically neon sign on me that says, "Bridger Was Here". It also makes me want to laugh, because this man… who hands out pain to women with whips, left a mark on me that was neither painful nor scary.

Talk about irony.

In fact, his mouth on me felt too damn good. Even as he was sucking on my skin, I knew it would be visible to everyone, I couldn't find it in me to care last night. While his fingers were in me and on me, and his mouth was on my neck, I didn't have one single worry in my world. He made me forget everything.

Except this morning, those memories are dulling and I'm left with the brutal reality that Bridger doesn't want anything from me in return. I was positive last night after the last rumbles of my orgasm faded, he'd fuck me… make love to me… whatever. It totally stung in a humiliating way that he walked out. I didn't wait up for him to return, knowing when Bridger draws a line in the sand, he sticks to it.

It's been evident all morning as we drive northwest across Idaho. It's not been a silent and tense ride so far, but it's been absolutely devoid of any conversation that would even remotely come close to what we did last night. I am too afraid to bring it up, and he's clearly not going to.

Bridger had me pack an overnight bag as it is a good eight hours to Coeur D'Alene, Idaho where Aunt Gayle lives, and his plan is for us to stay the night after we pick up Belle before heading back. He ushered me into his sleek red Corvette I've seen but never ridden in, as I've been in hiding. We then drove a back road made of dirt and gravel that scraped on the undercarriage of his car, through the Double J Ranch, and came out at Woolf's house, which was a massive monstrosity set atop a butte.

I stared at it with my jaw hanging open and asked, "I assume ranching is a profitable business?"

Bridger gave a snort, not quite a laugh, and said, "Double J is the largest cattle ranch in the U.S. and he also owns oil fields. Woolf's pretty fucking rich."

Woolf was waiting on the front veranda of the house, and he met us at our car when we pulled up. When we got out, he handed Bridger a set of keys. "It's in the first garage bay."

Bridger grabbed our bags from the tiny trunk space in the Corvette and led me over to a detached garage done in pine logs that matched the house and held several bays. We walked in and Bridger went straight to a black Range Rover that was backed in.

"We're taking Woolf's SUV, not only so we can fit Belle's car seat, but also because if someone's watching me, they won't be expecting it."

"You think someone's watching us?" I asked tensely. "You mean Zeke?"

He shrugged as he opened the door for me. "I don't think so, but last night, something about Kayla put me off. She saw Kyle and me talking to each other and looked skeptical about it. We're just being safe. There's probably nothing to worry about."

And even as he said those words, he reached into his

overnight bag and pulled a handgun out. Opening the glove compartment in front of me, he slid the gun in and snapped it shut.

"Nothing to worry about?" I asked skeptically.

He flashed me a tight smile. "Not with that gun I'm not."

Bridger snaps me out of my memories by handing me his cell phone as he keeps one hand on the wheel. "It's a decent hour. Call your parents."

I've been dreading this. I need to do it, but my relationship with them is complicated and messy. I haven't talked to them in almost six months. I send them periodic cards with pictures of Belle, but I never provide a return address because I'm too ashamed to have them see me living at some motorcycle compound with their only grandchild. They don't approve of my lifestyle— what little they know of it, anyway—and now as a new mother who understands the worry a parent has, I can't say as I blame them. My calls to them have always been stilted, awkward, and so very short. They always took the time to remind me of their disappointment, but they would also invite me back home. I never accepted, and it's probably something I'll regret for the rest of my life.

My mom answers on the second ring. "Hello?"

"Mom… it's Maggie," I say hesitantly, wondering what type of reaction I'll get. Surprised delight or resigned disappointment.

"Maggie," my mom says, almost in disbelief, and then a long pause of silence before she says, "How are you doing?"

"Not so well," I say in a tremulous voice, and I have to give a slight cough to clear my throat. Bridger's head swivels my way, but I don't dare look at him. "Um… listen… I'm in some trouble and—"

"Honestly, Maggie," my mom says in a brusque voice, and it's clear I'm getting resigned disappointment today. "You're always in some sort of trouble."

"I know," I say, and there's no hiding the shame in my tone as I look down at my lap. "But this time it's pretty serious, and it might involve you."

"Oh no, you don't," my mom snaps. "We are not cleaning up a mess you've made. Are you in jail?"

"No, Mom," I say with swift frustration, curling my free hand into a fist. "I'm actually in some danger, and so is—"

"For heaven's sake, Magdalene," my mother says in that "mom" tone. "You can be so dramatic sometimes—"

"Mom," I grit out, my voice rising slightly. "I need you to just listen to me for a minute so I can—"

"Jim," my mom calls out to my dad. "You need to get on the line… it's Maggie. I'm not sure I can handle her latest—"

"Mom," I yell at the phone. "This is serious—"

"Maggie?" my dad says as he picks up on the other line. "What have you done now?"

"She says she's in trouble," my mom interjects.

"Well, of course she is, Cindy," my dad says dryly.

"Mom... Dad," I say now in a pleading tone. "I really need you to—"

"Let me make this clear, young lady," my dad says in a harsh tone. "You go months without contacting us, and when you do, you really have nothing to say. You keep our granddaughter from us, and you refuse to act like a responsible person."

"That's not true," I whisper, but he rolls right over me. My hands start shaking.

"We can't keep cleaning up your messes," my mom adds.

"I've never asked you to—" I try to defend myself.

But he cuts me off again, going off on a rant about personal responsibility and a failure for me to abide by my moral upbringing. I listen to my father laying into me when what I really want to convey is that he needs to pack up and get out of the house before danger comes knocking on his door, but he's on a roll now.

My eyes mist up with tears at the futility of it, but before I can try to interject anything else into the conversation, Bridger snatches the phone from me while growling, "For fuck's sake."

I turn to face him, my jaw hanging wide open, and he puts the phone to his ear. "Mr. and Mrs. Waylon... this is Bridger Payne. I'm a friend of Maggie's."

His jaw locks hard when my father clearly interrupts him, but he can't get more than a word or two in because Bridger says, "With all due respect, Mr. Waylon... I need you to shut the fuck up and listen. Your daughter and granddaughter are in very real danger by a man who's being investigated by the ATF for all sorts of vile criminal activity. Now, you can save your soapbox rant on all the ways in which Maggie has failed to live up to your expectations for another time, but this call is just a courtesy to you to tell you that this man... who is the president of a very large and very dangerous criminal organization... could very well be on his way right now to extract whatever information about Maggie and her whereabouts that you may have. So, it would behoove you and your wife to heed this advice, pack a bag, and go somewhere for a few days. Hopefully, the ATF will be taking them down soon, and if you can just stay under the radar until then, everything should be okay."

I'm astounded over the way in which Bridger has commanded this conversation, and the succinct way he gave my parents the relevant information they needed to know. Bridger listens for a few seconds, and then nods in agreement with whatever my mom or dad are saying to him. "That will work. I'll call you on your cell phone a bit later so you'll have my number. We'll stay in contact about the situation."

Another pause, shorter this time.

"I'll call you tonight," Bridger says, clearly winding the conversation down, but then he adds, "And for what it's worth... you need to cut your daughter a break. She's not the same woman she was when she left your home ten years ago. She's survived something incredibly horrific and she's an amazing mother, so you should really look at the positive things in your daughter for a change."

Bridger doesn't wait for a response. He just disconnects the call, calmly setting the phone in a center console tray. He puts both hands back on the wheel and says, "Your parents are going to pack up and take an impromptu vacation to Florida until this dies down."

I continue to stare at him, perplexed over his swift defense of me to my parents, because I have not been a good daughter. Fuck, I haven't been a good mother in all possible ways to Belle as I let her live her first two years in a shitty motorcycle club.

"Why did you do that?" I murmur in confused wonder.

He gives me a brief glance before turning back to look at the road before us. "Because you don't need to hear whatever shit they were handing you. You made mistakes. You're paying for them. You're moving on and making things right. They need to grow the fuck up and move past it themselves."

"Well, thank you," I say hesitantly. "I've never had anyone defend me before."

Bridger snorts but doesn't say anything, a clear indication he doesn't want to hear my gratitude, and I'm thinking that's because he wants to maintain the distance he put between us last night.

"I'm going to call Aunt Gayle again," I tell him as I reach for his phone.

I'd called her as soon as we hit the road a few hours

ago, but there was no answer. I left a voice mail but we haven't heard from her, and of course, I'm imagining the worst.

I shouldn't be though. There's no way Zeke could know about her if he hasn't talked to my parents, and that is where Zeke would go first. I don't have any siblings, so they would be the ones he'd want to pump for information. And the minute he applied any pressure to them—a thought that makes me nauseous because his pressure would hurt—they would give up Aunt Gayle.

My great aunt Gayle is the one family member I do have who loves me unconditionally. Even during all those years I partied, fucked up, and got into trouble, she never gave up on me. When I was in between jobs and had nowhere to go, her home in Coeur D'Alene was always open to me. I'd stay for maybe a few weeks, vow to get my life together, and then let the lure of the next great adventure pull me away from her. She never chastised or judged me, but always accepted me back with open arms.

It's why I knew she was the one who would need to keep Belle safe.

I dial her number and listen to it ring, each successive one causing me more anxiety when she doesn't answer. My stomach flips when her answering machine comes on, and I have to leave another message for her. "Aunt Gayle… please call me as soon as you get this. It's really important."

I rattle off Bridger's number and hang up, not leaving any more details than necessary.

Placing the phone back in the center console, I turn to Bridger and say, "What if Zeke—"

"Just stop," he says gruffly. "No way Zeke knows about her when he's not even been to your parents."

"But what if—"

"Mags," Bridger says softly as he takes one hand off the wheel to grab onto one of mine. The gentleness and confidence in his voice immediately settles me, even if my heartbeat picks up a fraction from his touch. "Stop worrying. Why don't you just assume she's out shopping or something?"

"I guess," I grumble, and then immediately regret capitulating on my worries because Bridger gives me a quick squeeze and puts his hand back on the steering wheel. I gaze down at my hand, almost longingly, wanting that warm reassurance coating me again.

Wanting Bridger to want something more from me in return.

I DIRECT BRIDGER through Aunt Gayle's small neighborhood that's made up of mostly single-story homes built in the seventies. Her husband, who was a Coeur D'Alene native, died before I was even born, and Aunt Gayle's lived here ever since in their marital home. She's seventy-four years old but acts about half her age, and while her arthritis can limit her at times, she's strong as an ox. I had no qualms that she could care for an active two-year-old when I begged her to take Belle.

Of course, she begged me to stay, but I couldn't. I knew Zeke would put all his energy into finding me, so I ran in the opposite direction, hoping I was leading him as far away from Belle as I could. I had no long-range plan when I decided to run. Just figured I'd always be on the run and foolishly believed Belle would be safe forever. It was shortsighted on my part, and I consider it a tremendous stroke of luck that Zeke is in the middle of a huge criminal investigation. Hopefully, he'll soon be put away and no longer a threat to us.

"It's right there... on the left." I point to a small two-bedroom house done in tan plywood siding with dark mocha shutters and an open carport attached to the side. The yard is pristine with late-blooming fall perennials bordering a walkway from the driveway to the front porch. The first thing I notice is that Aunt Gayle's car isn't in the driveway, and this gives me some small measure of relief that I'm not going to walk in and find her dead on the floor.

Bridger pulls into the driveway, parking just beyond the edge of the carport. I hop out of the Range Rover and scurry to the front door. As there is no doorbell, I knock, and then put my ear to the door to listen. I give a tiny twist to the knob and find it locked.

Absolute silence greets me, so I knock again... louder this time.

Nothing.

I turn to see Bridger walking up the steps to the

porch. He cuts right to look in the front window that goes to the living room. The drapes are pulled shut, but there's a small gap that he peers through for a moment before turning back to me.

"She's obviously not here," he says. "But everything looks fine… nothing out of place I can see."

"Let's go around back… see if we can get in."

He nods and walks to the far end of the porch, hopping off and heading around the back of the house. Before I can even jump down, I hear a man's voice "Just what the hell do you think you're doing?"

Without any regard for my safety, I jump off the porch and turn the corner of the house where I see an old man with a shotgun trained on Bridger, who is standing tensely with his hands in the air.

"Jesus, Randall," I say in exasperation as I look at the spritely man who tops out at just a little over five feet holding the monstrous Bridger Payne at bay. "Put that gun down."

"Well, hey, stranger," Randall says with obvious delight and he thankfully lowers the gun. "Assume this guy's a friend of yours?"

Bridger's hands drop but he remains in place… seeing how Randall is still holding the gun with his finger on the trigger.

"Yes, he's a friend… Bridger, this is Randall, Aunt Gayle's neighbor," I say as I walk up to him.

"Pleasure," Randall says to Bridger with a wily smile, finally taking his finger off the trigger.

"Friend of Gayle's?" Bridger asks dryly.

"Oh, I'm Gayle's sweetie," Randall says and cackles, showing off his gleaming white dentures he proudly told me about when I was here a few weeks ago dropping Belle off.

"Randall lives next door," I explain. "They've been neighbors for years."

"More than neighbors," Randall says proudly, but then leans in to Bridger and whispers, "We've been sneaking over to each other's houses quite often since my wife passed a few years ago."

I give a cough and look at him pointedly.

"Well, of course not while she's looking after little Belle, you understand," he says with an unapologetic grin.

"Where is she?" I ask with worry.

"Oh, she went off with a group of her church ladies to Spokane. Some kind of book signing for a romance author they all like. Took Belle with her, of course, although I would have been right happy to watch the little monkey. I mean… that author they were going to see… she writes some really sexy stuff, if you know what I mean, and I wasn't sure Belle should be tagging along."

Bridger manages to suppress a laugh, and I roll my eyes. "When's she coming back?"

"Tomorrow morning," he says affably. "In fact, since you're here… maybe Gayle and I can go out on a date. It's been a while since we had some alone time since Belle's come to stay."

I cock an eyebrow at him.

"Well, not to say I begrudge Belle being here, you know," he says quickly with another unapologetic grin. "But we have to be... you know... respectful of the situation with the little monkey always around."

"Let's go get checked into a hotel," Bridger suggests to me. "We can come back in the morning."

"Aaahhh," Randall says with a waggle of his eyebrows. "You two taking advantage of some alone time as well, I see."

"No, it's not like that," I say quickly, despite the fact Bridger fingered me to orgasm last night.

"We'll have separate rooms," Bridger says tersely as he turns back toward the Range Rover.

My heart sinks with disappointment, and I stare after him for a moment.

"So," Randall says and I turn my attention back to him. He nods toward Bridger. "Y'all not together then?"

"Nope," I say in a matter-of-fact tone, hoping it hides my disappointment. "Just friends is all."

Chapter 11
Bridger

PACE BACK and forth across the hotel room, my head tilting every so often to look at the door that connects my room to Maggie's. It's fucking torture knowing she's lying just on the other side, nothing more than that door and probably a flimsy pair of panties separating us. I know her resistance isn't what's separating us because I remember the need in her voice as she called out to me last night as I was walking out of my house. She could be mine for the taking if I just knock on that door and let her know I'm willing.

Except I'm not.

Because as much as I suspect sex with Mags would probably ruin me for any other, I'm too much of a chicken shit pansy to act on it. I'm too insulated in my little cocoon of protection, hiding behind a whip, a sex club, and whatever desperate female is willing to suck my dick without so much as a thank you after. It's all I know, and it's comfort to me.

Maggie Waylon is the opposite of comfort.

She's intrigue, danger, and possibly redemption wrapped up in one killer, sexy package that makes my dick act on its own accord. Just like now… half hard ever since I imagined her in panties on the other side of the door.

"Fuck," I mutter as I stop my pacing and flop down on the bed. I put my hands behind my head and stare at the ceiling, trying to think of something else.

Does no good.

Maggie's face flashes before me, eyes closed, chewing on her knuckle… on the verge of orgasm.

Goddamn her.

I should just go over there, open the door, and fuck her. Get it out of my system. It's probably not as great as I've built it up in my mind anyway.

Except that's not true, and I know it's not true because the minute my mouth touched hers last night, it was a kiss that completely disturbed me as much as it compelled me. Those feelings were too intense to forget. The thought of just that kiss has my dick getting harder as much as it causes anxiety to rocket through me, and perhaps I just need a hot shower where I can jack off once… maybe twice… and then I'll be able to let her go from my mind for at least a good night's sleep.

A soft knock sounds at the connecting door. Even as a zing of adrenaline spikes through me, my cock goes fully hard and presses painfully at the zipper of my jeans.

I should ignore it. She'll think I've already gone to sleep and leave me alone.

"It's open," my traitorous voice says loud enough to carry to her.

Goddamn her.

The door pushes open, and Maggie sticks her head in just enough to look at me. "Did I wake you up?"

"Nah," I say as I push off the bed to stand up. "What's up?"

Maggie's gaze drops to the floor as she steps in before looking up at me with uncertainty. "Um… I was thinking… this might all be over soon if Kyle's close to taking the club down, and I'm trying to figure out what I should do after."

She steps in further and closes the door, looking utterly gorgeous in the stupid pajamas I bought her that are white fleece with a sushi print on them. They're a little too tight which yeah… I have shitty judgment when it comes to women's sizing, but I can't help but admire the way the soft material molds to her ass or how her fantastically big tits push against the button-up top so that it gaps a little bit to show me a peek of cleavage.

My dick, which is also enjoying the view, jumps in my pants.

"So," she says slowly as she walks to the edge of the bed I'd just vacated and sits down. I take a step back and sit on the other bed, facing her. "I don't want to impose on your hospitality any longer than necessary. Hopefully, this will all go down quickly with Zeke, so I need to come up with a plan for Belle and me."

"You're not any imposition," I say quickly, and then mentally kick myself in the ass. Of course she's an imposition. She's driving me fucking nuts in my desire of her.

She gives a soft laugh, and it's like a punch to the gut. I've never been swayed by a woman's laugh before.

Never.

"Well," she says, still chuckling, "you've clearly not been around a two-year-old. You'll be begging us to leave."

"I wouldn't," I say softly. But then, with a slight cough, I say, "I mean... it's not like you have to leave the minute he's arrested."

She nods with a smile. "Yeah... I've thought about going back to my parents, but I don't know that they really want me there."

"I'm sure they do," I say, even though based on what little interaction I had with them and what I heard of Maggie on the phone, it's probably not true.

"Maybe I could come here to stay with Aunt Gayle until I get on my feet," she posits.

"Could be a good choice," I agree, even though my stomach cramps at the thought.

What. The. Fuck?

"Or," she says carefully. "You could give me a job, and I could stay in Jackson."

My heart leaps with a joy that feels foreign and invasive, and I immediately quash it. I force myself to lie. "I don't have any bartending or waitressing openings right now."

Her eyes drop to the floor, and she nervously plucks at the blanket on the bed. When she looks back up to me, she says, "No. I mean, maybe at your sex club, you could give me a job. I'm sure it's way better money than waitressing or bartending."

"What?" I growl in disbelief, coming to stand from the bed where I hover over her.

She swallows hard but pushes past my obvious anger. "I'm sure I'd be good at... well, whatever it is the girls there do. I mean... if there's one thing I've learned over these last several years is that my body is at least good for something. It doesn't mean that much to me, really—my body that is—and I could provide for a really good life for Belle, you know?"

My mind goes white with fury, and my blood pressure spikes to the point of dizziness. How dare she think she could just give her body to anyone, and how dare she fucking think it's not worth anything? Without really knowing what I'm doing, I bend over and wrap my hand around a fistful of her fleece top, pulling her from the bed. Her eyes flare wide, and a small gasp of what might be fear pops out of her mouth.

I lean in, put my face right in front of hers, and grit out, "You are not working in a sex club."

"Why not?" she asks with her head tilted but her chin lifted up, eyes flashing with stubborn defiance. "I'm good... I swear I am. I'll please your customers."

"You did not just fucking say that to me," I practically spit out in disbelief, giving her a little shake from my hold on her shirt.

Maggie's eyes burst with anger, turning from summer green to dark emerald, and she tries to dislodge my hold on her top by pushing against my chest. I don't budge, and she makes a growl of frustration. "Why the hell would that even bother you, Bridger? For God's sake, you deal in the sex business. It's not like what I'm suggesting is weird or anything. It's a way of life, right? You apparently hand out orgasms like party favors and make a good living from it, so what the hell is wrong with me doing it to try to provide for my daughter and me?"

She's got a good fucking point. I struggle to find something reasonable to divert her from this path, but I'm coming up empty. I certainly can't tell her she can't do it because I couldn't bear to see another man's hands on her. So I hedge on a semi-truth as I release her from my grip. "I don't pay the people who work in the club, Maggie. That would be prostitution under the law."

"Oh," she says softly as her head bows down and her body seems to deflate before me. She tugs on her pajama top to straighten it out.

"Perhaps it's best you come back here to stay with your aunt," I suggest, my stomach again twisting hard over the thought of her being so far away.

She nods absently without looking at me, turning toward the door that leads to her room. I want to reach out and snatch her back, my hand actually starting to reach toward her. But I go utterly still when she murmurs maybe more so to herself than to me, "Yeah… staying with Aunt Gayle would be good."

I don't say a word because I'm afraid if I open my mouth, it will be to beg her to stay with me, which is beyond insane. She reaches the door, hand on the knob, but before she turns it, she looks over her shoulder at me. "Bridger, it might be best if I just stay here with Gayle now. I think we're relatively safe. I mean… my parents are packing up and leaving their house for a bit until this dies down, so that's really the only way Zeke would learn about my aunt. So honestly… this is probably the safest place for Belle and me."

"What?" I rasp out, my throat threatening to close on me.

"Yeah," she says a little more confidently, her shoulders actually relaxing. "I think that's probably the best thing. So maybe you can just give me a ride to Gayle's house in the morning and head back to Jackson after."

"Mags," I say… and fuck… is that pleading in my voice? "You'll be safer with me."

She gives me a sad smile. Turning from the door, she pads over to me and places both hands on my chest. Looking up at me, those green eyes now bright and clear, she murmurs, "Bridger… I'll never be able to thank you for everything you've done for me. You're an amazing man, but—"

"Maggie… what's really going on here?" I interrupt her, because this isn't making sense to me.

"Nothing," she says quickly and turns toward the door again. "I just… we should part ways now—"

I lunge at her, grabbing her by the shoulder and

spinning her toward me. The movement is so fast she goes reeling and falls right into my chest. Not a hardship at all, but I take her upper arms to push her back just enough so I can look her directly in the eye.

"What's going on?" I repeat more firmly.

"Noth—"

"Maggie," I growl at her, one of my hands moving to slide my fingers along her jaw, curling around the back of her neck. I grip her gently. "Talk to me.

With a strength that surprises the shit out of me, Maggie pushes hard against my chest and steps back, dislodging my grip. Her eyes flash with anger as she blurts out, "I can't be around you anymore, okay? So I just want you to take me to Aunt Gayle's tomorrow and leave me there."

It's suddenly clear to me what this is all about, and guilt floods my entire system.

I can't be around you anymore.

Because I walked out on her last night when she opened herself up to me and invited me into her bed… her body.

I rejected her, and she's hurt by it.

"Maggie," I say apologetically, and it's apparently the wrong tone to take with her.

"Don't you dare feel sorry for me," she says furiously as she backs up two more steps toward the door. "I've survived far worse than you."

That slices me deep, and there's no way I can let her feel as if she's not worthy of the likes of me. Hell, she should know it's the opposite. I'm not worthy of the likes of *her*.

"Maggie… come here," I order and reach a hand out to her.

She shakes her head quickly in denial. Takes another step backward to the door.

"Maggie," I warn in a low tone, making it clear she's not getting through that door and to the safety of her own room.

We stare at each other a moment, each of us drawing our line in the sand. Her foot moves slightly to take another step away from me, and I lose all patience with the situation. I lunge once again at her in a move so fast, she shrieks in fear as my hands grasp her face. I pull her roughly toward me, bend my head, and slam my mouth down on hers. She makes a tiny sound of protest that fades into a soft moan before she slams herself into my body. Winding her arms around my neck, she goes to her tiptoes and opens her mouth to give me unfettered access to the sweetness of her tongue.

God, it's just as good as the first time I kissed her. No, it's better. It's better because I never thought I'd have this opportunity again, and I know I should feel like a shit for playing with her feelings like this—for using her attraction to me against her to get something I'm desperately craving—but I can't. I want this too much and fuck all the consequences.

I spin around and push her onto the bed where she lands with a jarring bounce. "Don't move," I order.

Maggie watches with half-mast eyes as I take my

clothes off, her gaze roaming all over my naked body as each part is revealed and finally settling on my rock-hard cock standing straight up. I grab my wallet from my jeans, pull a condom out, and throw it on the bed beside her. She doesn't even flinch or look at it, eyes still pinned on my dick.

Maggie licks her lips and a thrilling ripple of anticipation courses through me, making my skin prickle and my balls tingle.

Stepping to the bed, I reach a hand out and wrap it around the back of her neck again. I pull her from the bed into a standing position and lean down for a brief kiss. She sighs and goes lax, but I release her and she wobbles a bit.

Taking two steps backward, I sit down on the opposite bed, take my dick in hand, and start to stroke it. "Get undressed for me, Mags. Let me see that beautiful body."

A quavering breath flutters out of her, but her fingers go immediately to her top and she unbuttons it slowly. My mouth waters as she reveals her breasts and drops the fleece shirt to the floor. Her hands go to the waistband of her pants, tucking her thumbs in. She bends over to push them off, stepping out of them carefully.

I grip my cock hard as I stare at her naked body, her curves and soft skin beckoning. Want to put my mouth to those nipples and rub my shaft all over that softly rounded belly that has faded stretch marks right across the bottom. Fuck… when had that ever turned me on? But it does for some reason, and I think it's because she stands there proudly as a mother who bore a daughter and doesn't give a fuck what it did to her body.

It's a perfect imperfection in my mind.

"Come here," I murmur. She obeys instantly, taking the few steps across the carpet to stand between my legs.

I release my cock, put my hands to her waist, and lift her so she's straddling my lap. She immediately pushes down to rub her pussy on me, but I hold her tight. She squirms, uttering a moan of protest.

"Slow down," I tell her, my fingers lightly brushing over her lower stomach... right over her scars, and then down between her legs. I push my fingers through the lips of her sex, feeling the slick wetness and she fucking purrs in satisfaction.

I can't decide what I ultimately want to do to her, but I know first thing on my agenda is to get her off. Want to hear my name when she comes. I know my fingers can do the trick, but that's already been done.

I drop my torso down to the bed, my hands gripping her thighs, and look up at her straddling over me. She looks down at me, her caramel-streaked hair falling over her shoulders but not hiding those magnificent tits peeking through. She's stunning and for a few moments, she feels untouchable, and that makes me doubt.

Then, an immediate feeling of foreboding courses through me, and Maggie's face morphs into hers.

She bounces harder and faster, and then she taunts me further by grabbing the ring swaying from the necklace in one hand and bringing it to her lips. Pushing it into her mouth, she sucks on it as she looks down at me in triumph before she spits it back out and pants, "You're so fucking good, baby. I'll never get tired of this cock, you know."

My fingers dig into Maggie's thighs, and I blink my eyes rapidly to dispel the memory. My eyes drop to her stomach to see the stretch marks. I start to get my bearings, and I know this is Mags, who's been abused and tortured, just as I was once, and I know she's not the same woman who destroyed me all those years ago. My stepmother never experienced the miracle of birth, and that's only because she was too fucking selfish to share her body with another creature.

In my heart of hearts, I know Maggie isn't her.

Still, her position on top of me causes anxiety to squeeze my chest so I slip my hands around the back of her thighs and pull on her. "Get up here," I tell her gruffly. "Want you to ride my face."

"Oh, God," she mutters as she crawls her way up my body. My eyes drop to that pussy getting nearer and nearer. Saliva floods my mouth, and that's something new. While I'm no stranger to handing out oral, I only do it for the benefit of the woman, never for me. It's no different from me striking a nipple with a whip.

But for some insane reason, my tongue tingles with the need to taste her and to experience the flavors of this woman.

Maggie places her hands on the bed above my head and with the urging of my hands on her ass, I pull her down to my mouth.

Chapter 12

Maggie

BRIDGER'S MOUTH ON me is like fire and ice all at the same time. Searing heat, chilly tingles.

A violent shudder rockets through me as he shoves his tongue inside, only to pull it back out and close his lips on my clit. I let out a horribly guttural groan that seems to fuel Bridger, as he starts to flutter his tongue over the sensitive knot in rapid succession. I can feel myself leaking all over him, but I can't find it within me to care, because this feels better than anything I've ever felt in my entire life.

My fingers dig down into the bedspread and my hips start to tilt and flex against his mouth. Wet sucking sounds fill the air along with approving groans from Bridger as I do, indeed, start to ride his face. I dip my head down, looking past my swaying breasts, but I can see nothing but the top of his head as he works his tongue against me. His hands massage my ass muscles, creeping inward with each flex and release on my butt.

Pursing his lips around my clit, he starts to gently suck against me and a jolt of pleasure bursts between my legs. His clever fingers burrow down in between my ass cheeks and he rubs them in alternating patterns right over my sensitive hole which puckers involuntarily because it's an incredible sensation. Zeke took my ass on occasion and I always hated any touch back there, but God… Bridger's touch is gentle yet commanding. He clearly knows how to make ass play pleasurable. I consider what his cock would feel like, but that's for another time.

Right now, he's feasting on me in a way that no man has ever done. I feel my orgasm already starting to gather, and I've been on his face probably less than thirty seconds.

His tongue starts lashing against my clit again, and he maneuvers one hand in between my legs to push two fingers into my pussy.

"Oh, God… Bridger, wait…" I cry out, because that is causing sensory overload and I don't want to come yet. This is too good to just let it come and go so fast.

He chuckles against me, pulling his fingers out, and I sigh in relief that I can enjoy this a little longer. But just as he decides to suck on me again, lips gathering tightly around my clit, his fingers, now wet with my desire, push back against my ass. I tense up as he pushes a single digit against my hole, and then go almost rigid when he pushes the tip of his finger in. At the same time, he bares his teeth and bites at my clit, and stars burst in my head as my orgasm rips through me.

"Fuck," I cry out, involuntarily mashing my pussy down hard on his face. His finger slips further into my ass, and my hips start gyrating to force more friction against his mouth.

Poor Bridger's probably suffocating down below, but I can't stop myself from rubbing myself all over his face while his finger starts to fuck my ass. Tremors peel up and down my spine, igniting every nerve within me. Bridger gives a hard suck again on my clit, which fires off a second orgasm before the first even fades away.

"Bridger," I scream as it all becomes too much and I actually fling myself off him, coming to rest on the mattress beside him. He growls in disapproval over the loss and rolls my way, pushing me right onto my back and coming to rest on top of me. I get a brief peek at his eyes, which are turbulent and swirling with dark desire as he stares down at me, then he's crushing his mouth against mine in a brutal kiss that tastes like Bridger and me.

We're like two horny teenagers at this point, our hands roaming roughly over each other's body. Bridger starts rocking against me. His cock is massive and emanates heat while he rubs it over my pussy. His fingers pinch and twist at my nipples. My hands go to his ass, and I try to press him harder against me, while we kiss and pant into each other's mouths.

Finally, Bridger rears up, comes to his knees in a straddle above me, and looks blindly around for a moment before locating the condom he had thrown there earlier. His fingers frantically tear at the package and when he frees it, his tongue actually sticks out of the corner of his mouth in a look of pure concentration as he rolls it over his thick shaft.

"Need to fuck you bad," he mutters, still watching his progress with the condom and once he's fully sheathed, he pulls my legs up and spreads me wide. With a quick dip of his hips, the thick head pushes against my opening, and I suck in a huge lungful of oxygen in anticipation of what I'm betting is going to be an amazing experience.

He's going to fuck me.

He's not going to leave me.

He really, really wants me.

Bridger's eyes slide up my body and his look is tortured when it meets mine. "This might be a little rough," he grits out. "I'm sorry."

Before I can say anything, he plunges all the way into me and my back arches off the bed as I moan my satisfaction out to the heavens.

"Christ fuck, that feels good," Bridger groans.

"So good," I agree as I tilt my head back to look at him. His gaze is so intent as he looks down at me before he drops his elbows to the mattress to press his stomach and lower part of his chest against me.

He doesn't kiss me again, but merely stares at me almost in confusion as his hips start to move. He pulls out of me to the tip, pushing back in with a shocking force that causes me to grunt.

Oh, God… that feels so damn good. I just don't think I can…

Bridger's hips start moving fast, pumping his cock in and out of me. I can hear the sounds of wet skin sucking and slapping as he fucks me. He closes his eyes, biting down on his lower lip, and his face morphs into a beautiful visage of pure pleasure. It's so stunning in its transformation that I bring my hands to his cheeks to touch him. He moans at the touch but his eyes remain shut tight.

God, he's incredible. Beautiful and strong and heroic.

My hands slip to his temples, my fingers brushing through his soft hair. He makes a sound… of pleasure? Of protest? I can't decide, but his hips start moving faster and his cock is punching into me with abandon.

My fingers curl inward, grabbing hunks of hair. He fucks me harder, hitting against a spot inside of me that starts another orgasm to brew. I can't help it. I pull on his hair, a silent urging to go even harder if he must because if feels that damn good.

Bridger suddenly rears backward, pulling his dick all the way out of me and my hands dislodge from his hair so I don't rip it out as he puts distance between us.

He kneels in between my spread legs and my pussy is aching over the loss of him inside me. He stares down at me with a mix of anger and bewilderment. "Don't pull my hair like that," he mutters almost to himself, but I know he's addressing me.

"I'm sorry?" I ask in confusion.

"Never mind," he growls. Then his hands are at my

waist and he's flipping me over to my stomach. I can feel the bed dip as he scrambles off it, and then he's pulling me backward until my knees are resting right on the edge.

I don't even have time to process the sudden change of positions or the pervasively uneasy feeling I have that I've disappointed him somehow before he's slamming back into me from behind. My pleasure is immediately reengaged as I groan from the fullness, and he starts to fuck me again.

"Much better," Bridger groans as he tunnels in out and out of me, his breathing ragged and harsh. And yes… this feels amazing. Maybe not better, but just as good in a different way.

But something about Bridger's tone sets me on edge, because I don't think he's talking about the way this feels different to our bodies.

I crane my neck so I can get a look at his face. I need to know what's on his face so I can try to make sense of what feels to be a barrier between us now, but his large hand clamps on the back of my head and he stops me from turning. Then his fingers curl inward, grabbing a large hunk of my hair, and he holds me tight so I can't look at him.

Something's wrong.

I know it.

I almost demand he stop and talk to me, but then he takes his other hand, slides it to my front, and then down between my legs. He starts to rub at my clit and mutters,

"Want you to come again, Mags."

Okay, that right there… he's fully engaged with me.

He's back.

And because his fingers are magic and his cock is overwhelming me from this new angle, I start to fall under a fog of lust again. I concentrate on the amazing feeling he produces within me, and my heart starts a triple-time beat. Air seems to be a precious commodity as I pant like a dog on a hot day, and I start to pull and push my body against his, making his cock go deeper into me.

Bridger groans. "That's it, baby. Fuck me like I'm fucking you."

His words titillate and thrill me, because it sounds like he needs me the way I need him.

His fingers rub furiously against my clit, and he urges me in short, staccato bursts of words. "Come on. Mags. I'm close. Gotta come."

Oh, this man… doesn't want to leave me behind and the knowledge he wants me to have the ultimate pleasure again before he does sets me off. I go still, my back bowing from the force of the orgasm that tears through me, and once again, I cry out, "Bridger."

He pulls his hands from between my legs, confident my orgasm will continue to fire on its own, and puts both hands to my hips where he starts an all-out assault on my body. He lurches in and out of me, breath sounding like it's being ripped from his body, and then… he's suddenly gone.

His cock is gone and the last tingles of my orgasm fall immediately flat. I swivel my head and my heart clenches when I see the look on his face.

Pure agony and disgust.

Bridger isn't looking at me though. He's looking down at his cock where he rips the condom off and starts jacking himself. Three quick pumps and he starts to come, thick, pearly jets shooting out and hitting me on my ass and lower back.

Bridger head flies backward. He groans and squeezes his eyes shut as his hand flies over his shaft, viciously pulling and stroking... milking himself until every last drop is unloaded onto me.

I'm stunned as I watch his hand slow down. He strokes a few more times, squeezing the head one last time to pull a few more drops out. He even flexes his hips and wipes those drops clinging to his dick right onto my ass. His eyes finally open as he looks down at his handiwork of painting my backside.

Blank.

His eyes are flat, empty, and blank as they stare down at my ass, and a sense of anxious dread starts to fill me. Finally, he gives a deep sigh of... relief? Or is that regret? I can't tell.

Then his gaze slowly climbs up my body and locks with mine as I look at him from my position on my hands and knees. The cold flatness of his look melts away. He smiles at me sadly. "I'm going to get something to clean you up."

He turns away and walks into the bathroom, shutting the door behind him.

No post-sex cuddles.

No sweet words.

No soft touches or affirmation of what we just shared.

Just his cum on my back and ass now turning cold as the air flows over it, and I flop down to my stomach, incredibly confused and feeling utterly alone.

After a few moments, I hear the toilet flush, and then the sink running. My body braces when the bathroom door opens and I tilt my head, resting my cheek on the pillow to watch Bridger as he comes out. His gaze immediately comes to mine as he walks toward the bed, a wet washcloth in his hand. I stay still as he climbs onto the bed, leaning on his haunches as he comes to rest beside my body. My eyes close as he gently takes the washcloth, which is coarse, but also warm, and wipes the evidence of our union from my skin.

"All clean," he murmurs as he pulls it away and cool air immediately causes a chill to race up my spine. My eyes open and meet with his once again. No mistaking the look of contrition on his face, and I have to wonder what he feels sorry about.

For fucking me?

For being connected to me, not just physically but mentally, and then ripping it away from me mid-orgasm?

"What was that?" I ask softly.

His face is a mask of shrewd calculation as he looks at

me. "It was sex."

"But that's all it was?" I ask for clarification, already bracing for the answer I know is coming.

"That's all it was," he confirms, and his eyes fall away... not able to meet mine as he lies to me.

"No," I say firmly, pushing up to my knees and turning to face him. His gaze snaps back to mine with surprise. "It was less than sex."

"Excuse me?" he growls.

I scramble off the bed and bend down to my panties, tugging them on. Without looking at him, I grab my pants and put them on too. "Sex implies there's some level of intimacy between two people. And I think there was... to start. But then it became less than that. It wasn't anything more than a release for you by the time you finished."

"Seems to me you got off too," he snaps as he rolls from the bed. "Three times as I recall."

I don't even look at him though, gathering my top and shoving my arms through the sleeves. I don't take the time to bother buttoning it, just overlap the two sides of the opening over my breasts and wrap my arms protectively around myself to keep it closed.

"That's right," I sneer at Bridger, my anger starting to bubble and froth at the way he's discounting my feelings. "Three orgasms that were amazing—until they weren't. The only thing I remember about that experience is the look of disdain you had for me when you jacked off onto my back."

"Not for you," he growls as he stands before me naked and unabashed. "Not ever for you."

"Then who?" I shout in frustration as I throw my arms wide, my pajama top falling open. To Bridger's credit, his eyes don't drift down to my breasts but hold me pinned in place.

"For me," he says softly.

I can't help it. The pain those words cause propel me across the carpet until I'm right before him, my palms to his cheeks. He flinches but never breaks eye contact as he stares down at me.

"For you? Why?" I ask in bewilderment.

His hands come up, take my own, and pull them away from his face. He cradles them gently when he says, "I don't come inside of a woman. Not ever."

"I don't understand. Is that some kind of fetish or something? Like… I know it can be hot for a guy to come on a woman."

He gives me a soft smile. "Yeah, that can totally be hot and I like that, but that's not what I mean."

"What then?" I push at him, taking advantage of his willingness to open up to me.

"Mags," he says, giving a squeeze to my hands. "You're a very sweet woman, and I don't want to hurt you. But I'm going to tell you something about myself that people only suspect about me."

My stomach drops over the ominous tone, but I nod my head to give him permission to possibly hurt me further.

"I am beyond fucked up in the head when it comes to fucking and intimacy," he says in a flat voice. "They are two entirely different things to me. One I crave... that's the fucking... and one I cannot stand... that's the intimacy. Coming inside of a woman—inside her mouth, her pussy, her ass—it's just too much for me. I can't do it."

"Can't or won't?" I ask, because I get the sneaking suspicion this may be a cop out.

"Won't," he admits with a hard glint in his eye. "Not ever again."

"That's... that's... ridiculous," I sputter. "Every man who has sex will eventually come inside of a woman—or a man as the case may be."

Bridger's hands release mine as he steps back. "Well, I don't. I don't like it, and I never will."

"So you've done it before... orgasmed inside of a woman?" I press, because we're clearly getting to the root of the issue.

Finally, he looks away from me, searching the floor for his clothing. I can see an invisible wall being raised between us, and I feel like I'm losing him. I can't for the life of me figure out what happened to this beautifully fucked-up man to make him feel that way, but it breaks my heart in two.

I lunge forward, taking his forearm just as he starts to bend over for his jeans. "Wait."

He goes still, straightens, and turns to me, a look of wariness on his face.

"Was this a one-time only thing between us?"

Bridger's entire body locks tight and his lips flatten out. "That was the plan. I can't give you what you want."

"Maybe I'm willing to accept only what you can give me," I counter, stepping in closer to him, desperately offering myself in the only way I can apparently be united with this man. "We're going to be stuck with each other a little bit longer. What if I'm okay with how things just played out? I mean... you do give good orgasms, and I know what to expect now."

He cocks a skeptical eyebrow at me. "Mags... come on. You're an incredibly warm and open person. You don't want what I can offer."

My lips tingle with the out-and-out lie I tell him. "You're wrong. I'm okay with some raunchy, impersonal sex if that's all this is. Truth be told... even you pulling out and coming on my back was a lot better than what I've had in my life. I've lived in a world where men just use women for their own pleasure."

"Isn't that what I just did to you?" he replies sardonically.

"No," I say matter of factly. "You had me ride your face and gave me three massive orgasms. Doesn't sound like you were using me at all."

Bridger remains unconvinced, still staring down at me with a healthy dose of reluctance on his face. "I'll use you up and spit you out when I'm done, Mags."

His warning holds no punch, because he made the mistake of calling me Mags, which he uses like a term of endearment every time he says it.

"I can accept that," I tell him with my chin lifted.

But I won't.

I will not ever accept that from you, Bridger, and I'm going to make you see that there's more to sex than your narrow little world defines for you.

"I'll hurt you," he says as a last-ditch effort to put me off.

I give him a sensual smile, step in closer to his body, and drop my hand down to grasp his cock. It's still quite large even in its softened state, and my heart leaps with satisfactions as it starts to swell in my grasp. "Maybe I'll be the one who hurts you," I whisper to him. "Do you want me to hurt you, Bridger?"

He takes in a ragged breath, flexing his hips so my hand moves against him. "Yes," he growls, and I can't tell if he's talking about right now in this moment, perhaps some pain the way he likes to dole it out to other women, or if perhaps he's secretly hoping I can hurt him on a deeper level to prove to him that he's not as insulated as he likes to believe.

Chapter 13
Bridger

MAGGIE IS ALMOST bouncing with anticipation as I pull into Gayle's driveway and she sees her sedan under the carport. This is a change from the mellow and relaxed Maggie I had dealt with this morning when we rolled out of bed.

It wasn't my intent to sleep with her all night, and in fact, I had told myself I was going to kick her out after we'd had sex for the third time. But I was exhausted after having blown three successive nuts and given her twice as many orgasms while we frantically fucked all through the night. There would have been a fourth time, but I didn't have any more condoms on me. I thought perhaps I'd just fuck her without one because I knew she was clean. Jared had run a full blood panel on her when he first examined her, and I had him include an STD test in the workup. Not because I was thinking about fucking her then, because no… that was nowhere on my mind, but she had been held hostage in a biker compound and I knew those guys didn't take safe sex seriously. I figured she'd want to know if she was carrying anything, but apparently, she wasn't. I suspect that's because Zeke was the only one who touched her, and I knew he always wrapped up when he fucked pussy that wasn't Kayla's.

But after that third time, we'd both collapsed on the bed side by side, Maggie clearly not caring I'd come all over her stomach that time. I had also proved to myself that I could fuck her face to face with no impunity.

Well, that's not quite right. I was completely affected by kissing her the entire time and watching her face as she came with my cock wedged in deep, and I was barely able to pull out in time to avoid the dreaded "coming inside of a woman". But I'll never admit to myself that I kept wondering… what if I tried it just once to see what would happen?

Regardless, I didn't give in to that insane curiosity and we both fell asleep on top of the wrinkled bedspread and stayed that way until the light peeked in through the curtained windows. I found Maggie curled into my side, sleeping like the dead, and a not exactly unpleasant feeling of belonging pulsed within me as I took stock of her warm skin pressed against mine and the way her breath feathered over my chest. I relished it for a moment, completely accepting that this was an intimate moment, but not being entirely too wigged out by it. I was way too sated and mellow from great, all-night sex, which is something I've never had because I've never stuck around that long to go more than once.

"God, I think I'm going to pee my pants," Maggie says in an almost whispered squeal, and I can't help but laugh. I also can't help but be a little envious as she bounces up and down on the passenger seat, her tits jiggling, and I wonder if I could handle her riding my cock. I don't ever let a woman on top because bad memories and all that, but for some reason, I'm very curious as to what it would be like to have Maggie riding stick and letting me palm those beauties at the same time.

Shaking my head, I bring the SUV to a stop and put it in park. The front door opens and a little girl comes flying out, followed by an older woman who is rail thin but carries her posture in a way you know there's strength—both physical and mental—within. She stands on the porch with her iron-gray hair in a bun and watches with a smile as Belle jets down the front steps. Maggie's out the car door in a flash, and my throat turns dry as I watch her fall to her knees on the ground just as Belle slams into her, screaming, "Mommy."

My hand involuntarily rises, and I rub my knuckles across the ache right in the middle of my breastbone. I don't have much experience with moms and little kids. None of my friends have children, and my only experience is what I've seen on TV or in the movies. But I can tell you… I never had a reaction to a moment of parental bonding like I'm having right now. I remember those stretch marks on Maggie's stomach, and I look at the way she buries her face in Belle's neck. For the first time in my life, I have a true glimpse of what being a mother is all about. This is shocking to my senses because to me, mothers sexually abuse their boys and brainwash them into thinking beatings and pain enhance the sexual experience. I mean, my stepmom didn't bake me cookies but she got me off regularly, and that was something, right?

I feel a dark bitterness start to overtake my senses, and I force myself to push those thoughts aside as I step out of the SUV and onto the driveway. Glancing up at Gayle, I see she gives me a little wave of her hand to join her in the house while Maggie plops her butt on the browning front yard grass and pulls Belle onto her lap without even looking at me once.

I smile and walk past them, following Gayle into the tiny brown house and into the little kitchen decorated with cheery yellow curtains over the windows and the faint odor of lemon cleaner and fresh-brewed coffee.

She turns her head and smiles at me over her shoulder, pouring a cup of coffee from a half-empty pot. "I'm Gayle, Maggie's great aunt, and you must be the man that my Randall held a gun on yesterday afternoon."

I chuckle as I accept the cup from her. "Yes, ma'am. Bridger's the name."

"Well, welcome to my home, Bridger," she says with a grin and I find myself instantly connecting to this little spitfire of a woman. She's wearing faded jeans, a pair of worn crocs on her feet with white socks underneath, and a plaid, button-down flannel about three sizes too big for her.

Gayle pours herself a cup of coffee and then heads to the small, round table that takes up at least half of the tiny kitchen space. She inclines her head and I follow suit, taking the chair opposite her. "So, what type of trouble is Maggie in now?"

Her voice is not judgmental or admonishing, more worried than anything, and that puts me at ease. I would not take kindly to anyone placing any blame on her shoulders at this point of Maggie's torturous journey out of captivity.

And that's so weird… this all-encompassing protective instinct I have where she's concerned.

I take sip of coffee, put it down on the table, and tell her the truth. "Belle's father, Zeke, captured Maggie after she brought Belle to you."

"Oh, my God," she gasps, bringing her hand over her mouth. "What did that animal do to her?"

I decline to tell her the truth, because I don't want to cause any anxiety or stress on this woman. So I merely say, "She's fine. She was able to escape with the help of a friend, and I've been keeping her safe."

Gayle narrows her eyes at me and her voice is pure forged steel when she says, "Now you listen here, young man… don't you sugarcoat things with me. I want to know what happened to my Maggie."

Her ferocity is adorable and equally respectable, and I see a strong backbone and fortitude emanating from this woman. So I give her the truth. "He beat her. Tried to get her to tell him where Belle is."

Gayle swallows hard, but otherwise doesn't flinch.

"Then he left, and his old lady, Kayla, tortured Maggie," I continue, because for some reason, I just know this woman needs to be fully apprised of the situation so she can give the proper guidance and support to her great niece. "It was bad, Gayle. I mean, really bad."

"But she's okay now?" she asks fearfully, and I'm grateful she doesn't want more details than what I just gave her.

"Yes," I tell her with a reassuring smile. "She's fine, strong, and now very happy to have Belle back."

Another delicious squeeze of joy deep within my chest as I recall Belle flying into Maggie's arms.

"So everything's all settled?" Gayle inquires. "Zeke's not a threat anymore?"

"No, he's a very big threat," I tell her bluntly. "He's doubling up his efforts to find them both, and we're afraid he might start targeting her family. I've talked to her parents… they're going to leave town for a bit."

"Oh, dear," she murmurs, her eyes sliding to the front door where Maggie and Belle are reuniting on the other side. "Should she be here?"

"I think it's best she come back to Jackson with me," I tell her bluntly.

"But that's where Zeke is."

"And it's the last place he'd think they'd be. I can keep her safe until he can be taken down."

"And just who is supposed to do that?" she asks skeptically.

"There's a guy who's undercover ATF. Been inside the club for three years. He's the one who rescued

Maggie and got her out of there. Brought her to me. I think a huge bust is going to be going down very soon from what I've been told. Once that happens, they'll both be safe."

Gayle nods, instantly looking relieved. She stands up from the chair and heads to the refrigerator. "I'm going to make breakfast for everyone so you can have full bellies for the trip back."

I watch in silence as she pulls eggs and bacon from the refrigerator, and then a bag of frozen hash browns from the freezer. She gets out an electric griddle and loads it up with the bacon, takes another skillet from a cupboard, and heats oil in it on the stove. As she moves efficiently around her kitchen, she says, "Maggie's a good girl."

Oh, Gayle... if you knew the things she's let me do to her, you wouldn't say that.

"Yeah... she is," I agree softly, a secret smile hidden deep within me.

"Her parents are too tough on her. They never understood that children could be stubborn, rebellious, and willful, and that they just sometimes need to find their own way. She made a few mistakes, and they've pretty much written her off... made it impossible for her to return home, so she really didn't have a home. That's never a good situation to be in."

"But she kept returning to you," I point out. "You were her home."

Gayle nods as she takes a fork and starts flipping the

bacon. "That child knows she's always welcome here for as long as she wants. I tried to get her to stay when she brought me Belle a few weeks ago, but she didn't want me in danger. I assured her Randall's gun was plenty of protection."

"I don't think Zeke could find you if he can't get to her parents, but maybe you should go stay with Randall just in case," I suggest.

Gayle snorts. "That randy old toad would love to hear you say that. He'd tie me to his bed if he got the opportunity."

Wincing, I try to mentally scrub out my ears. I don't want to know these things about dear Great Aunt Gayle.

She spins on me, holding a fork up as she stabs it in my direction. "You promise me you'll protect them with your life if it's necessary."

"It won't be," I assure her, because I'm pretty confident Zeke has no clue I'm helping her and that he's going to jail soon anyway. "But I promise… he's not getting anywhere near Maggie and Belle."

She stares at me a hard moment, either trying to determine if she believes me or she's trying to convey some brutal message that she'll castrate me if I let her down. Finally, she gives me a smile and says, "You're a good man, I can tell. Strong and with character."

I drop my gaze from her so she doesn't see the cowardice within. That I'm not strong or else I wouldn't let the ghosts of my past dictate how I treat Maggie. I have no character because I'm unwilling to trust that Maggie just might be different. I'm definitely not good, having done things in my life that would turn her gray hair pure white if she knew.

The front door swings open with a resounding bang. Gayle jumps about a foot high, and then brings her free hand to her chest as if she's staving off a heart attack. She glares at Belle, who comes flying into the kitchen. "Aunt Gayle… Mommy says I go with her. Go with Mommy. Go with Mommy. Go with Mommy."

The little girl, who is the spitting image of Maggie, runs straight into Gayle's legs and wraps her arms around them before lifting her face and beaming her happiness upward. Gayle's weathered hand goes to Belle's fine, blonde hair that sits just below her shoulders. It's pinned back from her face with a pink bow, and Gayle strokes the top. "Gonna miss you, child."

"Miss you," Belle says with a grin on her face, but you can tell she doesn't really know what that means and is more parroting her aunt.

I feel Maggie's presence behind me before I see her, and then feel her hand come to my shoulder where she squeezes me briefly before walking past. She leans down, picks up Belle, and turns to face me. "Bridger… this is Belle. Belle… this is my friend, Bridger."

Belle puts her hand in her mouth and lowers her face shyly without looking at me.

"Belle," Maggie says softly, tickling at her ribs a bit. "Can you say hi to Bridger?"

She finally looks up at me. I get an up-close look at

the same fern-colored eyes as Maggie's.

"Hi, Bwidg-uh," she says, and I actually feel my insides go a bit gooey. I think this may be the first conversation I've ever had with a two-year-old, and she's fucking cute as all get out.

"Hi, Belle," I say as I reach out and hold my hand up in front of her. "Got a high five in there for me?"

She looks at me in confusion before looking to her mom, and then back to me. I lean forward in my chair, take her hand, and gently flattening it out before I slightly smack it to mine. "See… that's a high five."

I let her hand go, and she automatically slaps it to mine again. "High five," she says with a laugh.

"Or," I say as I curl my hand into a fist, taking hers to do the same. I then bump my knuckles against hers. "You can do a fist bump."

I let her go, and she knocks her fist against mine on her own. "Fist bump."

Laughing, I look to Maggie and say, "Smart kid."

"Gets that from her mommy," she replies tartly.

My phone chimes with an incoming text. Maggie sets Belle down so she can pour a cup of coffee for herself. The little girl immediately scrambles up on one of the kitchen chairs beside me where I feel the weight of her stare. I give her a smile as I pull my phone out, and then glance down at the text.

It's from Cal. *We are flying in tomorrow. Already booked room at Wort. Like to do club Sunday night.*

"Fist bump," I hear Belle say and I look up to see her

little hand hovering in midair. I make a fist and knock it to hers. She giggles, and I can't help but laugh.

There's a smile lingering on my face as I bend over my phone and shoot a quick response back to Cal. *Sounds good. Let's do dinner first.*

"Fist bump," Belle says, and I look back up. She's looking at me expectantly, fist hovering in the air. I touch my knuckles to hers, and she starts giggling uncontrollably.

"You've created a monster," Maggie says, and my gaze slides to hers. But she's not looking at me. She's looking at Belle with such uncontrolled love in her eyes that it makes me want to start crying for some reason.

"Fist bump," Belle says, and I give it to her again.

She laughs and laughs, and that makes Maggie laugh, and I realize I'm feeling something I've never felt in my entire life.

For the first time… ever… I feel charmed, and I get the distinct impression that there isn't anything Belle would ask of me that I wouldn't give her.

Little brat.

Chapter 14
Maggie

I PULL BACK the covers and place Belle in the middle of the bed in Bridger's guest room where I'd been sleeping. She normally sleeps in a crib, even though it was a ratty old one that Zeke had one of the guy's get for her from some yard sale, but Aunt Gayle assured me she'd been sleeping in her bed just fine without falling out. Besides, Belle has gotten to an age where she's climbing up and down on furniture and seems to have a little better grasp of gravity and such. I'm not so much worried about her falling out of the bed as I am of her waking up in the middle of the night and slipping out to roam the house where she could get in all kinds of trouble. Bridger actually had the same worries. As soon as he carried our bags inside while I carried a sleeping Belle, he went around the house and removed all the guns he had hidden around, locking them up in a cabinet in his bedroom. I could tell this weighed on him a bit, but he told me he truly felt the greater danger was in Belle messing with a gun than Zeke ever showing up here, so he felt the smart thing to do was secure them.

That warmed me… that his first thought was of Belle

and nothing else, and that's exactly as it should be. I know he met her only about nine and a half hours ago, but those two just clicked. I know I shouldn't read anything into it, but Bridger... the man who holds himself so removed from intimacy that he has to come on my stomach or my back has had no problem in letting Belle walk all over him.

The entire drive from Coeur D'Alene to Jackson, Belle made Bridger sing songs with him. I was surprised he even knew some of the basics, because I can't begin to imagine what his past is like given some of his social hang-ups right now. But his childhood apparently revolved around some kid's songs because he easily pulled forth awesome renditions of "Bah Bah Black Sheep", "Twinkle Twinkle Little Star", and "The Wheels on the Bus". Now, granted, those were really the only three he knew, so they got sung over and over again on the drive, but Bridger didn't seem to mind. While I was getting sick of hearing the same tunes repetitively sung, they'd finish a song and Belle would cry out from her car seat in the back, "Again."

And Bridger would sing with her again.

I'm not sure I've ever been as grateful as when Belle fell asleep after we stopped for a quick lunch at McDonald's—where Belle insisted on sitting in the booth beside Bridger—and I eagerly turned on the radio so I could listen to some adult music for a bit.

Pulling the covers up to her chest, I lean over, kiss her head softly, and whisper, "Goodnight, sweet pea. I love you." She's so exhausted from the long trip that she doesn't even stir.

When I step out into the hallway, I glance down to Bridger's room and see his door is shut. He'd said he was going to take a shower and that actually sounds like a good idea. I head across the hall into the bathroom I use. Within moments, I have my clothes shed and I'm standing under a steady spray of hot water while I consider everything that's happened during the past thirty-six hours.

Mostly, I think about Bridger and me and what transpired between us last night. The bridge we crossed when he finally fucked me, only to find myself standing across a chasm from him when it was all said and done. He said he's fucked in the head, and that his ideas of sex and intimacy are twisted. My heart aches when I think of him pulling out of me before he comes, because he says he doesn't like it, and that makes me feel wretched about myself because I know I'm not imagining the connection I have with him. He says he hates intimacy, yet he shows it to me all the time. I feel it in the way he kisses me or runs his fingers over my stretch marks while he stares at me with unbridled lust. The way he makes me come... like it's vital to him that I feel pleasure. Even the way he gently cleans me off after he spills himself onto me is an intimate act, but he doesn't seem to get that.

Regardless, I am not giving up on him. The man has the potential inside of him, I just know it. He's saved me, and now I want to do the same for him.

I finish my shower and take a moment to blow dry most of the dampness from my hair. After slipping into a pair of clean panties and a tight t-shirt, I make my way down to his room. He hasn't invited me there, but he didn't say he didn't want me either. While our trip today was filled with clean conversation in between "The Wheels on the Bus", I could still feel the current of attraction running between us.

I don't bother knocking on his door because I am not ready to hear him tell me to go away, so I open it gently and peek my head inside. His room is lit in a soft glow from the bedside lamp he has on, and Bridger lays there totally naked on his bed, propped up against some pillows and his headboard.

My heart stops beating in my chest as I see him stroking his cock, his eyes heated with lust as he looks at me.

" 'Bout damn time you got in here," he growls.

"I wasn't sure if you—"

"Don't ever doubt my want for you," he says in a low voice, like smooth stones are tumbling within his throat. "Now get over here."

My panties immediate get soaked just from the naked need in his voice, and I hurry into the room, leaving the door open slightly so I can hear if Belle calls out to me.

"Ditch the shirt and panties," he orders me, his hand slowly working his hard shaft.

I scramble to comply, totally looking awkward and

not sexy in the slightest, but the desire in his eyes doesn't dull and he looks like he wants to attack me. When I pull my panties clear, he holds his hand out for them.

I don't hesitate; I just place them in his palm. His fingers rub along the crotch, and he gives me a feral smile as he feels the wetness there. "Did you know it was torture all day today, sitting next to you in that car… smelling you… but not being able to touch you?"

See… that's intimacy, Bridger, whether you admit it or not.

I shake my head and he gives a dark laugh, crooking his finger at me to come closer. My feet obey and my heart feels like it's going to burst from my chest. Before I reach the bed, Bridger pushes off it and reaches into the drawer of the bedside table. "Get on the bed. On your hands and knees."

My stomach flips when he turns to me, a bottle of lube, a butt plug, and my panties held in his hands. My throat goes absolutely dry. "What are you going to do with those?"

"I'm going to shove these panties in your mouth so you don't wake up Belle when you scream, then I'm going to slide this plug into your ass before I fuck you," he says with dark promise. "And I promise… it's going to feel really good."

A cramp of longing hits me square between my legs, but I don't get on the bed as he demanded. Instead, I ask, "That the kind of kinky stuff that goes on at the club?"

He laughs, and it sounds amused and sinister all at the same time. "This doesn't even come close to the kink that happens at the club, Mags. Now get on the bed."

I let out a rush of nervous breath and do as he commands, not because I don't have the fortitude to say no, but because I most definitely want to say yes. I crawl onto the mattress, facing away from him, and raise my ass into the air as I go down to my elbows. I bow my head, look at the navy comforter, and wait to see what he does.

The first sensation is the soft glide of my silk panties across my ass just as the bed dips and Bridger comes up behind me. "You're fucking gorgeous, Mags," he whispers, and my heart flutters.

Then a hand is sliding down my butt, in between my legs, and his fingers softly rub against my pussy. He just circles them lightly against my damp flesh, driving me crazy for more of his touch. Finally, he dips a finger inside of me, easily sinking in because I'm soaked, and then pulls it back out. Dragging it up the crease of my ass, he taps the tip against my tight hole.

I gasp and squirm, both nervous and excited to see what he does.

"Open your mouth," he tells me.

I don't hesitate, raising my head and turning it to him so he has access. In goes my panties and I have a moment of panic that I won't be able to breathe, but he doesn't push them in far, only enough to muffle my screams.

"Only thing that would be better is if I had the time to tie you up, but we'll save that for some other night," he murmurs to me.

I lower my head again, staring at the comforter, and my skin starts to prickle with apprehension when I hear the click of the lube cap and then feel a warm stream right over the crack of my ass. Bridger's finger is next, pulling the slick gel down and massaging it all around my hole. I can't help that my body pushes back against him... seeking more.

"Is your ass cherry, Mags?" Bridger whispers as he pushes the tip of his finger in.

I shake my head frantically, thinking of the times that Zeke fucked me there. He always used lube, thank God.

"Good to know," he mutters, pushing his finger all the way in. I gurgle against the panties, the feeling of his finger far too good and causing a burning need in me for more.

"I would fuck your ass right now," Bridger says, voice dark. "But I want that pussy too bad. I want that sweet, wet, tight Maggie pussy wrapped around my cock."

Oh, God. Oh, God.

Bridger's words are like ear porn, and I can feel wetness leaking out of me between my legs. I start panting against the silk in my mouth and if I were able to, I'd scream at him to just fuck me already.

But he has something else to do first.

Bridger removes his finger, and it's immediately replaced by the cool tip of the butt plug. I've never had one of those before, but as he slides it into me, my tender flesh stretching and then forming around it, I think to myself that I've not led a very full life without experiencing this. It feels amazing as he slides it into the hilt and then taps his finger against it a few times. That action makes me squirm and moan against my gag.

"Fucking beautiful," Bridger mutters, and his voice sounds strained.

I hear him rip into a condom and in my mind, I can see him rolling it on that long, thick cock of his. My mouth would be watering hard right now if the silk weren't sucking everything up. I wait for it… for him to slam into me from behind, but instead, he flips my body over until I'm lying on my back and he's looming over me.

He leers down at me, in a totally sexy way, and taunts, "Want to watch your face while I fuck you… want to see how good that plug feels in your ass while I'm doing it."

Oh, God. Oh, God.

I have never in my life had a man so focused on making me explore my kinky side and wanting to make sure it feels good to me. My experience with men is that it's all about them, and they couldn't give a fuck if I enjoyed it or not. All they cared about is if I moaned at the appropriate times and stayed wet throughout.

Bridger spreads my legs, uses a hand to guide the head of his cock to my pussy, and then he sinks into me slowly. His eyes stayed pinned on me the entire time, and mine immediately water from the overload of sensations. His cock stretching and filling me, rubbing against the plug that's separated by the thin veil of tissue in between, and pressing it further into me once he bottoms out. My forehead furrows, and I blink my eyes to dispel the moisture. Bridger's own eyes become worried as he asks, "You okay?"

I nod my head frantically, lest he thinks I want him to stop. I try to say, "I'm good," against the panties in my mouth, but it's absolutely unintelligible. Still, he accepts my nod and his face smoothes out.

"Good," he praises, lowering his elbows to the mattress by my ribs. "I'm going to fuck you so slow, you won't know where time has gone. Not going to touch your clit. Going to just make you come with the power of a slow fuck from my cock and that plug deep in your ass. Think you can do that for me?"

I nod vigorously again. He smiles so beautifully at me that the wind is knocked from my lungs. Bridger bends down, places a kiss on my cheek, and then starts to move inside me.

And oh my word… nothing has ever felt like this. Every nerve in my body seems to fire, and the sensation of his cock sliding in my pussy, rubbing against the plug, jamming it into my ass every time he sinks to the hilt… He's only about five strokes in and I already feel my entire body tightening with the need for release.

Bridger's hips swivel and gyrate, sinking into me

from various angles. He stays slow and steady, and I marvel at his control and power. But for the sheen of sweat that immediately breaks out onto his forehead, I wouldn't know he was affected at all by this sensuous fuck.

But then he pulls out, and instead of a slow slide in, he punches his hips and drives into me hard. The plug jostles in my ass, his pelvis presses on my clit, and stars explode behind my eyes because the feeling is so intense. I scream against the panties, but it stays locked in the top of my throat with no means to escape.

A flash of triumph spreads across Bridger's face as he increases the power of his thrusts, seemingly forgetting that he promised me a slow fuck. I watch as his eyes start to flutter closed. He bites his lower lip, and I know he's starting to get lost to the pleasure along with me.

"Christ, Mags," he whispers in between panting breaths. "Why in the fuck do you feel so good to me?"

He sounds so wondrous and lost all at the same time. It makes my heart hurt a little. Bridger leans down and places his forehead against mine, his rough breathing feathering across my face.

"So good, baby," he whispers and starts to fuck me harder.

My orgasm brews... bubbles... churns hotly at the base of my spine. Bridger rotates his hips again, pressing down on my clit once more, and the pleasure jolts through me so hard that my hands fly to his head. I burrow my fingers into his hair. As he slams into me again, I scream against the panties and yank viciously at his hair without thinking what I'm doing.

Bridger's movements slow and he pulls his head up, twisting his neck and dislodging my hands as he pushes up and places his hands at the back of my thighs, giving him better leverage to start pounding at me again.

My orgasm curls inward... pulses a few short times as if it's gearing up to break free of a starter's gate, and with another slam of Bridger's cock into me, it springs forth and decimates my entire body. The minute I start shaking, Bridger quickly pulls out of me. I think he's going to come too, but, instead, he reaches down and jerks the plug out of my ass.

I shriek against the silk in my mouth, my orgasm going from a mere burst outward to a nuclear explosion. Then Bridger's cock is back in me. As I shudder and shake and lose all control of while the world's strongest and longest-lasting orgasm rages through me, Bridger raises my legs and almost folds me in half so he can fuck me even harder.

He pounds my body brutally, but it hurts way too good. I can feel him everywhere, with every stroke... even deep in my heart as crazy as that sounds.

His face becomes pinched, and I realize he's close to coming. I stare at him, his eyes lock with mine, and I beg him with just the power of my gaze to stay inside me. I tilt my head, raise my eyebrows, and grip desperately at his ass with my fingers to hold him to me.

And I think he may do it. I see a flash of determination bolstered by some out-of-this-world fucking, and my heart starts to feel like it's going to have its own bursting orgasm. Bridger's breath becomes choppy, his face looks almost pained, and just when I think he's going to plant deep and let loose, he jerks all the way out of me as he starts to come. He orgasms so hard and fast, he can't even get the condom off. Instead, he just falls on me where he dry humps the outside of my pussy while he shudders and groans his release.

"I'm sorry," he mumbles with his face pushed into my neck, his hips still gyrating slowly against me as he trembles. "I'm sorry."

I pull the panties out of my mouth and let the flood of saliva coat my tongue. My arms wrap around his broad shoulders, and I press my fingertips into his shoulder blades. "It's okay."

"I thought I could," he mutters, his breath still coming out in short bursts, which seem more panic filled than sex filled.

"It's okay," I say again softly, my hands flattening and stroking the skin on his back. "It's okay."

Eventually, his breathing evens out and he finally lifts his head to peer down at me. "Maggie... that's all I've got to give you."

I smile at him, and I make it an accepting smile so he doesn't feel worse than what I already see deep in his eyes. "Then I'll gladly take it if that's all there is."

"It won't be more," he says almost sternly, making sure expectations will never be failed.

Stupid, foolish man.

"It's already more, Bridger," I reprimand him. "You're already more than what I ever had."

"You deserve more than that though," he whispers harshly.

"I've had so much less," I remind him with brutal honesty.

That doesn't reassure him as I see him wince and pain fill his eyes. He stares at me a moment more before rolling off me and heading into the bathroom to get cleaned up.

Chapter 15
Bridger

I OPEN THE front door of The Wicked Horse, the loud music washing over me. Cal and Macy follow me in. Turning to them both, I lean in and speak loudly. "This is the main club area. We have a full-time DJ but a live band on the weekends. Full-service kitchen over there."

"It's amazing," Cal says back with an appreciative smile as his eyes roam.

"Maybe we can try to two-step later, honey." Macy laughs as she snuggles into him.

I'm not sure if that was a serious offer by Macy or that's a euphemism for fucking, because they're not here for the nightclub. No, they flew from New York City to see the kinky grandeur of The Silo. We'd just arrived from having dinner in Jackson with Logan and Auralie, and while I invited them to the club with us tonight, they both declined. Again, no surprise. All my best Fantasy Makers falling to that crazy little thing called love, and while I don't think any of them are necessarily adverse to what goes on here, I think they're just so far up each other's asses right now with the newness of their relationships that The Silo has no appeal for them.

Not so with Cal and Macy apparently. While I get the impression they don't do this often, they still keep their sex life spicy by doing things like this. I lead them through the throng of nightclub patrons, down the back hallway, and out the rear door. We navigate the stone slate path aglow with landscape lighting to The Silo that sits a few dozen yards behind.

The Silo is exactly what it sounds like. A tall, round building done in white concrete staves with an authentic grain elevator running up the outside. Inside is a little different though.

I check my security fob, punch in the random key code it assigns, and pull the door open for Cal and Macy. They enter, walk down the short hallway to the interior, and Cal gives a low whistle of appreciation as they look around. It's a far cry from the sex club where we met in New York, which was a huge mansion filled with elegantly decorated, private rooms. The Silo is a bit more open and transparent. A huge, circular space with glassed rooms around the perimeter so everyone can watch the action inside.

Macy's head turns to the left, taking in the closest set of glassed-in rooms. It's still fairly early at ten PM, so the crowd is a bit light, but the rooms are already sporting some major action. The first room to her left is occupied by a couple fucking on a mattress with black silk sheets. It's a spotlight display room and only meant for a twosome or threesome who want to keep the group intimate but still be seen. The next room houses the stockade I'd built for Cat when she was an active partici-pant here, and I'm surprised to see Jared Crossgrave in there. He's shackled tight in the stockade. One of the patrons is fucking his ass while another one has his dick shoved down Jared's throat. Again, not interested in guys, but there's no denying it's a hot setup. Macy must agree because she reaches back to squeeze Cal's hand when her eyes land on the scene.

Finally, she cranes her neck and takes in the next room, which is the Orgy Room. There are probably ten or so people in there, all naked and engaged in various stages of fucking.

"You two want a drink?" I ask, but Macy shakes her head without taking her gaze off the orgy room.

"I think my girl found the room she wants," Cal says with a husky voice. "We'll join you for a drink… after."

I laugh and clap Cal on the back, then turn toward the circular bar in the center of the room. Finding an empty stool near the Orgy Room so I can watch, I sit down and order a beer from one of the bartenders. When she sets it in front of me, I throw a ten-dollar bill down and tell her to keep the change. I may own the place, but I pay for everything here, just so my staff knows nothing is free.

After taking a sip, I swivel the stool and look toward the Orgy Room. Cal and Macy are already inside, but they are doing nothing more than reclining on a double-wide lounge chaise and making out. They don't look to be in a hurry to do anything, and I watch them with interest.

I learned a lot more about them personally at dinner tonight. Cal's best friend and law partner, McKayla Connover, is also Macy's best friend. Apparently, Cal and Macy used to hate each other, and then became passionate secret lovers before falling in love. Macy was an heiress turned practically penniless when her father was convicted of so many white-collar crimes that he's spending the rest of his life in prison. But you'd never know it from looking at her or talking to her. The statuesque redhead is sweet, humble, and works full time for a non-profit outreach program. Cal, of course, is a distinguished attorney, and now the two of them are getting ready to get their freak on in front of a crowd of strangers.

It's titillating, no doubt, the things that go on inside this club. But I rarely feel anything as I watch the action. It's business to me. So I can look with a somewhat dispassionate eye as I watch Macy roll over on top of her husband, her red silk dress riding high up a pair of spectacular legs.

Not as spectacular as Maggie's but still… not a hardship to look at.

I don't even chastise myself for thinking of Maggie because I've just accepted that's the way things are. I can't go five minutes without seeing her face, remembering how fucking fantastic her pussy feels, or the way she carried a sleeping Belle into the house last night with the look of such pure completeness on her face. It made me a little jealous I'm not the cause of that look.

So I've given up trying to banish her, and I've decided to accept things for right now. She's in my house. She's in my life. She has said unequivocally that she accepts what I can offer her—which isn't much in my opinion—but she seems to think it's enough for her. Selfish bastard that I am, I'm going to take her at face value. I'm going to continue basking in the goodness of Maggie while I can. I know she's not a permanent fixture, and I know I can't offer her a happily ever after, but I can give both of us a happily for right now kind of existence.

Memories of last night wash over me as I keep my gaze pinned on Cal and Macy. She's now pulling her dress over her head, dropping it to the floor, and Cal's hands go to his wife's breasts. She throws her head back and I can imagine the moan he's provoking. I'd done the same to Mags last night, although most of her sounds were muffled by the panties I'd stuffed in her mouth.

Last night, Maggie made me feel things that were horrible and wonderful all at the same time. Once I'd pulled the plug out of her ass, I marveled at what I believe to be the strongest orgasm I've ever seen a woman have at my hands. For a moment after I shoved my cock back inside of her, I wanted to experience it all. For a brief but insane moment, I thought to myself that perhaps my demons weren't worth fighting. As Maggie dug her fingernails into my ass in a silent plea to stay inside of her, I resolved that I was going to do it. I was going to say to hell with my past, my bitter memories, and most of all my shame, and I was going to come deep inside that beautiful pussy. I held strong and true and I slammed into her hard when I felt my orgasm starting to break free.

But then I saw something in Maggie's eyes. It was probably nothing more than sweet happiness that I'd give her the intimacy she was craving, but my twisted mind chose to see it as triumph. And then I was seeing nothing but *her* face giving me that evil look of victory. In that suspended moment between amazing pleasure and all-consuming release from orgasm, I became terrified that if I came inside of Maggie and then experienced the disgust and shame I had felt all those times my stepmother made me come inside of her, that I'd transfer those feelings to Mags.

I wasn't afraid of Maggie falling for me if I gave her that intimacy.

I was afraid I would hate her for it.

So I pulled out, humped her like a horny twelve-year-old boy, and came within the confines of the latex condom while Maggie whispered to me that it was okay.

My stepmother wasn't always evil. When my dad started dating her just over a year after my mom died, she was actually quite nice to me. She didn't try to be a replacement, but she took great efforts to show me I could rely on her. From the ages of seven to nine, we had a decent relationship.

Then my father died and she was appointed as my

guardian, which were my father's wishes according to his will.

Her change from suitable stepmother to abusing monster was gradual, although in my heart of hearts, I think she was always a monster. I even believe had my dad lived, she was going to abuse me no matter what. She'd just do a better job of hiding it.

When my father died, she became cold and distant. The only interaction that came from her was when she yelled at me for the smallest of infractions. By the time I was ten, she was beating me regularly, usually for no reason at all. These beatings were always followed up by ostentatious shows of apology from her, usually in the form of hugs, kisses, and bribery gifts.

She first started touching me inappropriately around the time I was twelve, using her affection after a beating as an excuse to put her hands on me in a different way. Likewise, she encouraged me to reciprocate. I was old enough to know it wasn't quite right what she was doing, but I was also scared enough of her and too young to question.

I remember having my first wet dream when I was thirteen, and my stepmom having a gleam in her eye when she saw the sheets. By this time, she was regularly using drugs, which was sometimes fine by me. When she was so out of her mind on heroin, she'd ignore me for days at a time, and that was when I was happiest. But when she was in between fixes, she came on to me stronger than ever. In fact, I think she considered me a "fix". One night, after a particularly vicious beating, she gave me my first blow job and I learned to equate the pain of punishment with a pleasurable reward. I still knew it wasn't quite right, but I also took the good feeling to try to compensate for how bad it was at all other times.

By the time I was fourteen, my stepmom didn't need me to fuck up to give me a beating. She had regularly started making it a part of foreplay for me, using ropes to tie me up with the promise that I'd have a bit of pain before my sweet reward. Her favorite tool was the belt—which is an implement I never use in my work—and she spared no part of my body from its fury. I became so conditioned that this was my way of life, I didn't question it anymore. None of my friends at school would ever believe the horrors that happened in my house, and I was too ashamed to admit I'd reached the point where my stepmom didn't even have to tie me down. That there were many times I'd get on the bed just from her command, letting her whip the shit out of me before she fucked me.

Throughout every single loathsome encounter with her, she tormented me by having complete control over my body. And her sick, twisted games included telling me how much she loved having my cum inside of her. She'd ride my dick, taunting me, knowing I'd give it up to her, and then she'd shame me with it afterward.

"Look, Bridger… look at your cum dripping out of me. Isn't it beautiful?"

If Maggie knew all that shit, she'd understand why it's taboo to me to share that with a woman. Why there's nothing beautiful about it to me. Why instead, I get a little bit of vindication by denying that to a woman, and in turn, perhaps giving her a little humiliation by marking her with my semen when I come. God, fuck me in the ass as I deserve, but yeah... even with Maggie. I come on her in part so she knows I don't respect her enough to do otherwise.

I'm a shameful, heartless fuck, no doubt, but I'm also selfish as I mentioned. As long as Maggie wants me, I'm going to give it to her in the only way I know how, and the reason I'm doing it is because I've never had pleasure the way I experience it with Maggie. My orgasms are strong and vibrant and transport me to a place I've never been before. I crave that with her so the one thing I vow to myself and to her, although she'll never know it, is that I'll kill myself to make it pleasurable for her in return. I'll go to the ends of the earth to at least make her feel the best she's ever felt. To make her orgasms forever be unrivaled.

It's the very least I can do for her for the amazing pleasure I'm receiving.

I watch with interest as Macy scoots down Cal's body, her hands deftly working at the belt to his pants. She gives him smoldering glances as she frees his cock and takes it in hand. He says something to her. She tilts her head back and laughs, and I can't help but envy their easygoing yet incredibly trusting relationship. What I wouldn't give to purge every bit of doubt and shame out of me and have the ability to laugh with Maggie like that.

Macy bends over her husband and takes the length of him in her mouth. Her long hair is pulled into a low ponytail at the nape of her neck, so I have an unobstructed view of her cheeks hollowing as she sucks Cal's cock. She's a natural and takes it deep with no gag reflex. Very impressive.

Cal lifts up on one elbow to better watch her, reaches a hand out, and touches her cheek. It's sensuous and intimate even as it's filthy kinky because they're doing it in front of strangers. I half expect them to start fucking—perhaps even Cal suggests it as he says something to her—but she gives her head a shake before starting to bob over him faster and faster. Cal's eyes blaze with lust as he gives himself over to the pleasure of his wife's oral skills, his mouth moving in what I bet are whispers of encouragement.

Macy sucks and jacks him, every once in a while peeking up at her husband with pure devotion burning in her eyes. It's their communication between each other that I find sexy, and my cock starts to perk up a bit.

Odd. I've seen a thousand blow jobs and they haven't motivated me. But watching Cal touching his wife's cheek while she gobbles up his cock with that look in her eyes like he's the only man on this earth touches me in some way. It makes me wonder if Maggie would ever look at me like that, and what I would give her if she did.

Staring at them, I contemplate all these unknowns. I don't move my gaze once, watching Macy's cheeks hollow and Cal's head fall back as he starts to lose himself. I watch his hips punch upward as he shouts in abandon, and I watch Macy's throat move up and down as she swallows her husband's gift to her.

Fuck, I want to have that.

I know I can't... afraid it will feel awful, all evidence to the contrary, as I watch Cal coat Macy's tongue with his cum and the pure pleasure etched on his face as it happens. I suppose that occurs because they have trust between them.

Trust is not something I give to anyone save for Woolf and maybe Father Adrian.

I've known Maggie less than two weeks, and I certainly don't trust her. I don't know her, really.

Except, she's never given me any reason to doubt her. She's shown herself to be an amazingly resilient woman, a devoted mother, and a caring individual who doesn't hold my deficiencies against me.

Those things aren't enough to warrant trust, but maybe they're enough to warrant me giving a little more of myself and seeing what happens with her.

Chapter 16
Maggie

"**F**ULL HOUSE. READ 'em and weep, ladies," Sloane says as she lays her cards down with flourish. And yup… three jacks and two nines. The petite blonde with blue eyes flashes a grin as she rakes the large pile of chips in the center of the table toward her staggering pile that's almost cleaned everyone else out.

"Damn it," Callie says as she tosses her cards facedown. "You are the luckiest bitch I've ever seen."

Callie is absolutely gorgeous with her chocolate-brown hair and eyes that are green like mine but much lighter, so they absolutely pop on her face. She belongs to Woolf, who I've come to learn a lot more about tonight as I'm treated to my first girls' poker night. Bridger had plans with some friends who flew in from New York City. He was going out to dinner with them and then was going to take them to The Silo. I'd lie if I didn't say I was jealous.

Jealous that he didn't ask me to go out to dinner with his friends and jealous he's going to be hanging out in his sex club tonight, both of which ridiculous because I'm in hiding and can't go out in public. I wanted to question him about the club though… get reassurances he wouldn't fuck someone else, but in the end, I didn't have the guts. He owes me nothing, and he's made it clear he has hang-ups when it comes to relationships.

Besides, it's not like I could go anyway. I had Belle to watch, and that was fine by me. I couldn't get enough of her, and I spent most of the day annoying her because I constantly wanted to cuddle when all she wanted to do was play. I had to satisfy myself that at least when she took her afternoon nap, she did it in my arms while I sat happily for almost two hours while she slept.

Bridger had been doing some work most of the day out in a large, detached shed that sits off the back of the house, but he came in before he got ready to leave for the evening. He advised me he'd invited some friends to come over and sit with me tonight. I was a little pissy that he was going out and I was staying here, and I assured him in what I think was a snotty tone that I didn't need babysitters.

He cocked a gorgeous eyebrow at me and said, "They're not babysitters, Mags. They're a group of girls I think you'd get along well with so you can have some fun for a change."

That made me feel like shit for all of about five minutes, but then I got jealous again when he said he was going to take a shower before he had to leave for dinner.

Ugh.

Why does he have to be so complicated?

Why do I have to fall for a complicated man?

"Let's open another bottle of wine," Cat says as she stands from the table.

The final member of our girl's gang, Auralie, also stands up and says, "I'll help you get it and some more snacks."

These women showed up about four hours ago with pizzas, chips, and wine, and I was immediately over-whelmed. It's clear that Callie and Sloane are very close, and I later learned they've known each other the longest. Callie is the governor's daughter, and Sloane was work-ing undercover for a magazine trying to expose both the governor and Callie for their ties to The Silo through Woolf. Talk about a rocky start, but they both laugh when they talk about it.

I also learned with interest that Bridger's best friend, Woolf, left The Silo and gave it all up so he could be with Callie, whose dad is up for re-election. That's true love, indeed. Sloane ended up falling in love with a man named Cain who is head of security for both The Wicked Horse and The Silo. She was apparently using him to try to get dirt for the story. He's obviously forgiven her, and so it goes without saying… that's true love as well.

Cat and Auralie are a bit more closed off, and they're not as close to Callie and Sloane, but that doesn't mean they don't get along. They all have one interesting thing in common, and it's that they fell in love with men who worked in The Silo. Cat is an exotic woman with long, dark hair, beautiful brown eyes, and high cheekbones that proclaim some American Indian heritage. She was actually a member of the club until her late husband died. He was apparently an abusive prick, and her man Rand pulled her up by the bootstraps and taught her how to lead a new life. Auralie is the newest to the group, only moving to Wyoming a few weeks ago to permanently be with her man, Logan. She looks all of about eighteen with her porcelain skin, black-as-midnight hair, and innocent blue eyes, but I was surprised to learn she's actually twenty-six and was a professional con artist prior to meeting Logan.

Yes, they are a fascinating group of women. Every one of them funny and outgoing, although Cat is the most reserved of the group. They made me feel instantly welcomed. With the help of the first two bottles of wine, I told them my story after I put Belle down to bed.

And I didn't hold anything back except for Kyle being undercover ATF. I'm pretty sure Callie knows though, since Bridger had told Woolf that part, and I don't think those two hold anything back from each other.

The girls all rallied around me, threatening to castrate Zeke if he came anywhere near me and vowing to kick Kayla's ass if they ever saw her around town. We then decided to play poker, which was nothing more than an excuse to sit around Bridger's kitchen table while we gossiped and drank wine. None of us—well, except

Sloane—were really into the game, and we were playing with chips and not money anyway.

Cat and Auralie uncork two more bottles of wine and bring them back to the table along with a new bag of potato chips. Cat tops off all our glasses while Callie grabs the bag of chips from Auralie and pours out a pile right onto the table by her poker chips.

"Poker chips and potato chips," she says with a goofy grin on her face.

Yeah, we're all slightly tipsy.

Cat and Auralie take their seats again, and we all take a unanimous sip of wine. When the glasses get set back down, Sloane says, "I'm tired of playing poker. You gals suck and it's no fun."

"You suck," Callie mutters as she munches on potato chips.

"I know," Sloane says with a devilish grin. "Let's play truth or dare. Maggie can go first. I think you should choose truth, so we can get to know you a little better."

My head snaps her way, and I narrow my eyes at her as this game sounds dangerous. "Out of curiosity, what would the dare be?"

"Um… you have to text a naked picture of yourself to Bridger, right now," she says deviously.

"I choose truth then," I say quickly. No way would I ever do that.

Except… I'd love to have that type of relationship with someone. Fun and flirty that I could sext with. Drive him crazy until he could get home to me. But

Bridger is most definitely not fun or flirty.

"Okay, truth," Sloane says as she rolls her eyes up to the ceiling, pondering a good question. When her gaze comes back to mine, there's a shimmer there that makes me have no doubt she was a good reporter and would delve to find the truth. I brace for it. "Tell us the truth—are you having sex with Bridger?"

Fuck.

The other girls all lean forward, interested in my answer.

I look around at their faces, all eager with something, but it doesn't look like the need for gossip. Actually... it looks more like a deep respect for this man with an insatiable thirst to know more about him.

With a sigh, I drop my gaze and fiddle with the stem on my wineglass. "Yes. We're having sex."

"I knew it," Callie says smugly.

"How did you know it?" Cat asks.

"You should have seen the way Bridger fretted over her before he left tonight," she says. And only Callie would know that because she arrived first and was the only one to see Bridger before he left.

"Oh, tell us the details," Auralie says. "Because there's no bigger mystery than Bridger Payne."

Tell me about it, Auralie.

"Well," Callie says slyly. "He must have asked her a dozen times if she was okay that he was leaving, even once told her that he'd cancel his plans and stay."

"He didn't say it exactly like that," I mutter.

"He said it in those exact words," Callie argues. "And when you weren't looking because you were getting some pizza for Belle to eat, he was eating *you* up with his eyes."

"There's no way—" I mutter.

"Okay, tell us details," Cat says softly as she leans forward. "Auralie and I haven't had the pleasure."

My jaw drops open as my head snaps first to Callie and then to Sloane, who both look at me with flame-red faces. "You two have been with Bridger?"

A furious wave of jealousy crests within me, and I swear I can feel steam coming out of my ears, although I don't know why. It's not like I have any true claim on him.

Callie holds up her hands. "Relax, Maggie… it was long before he ever met you and it was in a three-way with Woolf."

That mollifies me somewhat, but the jealousy still gurgles. My gaze slides to Sloane. "And you?"

Her face goes redder, but she gives me a sheepish grin. "Also long before he met you and I fell in love with Cain. But it… um… was a five-way."

"A five-way?" I blurt out in astonishment.

I didn't think it was possible, but her face goes even redder. "Yeah. Me, Cain, Bridger, Logan, and Rand."

My head swings in the opposite direction, and I stare agog at Cat and Auralie. "Your Logan and Rand?"

Cat smiles understandingly at me. "Long before I ever fell in love with Rand."

My eyes cut to Auralie, and she admits, "And long

before Logan came into my life. But... um... I was sort of with Bridger."

"Well, hell, Cat," I say sarcastically, throwing my hands up. "You should just fuck him when he gets home tonight. Then he'd check all five of us women off his list."

"No way," Cat says with a vigorous shake of her head. "I'm completely satisfied, thank you."

"And technically," Auralie says timidly. "I didn't fuck him."

"Well then, what did you do with him?" I ask hesitantly, not really wanting to know the details but asking all the same.

"He... um... sort of used a flogger on me," she says with her cheeks also turning pink. "And he um... got me off with his fingers."

I push the chair back from the table to stand up, pick up my full glass of wine, and chug it down. When it's empty, I set it back on the table, grab the nearest bottle, and fill it back up. I grab it, intent on getting shitfaced drunk, but Sloane reaches over and pulls it toward her—out of my reach.

I glare down at her and then around the table in succession. "This is messed up. And I know messed up. I've been held captive in a biker compound for three years, and I've seen all sorts of fucked-up shit. But this... you people are all friends and sleeping with each other, and no one seems to be bent out of shape about it."

"We don't all sleep with each other now," Auralie

points out. "That was in the past, but I'll maintain to you… there's nothing wrong with it if we did decide to do that. As long as everyone is consenting and understands the consequences."

"We've all felt what you're feeling," Callie adds on softly. "The jealousy and guilt that comes with sexual freedom and exploring your desires. It's hard when your heart belongs to someone, but if there's trust and care, you can explore those freedoms with other people who are within your circle of trust."

"I'd never share Bridger with anyone," I say vehemently.

Sloane cocks an eyebrow. "Even if he asked you to? Said it would turn him on? That it would be a special gift if you'd agree to it?"

Would I? Would I give that to Bridger if he asked me? I yearn for a connection so badly with him. What would I do if he came to me and asked me to have a three-way with another man? Or another woman?

Could I do that?

The answer comes to me with utter clarity. Absolutely not.

No way.

"I may have made some poor choices in my life, but I've always been loyal to the man I've been with," I say with my chin held high. "I just couldn't."

"And that's a fair statement," Cat says softly. "But maybe you could try to understand that some couples are so secure within their bond that it's not a breach of loyalty. It's actually quite an intimate experience."

My head hurts from the implications. I sit back down in the chair, actually slumping down. "Do you think Bridger's going to expect that of me?" I ask in a quiet voice.

A warm hand covers mine, and I look up to see it's Callie's. She gives me a confident smile. "I don't know what's in Bridger's head, but I can tell you… each one of the experiences we've had with him have come at the request of our men. It wasn't Bridger's idea. He was only accommodating his friends' requests. But what I do know is that Bridger has never shown interest in a woman before in the way he has you. He clearly has feelings for you."

"I don't know about that," I mutter, thinking of the fact he can't even stand to come inside my body.

"Well, I do," Callie says firmly. "I know Bridger better than any of you, except maybe you, Maggie. You might actually know him better, but if you think that man isn't interested in you, you are truly blind to what's right in front of you."

"It doesn't matter," I say glumly. "He's made it clear he has limitations, and that what we have now is about all he has to give."

"I don't believe that," Cat says, and I turn to look at her. "I may not have been intimate with Bridger, but I know him quite well. I've talked to him a lot, back when my husband was parading me around The Silo as his sex toy on loan to anyone who wanted to fuck me. He's a good man. I mean, he's really deep down decent. He is devoted to those he cares about, and I think he's shown he cares about you based on how he's helped you. I think people see Bridger as this mystery because he's intimidating and withdrawn. But I think he probably has the biggest heart out of all of us. He just keeps it locked up for some reason. If I were you, I'd figure out that reason and then how to bust that lock."

A small flicker of hope burns bright in the center of my chest. "Do you really believe that?"

"I do," Cat says with an encouraging smile.

"Me too," Callie says. "He's an amazing man, but I think you're an amazing woman. He's lucky to have you."

A key rattles in the front door lock. We all freeze as if we're caught robbing a bank, and then slowly turn toward the door as it opens. Speak of the devil, Bridger walks in with Woolf right on his heels.

"Now there's the hottest man to ever grace the Teton mountain range," Callie says in surprised delight as she gets up from the table and saunters over to Woolf.

He puts a hand behind her neck and pulls her in for a slow, hot kiss that makes me yearn for that type of reaction from Bridger when he sees me. As it is, he looks at me sternly, eyes taking in the wine and chips spilled all over the place.

When Woolf lets Callie up for air, she places her hands on his chest and asks, "What are you doing here, babe?"

He nods over to Bridger. "He asked me to come over and take you ladies home. Figured you'd all be too tipsy to drive."

"But we're having fun," Sloane says with a devilish smirk. "Bridger can just haul himself off to bed and us girls will hang out. We can all crash here, right?"

"Wrong," Bridger says curtly. "Now clear out."

"Mr. Grumpy Pants," Callie challenges him, and then bats her eyelashes. "Come on, Bridger. You can party with us. I'll get you a glass of wine. You can hang out with the girls tonight."

"The only one I want to hang out with is Maggie," Bridger says with his eyes narrowed at Sloane. "And I'd like to do it alone, so you ladies get your purses and your half-empty wine bottles and get home to your men."

Callie snorts but then Woolf is pulling her toward the door. "Come on, girls. Let's get going."

Callie jerks away from Woolf, and says, "Wait a minute. I need my purse."

She hurries over to the table where her purse is draped over the back of her chair and leans in to whisper to me excitedly. "He wants to spend *alone* time with you."

"Yeah, I got that, Callie," I say dryly, but I'm not denying the butterflies zooming around my stomach when he said that.

She gives an excited little squeal and gives me a hug. It's obvious to everyone, including Bridger, that she thinks there's a love match occurring. While I want to share her enthusiasm, I remember all too well how firmly

Bridger sets himself apart from me, unwilling to give himself to me completely.

The girls all grab their purses, stepping up to give me hugs and whispered words of encouragement. Bridger watches all of this with an impassive face. He doesn't even flinch when Woolf walks by him and punches him in the arm, stating, "Have fun, dude."

When they're all cleared out, he locks the door and sets the alarm code.

"Been talking about me, I see," is all he says when he turns to face me.

I shrug, although my heart is racing. I don't know if he's mad or what, but he's making me incredibly nervous. "Women drink wine, we talk."

Bridger saunters up to me until we're standing almost toe to toe. He looks down at me, taking a lock of my hair and rubbing it between his fingers thoughtfully. "And did you learn anything new about me?"

"Only that you're a seriously complex man who has apparently been with every woman who was just in this house," I say tartly.

His eyes slide up to mine lazily, and he smirks at me. "Not Cat," he says without apology about the other women.

"That's all you have to say about it?" I ask in disbelief.

He drops my hair, but the smirk stays in place. "What do you want me to say, Maggie? Should I apologize to you for every woman I've been with before you? Or should you be happy in the knowledge I haven't been with anyone since you and I were together?"

"No one?" I ask suspiciously, because he did just come from spending several hours in a sex club.

"No one," he affirms, although he adds on in a move I'm sure is meant to test my resolve to be with him. "Well, I did get my dick sucked by one of my bartenders after Kyle dumped you on my doorstep, but it was before I ever touched you. But if it helps, I was thinking about you the entire time she was getting me off."

Emotions rage within me. I'm ecstatic he's not been with anyone since me, but a little put off that he talks about casual sex so… so… casually. It's just another reminder that he's so far removed from the intimacy of it that I fear he can't be reached.

I could argue with him about this, and I could act like a bitter shrew who has lost her footing and doesn't know where she stands, but it won't do any good. Bridger is comfortable in who he is and no amount of unease on my part will change that.

So instead, I step into him and put my hands on his hips. In a husky voice, I remind him, "You said something about wanting to be alone with me. What did you have in mind?"

He leans down and gives me a soft kiss before he says, "I've got something I want to try with you. Got a little inspiration at The Silo."

"Whatever you want to try, I'm all in," I tell him as I flex my fingers into his hips. His eyes flash hot, and then he pulls me toward his room.

Chapter 17
Bridger

"*WHATEVER YOU WANT to try, I'm all in.*"

Maggie's words continue to echo in my head as I lead her by the hand back to my bedroom. She pauses at the room she shares with Belle, peeking in on her. A soft, luminous smile graces those perfect lips when she sees her daughter, and I wish I could capture that look. It speaks everything about motherhood that I don't understand but find deeply touching. I'm extremely happy Maggie has reason to smile like that.

The minute we cross the threshold of my room, I turn to Maggie and kiss her. It's as wondrous and volatile as the other times my mouth has been on her—fueled by desire and sheer lust for her taste. She moans, reciprocates, but before we can get going, I pull away and start to remove her clothes. It takes me no time at all to get her naked, and then I swiftly dispose of mine.

Maggie unabashedly looks at my body, eyes roaming all over. Her eyes hesitate over the flock of blackbirds flying up from my rib cage before turning in toward the center of my chest. Her eyes linger on the one near the center that explodes in a puff of black feathers, and then her eyes drag downward, following the inked feathers that float down the front of my abdomen.

Her eyes travel even further down. She stares with no shame at my cock, which has been in a state of semi readiness since I walked in the door and laid eyes on her, and then went fully hard when I kissed her moments ago.

"I want your mouth on it," I say in a low rumble of need, and Maggie's eyes snap back up to mine.

"You just want a blow job?" she asks incredulously, as if she was expecting me to ask for so much more. Yet, she has no idea.

I step up to her, slide my fingers around the back of her neck, and pull her in closer to me. I lean down and place my lips near her ear. "No, Maggie. I want your mouth. Your tongue. Your throat. I want all of that on my cock, and I want your eyes on me as you suck it. And if there's a God who's willing to give me this, I want to come on that pretty tongue and watch you swallow me down."

Maggie's eyes round in shock, and she whispers, "Oh, God."

She actually sways a bit, and I tighten my grip on her neck. "Wanna give it a try?"

"More than anything," she whispers, and she punctuates that desire by licking her lips. The head of my dick starts leaking at the promise in those words.

I kiss her again, very briefly, just to get a measure of control before turning to the bed. After I grab a pillow, I turn back to her and drop it on the floor. I flash a grin. "Don't want your knees to get sore."

She manages to smile, but I can tell she's not falling prey to my little bit of levity to lighten the situation. It's just as well. My attempt at humor was nothing more than a way to help distract me from the curl of fear deep in my belly. There have been times in my life where I've been scared… mostly when I was younger. But most things in adulthood don't cause me much pause.

Except right now.

I'm terrified this could disastrously spell the end of us. It's one thing for me to hold myself back from Maggie because I'm too scared I'll be disgusted by coming in her mouth. It's an entirely different prospect that I might have the figurative balls to shoot down her throat, but if I'm disgusted by it, I won't look at her the same way again. If that happens, I'm quite positive it's all over for us.

"I'm scared," Maggie admits to me in a whisper. "What if I'm not good enough… to you know… make you want to…"

I reach out and jerk her softly to my body, my need to assuage her fears more powerful than trying to talk me out of my own. I wrap my arms around her and press a kiss to the top of her head. It's the single most intimate thing I've ever done with a woman, and I'm bolstered by the fact that it doesn't feel strange, just right.

After a moment, I release her to peer down at her again. "Mags… anything you do to me will be the best

I've ever had because it's you. If there's any failure tonight, it's on me... not on you, okay?"

She nods with quiet acceptance, but then says with a bashful smile, "It's a lot of pressure."

I grin at her, for real this time. "There's a lot of pressure in my dick right now. I bet you could alleviate it if you'd just get down on your knees."

Her smile widens and I see mischief in her eyes for a moment before they sober a bit. "No matter what, Bridger. Promise me that if this isn't something you can do, you just pull out and do what you need to do. It doesn't change how I'll feel about you."

I brush my cheek against her face, and I lie to her. "I promise."

But if this doesn't work, I'm done. I can't continue to torture myself by wanting something desperately that I can't have, and I can't continue to hurt Maggie by not being able to give her what she so needs and deserves.

Maggie leans into me, placing her hands on my chest. My pecs jump from the contact and a bolt of lust courses through me when she places her lips right over my heart and gives me a soft kiss. Then she slides that mouth down my stomach, nibbling and licking at my skin as her fingers travel right along down.

When she gets to my pelvis, she veers around my dick, which is bobbing in front of her and angled to the ceiling, kissing my hipbones while her fingers press into my thigh muscles. She slips a hand in between my legs and fondles my balls, and fuck yeah... that feels damn good.

My arms stay loose at my sides but my fingers curl inward, mainly to prevent myself from grabbing onto her head and demanding she give my cock some attention. I stare down at her as she works slowly with her mouth, tasting and exploring my body. Her hair shimmers, streaks of chocolate, honey, and caramel, and my fingers also itch just to slide into that softness I know smells like the pear shampoo and conditioner I bought her.

Maggie pulls her lips away and focuses in on my cock, which hovers in front of her face. Her delicate hand circles the base. A rumble of lust ripples through me as she sticks her tongue out and laps at the clear liquid seeping from the end, wiggling it against the slit. Electric pleasure shoots through my dick and travels up my spine from that tiny touch, and a deep groan slips out of my mouth.

Maggie looks up at me, those green eyes shining with desire, and whispers, "See… you're already on my tongue now, and I have to tell you… you taste amazing, Mr. Payne."

Pure joy radiates through me as I realize she's right. My cum—pre as it may be—has touched her tongue, and I liked it. No, I loved it—that soft feeling like heaven against me. My hands reach up and grasp the sides of her head. In a voice hoarse with lust and tinged with a bit of fear that this will still result in failure, I barrel forward and say, "Let's get more of that mouth on me then."

"My pleasure," she says, her voice raspy with sex and promise.

Then her mouth opens, and she pulls my cock into her soft warmth.

My legs almost buckle at the first contact… the pure, unadulterated feeling of skin-on-skin contact with Maggie. She pulls me straight back until my head bumps against the back of her throat. She opens up, makes a swallowing motion, and takes me back even further.

"Goddamn." I groan at the sensation of her throat accepting my cock. She moans, sending vibrations of pleasure through me, and my fingers tighten against her head unintentionally. I have to force them to relax and fight against the overwhelming need to hold her tight and plunge further down her throat.

Maggie pulls back, her tongue massaging the underside of my dick as it slides free. She sucks greedily on the tip, pulling more pre-cum into her mouth, and I'm astounded that the thought I'm passing my liquid into her body is turning me on rather than off. She spends moments working the head of my dick, licking furiously against the sensitive underside and prodding my slit with the tip of her tongue while her hand squeezes and strokes the base. My balls tingle and rage with the need for more.

I need more from her now.

I need it with a blazing intensity that is threatening to unravel me.

Maggie's eyes peek up and I'm not sure what's written on my face, but I think it might convey the fact I'm on the very edge of losing control because she immediately pulls her mouth off me and asks, 'What do you need, Bridger?"

God, what do I need?

I need everything from you, I want to say, but no way I'm letting her that far in.

My voice practically croaks. "I want to fuck your face, Mags. You can clearly take it deep, and I want to possess that throat. Give me the control."

So what if that sounded like begging?

Maggie smiles at me, her eyes shimmering with lust, relief, and adventure.

No triumph though. I don't see a flicker of that anywhere, and that makes me even hornier for her.

"Take it," Maggie whispers before opening her mouth and sucking me down deep.

I give a bark of relief, my hands holding her head steady, and I start to move my hips.

Slowly at first, to gauge her level of flexibility, going a little deeper with each stroke. Maggie hums against me, her eyes looking up and telling me to go harder.

Deeper.

Faster.

Her throat opens up, takes the head of my cock on one stroke, then takes another inch on the second. Maggie sets an easy routine, sucking in air through her nose in perfect synchronicity to my thrusts. I am fucking that beautiful face in perfect harmony with her body's acceptance of my cock.

Soft tongue grazing the underside.

Tightness as I push into her throat.

Her hand squeezing and twisting my shaft as I pull back.

The complete acceptance of me into her while letting me dictate how this is being done.

Best. Fucking. Blow Job. Of. My. Life.

I move faster, my body giving all signs that it's ready for release. My lower back muscles get tense, my balls tighten, and the blood in my veins races with every furious pump of my heart. I actually go a little dizzy with the need to come, and yet the desire to prolong this exquisite face fuck of beautiful, sweet Maggie wars within me.

She hums again in appreciation, taking my cock deeper than ever, and puts her hands to my ass to pull me even deeper than that.

"Christ," I mutter as my hips pick up the pace, not wanting to choke her but also desperately needing to get to the finish line. It's in sight, and I know I can do this.

I look down at Maggie, find her eyes on me as I told her to put them, and I see encouragement and tender care in that gaze. It's the only thing I see, and it gives me renewed desire to coat her mouth with my semen.

"Going to come, Maggie," I groan as I hold her head and pump in and out of her mouth.

Her fingers flex into the muscles of my ass, and I feel the sting of her nails. My balls tighten further, aching with the need to give it all up to this woman who is starting to worm her way deeper into my life.

Into my heart.

I falter over that thought, actually causing a stumble in my measured strokes, and I go a little too deep. Maggie makes a slight gagging sound and I immediately pull back, grazing my thumbs over her cheeks in apology. I slow my thrusts a bit, making sure she's able to breathe. Her eyes are warm as she stares at me... my veined cock pushing in and out past those swollen lips.

But is that...?

Begging I see in her eyes?

Is she begging me to give it up to her?

Confusion courses through me as I try to forget that *she* used to beg me to give it up to her. She really didn't need to, knowing my body would ultimately betray me, but it always made me feel that it was my choice to give her what she wanted. With that came extreme humiliation after the last shudder left my body and I plummeted from the sexual high.

I stumble again, pull almost all the way out of her mouth, and Maggie senses my turmoil. She takes the base of my cock again, squeezing it gently. She pulls her mouth free, licks her lips, and whispers, "Stay with me, Bridger. This is just me, and this is all about you."

I stare down at her, my cock aching with need. I could easily jack off my conclusion and bathe her face, or I could barrel past this fear and take mine and Maggie's fates in my hands.

She looks at me patiently, with no recrimination if I don't choose her, and that makes my final decision. She's giving me the control, and that makes all the difference to me.

"Open back up," I order her and she does so quickly, latching that gorgeous mouth back onto my dick.

I set back up a quick pace, and she falls in with me, sucking and licking and letting that throat work tight magic on me. Maggie's eyes shimmer with reassurance, and they never give up their hold on mine.

We stare at each other while I pump into her mouth and I willingly give myself permission to orgasm while lodged deep inside of her. Pure passion erupts and I pull back slightly so the head of my cock sits against her tongue as I start to come. I don't want it in her throat. I want her to taste it. I want her mouth awash with my semen, and I want the knowledge I'm giving it up freely with no fears holding back a single, precious drop of my lust.

I spend myself in Maggie's mouth, and it is utterly fucking divine.

"Mags," I groan as my entire body quakes with release and her hands come back to my ass where she lovingly presses against my muscles, indicating for me to give her more.

I push further into her. She swallows down the head of my cock and the mouthful of cum.

She swallows my fucking soul.

Everything goes still around us and I focus in on her

face, my dick still stuffed inside of her. Her eyes are aglow with respect for me. *You did it, Bridger. And I loved every drop you gave me.*

I pull free from her warm hold, tingles still rippling through me, and haul her up from the floor. My mouth crashes on to her and I swipe my tongue inside, seeing if she left any part of me behind. I get a vague taste of my cum, and she swipes her tongue against mine as if she's claiming every last bit of it back.

I feel sated and energized all at once, knowing something monumental has just happened to me. I've spent years fighting against invisible chains that have held me back, learning to live an unrealized existence. But tonight… Maggie's busted those chains and I eagerly wonder what else I can willingly give to her without destroying myself at the same time.

Bending down, I lift Maggie into my arms and carry her to the bed. I lay her down and climb onto her, holding my weight so as not to crush her body.

She puts a hand to my cheek. "That was beautiful."

"You're beautiful," I tell her honestly. I've never said that to a woman with such brutal truthfulness before.

"I hope we can do that again," she says with a shy smile, and I realize a travesty is occurring.

Sweet, beautiful Maggie is left wanting.

"I have something else I need to do first," I tell her with a promising glint in my eyes.

"What's that?"

I push down her body and spread her legs. My only

answer is when I put my mouth on her pussy and dive in. Maggie moans and her hands go to my hair, and for the first time, I don't seem to mind. Maybe I'm too sated by that amazing orgasm or I'm on a metaphorical victory lap since I just battled and persevered over some pretty fucked-up demons. Regardless, I let Maggie's fingers grip into my hair and I let her push my face down into her sweetness, while I lick and suck her like a starved man.

"M-o-o-m-m-m-m-m-y," Belle cries from her room down the hall.

Ordinarily, nothing would distract me once I was on a mission for some great sex, and I've fucked my way through all sorts of attention breakers. But the minute I hear Belle's voice, I rear off Maggie and scramble off the bed. She does the same, deftly grabbing my t-shirt from the floor and throwing it on as she runs out the door. I manage to hop into my jeans and have them zipped and buttoned by the time I make it to Maggie and Belle's room.

I find Maggie on the bed with Belle cradled in her arms, her little face pushed into Maggie's neck. The bedside lamp casts them in a warm glow, and my chest aches at seeing Mags comforting her daughter.

She turns her head and gives me a smile. "Nightmare."

Part of me feels like I'm intruding, and yet part of me feels the need to offer assistance. Belle's been in my house less than two days and I've already fallen for the little brat, my first real experience with a kid. She's terribly funny for a two-year-old and smart as hell, and she could easily provide me ceaseless hours of entertainment. I never knew I could be so easily captivated by a kid.

I push past any uneasiness and walk into the room, setting my ass on the edge of the bed near Maggie's bare legs. Luckily, my t-shirt swallows her and she's adequately covered. I place a palm on the mattress on the other side of her hip and lean in to look at Belle's face.

She stares at me with luminous eyes the same shade of green as her mom's.

"You okay, kiddo?" I ask as I touch the tip of my finger to her nose.

She nods up and down at me, but she doesn't give up the clinging hold she has on her mom.

My gaze slides to Maggie, who peers at me over the top of Belle's head. Her eyes hold a look of amused frustration for our interruption. I answer her by moving my hand and grazing my thumb down the side of her hip, letting her know it's okay. I'll make it up to her.

"Need anything?" I ask her as I stand from the bed.

She shakes her head at me before laying her cheek on top of Belle's head and closing her eyes in blissful happiness that she can provide comfort to her daughter.

"Okay," I say, hating to leave Maggie's side but also sensing this is a moment that she and Belle should have alone. "Goodnight."

"Goodnight, Bridger," she says softly.

I go back to my room and shed my jeans before

crawling into the bed. The taste of Maggie is still on my lips and I'd give anything for her to come back in here after Belle falls asleep. I wait, wondering if she'll want me to finish what I started, and then I wait some more. After about half an hour, I creep down the hallway, the soft glow of light spilling out from the room. When I turn the corner, I see Maggie on her back, sound asleep, with Belle curled into her side. My cock is sadly dejected even as my heart warms.

Stepping into the room, I pull the covers over both of them before turning out the light and returning to my room. I go to sleep with the memories of me coming inside of Maggie's mouth.

Chapter 18
Maggie

B RIDGER PULLS THE Ford truck to a stop before a massive barn weathered gray from the elements. I see Woolf standing out front in a pair of well-fitting jeans, a plaid western shirt, and cowboy boots. He looks good, but not as good as Bridger who is in the same attire.

When he came out of his room this morning, he was dressed like a true cowboy, even carrying a cream-colored Stetson in his hand. I'd never seen him dressed this way, as he tends to wear dark jeans with fitted t-shirts along with heavy, biker type boots. I was in the kitchen feeding Belle some cereal when he walked in and advised us he was taking us horseback riding.

I didn't argue because I was getting sick of this house and Belle who has far more energy than me was going stir crazy as well.

I didn't know Bridger had a truck as he kept it parked behind the work shed, but it totally fits him, way more than the flashy Corvette. He'd even had Belle's car seat strapped in, which meant I had to sit beside him on the drive to the Double J. We took the same back road we'd taken the morning we'd left to get Belle. As the truck bumped and lurched over the gravel and dirt road, I tried not to get too hot and bothered by the way my leg pressed against Bridger's.

To say last night was a miracle realized is an understatement. Bridger totally gave into intimacy. The moment we shared when he came in my mouth was beautiful and wondrous. Granted, the evening didn't end on a perfect note as Bridger was well on his way to giving me an orgasm when Belle woke up from a nightmare, but regardless… it was one of the best nights of my life.

Bridger's different today as well. He seems more open and laid back. He's wearing a smile, and I wonder how much of that is to my credit or his own. I also wonder when we'll be able to explore his new adventurous side again, and if he is willing to take it even further.

After putting the truck in park and cutting the ignition, Bridger hops out and rounds to the passenger side to get Belle out of her car seat. I get out on the driver's side and wave to Woolf as he walks toward us.

When I turn back to the truck, my breath hitches as Bridger shuts the door and carries Belle perched on his hip. She's chattering away at him in that new language she's developed that's filled with clearly annunciated words mixed with babble. He smiles at her and says, "Oh, really? I had no idea."

I put my hand over my mouth and suppress my laugh, as he clearly has no idea what she's saying but is valiantly trying to carry on a conversation with her.

We all come to a stop at the front of the truck. Woolf leans his face into Belle's and says, "Hey pumpkin… what's your name?"

"Belle," she says with a giggle.

"Pretty name for a very pretty girl," Woolf says, and that makes Belle go all shy. She tucks her face into Bridger's neck to hide, and my breath hitches again when Bridger's hand comes to the back of her head to hold her there.

Woolf smiles at me. "Hey, Maggie."

"Hey, Woolf. Thanks for inviting us over."

"Sure thing," he says as he turns and heads into the barn, but he speaks to Bridger over his shoulder. "I saddled Lucy for you."

"Perfect," Bridger says, clearly at ease with the horse chosen. He told me on the way over here that he works on the range for Woolf sometimes, so he truly is a cowboy as well as a sex club owner.

Again, complex man.

Inside the barn, a dove-gray horse stands placidly outside of one of the stalls. The barn is long and has at least ten stalls on each side. Every one appears to hold a horse.

Bridger walks up to Lucy, and Belle's eyes go wide with wonder.

"Ho-sie," she says as she points to it.

"That's right," Bridger tells her and sidles up closer to her head. "Her name's Lucy, and you can pet her."

Bridger puts his hand on Lucy's muzzle, encouraging Belle to do the same. She hesitantly reaches out and strokes the horse with a bright smile on her face.

"Want to go for a ride?" Bridger asks Belle.

For the first time, a moment of doubt courses through me. I mean... this isn't a little pony but a full-size horse. And my daughter is only two and is oh so very small.

"Bridger," I say hesitantly. "Um... I'm not sure she should..."

"She's going to sit in my lap," Bridger says, shooting me a glance and then looking back to Belle. "Want to ride with me?"

Belle nods her head furiously, but I'm still uneasy. I reach a hand out to touch his arm, and he turns to me.

"She's only two," I say with obvious worry. "And if she were to fall... I just... I don't know if she should..."

My words trail off, torn between wanting to give in to that look of delight on my daughter's face and my need to protect her from danger.

Bridger takes his free hand and puts it behind my neck. His fingers grasp me gently and his thumb strokes the back of my neck. "Maggie... I promise it's safe. Lucy is the gentlest horse known to mankind, and I swear I won't let her fall. I'll only walk around the paddock and I won't do anything crazy, I promise. She'll be totally fine."

I chew at my lip, my gaze going back to the large horse and then back to Bridger, who waits for me to make a decision. I can tell he'll abide my wishes, but I can also tell he really wants to get on that horse with my daughter.

Ultimately, I decide to trust in Bridger, knowing he's been our protector from the start, and he wouldn't ever do anything to harm a hair on her head.

"Okay," I say with a tremulous voice.

His eyes soften. He then shocks the hell out of me by leaning in to give me a soft kiss on my lips. I'm shocked he does this in front of Belle and I'm even more shocked he does this in front of Woolf. I just didn't think Bridger was in to public displays of affection, because hello... man averse to intimacy.

I gasp in surprise as his lips graze against mine and let out a sigh of sweet joy. When he pulls away, he turns to hand Belle to Woolf and then with one hand on the saddle horn, he hauls himself up into the saddle.

And damn... no man should ever look that fucking sexy.

Bridger shoots me a grin and it's knowing. He can tell by the look on my face I'm lusting after him at this moment, and if he were so inclined to check, he'd find my panties wet. He then turns to Woolf, who hands Belle up to him. He actually sets her sideways on the inside of his thigh where he can wrap one large arm protectively around her. Then he takes the reins. With a soft cluck and tap of his booted heels to Lucy's flanks, the horse starts plodding out of the barn. Woolf and I follow them, watching as Bridger directs the horse into a grassed paddock whose gate is already open.

Woolf and I stand at the fence, resting our forearms on the top as we watch Bridger patiently walk the horse in a large circle while Belle laughs and giggles in unrestrained glee. By the second lap, the knot of anxiety in the middle of my chest starts to loosen and I actually start to enjoy watching them together.

"I've never seen Bridger with a kid before," Woolf says out of the blue. He doesn't turn to look at me but keeps his eyes on the horse and its riders. "He's damn good at it."

"Total natural," I agree.

"I've also never seen him kiss a woman before," he observes.

"Really?" I ask, turning my head to Woolf.

"Well," he says with a sly glance at me before turning back to look at Bridger. "I've seen him kiss a woman with the expectation of blowing a nut after, but never seen him kiss a woman just because he wanted the kiss and nothing else."

I don't know what to say to that, but my heart flip-flops over the implications that the kiss I just got was apparently very special indeed. I watch Bridger slowly walking a horse around in circles to entertain my daughter, and I realize how lucky I was to get that kiss.

"Maggie," Woolf says softly and I turn to look at him. His face is somber, and something bottoms out in my stomach from that look. "Bridger has some seriously dark demons. His past is... well, it's really bad. I never thought there would be a woman who would have the ability to push him past that, but I think that might be you."

"You do?" I whisper, wanting to believe him because it's what I want.

"I do," he murmurs. "But it's not going to be easy. You've clearly made some breakthroughs with him, but it's going to get harder before it gets easier."

"What happened to him?" I ask, hoping a clearer understanding of the mystery of Bridger Payne will let me help him.

Woolf shakes his head. "Not for me to say. But I'm just telling you... if he slides back into that closed-off person... have patience with him, okay?"

"Of course I will," I tell him reassuringly. "He knows I'll accept whatever he can give me."

"Well, I hope that's not true. I want you to push at him for more, but just be cognizant of the fact that he's got a lot of years of being a certain way, and what you're offering him is probably as terrifying as it is thrilling. Bridger's happiest in his darkness, and while he might be enthralled by the light you're casting, he's going to be distrusting of it."

I turn back to look at Bridger, his smile even wider than it was minutes ago. My daughter secure in his arms. I see perhaps a future there in that paddock and wonder if I have the fortitude to grasp onto it.

"What's the best way I can help him?" I ask Woolf without taking my eyes off my daughter and the man who may be what dreams are made of.

"Let him lead the way. Let him be in control. And don't push him too hard."

"I can do that," I say with resolve.

"Even if it takes forever," Woolf adds on.

"Even if it takes forever," I agree.

The commitment is made. I'm in this for the long haul.

Bridger continues to walk Lucy around the paddock, a few times even breaking into a little trot that caused Belle to shriek first in terror and then uncontrollable laughter. I almost shrieked too the first time he did it, but I luckily maintained my composure.

Finally, Bridger walked the horse back through the gate and handed Belle down to Woolf, who sets her on his hip. She looks over his shoulder at me and exclaims, "Mommy… you see me on ho-sie?"

"I did, baby," I tell her with clear pride in my voice. "You were so brave, and that was amazing. Can you tell Bridger thank you?"

Belle looks up to Bridger and says, "Tank you, Bwidg-uh."

"My pleasure, darlin'," he says. He even tips his hat at her, and oh man… I swear my ovaries just combusted.

Bridger turns his eyes to me and holds his hand down to me. "Come on. Your turn."

"What?" I ask, taking a step backward. "No way."

"Yes," he says, snapping his fingers before holding his palm out again. "Get that gorgeous ass up here."

Woolf turns and walks away with my daughter, calling over his shoulder. "I'm going to take Belle up to the house. Callie will have lunch ready in about an hour."

I look at Woolf's retreating back as he walks to Bridger's truck and puts Belle back in her car seat. "But… but…"

"Come on, Mags," Bridger says in a low voice.

I chew on my lip again, all the same fears I just had for Belle coming to the front of my mind. Except this time, it's me I imagine falling off the horse and getting trampled to death. "I'm scared of horses."

"You're scared of nothing," Bridger says with a pointed look. "And I'll go just as slow as I did with Belle. I promise."

With a pained sigh, I give him a nod and say, "Okay… how do I get up?"

Bridger considers me for a moment before he dismounts. "I was going to just swing you up behind me, but now that I think about it, I'd rather have you in front of me. Means I get to wrap my arms around you."

Oh, swoon. Did he just say that?

Now all of a sudden, I'm dying to get on that horse.

Bridger comes up behind me and with hands to my waist, helps to lift me easily into the saddle. The horse stands completely still and then Bridger's hauling himself up behind me. Two of us can't really fit in the saddle so with an arm around my waist, he hoists me up a bit and sets me down right over his crotch.

This, of course, makes me think lewd thoughts.

They're immediately driven away when Bridger clucks and taps the horse's flanks with his boots, and the horse starts walking. My hands go to the saddle horn. I latch a death grip on it as Bridger leads the horse away from the paddock and onto a trail that starts on the far side of the barn. The Teton Mountains loom straight ahead with gray, craggy peaks covered in snow.

Bridger chuckles and tightens his arm around my waist. "Ever been on a horse before, Mags?"

I shake my head. "Nope. It wasn't high on my bucket list."

"Well, try to relax. You're stiff as a board."

I try to relax, but I can't seem to remove the steel pole out of my spine. I try to concentrate on the sway of the horse so I can make sure I counter sway and maintain the best stability.

"You need an orgasm," Bridger whispers in my ear.

"What? Huh?" I ask, startled, my hand gripping onto the saddle horn even tighter.

"I was going to tell you to put on your jeans when you got dressed this morning, but I couldn't resist the easy access these little stretchy pants you wear would provide," he says, and then his hand is slipping down the front of said stretchy pants.

"Bridger," I hiss at him. "Stop. Someone might see us."

"So," he says dismissively as his finger scrapes against my clit, but I know he's being dismissive because my concern is ridiculous. There's no one out here, and Woolf has already left with Belle.

My head immediately falls back onto his shoulder, but I don't give up my death grip on the saddle horn.

"That's it," he urges me. "Just relax and let me make you feel good."

The tip of his finger dips into my pussy, which is flooded, and he pulls that wetness back up to my clit, rubbing in quick circles.

Then comes the ear porn.

"Wanted to do this last night," he growls near my ear. "With my mouth. Wanted to lick this clit and suck you absolutely dry until you couldn't possibly give me another orgasm. Then I'm pretty sure I was going to fuck you after and make you come again."

"Oh, God… just damn, Bridger," I say in a complaining voice. "You are way too good at dirty talk."

He laughs darkly and flutters his finger over me faster. I give into the sensation, let the sun warm my face and I listen to his continued filthy talk while he finger fucks me to orgasm. It doesn't take long and Lucy, God love her gentle soul, doesn't even flinch when I scream out my release.

Bridger pulls his hand out of my pants and licks it clean. All I can do is lean back into him, utterly relaxed and ready to enjoy the rest of the ride.

We're silent for a moment, but because I'm feeling so mellow and Bridger's in such a good mood, I ask him, "So last night… it was good?"

"You mean am I good after coming in your mouth?" he asks, and I don't miss the humor in his voice.

"Something like that," I mutter.

"I'm good, Mags," is all he says, but he doesn't elaborate.

So I push forward with another question that's been eating at me. "The tattoo... the birds on your torso. Those have special meaning?"

"They do," he says, but then nothing more.

"Will you share the meaning?" I ask hesitantly, fearing his rejection.

It comes swiftly and simply. "Nope."

That should be enough to dissuade me from trying further intimate conversation, but I'm not going to give up. I promised Woolf I wouldn't, and I'd rather not wait for "forever" to break through to him completely.

"Then tell me about The Silo. Why did you open a sex club?"

I hold my breath and brace myself for his rejection. He's silent for a long moment but finally, he takes in a deep breath. When it's released, he says, "You already know I've got some screwed-up ideas when it comes to sex, so I guess the easiest way to explain The Silo is that it's able to sort of bring order to my thoughts about sex."

"Like how?"

"The Silo is about freedom. About doing things that make you feel good with no guilt or shame. It's about expressing desires, passion, and lust, and doing it in a way that lets you sleep soundly at night because there's no judgment."

"Have you been judged?" I hazard a tentative guess.

"Not for expressing my sexuality," he responds confidently.

"Ashamed?" I whisper.

"Every fucking day," he says.

I sit straight up because I'm so stunned. Craning my head to look at him, forgetting my fear of falling, I ask him, "Why? Why would you ever be ashamed?"

His eyes bore into me, and I immediately regret asking him such a personal question. I expect him to tell me to mind my own fucking business, but he doesn't.

But he also doesn't answer my question.

Instead, he asks one of his own, "Would you ever go to The Silo with me? You know… after this shit with Zeke gets sorted?"

"Sure," I say with a quaking voice as I turn around and face forward again. But the thought of going to a sex club terrifies me. I'm terrified of what I'll see… namely that Bridger might like the things that go on there better than he likes just plain old sex with me.

"Would you let me fuck you in The Silo?" he presses me, arm tightening around me again. "In front of all those people?"

"I… I…" The words won't come out, lodged deep in my throat.

But he moves on, and I'm starting to understand he's trying to make a point to me.

"Would you let me lock you in a stockade, fuck you in front of everyone, and then invite all my friends to come and do the same?"

My stomach rolls.

"Or maybe I can put you on my St. Andrew's cross, and I can stripe your skin with a whip? How about that, Mags? Would you let me do that?"

"Bridger," I say with dismay.

He growls low in his throat and puts his lips near my ear, causing a shudder born of fear and anxiety to ripple through me.

"I'm ashamed, Mags," he murmurs in my ear. "Ashamed because I want to do all those things to you, and I want you to love it. I'm ashamed because I want those things, and I know you can't ever give them to me because they'd cause shame in you. And mostly, sweet Maggie, I'm ashamed that I'm even torturing you with this, because when it boils right down to it, I'll never act on these desires. You and I are just too different, so it's all moot."

"No," I automatically say in denial, because I don't want to believe we can't have common ground even though what he wants to do to me is beyond my comprehension at this point. "I could try."

"I wouldn't want you to try, Mags," he tells me with brutal honesty. "I'd want you to beg for it."

"Why are you telling me this?" I ask him with a hard edge to my voice. "Truthfully, Bridger… why are you saying these things?"

"Because, babe," he says before nipping my ear. "I'm trying to make you see that while I'm enjoying you immensely right now, The Silo is my life. It's how I survive, and that makes us too different in the long run."

Chapter 19
Bridger

I ADD A little more chili powder as well as some cumin and give the chili a stir. I'd put the pot on not long after we got back from Woolf's, figuring that would feed us for a few days. Of course, Belle wouldn't eat it as I've figured out she's a picky little eater. So the fridge is stocked with some deli turkey, yogurt, and raspberries, three things that she can apparently eat for every meal.

My eyes keep flicking down the hallway to Maggie and Belle's room. Maggie had put Belle down for a nap over an hour ago and had lain down beside her for a bit. When I went to check on them a few minutes ago, I saw Maggie was fast asleep.

I watched her like a certified creeper for a few minutes, my heart torn in a million different directions while my mind kept interjecting its own opinions.

I want Maggie like I've never wanted another woman. I want her so bad my teeth hurt, and I'd probably give my right nut for her. But fuck if I wasn't telling her the truth today… in the long run, we're too different.

Or rather, I'm too fucked up to ever really have a chance at a normal relationship. I might have gotten past a sexual hang-up by coming in her mouth, and I want to come in other places in her body too, but that's all it is. A hang-up.

Poor Maggie would still have to deal with my entire fucked-up state of mind. That's just not something that's solved with an orgasm in the right place. Coming in her mouth, her pussy, or her ass if she gives it to me isn't going to stop me thinking about my stepmom every day. I think about the things she did to me and how I caved to those things on a daily fucking basis. They are a part of me. The shame is a part of me. The nightmares are a part of me.

Just like The Silo is a part of me. I need The Silo like I need air. I need that place to constantly remind me that sex is good and real and should be enjoyed. I might not partake in much fucking that goes on there, but I need the existence of it to ground me. I need it to help ease the shame that seems to be immersed into my very skin.

Why did I say those things to her today?

I could easily blame it on her and the way she pushed at me for personal information, but truth be told, I knew I had to say those things to her when I was giving Belle a ride on the horse. I happened to glance over at Woolf and Maggie as they stood at the fence and watched us, and I knew they were talking about me. I know Woolf well enough to know he was probably giving her advice on how to handle me, and what I saw in Maggie's eyes about slayed me.

I saw hope and determination, and I knew Woolf

was egging it on too.

So I had to say those things so I could keep her expectations realistic and hopefully cut down on some of the hurt when she realized her ultimate efforts would be futile against someone as twisted as me. I did it because I wanted to save her pain and humiliation, two emotions I've felt plenty in my lifetime and would never wish on her.

But mostly I said those things so I could ground myself. I need a reminder that I couldn't let things get out of control with her. I had to temper this insane need I seem to have for Maggie with the brutal truth that I ultimately don't deserve her brand of beauty and light.

I hope I have her on track.

I feel like I'm back on track.

Doesn't mean I'm still not going to have her though. I told her today, as we rode the horse up to Woolf's front porch, that while we were too different for the long run, I was by no means finished with her yet. Because I'm not. Not ready to give her up until I've had my fill of her, and that's the Bridger Payne who's the selfish bastard coming out to play.

But at least expectations are clear and my line has been drawn in the sand. I'll just have to tread carefully with her heart and make sure I never forget who I truly am.

I put the lid back on the chili pot, set the spoon down in the sink, and turn to the fridge for a beer.

But then my body freezes as I hear a low rumble of

what sounds like thunder at first.

Then I realize it's not thunder—it's motorcycles. Harleys to be exact, and my blood pressure spikes. I run through the living room, peer out the front blinds, and count three Harleys coming down the driveway, kicking up a slight blowing of dust that's settled over the pavement. Leading the trio is unmistakably Zeke Powell, President of Mayhem's Mission.

"Fuck," I mutter as I quickly turn the stove off and haul ass through the living room to the hallway. Maggie meets me, holding Belle in her arms with a look of utter fear on her face. "My bedroom. Now."

Maggie turns and flees into my room with me hot on her heels. I go to the gun cabinet and unlock it, pulling down a shotgun. I quickly load two shells, cock it, and hand it to her. "Get in the bathroom. If anyone comes through that door that's not me, you shoot first and ask questions later, okay?"

She nods furiously in agreement, and I see a determined gleam in her eye. It's of a mother protecting her daughter and I know if Zeke makes it past me, Maggie sure as shit isn't going to let him get his hands on Belle.

Reaching back into the cabinet, I pull out a pistol and quickly slam in a cartridge. I pull the slide back and chamber a round before tucking it into my waistband at my back. I turn toward my bedroom door, but Maggie calls, "Bridger."

I turn to her and she whispers, "Please be careful."

"I will," I tell her. Then I race down the hallway and

through the living room. I can hear the bikes come to a stop and the engines cut, making the air heavy with the silence. I take a deep breath, let it out, and open the door to step out on my front porch.

Zeke dismounts his bike and removes his sunglasses, hanging them from the collar of his black t-shirt. The other two guys, who I recognize from the club but don't know their names, remain on their bikes.

Zeke walks to the bottom of the porch and looks up at me. "Bridger."

"Zeke," I say in acknowledgment. "What can I do for you?"

He looks off to the side of my yard, taking in the work shed before turning back to me. "Looking for Kyle… seen him around?"

"Nope," I say and it rings with truth because it *is* the truth.

"Kayla seems to think you're pretty buddy-buddy with him," Zeke says as if he's just attempting some casual conversation with me, but I don't buy it for a second.

"No more than I am with you," I tell him.

Zeke nods, glances back at the two other bikers, and then raises a booted foot to rest it on the bottom porch step as he looks back up at me. "Something was taken from me… something very precious, and it seems that maybe Kyle had a hand in it."

My fucking stomach cramps and sweat breaks out on my forehead. Still, I try to keep a level voice when I say,

"Got nothing to do with me."

"Kayla says you were in a fairly private conversation with Kyle the other night at the compound," Zeke says, his eyes boring into me with cold calculation.

"I shared a joint with him on my way out to my car, Zeke," I say with annoyance. "Would have done the same with you if you'd been there."

He makes a low hum in his throat and gives me a tight smile. I'm not sure if he's buying my shit or not, but I'm tensed and ready for a battle if need be.

"Alright," Zeke says, putting his sunglasses back on his face. "You see Kyle… give me a call, will you?"

"Sure thing," I say as my stomach unclenches slightly.

Zeke nods and turns toward his bike. Then, as if he has a second thought, he turns back and says, "You know… I could stand a stress reliever now that I think about it. Why don't you come out to the clubhouse tonight… work Kayla over a bit?"

Every instinct in me wants to tell him to go fuck himself, but I know I'm walking a very dangerous line right now with this man. I give him a nod. "What time?"

"About eleven," he says and turns away, satisfied with my answer.

I stay on the porch and watch Zeke mount his bike. All three men kick start them to life. They carefully back their bikes up, maneuver them into turns, and then head back down my long driveway that winds at least a full half mile before it connects to the main highway.

As soon as they're out of sight, I turn back into the house and call out to Maggie as I close the door behind me.

"Mags… it's all clear," I shout as I walk back toward my bedroom. She comes out of the master bath, Belle toddling behind her, and hands me the gun with the barrel pointed downward. I uncock it but leave the shells inside.

"Go get packed up. Two separate bags, one for you and one for Belle," I tell her as I lay the gun on the bed and go to my closet to pull out a large duffle bag.

"Why?" she asks fearfully. "What happened?"

"He knows," I tell her as I go back to my gun cabinet and pull out three more guns. I put them in the duffle and head to my dresser to grab clothes.

"Knows what?" she whispers.

"He knows I know where you are," I say confidently. "He might even have a clue that I have you."

"Then why didn't he just bust in and take me?" she asks, and it's a good question.

But I saw how Zeke was checking out the landscape and figuring out how it would look to find my dead body and possibly Maggie's once he had Belle. He wasn't going to risk that move right then.

"He wants me to come to the club tonight," I tell her. "He wants to lure me there; I'm sure he thinks it's better to kill me on his turf rather than mine. They can dispose of me quietly and then come get you."

"Please tell me you're kidding me," Maggie begs.

I stop pulling clothes out and turn to face her. "I'm dead serious, Mags. Just trust me on this. Now, we're leaving immediately, so go get bags packed."

She hesitates only a moment before she races out. I throw the clothes in the duffle and grab several boxes of ammunition from the cabinet. When I turn to toss them in the bag, my eyes lock on Belle still standing there, watching me curiously. My heart fucking squeezes at the thought of Zeke getting his hands on her, and I double my efforts to get packed.

"Don't worry, Belle," I murmur more to myself than to her. "I'm not going to let anything happen to you or your mommy."

I zip the bag, grab it and the shotgun with one hand, and then bend to scoop up Belle. Her little arms go around my neck, and I'm amazed at her trust in me. I hope to fucking God I don't let her down.

I pause just outside of Maggie's bedroom door, noticing her zipping up a backpack before grabbing a small tote from the bed and turning to me. She looks determined but fearful, and I want to kiss her to reassure her, but we don't have time. For all I know, the entire club might be rumbling down my driveway in seconds.

I lead Maggie out the back door of the house and we trot to the truck, throwing our bags in the back. I get Belle quickly buckled into her seat while Maggie scrambles in from the driver's side. No more than five minutes after Zeke left, I have the truck pointed down the back road that leads to Woolf's house on the Double J.

He's the first person I call and he answers on the second ring with a, "What's up?"

"I'm headed to your house now. I need you to take Belle and head to Cheyenne," I tell him, my voice conveying the urgency of the matter.

Maggie's hand grabs my arm and she says, "What? No. I'm not leaving Belle."

I shrug her off and ignore her, continuing my instructions to Woolf. "I'm pretty sure Zeke knows I have them, so I need you to take Belle in one direction and I'm taking Maggie in another. They'll hopefully follow us if we're spotted."

"I'll be ready when you get here," is all Woolf says before he disconnects the call, and that is the power of true friendship right there. I know he'd lay down his life for me if I asked, and he'd do it for someone I care about too.

"Bridger," Maggie says in a panic. "I don't want to be separated from Belle."

"Mags," I say softly, taking my hand and putting it on her thigh to squeeze reassuringly. "I can't protect you both, and if we're being actively hunted, I'd rather lead those fuckers as far away from Belle as I can get them. That means you're bait."

I look over at her and I see awareness dawn on her face as she understands what I'm saying. I hate myself for calling Maggie "bait" to her face, but I knew she'd understand me. Maggie will do anything to protect her daughter, and she withstood torture in doing so. She would have no qualms about leading an entire gang of bikers on a chase if it would put distance between them and Belle.

"Okay," she says with a shaky voice. "I understand."

"Good," I say with another squeeze to her thigh and I about lose it when she leans her head on my shoulder.

"Thank you," she says quietly.

I don't take my hand from her thigh.

"Wheels on the Bus," Belle cries out, and Maggie and I burst out into nervous laughter. Then we sing "The Wheels on the Bus" three times on the way to Woolf's house.

As promised, he's waiting in front of the detached garage with two bay doors open. Maggie wrestles Belle out of the seat while I collect the bags from the back of the truck. Woolf walks into the garage and around the back of a vintage Hummer. It belonged to his dad and sometimes we'd take that bad boy out four-wheeling on the ranch.

"You take the Hummer," Woolf says. "If those fuckers come after you, you run them right over."

"What are you taking?" I ask as I throw the bags in the back, and then walk out to the truck to get Belle's car seat. Callie's already out there, holding a large duffle bag in her hands, so clearly she's going with Woolf and Belle.

"I'm taking the G550," he says stoically. "It can run motorcycles over too."

I unlatch the car seat and tug it out, walking in long strides to the G550. Woolf opens the back door while

Callie, Maggie, and Belle follow. As I'm putting her car seat in the back on the passenger side, I tell Woolf, "I probably bought some time so I don't think they'll follow us. I'm just being more safe than sorry."

"How's that?" Woolf asks as he watches me work.

"Zeke invited me out to the club tonight to work on his old lady," I tell him as I maneuver the seatbelt to secure the car seat.

"Kill you deader than a doornail if you went," Woolf posits.

"Yeah," I agree. "Figured that much. Just hope he believed me when I told him I'd be there. If he does, we have a good head start. It'll also help we'll be in vehicles they don't know and coming out of the Double J main entrance versus my driveway."

"Where are you going?" Woolf asks as I finish and turn toward him.

"Salt Lake City," I tell him. "Long, flat roads in between so I can see what's coming."

"Good idea," he agrees.

"You locked and loaded?" I ask him.

"To the hilt," he assures me. Woolf owns as many guns as I do. It's what Wyoming men do.

"Thank you, brother," I say, my voice getting a little choked.

Woolf studies me for a moment before he pulls me into a hug. He claps my back roughly a few times before holding me tight. I'm not weirded out in the slightest and return the hug hard.

"Do me a favor," he mutters so only I can hear him. "Try not to get killed. I think you might finally be on your way to a fulfilled life, if you know what I mean."

I do know what he means.

He means Maggie, but I'm not about to tell him I have serious doubts about that. Instead, I clap him on the back a few times and pull out of his embrace.

Woolf turns and holds his arms out to Belle. Maggie hugs her fiercely for a moment, and then kisses her cheek. "I love you, Belle."

Belle smiles back at her mom and says, "Chee-chew."

It's Belle talk. I love you is "chee-chew," strawberries are "joppies," and for some weird reason, cereal is "bee-boss". I hope to fucking God I get to hear more Belle talk in my future.

Chapter 20
Maggie

WITH MY ELBOW propped up on the passenger window ledge and the side of my head resting against the glass, it's easy for me to keep my eyes on the passenger side mirror and look at the long road behind us as we drive through Idaho. We could have cut south through Wyoming on our way to Salt Lake City, but the road tends to be more winding around the buttes. Cutting southwest through Idaho wasn't as direct a route to Salt Lake City, but the terrain was flatter with wide-open spaces so you could see if someone was following you.

We've lapsed into silence, part hypnotized by the bland terrain and flat roads as well as being lost within our own thoughts. I wasn't expecting this to happen. I'd been lulled into a false sense of security thinking that Belle and I were safe at Bridger's and that it was just a matter of waiting until Mayhem's Mission could be taken down. I'd forgotten the hours of torture that Kayla put me through, and the beatings I took from Zeke when he first caught me without Belle. It was all so easy to put that shit behind me because I had the bright, dazzling persona of Bridger Payne distracting me.

That, of course, makes me feel incredibly guilty. I should have been more worried about Belle and less worried about whether Bridger would ever fully open up to me. I should have never gotten involved with him on a sexual level and just accepted his hospitality and protection until I had Belle firmly in hand, then I should have taken off and gotten far away from Zeke and Kayla.

Except I know deep down that wasn't a plausible scenario. I had nowhere to go. No money. No credit. No car. I had no way to support my daughter and ensure her safety. I was stuck depending on Bridger for my entire well-being and that of Belle's.

Which brings me right back to the beginning, and that is living in Bridger's home, seeing what I want right there in front of me, and acting on it.

Of course, there is the tiny little fact I need to consider that just this morning as we were riding Lucy together, he was essentially telling me he's not in this for the long haul. He specifically told me that we were too different for this to work out in the end.

Is he right about that?

Are his demons better controlled with the way he lives his life now, or can I chase them off? Does he really need The Silo the way he says he does, and if so, could I ever reconcile that fact? Could I share him with that lifestyle?

Bridger doesn't seem to think so, and that's really the reason he laid things out for me so clearly today.

I sigh, cut my eyes forward for a few moments, and then gaze back into the side view mirror.

"You're a very brave woman, Mags," Bridger says softly, and my head swivels to the left to look at him. He has his right hand gripping the top of the steering wheel and his left arm casually resting on the window ledge. He looks so calm and in control right now, and I feel like I'm going to splinter into a million pieces.

"I don't feel it," I murmur, directing my gaze back out the windshield.

"You could have insisted on going with Belle," he says softly. "You would have been safe at the governor's mansion."

I didn't understand at first why Bridger told Woolf and Callie to head to Cheyenne, but he told me as soon as he got in the Hummer and we were heading out of town. He'd told me that Belle would be protected by the governor's security detail. As long as she was inside that house, no one was getting at her, and I marveled at Bridger's brilliance and quick thinking.

We didn't see one single biker as we left Jackson, and once we crossed over into Idaho, it was pretty clear no one was following us. Still, it was a wise decision for us to split up from Belle because if we'd stayed together and were followed, we were all unsafe until we got to Callie's father. At least this way, there's a very good chance they'll come after me, assuming Belle would be in the back of the Hummer and not well on her way to Cheyenne in the back of a G550 that would never be on

Zeke's radar.

"What do you think's going to happen?" I ask him curiously.

"Well, if Kyle's ATF handler will call me the fuck back, we'll have a better idea, but you and I will lay low until we figure it out."

Bridger's first course of action after we crossed into Idaho was to try to get up with Kyle's ATF handler. He'd told Bridger his name was Joseph Kizner and he was working as a used car salesman in Driggs. It only took Bridger a few phone calls to locate the dealership he worked at, as well as a crafty message on the man's voice mail, and we were hoping to hear from him at any time.

I nod in acceptance. He's basically telling me what I already know, and that is we don't know jack shit. We're flying by the seat of our pants and have no clue if we'll stay hidden for two days or two weeks.

So that discussion is out, but I might as well turn the discussion back to something we could at least air out. "What do you think will happen with us?" I ask him.

He doesn't even flinch, but just turns his head lazily to look at me. "Haven't given it much thought."

I grimace and look away from him. Nice to know I plague his mind so much. I open my mouth to tell him I should definitely move to Coeur D'Alene, but he's apparently not done.

"I have no clue what your expectations are, Mags," he says softly as he reaches across the interior and gives my thigh a squeeze, all while keeping an eye on the road.

"But I'm not ready to give you up yet. Haven't even begun to get my fill of you. So I guess for the immediate future, I'd like you to consider staying around Jackson."

"In your home?" I ask bluntly. "Me and my two-year-old daughter... you want us to stay?"

I can tell he wasn't lying when he said he hadn't given it much thought because he sort of blanches at the thought of us being there permanently. In fact, he doesn't even need to answer my question as I see his lack of commitment to that deep of a relationship written all over his face.

"I'll think about it," I cut in before he can say anything, turning my gaze back to the side view mirror after leaning my head against the window again. "Staying in Jackson, that is. But I'd have to find a job and a place for Belle and me to live."

I can almost see feel his body exhale with relief, and yeah... that hurts. He wants me close enough to fuck me but not so close as I become a burden on him and his single lifestyle.

But life hurts sometimes, and I've got bigger things to worry about than whether or not Bridger cares enough about me. Right now, he's doing right by Belle and me by keeping us safe and protected. I owe him the world for that, but at the least he deserves my respect. Said respect will cost me some chunks of my heart being carved out the more I come to realize he's a tougher nut to crack that I'd supposed originally.

Bridger's phone rings, and he picks it up from the

center console.

"It's him," he says after looking at the incoming number. "Him" being Joseph Kizner.

After he connects the call, Bridger hits the speaker-phone button so I can listen to the conversation. I sit up straight and lean toward the phone as Bridger holds it up in between us.

"Bridger Payne," he says by way of identifying himself.

"Yeah… Mr. Payne, this is Joseph Kizner, calling you back."

When Bridger had left a voice message, he'd didn't bother to make up a story about selling a car. He needed something a little more enticing to induce Mr. Kizner to call him back as quickly as possible. So his voice mail merely stated he was trying to reach a high school friend by the name of Kyle Sommerville and that he'd heard Joseph had served with him in the army. All completely fictitious, but it got Kyle's name out there. Anyone in the office who might have listened to the message wouldn't be any the wiser that Mr. Kizner was not a salesman but was in fact an ATF agent.

"Do you know who I am?" Bridger asks him. "Has Kyle mentioned me?"

"He has," Kizner affirms. "Mentioned you several months ago as someone we could potentially use to gather further info on Mayhem's Mission."

"Yeah? Well, I would have declined had you approached me," Bridger says dryly, "but Kyle got me messed up in this shit all the same."

"What do you mean?" Kizner asks with obvious worry in his tone.

"Zeke was keeping a woman prisoner at the club… name of Maggie Waylon. She and Zeke have a two-year-old daughter together named Belle. Maggie escaped with Belle and got her to safety, but Zeke caught Maggie. Had been beating her, and his old lady took matters into her own hands when Zeke went on a run here recently. Was torturing her and was going to kill her. Kyle got Maggie out and asked me to take care of her."

"Jesus fuck," Joseph growls into the phone.

"I take it you didn't know any of this?" Bridger asks.

"We don't meet often. It's too risky, and we were supposed to meet yesterday, but he never showed. Wasn't anything I would be worried about though. We've had meets before where he doesn't show because something came up, but I figured I'd hear from him soon."

"Well, something may be wrong," Bridger says somberly. "Zeke showed up at my house a bit ago looking for Kyle—said he hasn't seen him. I can't tell you why, but it didn't sound right to me. It's like I got the impression he knew exactly where Kyle was but was trying to figure out what I knew. I think he knows Kyle took Maggie out of there, and I think he knows I was hiding Maggie and her daughter, Belle."

"Do you think he knows Kyle is working undercover?" Kizner asks, his voice now on full alert.

"I don't know, but my gut says no," I tell him. "If he suspected that, wouldn't he be getting the hell out of dodge?"

"Good point. Where are you?"

"We've only been on the road a few hours. Heading to Salt Lake City, but we're not far from Montpelier, Idaho. I've sent Belle to Cheyenne with a friend whose father is the governor. She'll be well protected."

"Okay," Kizner says, his voice now taking charge and brooking no nonsense. "We've got Zeke under constant surveillance as well as his higher-ups in the club. I'm going to check in with them, see where they are."

"I don't think they're following us," Bridger supplies.

"Then go ahead and pull off in Montpelier. Get a hotel and wait to hear from me."

"What are you going to do?" Bridger asks pointedly. "Because we cannot stay on the run. I've got a business… Maggie wants to get back to her daughter."

"I get that, and things are going to move fast. We're actually ready to take them down. All supporting agencies are in place, and we have enough agents ready to go. We were just waiting on this last meet with Kyle for the go-ahead. But if you think he's in danger, then we have to move now."

"Like as in 'now', right now?" Bridger asks, his eyes cutting to me briefly.

"As in a few hours," Kizner says. "It will go down tonight probably, after it gets dark. Probably let them party a bit… get relaxed."

Bridger nods in understanding, but he adds on for Kizner's planning benefit. "Zeke invited me to the club. Expects me there at eleven PM. If you don't do it by then, he'll send some people out for me, I'm sure."

"Then we'll have it go down before then," Kizner says. "This number I'm calling you from is my cell. Text me the hotel you're at and I'll let you know as soon as we have the club members in custody. We'll need you to come back and give a statement and such, but we'll worry about that later."

"Got it," Bridger says, and then adds on, "And just so you know… if they are following us and come anywhere near Maggie or me, I'm going to shoot."

"Wouldn't expect otherwise," Kizner says. "Talk later."

And then he hangs up.

Bridger draws his phone to his face, rubs the edge thoughtfully against this chin. "I wonder if Zeke knows Kyle is undercover or he just thinks he helped you escape?"

"I don't know," I tell him. "But I can tell you this… Kyle was good in his act. I would have never thought he was a cop. He was an asshole, and like I said… he egged Kayla on when she was torturing me."

"You know he was doing that to maintain his cover," Bridger points out.

"Yeah, I get it," I say with a smile. "And I will totally give him a hug when this is all over."

Bridger doesn't respond but puts his blinker on as

the exit for Highway 30 looms ahead. He then holds his phone back out, chooses a contact, and dials, also putting it on speakerphone so I can listen.

Woolf answers almost immediately.

"Just checking in," Bridger says. "Where are you?"

"About half an hour outside of Rock Springs," Woolf says. The trip to Cheyenne is over six hours in length so it will be at least four more before I know Belle is to safety.

"Anyone following you that you can tell?" Bridger asks and I hold my breath waiting to hear his answer.

"Nope," Woolf responds casually, and then adds on the best news I've heard yet. "Callie called her father and filled him in on what was going on and that we were heading his way. He arranged for the state police to escort us county by county to Cheyenne, so you don't have to worry about Belle."

"Oh, thank God," I murmur, but Woolf apparently hears me loud and clear.

"I'll take good care of her, Maggie. I promise," he reassures me.

"Listen," Bridger says. "I just got off the phone with Kyle's ATF handler. Filled him in on what was going down, and they're concerned about Kyle. They're going in tonight to make the bust."

"Thank fu—" Woolf starts to say, but then he stumbles and says, "Fudge."

Bridger turns to me and we smirk at each other, because yeah… sometimes you have to watch your mouth when you have a two-year-old in the car.

"At any rate, at his suggestion, we're stopping in Montpelier," Bridger continues, "but you should head on to Cheyenne. It'll hopefully be over by tomorrow, and then you can start back."

"Sounds like a plan," Woolf says.

"Later," Bridger says.

He disconnects and puts the phone back in the console, his hand going to the top of the steering wheel again to resume his casual pose.

Now that I know Belle is utterly safe and has police protection even as we speak, all of the tension I'd been carrying just melts away from my body. I don't care if I'm bait and Zeke comes after me, but knowing that Belle is safe right now makes me incredibly happy.

"We'll Facetime with Belle once they get to Cheyenne, okay?" Bridger asks, glancing at me again.

"Sounds good," I say as I lean back in my seat and look straight ahead. I don't bother looking at my side view mirror anymore, because it seems we're good.

We're safe.

Zeke's going down tonight.

Belle and I will be reunited.

And then I'll figure out what to do about Bridger.

Chapter 21
Bridger

MAGGIE DOESN'T SAY a word as I pull the Hummer around the back of the Clover Creek Inn to the room I'd secured for the night. I handed her the magnetic key when I got back into the vehicle, wondering if she cared that I only got one room.

I wondered because I'd laid my speech on her earlier today about us being too different from each other to survive in the long run. I figured my proclamation would send Maggie scurrying away from me, which is not something I wanted, but something I figured would happen since well... she's a woman. Women take more stock in the future and looking past a single night—or just a few nights—of pleasure.

But it made sense, only having one room, because there was still a danger presented from Zeke. Granted, I didn't think it was a big danger and it's pretty obvious we weren't followed. But still, it was a good excuse to insist we stick together.

And I do want to protect Maggie. Wasn't lying to Kizner. I will shoot anyone that comes through that door after we get inside. But my ulterior motives are more because while I certainly will see to Maggie's protection, I want to be in the same room tonight because I intend to fuck her.

I stand by my words to her. There are certain things I need in my life. I have certain demons I've learned to live with rather than abolish. Those things are probably not going to change about me, and Maggie is too sweet to have to deal with them for her future. She'd be hurt by me eventually, so I wanted to start getting her expectations set that this... whatever it is we have... has an expiration date on it. I'm just not sure what that date is right now.

But it's not expiring tonight. We'll be staying here for at least the next twelve hours, and I intend to fuck her more than once. Belle's safe, we're safe, and the next logical priority for me is seeing how far I can take it with Maggie. I am way more excited and turned on by the prospect than I am fearful of it, and this is pushing me forward.

Can I do in her pussy what I did in her mouth? I'm definitely bolstered by past success, and I'm not going to lie... I'm dying to feel her wrapped around me when I release. I want to feel the electric moment I felt when I was in her mouth. The orgasm was glorious, long-lived, and almost brutal in its power. Not like the flatlined orgasms I usually have that give me two to three seconds of mind paralysis at best. As much fucking as I do in my lifetime, I want it to be spectacular rather than ordinary just once.

I pull the Hummer into a parking spot and get out of the vehicle. Maggie follows suit but waits for me while I get the bags out of the back. I then follow her to the room and wait while she unlocks the door. I stand close enough to her backside that I can smell the faint smell of her pear shampoo and the very vague odor of saddle leather from our ride this morning.

When the door opens, she jets inside and heads straight to the bathroom, which tells me she's nervous. More importantly, she knows what my intentions are. I drop the bags on one of the beds and remove the guns. I do a quick check to ensure they're all loaded and ready, then I take my clothes off. I'd considered doing a slow seduction of Maggie, but then immediately discarded it. She knows I want her, and she wants me too. It's a waste of time, so I did away with it.

I wait by the bathroom door patiently. She finally opens it to find me looming there naked. I expect her to jolt or even scream, but instead, she lets her eyes roam down the length of my body almost dispassionately before coming back up where she cocks an eyebrow at me. "So, that's how we're playing this?"

"You mean by jumping right into bed and fucking? Yeah, pretty much."

I wait to see how she'll take this. Will she smile, give me a small laugh, and jump into bed, choosing to show me a bit of levity over my brashness? Or will she be disappointed? Fearful? Disgusted?

She grimaces at my remark, and there it is... an obvious flash of disappointment in her eyes. Fuck if that doesn't feel a lot like guilt brewing at the center of my chest, but I push it away as I wait to see what she does. I swear to fucking God, if I see a glimmer of a tear over my somewhat callous treatment of our relationship, I'm going to throw my clothes back on and just sit outside the hotel door all night, keeping myself far away from Maggie.

"Fine," Maggie says pertly as she pushes by me, giving a slight elbow to my ribs so I'll move out of her way. She starts jerking her clothes and shoes off until she's as naked as I am. She then crawls onto the bed that doesn't hold our bags, and lies on her back, staring at the ceiling. In a voice that sounds intentionally robotic and uninspired, she says, "Oh, Bridger. Come and do me, you big stud. I can't wait."

I don't know how to take that. Is she teasing me? Is she making a point?

I walk across the room and hop on the bed, straddling her waist. She glares at me, although her eyes do drop to my dick, which is hard and ready, before peeping back up to me. She waits for me to make a move, and although she's acting put out, I can see the pulse in the base of her neck jumping and her nipples are beaded tight so she's not as unaffected as she wants me to believe.

"Any chance you're on some form of birth control?" I ask her. "I know you're not on the Pill."

She looks confused for a moment and then nods her

head. "IUD. I got one after Belle was born. Wasn't about to give Zeke another child and tie me to him further."

"Then we're fucking without a condom," I announce to her and wait to see her reaction.

"What the fuck, Bridger?" she says in exasperation, but there… right there… I see her eyes flame with lust. But she retains a little bit of common sense when she says, "You don't even know if I'm clean."

"You realize you didn't even bother asking if I am," I point out.

"Well… I assume if you said you didn't want to use a condom it meant you were clean. I don't think you'd do anything to ever intentionally put me in danger."

Fuck… that admission right there. It's exactly what I was seeking when I broached this subject. I wanted to know the depth of her trust in me. No particular reason for it, other than to stroke my ego where Maggie's concerned, because even though I have a connection with her that's different from all others, I still sometimes wonder exactly how she feels.

And, of course… I couldn't do something as simple as just ask how she feels. No, that would be way too easy.

"And you trust me?" she asks in what is a sweet, hopeful voice that lets me know right there… in addition to wanting me, Maggie is not taking my proclamation that we're too different to heart.

But I fall prey to the tone of her voice, not wanting to hurt her. Never wanting to hurt her.

"Mags," I say softly, placing my palm right over the

middle of her chest. "If you were to sit here and tell me to my face that you're clean, I'd believe you wholeheartedly."

Her eyes go round, but then slide off to the side to stare at the bedspread. In a small voice, she says, "I'm not sure. I mean… Zeke always used a condom, but that one time it broke. I've never been tested, but I've also never had any symptoms of anything."

That right there is the truth, and she gave it to me point blank. Something shifts inside of me, and my respect for Maggie grows.

"Well," I say carefully. "I do happen to know for sure you're fine. Jared ran a full workup on you when he first treated you, and I had him include an STD panel. I had no clue what your backstory was at that point, and I wanted to make sure you got proper medical attention."

"Oh," she says as her eyes come back to mine. "Well… thank you."

"So, the condom issue is dispensed," I tell her with a pointed look. "But we have one other thing that we need to talk about before we get started."

"You make it sound like we're getting ready to start a board meeting or something," she mutters, but there's a pouty tone to it and it lightens the mood somewhat.

"It's true what I said in the car a bit ago," I tell her as I move both my hands to the mattress by her head and dip my face down over hers. "I haven't given much thought to what you and I are, or what we'll do going forward. But it seems like things with Zeke are going down fast, and come tomorrow morning, you might not need me anymore."

"Agreed," she admits, but fuck… it kills me how sad she sounds.

"So I'm thinking about it right now," I explain my rationale. "And the one thing I know right now is that I really want to fuck you, and I hope it's going to be just as amazing, if not more so, than that stellar blow job I got last night. I expect I'm going to come deep in your pussy and I'm going to love that feeling, so I expect I'll do it again. I also expect I'll want you tomorrow, and the day after, and the day after that. But truthfully, that's as far as I've gotten, Maggie. I just don't have it in me to look too far into my future. I've got doubts and insecurities just like anyone. So if you want to keep on with me, to see where it goes, that's great. But if you don't want to, because I can't give you more than what I did just now… I'll back off and put my clothes on. The choice is yours."

She doesn't say anything right away, just looks at me without breaking eye contact. Finally, she says, "That's quite a speech, Mr. Payne."

"Did it make sense?" I ask.

"It did, and as it stands… I can appreciate you not knowing what you want. I can also appreciate your doubts," she says coolly, and my chest gets tight with anxiety that she's going to tell me to put my clothes back on. But then she gives me a sassy grin and her eyes sparkle playfully when she says, "I can appreciate those things as much as I can appreciate that fabulous cock that you're practically waving in my face right now, and I'm really wondering what it will feel like inside of me without a condom."

Every bit of tension drains right out of me. At the mention of my cock, it stands a little straighter as if it's preening, and then starts to weep for her with eagerness. My chest also squeezes with the realization this woman is trying to make this easier on me.

"You're just saying that to let me off the hook, aren't you?" I ask her.

"I'm saying that simply because I understand your limitations, and right now... I'm okay with that. I'm also very okay with us having sex and seeing what happens after. It's just that simple."

I smile at Maggie, immediately stretching my body down the length of hers. Her legs part for me and my hips settle in between, my dick laying heavy over her pubic bone.

I look down into Maggie's green eyes as I hold myself off her somewhat by my elbows digging into the mattress. "I want you so bad, Maggie. When I came in your mouth last night, it busted me out of some shackles for sure. I want to know if they're completely banished."

"Then you should probably get on with fucking me," she says impishly, and I appreciate her attempt to further lighten the mood.

But I need her to know one more thing. "I think I'm good, Mags. I think I can do it. Hell, I want to do it so bad... come inside you. But same warning as before... it might not happen."

"And I'm good if that's the case," she assures me with a smile.

"All right then," I say with a return grin. "Let's proceed to the fucking."

"Let's," she says saucily.

"But first," I say before pressing my mouth against hers and giving her a slow kiss. "Lots of foreplay."

I kiss her again, and she mumbles against my mouth. "Sounds good."

And so I spend a very long time getting Maggie worked up for me. Well, hell… getting myself worked up. I roll us to our sides and we kiss and make out like two horny teenagers in the back of a car. Our legs intertwined together, my dick pressed in between our bodies, and some humping as well. But then I get down to business, sliding my hand to her pussy and engaging her clit. I move my mouth down to her breasts, lick and bite at her nipples—which I know would look amazing with some clamps on them—and finger fuck her to a quick orgasm.

I think about bringing her to a second orgasm, but then her hand is on my cock and she's stroking me a little too good and getting me a little too worked up. I briefly consider flipping her on her stomach and riding her that way, but determine that would make me a pussy. If I'm going to confront my fucking cum demons, I'm going to do it face to face with her so I can look into her eyes and assure that Maggie's motives are pure.

Pushing Mags onto her back, I position myself over her, knocking her hand away from my cock. She spreads her legs wide and raises them high, opening herself before me in silent invitation. I look down at her cunt that's wet and swollen with need, and it seems to call out to me. This is it… it's where I bust past my reservations and make this pussy mine. It's where I take back a little bit of what *she* took from me.

I fist my cock and bring the tip to her slit, rubbing the head up and down a few times. The feeling is exquisite and my nerve endings so receptive that the pleasure is almost unbearable. But I also remember this feeling from my past… this completely bare and un-dulled feeling of flesh on flesh, and I flashback to *her* on top of me.

Her sinking down on my cock and the terrible groan she'd always produce from within me because it felt so fucking good even as it all felt so very wrong.

Nausea wells up inside me and I pull away from Maggie so my cock's not touching her.

"Bridger?" Maggie murmurs, and I feel her palms on my cheeks. "We can stop if you want."

I shake my head, blink my eyes, and stare down at Maggie. I take in her beautiful face… her gorgeous hair all fanned out. Those green eyes sparkling with desire and understanding, and, most importantly, with acceptance of whatever I'm able to give her. Despite how little it may actually be.

Before my fears can get the better of me and before I

can change my mind, I put my cock back at her entrance and with one slow but very assured move, I sink into her until I bottom out, all while maintaining eye contact with her.

Pure, electric bliss sears my entire body from the inside out, and a massive rumble of pleasure bolts up my spine. I go absolutely dizzy from the overwhelming physical sensations assaulting my body, and I feel something pulling at me to let go… to become an animal and take what my body demands.

Maggie's eyes flutter, but she forces them to stay open so she can keep my gaze. I hold absolutely still, taking in everything about this moment and trying to control an urge to unleash myself on her.

Maggie's warm eyes filled with desire and acceptance.

Hot, wet flesh tightly wrapped around my cock.

Immense pleasure.

Eagerness to come.

Not a single bit of shame.

No nausea.

No guilt.

Balls already tingling because I want to come really fucking bad.

I want to come inside of Mags.

Tentatively, I pull my cock back and fuck… what a feeling. The bare sliding of her flesh against mine and the tightness almost refusing to let me go. It feels so good it's almost unbearable. I don't want her to let me go.

Slowly, I slide back in… that hot, wet channel sucking me back and squeezing my dick deliciously. I groan over the sensation… all these feelings just beautifully raw and completely overwhelming. I feel like I'm falling into a deep ravine of lust and pleasure mixed with complete gratification, and the only fear I hold at this point is that once I make that fall, I'll never want to crawl out again.

Maggie watches me, her lower lip held between her straight white teeth. Her hands rest at my shoulders, lightly waiting to either grip me in pleasure or console me in failure.

"Feels fucking good, Mags," I tell her in a gruff voice, and I see instant relief flood her face.

"Will feel better if you move," she says with a smile, her hands wrapping around my neck and her knees pressing into my ribs as if she's gearing up for a ride that she knows she'll need to hang on hard to.

I know it will.

Feel better.

Feel better than anything I've ever felt, and I think I'm ready for it.

I hope to fucking Christ I'm ready for it.

I push up and brace my hands on the mattress, using the leverage to start a rhythmic dance of my hips by pulling out and then punching back in deep. Holding a few seconds so I can savor the tremors of pleasure it produces, then I repeat, but a little faster with the next successive thrust.

With each push back into Maggie's sweet pussy, she moans and pants and her fingers press into my neck muscles. With each thrust of my cock, my pulse fires hotter, faster, more erratic as the pleasure builds inside of me. I fuck her harder, and harder, and then harder yet, until I feel like I'm trying to throw myself deep into her. My chest heaves, my throat works overtime to swallow the grunts and curses that try to escape, missing far more than it contains, and my balls actually start to ache with the need to come. I want to hold it off, but there's no putting a lasso on this runaway train. My body has taken over, and it wants to know what this buildup is all about. It's demanding to experience the explosion that it inherently knows is going to be brutal and transcendent all at the same time.

My body begs me to give it up to Maggie. Give her my offering of my own free will. Watch as she accepts, not because it gives her power but because she revels in me.

I pick up the pace, fucking her deeply… completely.

I fuck her on my terms.

"Bridger," Maggie breathes out on a moan as I hit her sweet spot over and over again. "Feels so good. So damn good."

A weird pulse of tension knots in my chest.

"Give me more, Bridger," Maggie says, her hands sliding into my hair and fingers curling to grab hold.

Give it to me, Bridger. Give it up to me. You know you want to.

My thrusting falters, my head twists on its own accord to dislodge her hands from my hair, and I pull my hips back too far, causing my cock to come all the way out of Maggie's sex.

Immediate relief I'm out of her.

Immediate hell that I'm out of her.

My body wars with the need to finish and the compulsion to scramble away. I shake my head to clear my thoughts, but my body takes over and my hips thrust forward involuntarily to sink back into her wetness. I groan because the pleasure from her pussy gripping tight is beyond amazing, and the knot of anxiety lessens somewhat. With a quick pulling back of my cock and another punch in deep, the pleasure sizzles hot again and the remaining anxiety melts away.

I'm okay.

It was just a stumble.

Let it go.

I start thrusting in and out of Maggie, the euphoria once again grabbing hold of me and urging me to completion. My pace is fast, my thrusts deep. She looks at me with a touch of trepidation clouding her normally bright eyes. Her hands come back to my shoulders, her touch tentative.

I don't want her to be tentative.

But I don't want her to be controlling.

I want her to want me like no other woman has, yet it has to be a genuine desire and not born of a self-serving, sociopathic need for dominance.

But no… that's not Maggie.

It could never be sweet Maggie.

Bending down, I place my mouth on hers, giving her a kiss that says how much I love the feel of her under me… around me. I tell her from the depths of the kiss that she is amazing, gorgeous, and sexy, and she is rocking my world right this moment.

I fuck her hard, feeling her breath quicken as she pants into my mouth and her body starts to tremble. I heave my body against hers, lurching almost so that my cock can grind deeper and deeper into her. My own head spins from the dizzying heights I'm being propelled to, and my entire being aches with the need to give it all up right here and now.

I thrust in particularly deep. Maggie's mouth tears away from mine as she throws her head back and screams her release. I'm amazed that I can feel her pussy rippling all around my cock as she comes, and that right there ignites my own orgasm.

I don't even suspect it coming up on me, but rather it seizes me blindly and takes my entire body hostage. I stiffen, one moment suspended in time where I see Maggie's lust-glazed eyes smiling at me and I feel her body's tremble, and then I start to come viciously inside of her. I shoot so hard, my vision darkens for several moments. The pleasure that bursts outward from what seems like every molecule in my body robs me of my breath… to the point where I don't think I'll ever be able to breathe again.

But that's okay, because as good as this feels, I don't need oxygen to survive. I can survive on sex with Maggie alone.

My head drops to her shoulder, and I close my eyes to enjoy the lingering pulses of pleasure that seem to be without end. If my prior orgasms during sex seemed gray and lackluster, these feel like the burst of color that occurred when Dorothy stepped out of her house in Oz.

Maggie's soft hands stroke my shoulders, and I lift my head up to look at her.

"Hey," she says with a soft smile.

"Hey," I mumble back to her, my heart still beating frantically.

"Good?" she asks hesitantly.

"The best," I tell her truthfully.

"Really?" she asks, her smile now wider than the Wyoming prairies.

"Wouldn't lie," I mutter. But I won't elaborate either, because I'm afraid of what a pussy I'd sound like if I tried to wax poetic about that transcendental experience.

Instead, I roll us to our sides, keeping my cock still wedged inside of her. It still has little tingles of pleasure coursing through it, and I'm completely fine by that.

"What do you want to do?" Maggie asks as she wraps her arm around my waist and burrows into me closer.

I don't even hesitate. "Want to get a second wind, and then I want to do that again. Then maybe we'll grab some dinner, and then I definitely want to do it again after that."

"Insatiable," she murmurs, leaning in and pressing a kiss at the base of my throat.

With you, *Maggie,* I think to myself. *Absolutely with you.*

THE CALL COMES in at 3:10 AM and wakes me from an exhausted sleep. I'd fucked Maggie four times in this hotel bed, the last only about two hours ago, and that, coupled with the stress of our situation and the travel, had me falling into a slumber that resembled a coma.

It's why my voice is hoarse and my speech is a little slurred when I answer, "Hello."

"It's Joseph Kizner," I hear and I sit straight up in bed, instantly awake. "It's done—went down a few hours ago. Zeke's in custody as well as several members of the club. Raids went down in several other clubhouses across the United States. Would have called earlier but I've been slammed with getting all the arrests processed and everyone booked properly."

I let out a sigh of relief and scrub my hand through my hair. Maggie doesn't even stir beside me.

"I've got to go; got a shit ton more paperwork. Just wanted to let you know," Kizner says. "You should head back to Jackson once you both get up and moving. We're going to need you and Maggie's statements."

"Will do," I murmur into the phone before disconnecting. The relief that this nightmare for Maggie is finally over and my sheer exhaustion compels me to sink back down beside her. After placing my phone on the bedside table, I roll over and curl my body around Maggie's. We'll sleep for a few more hours, but then we need to hit the road.

It's time to get my life back on track again.

Chapter 22
Maggie

JUST AS THE clock hits three PM, I hear the scrape of tires on asphalt and shoot up off Bridger's couch. I race to the front door, throw it open, and fly down the steps before Woolf can even get the G550 to a complete stop. I've been a bundle of nerves waiting for them to arrive from Cheyenne, because although I logically knew Belle was safe, I had to see it for myself. I also had to feel it, and by that, I needed to hold and squeeze her to death.

Bridger and I got back to his house around ten AM as we were only a few hours away. Woolf, Callie, and Belle had a lot further to travel, of course, so it's been a waiting game through the morning and early afternoon. Which sucked because that left me way too much time to think about Bridger and where we stood.

Last night was unbelievable. The most prolific and sublime sexual experience of my life. I almost don't want to ever have sex again because I don't think what we did last night can be topped. Sure, we got off to a rocky start and Bridger had a few stumbles that first time, but after that, he was a man on a mission. He'd just discovered the holy grail of sex, and he was determined to reach that pinnacle again and again. If I can believe the man as he muttered the fourth time he came inside me, "Get's better every time; can't wait to do it again," I'd say Bridger was now a fan of coming inside of a woman.

Well, I hoped his fandom was really reserved for coming inside of just me.

So yes, I replayed those memories over and over in my head today. Bridger went into his office for a few hours late this morning, so I may have used my fingers on myself while I replayed those memories. I was in a constant state of arousal around the man, knowing what he could do to my body, and I couldn't wait to be with him again.

Sadly, I thought he might take me again this morning when we woke up, but he just hurried me into the shower, stating he wanted to get on the road. This bothered me because I was there, I was warm, and I was ready for the taking. But his desire to get on the road trumped his desire for me, and I'm not sure that bodes well.

Regardless, the G550 comes to a stop and I pull at the back passenger door, opening it and staring at Belle's beautiful face. Her eyes light up with happiness and she yells, "Mommy" as she stretches her arms out to me. I practically tear at the harness restraint to free her, and then I'm pulling her out and squeezing her to me. Her little arms go around my neck and she lays her head on my shoulder. It's the best feeling in the world.

Yes, better than being with Bridger, but that's the

second best feeling in the world.

I spin around and around, holding my baby, vaguely taking in Bridger as he stands on the front porch and watches our reunion. When I stop spinning, I see Woolf walking up to Bridger, clapping him on the back as they talk quietly. Then Callie's arm comes around me, and she gives me a side hug, "It's over, toots. Time to finally relax."

And she's right. Zeke is in jail, and Belle and I are free. It is definitely time to relax.

Except even as I think that, I hear more scraping of tires on asphalt. I turn to see a clichéd black Suburban coming down the long driveway that's clearly government issue, and as it gets closer, I can see blue lights on the dashboard.

"About time," Bridger mutters from the porch.

Bridger called Kizner today when we hit the road to find out when they wanted to interview us, but got his voice mail. He didn't call us back, but sent a terse text that said, *Sorry—slammed with processing and transport of prisoners. Someone will be out this afternoon.*

And that was it. We didn't hear anything else from him, and we certainly hadn't heard anything from Kyle. Bridger and I just assume Kyle's more slammed than Kizner, since he's the guy who brought the entire club down. We imagined he'd have debriefings upon debriefings and wouldn't surface for a while. In fact, I wondered if I'd ever get to see him again and thank him for saving me.

The Suburban comes to a stop beside Woolf's vehicle. A tall, gaunt man with thinning dark hair streaked with silver gets out. He's wearing a black windbreaker, jeans, and what looks like a button-down dress shirt underneath in pale blue.

I start walking toward the porch as he does, and he gives me an uncertain smile. "I'm guessing you're Maggie?"

When I nod, he reaches his hand out to me. I shift Belle up higher on my hip and shake with him.

"I'm Joseph Kizner," he says before turning his attention to the men on the porch.

Bridger steps forward and introduces himself, and then Woolf and Callie, before inviting Joseph into the house. We all trek inside and Bridger offers Kizner something to drink, but he declines.

Callie sidles up to me and opens her arms. "Why don't you let me take Belle back to the bedroom to play while y'all talk?"

I nod and hand Belle over. She doesn't need to hear any of this.

After Callie disappears down the hall, I go to my usual place on the sofa, and Bridger sits down beside me. Kizner takes an armchair on the opposite side of the coffee table, and Woolf stands behind the couch, maybe in a show of solidarity and support. I don't care if he hears the details of my story. Kizner said he'd want our statements so I'm going to have to disclose what happened to me. He protected Belle with his life and I owe him everything, so he's more than earned his right to hear the entire story.

Kizner dispenses with any small talk and gets right to it, "The raid went down quickly. They never saw it coming, never suspected. We had twenty-three arrest warrants for that clubhouse alone. Similar raids went down at clubhouses across the United States. We were able to serve eighteen of the twenty-three warrants, but that did include arresting Zeke Powell as well as his number-two guy, Arden Hayes."

"What were the charges?" Woolf asks from behind me.

Kizner looks at Woolf when he answers. "Murder, drugs, illegal guns, extortion, slavery. Charges that will ensure Zeke Powell goes away forever, and the other members for a very long time."

Kizner then slides his gaze down to me, as I'm sitting just below Woolf on the couch. "And I want to get your statement, Miss Waylon, and we'll amend charges to add kidnapping."

"And torture," Bridger growls. "Zeke's old lady, Kayla, beat her and cut her, deprived her of food and water, and threatened to kill her."

Kizner nods and takes out a recorder from a pocket in his windbreaker. "There are no arrest warrants for Kayla Powell at this time. She was there when the arrests went down though. Let me get Miss Waylon's statement, then yours, Mr. Payne, and we'll go from there."

And so I tell Agent Kizner everything. How I first

came to Mayhem's Mission and that Zeke claimed me as his property. I was embarrassed and ashamed to think of myself in those days, down on my luck but still loving to party and content with being someone's fuck toy so I'd have a roof over my head and booze in my gut. About getting pregnant and how it took me two years to get inspired to run with Belle. I tell him about Aunt Gayle and then how members of the Omaha chapter of Mayhem's Mission found me in Nebraska because I stupidly holed up with a girl who used to be one of the club whores here in Jackson, but wised up and got out. I naively felt it would be safe since she wasn't in that environment anymore, but she betrayed me.

Kizner asks me some follow-up questions, and then focuses in on what they did to me to induce me to give up Belle's whereabouts. I hear Woolf mutter a curse when I tell Kizner the brutal details of what Zeke did. Beatings with his fist and then a frustration fuck—which, let's face it, was rape because I didn't want it even if I was too beat down to say so. And how Kayla beat me with her own fists, or the handle of a broomstick, which is where I got the gash on the top of my head. I grit my teeth when I tell him she used a knife on me, and I even admit with shame that's when I almost broke and told her what she wanted to know.

"And how did you escape?" Kizner asks.

I shrug. "I don't know. I passed out from the pain during one of Kayla's sessions. I was in the basement and had lost track of time—didn't even know if it was day or night. I woke up here in Bridger's house. He said Kyle brought me here. I didn't believe it at first because Kyle watched what Kayla did to me, and he laughed. He even egged her on once when she was punching me. But I understand now that he was playing a role and he saved me."

Something flickers across Kizner's face, and I'm pretty sure it's guilt. I don't miss it, and neither does Bridger, who I can literally feel tense up beside me.

He leans forward and asks Kizner, "Where's Kyle? I get he might be tied up, but I'm sure Maggie would like to see him… to thank him for helping her."

There's another flash of guilt across Kizner's face followed by extreme sadness as his shoulders sag. He looks down at the floor and says in a low voice, "Kyle didn't make it."

"What?" Bridger growls in disbelief as I feel tears well up in my eyes.

Kizner looks up to me before sliding a morose gaze to Bridger. He clears his throat. "We found his body during the raid. It was at the back of the property. Single bullet to the back of the head—execution style."

A heavy silence fills the room. My head spins with the implication that the man who saved my life gave up his. That he was most likely killed because Zeke suspected he'd helped me. I know this because Kizner said the raid went easy; that they had no clue ATF was coming down on them.

I feel myself starting to fracture. Start to break into a

million pieces.

But then Bridger shoots off the couch with a muttered curse and stomps down the hallway to his bedroom without another word to any of us, leaving behind a physical wake of sorrow and anger. His bedroom door slams with such force, the house shakes.

I immediately stand from the couch and jet down the hallway. I don't bother with a knock. When I open the door, I immediately see him standing at the bottom of the bed, his chest heaving and his hands curled into tight fists. He emanates danger and raw fury, and I don't think twice before I run to him and slam my body into his front while wrapping my arms around his waist.

I press my cheek to his chest and whisper, "I'm sorry. I know he was a friend of yours."

"He wasn't a friend of mine," Bridger growls, his arms staying tense at his side rather than returning my embrace. "I drank a few beers with him. Fucked a few club whores with him."

I flinch, not just because of the crudity of his words, but because there's no doubt in my mind Bridger mentioned fucking other women because he's using this as an opportunity to remind me that he's not a long-term commitment kind of guy. He's also taking out his pain and anger on me, and I choose to think he does so because he trusts I will see it for what it is and not hold it against him.

So I just squeeze him harder and say, "He may not have been a friend, but he saved me. He was a good man, and it's okay to mourn him."

Silence except for the beating of Bridger's heart against my cheek.

Then his arms come around me and I feel him rest his own cheek on the top of my head. "He should have known they were onto him. He should have gotten out of there."

His words are gruff and although on their face they place blame on Kyle's shoulders, I know he says them merely out of disbelief that he's gone.

Bridger only holds me for a few moments before he pulls away. His hands come to my shoulders. and he says in a low voice, "Get back in there. I'm sure Kizner has more questions. I'll be in there in a minute."

I study him, wondering if I should refuse. Should I stay and console him more?

But I see a certain aloofness there now, and it's clear Bridger's taken all he will from me right now. I can only hope he doesn't use this as an excuse to freeze me out.

I nod and turn away from him, but his voice stops me at the door. "Mags?"

So confused and unsure. Filled with need for something, and I turn around expectantly.

Bridger swallows hard and looks at me with frustration. I wait patiently.

Finally, he just shakes his head and mutters, "Never mind. I'll be out there soon."

I don't press it. Bridger isn't a man to be pushed. He has to find his own way, and while I'll gladly provide whatever gentle encouragement I can, I also know there are boundaries with him that he's not ready for me to cross.

When I get back into the living room, I see Kizner holding a cup of coffee and Woolf doing the same, except now he's sitting on the cushion that Bridger vacated.

I take my spot on the couch, sitting next to Woolf. He looks at me expectantly. "He okay?"

"Sure," I say with a confident voice, but I can tell by the look on Woolf's face he doesn't believe me. "Just needs a minute."

Woolf stands and without a word, he walks down the hallway to Bridger's room. I'm glad... that he's a close enough friend that he looked past my false proclamation about Bridger and is going to offer his support as well.

"Miss Waylon," Kizner says and I turn my head to look at him. "Kayla Powell... what was her motivation in torturing you?"

"Well, I think she was taking up where Zeke left off. When he went on a run, she took it upon herself to continue to work me over to give up Belle. Or maybe he even asked her to do it, I don't know. But mostly, I think she did it because she hates me. I think she wanted to find Belle for Zeke, because she loved that bastard and couldn't give him a child, but I think mostly because she was jealous that I gave Zeke something she couldn't."

He asks me a few more questions before turning the recorder off and slipping it back in his pocket. "This is

282

more than enough for an arrest. It will be the local authorities though, and I'm sure they'll want to talk to you as well. Could take a few days as they got their hands full right now with the club members and waiting for the US Marshall's to fly in and take custody of them."

I nod before looking down at my hands clasped tightly together. When I look back up, I ask, "Did Kyle have family?"

Kizner nods. "A sister… in North Carolina. She's already been notified."

A lump forms at the base of my throat, and I swallow past it. "I'd… um… when the time is proper… I'd like to reach out to her. I want to let her know what Kyle did for me."

"I'm sure that would be a comfort to her," Kizner says, but I have to wonder if that's true. She may hate me because my predicament ultimately led to his death. Still, I need to express my gratitude and condolences to her.

Kizner leaves, telling me on the way out that the local authorities will get up with Bridger about a statement, mostly to nail down the facts about Kyle bringing me here and the condition I was in when he did. I tell him that's fine. He pulls out of Bridger's driveway, leaving behind a household filled with a mixture of relief that our ordeal is over and heavy sorrow that someone gave his life to ensure our safety.

Chapter 23
Bridger

I SCAN THE last page of the payroll summary report, feel satisfied it's in order, and then sign off on it. That task complete, I put it aside and my thoughts immediately go to Maggie. I growl in frustration, because I don't want to think about her. I grab the inventory order sheet that my senior bartender, Ted, had placed on my desk last night before he headed over to The Silo. In addition to being a fucking fantastic bartender, he's one of my best Fantasy Makers as well. All the ladies and men love Ted and his eight-inch cock. He doesn't discriminate where he'll stick it.

Perusing the inventory sheet, I make a few notations in the side column, noting our stock of white wine has been depleting faster than normal. Must be a run on tourists or something, but my mind involuntarily thinks of Maggie again because she likes white wine. This is something I learned about her just last night after I fucked her.

And what a spectacular fucking it was. I'm sure we were both overly sensitive to emotion based on learning about Kyle's death that day, but I rode her hard from behind, that same animalistic need overtaking me and causing me to practically try to crawl my way inside of her because it felt so good. But when I felt myself getting close, I flipped her over, because I really wanted to suck on those perfect tits because I'd come to realize they are very sensitive. I figure if I can ever get to a point where I can control myself around her, I'd want to see if I can make her come just by working her nipples over.

So I hammered into her, my teeth biting at her nipples before I'd suck on them, and it was well on its way to being another existential experience for me until she grabbed my hair again.

Maggie wasn't kidding. She's a hair puller.

I, however, am not a hair pullee.

Never will be simply because *she* got off on grabbing a fistful of my hair, which I'd always worn long as a kid, and she'd hold me there while she would alternate blows to my face with kisses. When I was twelve, she once dragged me through the house by my hair as I tried to madly scramble on my hands and knees to keep up with her. She dragged me right into the bathroom where she slapped the shit out of me repetitively before she put me in the bathtub and bathed me with apologies.

When Maggie grabbed onto my hair, my hips never missed a beat in their jackhammering and my hands pulled hers away from me so I could hold them pinned above her head until I came inside of her with a loud groan of stupendous relief.

After, I was feeling mellow and because I'd loved the

way Maggie's body felt against mine the night before when we slept in the motel bed together, I was content to let her cuddle into me.

As she stroked my stomach, she said, "Sorry about the hair thing."

"It's okay," I muttered, my own hand stroking her hip.

"It could be a repetitive problem," she said, humor in her voice, but I didn't reply.

And when I didn't reply, she asked me somberly, "Why does it bother you?"

I could have given her a million different answers. I could have lied a million different ways. But instead, I told her the truth. "My stepmom used to beat me. She often did so while holding me in place by my hair."

Maggie gave out a cry of protest. "Oh, my God. I'm so sorry."

"It's in the past," I mumbled as I reached for her hand and moved it from my stomach to my cock to distract her unwanted pity. I'd just got done coming in her not fifteen minutes prior, but the minute I made her fingers curl around me, I started to come alive again.

Because my body wants Maggie in a way that it's never wanted anything before.

I actually believe it needs her, because the thought of me getting this anywhere else is like shoving rancid meat down a starving man's throat.

So she got me hard with her hand, and then harder yet with her mouth. She gobbled my cock up and swallowed me whole, after which I ate her beautiful pussy still leaking with my cum. It was a beautiful experience.

Would have fucked her again this morning given the opportunity, but when I woke up, she was gone. I assume she slept with Belle, and I'm not sure if that relieved or irritated me. Regardless, I found them both in the kitchen when I came out, and Maggie served me eggs and bacon.

We all three sat at the table together and ate breakfast. I smiled appropriately and teased Belle. I helped Maggie clean up after. And the entire time, I analyzed every feeling running through me. Bodily repletion from amazing fucking. Companionship from a beautiful and kind woman. Joy from an energetic toddler who is cute beyond words.

And fear that I don't deserve a single minute of it.

I want Maggie, no doubt. For sure in my bed.

My heart? Not so sure.

She's so many wonderful things to me, but she's still a complication. My life is orderly. I have certain proclivities. I have unbearable demons that are well controlled with the very structured life I lead. The Silo gives me comfort, and it's a part of me.

I know for sure I cannot let this carefully ordered world deconstruct on me.

Maggie has the ability to tear it all apart.

Ultimately, I had no great epiphany as to what to do. My cock was winning my war of indecisiveness, and I left the house after breakfast to get some work done. I didn't kiss Maggie goodbye, but I did tell her I'd see her at dinner. It sent a message as mixed as my feelings.

I want you, but I don't. I like having you here in my house, but I'm just not sure I'd want it forever.

I didn't go straight to The Wicked Horse though. Instead, I drove into Jackson and went straight to my barber. Anyone who knows me knows I don't give a shit about my appearance. I'll often grow my hair long, and when it becomes a nuisance, I'll shave it all off and let it grow back again.

My hair is long, but not quite to the point where it's bothering me.

Still, I didn't hesitate a moment parking my ass in that barber's chair and telling him to take it all off. Took no more than ten minutes and some sharp electric blades before I had nothing but stubble over my entire head that looked like an early five o'clock shadow. I killed two birds with one stone. Got my haircut out of the way and ensured that Maggie's hands would never grab hold of my hair again.

Finishing up the inventory sheet, I put it on the edge of my desk. I'll walk out and hand it to Ted a little later. He'll call in the new stock order. I turn to my email, relishing in the minutes it gives me of Maggie-free thought.

There's one from Cal, letting me know again how much he and Macy enjoyed The Silo. I feel bad I didn't spend more time with them, but it was a quick in and out trip for them. Still, I should be the one thanking them. They inspired me to get up the courage to come down Maggie's throat and forever changed the way I would have sex.

At least I think.

Not sure I'd want to come inside another woman.

Not sure I could.

My phone rings. I grab it from the desk where it sits next to my laptop. Flipping it over, I see it's from Kizner.

"Payne," I answer the phone brusquely.

"It's Joseph Kizner," he says, although it's not needed as he's in my Contacts now. But still, in just those three words, my body goes stiff with alertness because there is no mistaking the urgency and concern in his voice.

"What's wrong?" I immediately ask.

"Local authorities still haven't processed a warrant for Kayla Powell's arrest, and probably won't until they actually interview Maggie," he says, and this doesn't surprise me. I didn't expect it to move fast. But his next words send a cold shiver of fear up my spine. "I interviewed Zeke today, and he made some threats against Maggie and Belle."

"What kind of threats," I ask thickly, my mouth suddenly dry.

"When we told him we'd be amending the charges against him to add kidnapping and assault, he didn't take kindly to it. When we told him we were going after Kayla, he just laughed at us. Said we'd have a hard time proving that against his old lady without any witnesses.

Threw it in our face that Agent Sommerville was dead and couldn't testify."

"But Maggie's a witness," I rasp out.

"I've got cops headed there now," Kizner says, but I'm already shooting out of my chair and running for the door.

"I'm closer," I tell him before I disconnect. I careen through The Wicked Horse and fly to my Corvette parked right at the front door.

Kizner calls me back as I toss my phone on the passenger seat, start the car, and peel out of the parking lot, leaving lots of rubber behind. When my phone goes silent, I grab it and dial my house phone. It rings repetitively five times until the answering machine picks up. It's a model that has a speaker on it so you can hear the person leaving the message.

"Maggie," I say in a voice that I struggle to keep calm so I don't freak her out. "Zeke has made some threats against you, and I'm headed there now. I want you to take Belle and go into my room. I have a shotgun on the top shelf in my closet. Lock yourself in the bathroom until I—"

The message cuts off. With a curse, I dial back. She doesn't answer this time either, and I hope to fuck she's just outside playing with Belle. I continue my message. "I'm sure it's all fine, but you never know with someone fucked in the head like Zeke. He has members who weren't arrested and were loyal to—"

The machine cuts off again with an offending beep.

"Fuck," I yell and throw the phone down into the passenger foot well.

It rings again. I almost drive off the highway trying to lean over and grab it because it might be Maggie. After I get it in my hands, I curse again when I see it's Kizner.

I connect the call. "I can be there in about fifteen minutes. Where are the cops?"

"At least twenty-five out," he says. "You armed?"

"No," I say, cursing myself for assuming Maggie and Belle were safe.

"If you can tell someone's in that house with them when you get there, you do not go in. You wait for the cops to get there," he orders me like an overbearing father.

"Not gonna fucking happen," I tell him.

He sighs into the phone, and I can hear the worry in it. "I'm headed that way too," he says softly. "Just in case."

"Got it," I mutter, and then disconnect. I put both hands on the wheel and bear down on the gas.

The fifteen-minute drive seems to take thirty, but in reality, I made it in eleven thanks to the power of my Vette and my erratic driving as I passed people on the highway without prejudice.

I barrel down my long driveway and my house comes in to view, my stomach sinking when I see a dark gray Dodge charger parked in front. I don't know the car and have never seen it before. It could be an undercover cop car for all I know, and that would be a welcome scenario. It could be one of Zeke's guys who didn't want the rumble of a Harley to scare Maggie off.

I pull my car up, turn the ignition off, and get out. I consider sneaking around the house and peering in windows so I can verify the house occupants. But that would take time and would also keep Maggie and Belle in danger longer.

Besides, I've never been one for subtle.

I gingerly navigate the front porch steps, skipping over the third one that creaks, and walk right into my house like a man on a mission.

I'm not prepared for what I find.

My eyes first land on Belle, who sits in the corner of the living room near the back door. She has tears streaming down her face. My gaze slides to the right, five feet from Belle, and Maggie is sitting in a kitchen chair with Kayla in front of her. Kayla's back is to me, but the minute the door opens, she swings around. My heart lurches when I see she has a gun in her hand.

I want to look back at Maggie, ensure she's okay. I want to go pick up Belle and comfort her. But I don't dare take my eyes off the gun that Kayla is now pointing at me.

"Oh goody," Kayla sneers. "I can knock two people off my list now that you're here, Bridger."

I slowly raise my hands up and to the side in a message that clearly conveys, *Just calm the fuck down and don't do anything hasty.*

"Come on, Kayla," I say in a calm voice that I hope is soothing in nature. "You don't want to bring this down on yourself, do you? Zeke's going down, but you don't have to."

"Do you think I'm stupid?" she hisses at me, waving the gun erratically around but still pointed in my general direction. "You don't think I haven't figured the cops are coming for me, too?"

And they should be here in hopefully about ten minutes, I think to myself. But I tell Kayla, "You don't want murder on your shoulders, Kayla. You'll go away forever."

"Think I give a fuck?" she yells at me. "Zeke's gone. He ain't comin' back. You think I give a rat's ass what happens to me?"

I take a moment to let myself look at Maggie.

Just a moment so I can assure she's okay as I try to figure out how to talk this crazy woman off the ledge.

And in that moment, I see everything clearly.

Maggie's eyes, which reflect to me the very depths of her soul, shoot a quick glance at Belle before looking back to me, and I see exactly what she's saying.

I am not going to sit back and let this bitch get her hands on Belle.

I give a slight nod, which is intended for Kayla to see that I've just had a very important communication with Maggie. As I hoped, Kayla twists her neck to look at Maggie behind her. The minute her attention is off me, Maggie kicks her legs out viciously and catches Kayla behind her knees.

Her legs fold and she starts to go down as the gun aims upward. A piercing shot rings out, and a flutter of dust from my ceiling comes down.

I take the opportunity to charge, just as Kayla starts to stand straight again. I jump right over the couch, the quickest way to my destination, and I lower my shoulder like an enraged bull going after the matador holding the bright red cape.

I see Kayla lower the gun and swing it my way. It goes off moments before I crash into her. A hot, burning flash of pain hits the outside of my right shoulder just as it plows right into Kayla's stomach. We go flying right past Maggie and into the heavy sliding glass door that leads onto the back deck. I'm immediately thankful it just shudders and doesn't shatter, as I'm not sure either of us would have survived that.

Kayla lets out a whoosh of breath as the gun goes flying out of her hand. Her head flies backward and slams hard into the glass, and she literally starts to sag downward.

I don't trust the murderous bitch, so I grab her shoulders, pull her away from the glass door, and slam her back into it. Her head hits against the window with brutal force, and she doesn't even make a sound of pain as her eyes roll into the back of her head. I let her go, and she slumps to the floor, out cold.

Maggie scrambles out of the chair and runs to Belle while I grab the gun, removing the clip and chambered round before tossing it across the room. My hands go to my belt where I quickly pull it off before squatting down and rolling Kayla onto her stomach. I don't feel an ounce of sympathy when I see the back of her head was cracked open and is leaking blood. No clue if I damaged her severely. Don't care.

I pull her hands behind her back and secure them with my belt. When I stand up and turn to Maggie, she's as pale as a ghost as she tries to console Belle. My hands are shaking as I reach them up out of habit to run my fingers through my hair, only to have them hit the bristles on my head.

Blowing out a breath of terror-filled air, I come to the realization that I almost just lost Maggie, and it scared the fuck out of me.

Scared the fuck out of me because I've never had anything matter to me that much, and I don't like the heavy burden of responsibility that weighs down upon me in this moment.

Chapter 24
Maggie

B RIDGER'S HANDS SHAKE as he drags the pads of his fingers over his buzzed-cut head. His hair is gone. All that beautiful, warm brown hair that was soft, silky, and slightly wavy... just, gone. Here I am, having just narrowly escaped death—because there's no doubt that Kayla was here to kill me—and all I can think about is that Bridger's hair is gone.

He's utterly magnificent, of course. With the hair gone, the golden hue of his eyes pop against his dark lashes. His cheekbones seem sharper, his jaw more squared.

His lips.

Those lips are fuller... more sensuous.

I just narrowly escaped death and all I can do is stare at Bridger with a dark shadow of bristles on his head, and think... he cut that all off because of *me*.

Belle's cries soften and she gives a small hiccup as she holds onto me tightly. Thank fuck Kayla didn't touch her as it was going to be hard enough moving her past this trauma.

"You okay?" Bridger asks gruffly as he raises his

shoulder and peers at it. My eyes drift there, and I gasp as I see his olive-green Henley dark with blood.

"Oh, my God, Bridger," I cry out as I rush over to him, Belle bouncing on my hip. "You're shot."

"Grazed," he says through gritted teeth as he fingers a jagged tear made by a passing bullet and tries to peer inside. With a grunt of frustration, he pulls his shirt off and tosses it to the floor where it lands beside Kayla's head.

I don't even spare her a glance. I scoot closer to Bridger and stand on my tiptoes so I can get a look at his wound. It's about a two-inch groove cutting through his skin that's about half an inch wide and oozing with blood. It's not deep. As he wipes a finger over it, I can see pink skin underneath before more blood oozes.

"Goddamn, I'm a lucky son of a bitch," he mutters as he barely gives me a glance and pushes past me to walk into the kitchen.

I watch as he grabs a kitchen towel and presses it to the wound before walking back into the living room and calling 911. I watch in shock as Bridger calmly tells the dispatcher what happened, and I'm surprised when he mentions that there are other police already on the way. I'm not sure how they knew what was going down, but before Bridger can even finish telling the full story, I see a police car pulling up behind Bridger's Vette through the living room window.

A flurry of activity ensues as uniformed officers come in and take stock of the situation before checking on

Kayla. Joseph Kizner arrives on their heels and goes immediately to talk to Bridger. Another car arrives, more local police, who, after talking to the first ones to arrive, stand around watching as one of the EMT's attends to Kayla, who is still unconscious. The other EMT goes to Bridger. After giving him a quick examination, he cleanses and bandages his wound. There's some words exchanged. Bridger gives a sharp shake of his head, and I hear him say, "I'm not going to the fucking hospital. It's a scratch."

Typical man.

The EMTs examine Kayla, who's still out cold, but then quickly load her up and cart her off to, I assume, the hospital in Jackson. The second set of cops leave to presumably follow the ambulance and the first set split apart, one going to Bridger and the other asking to talk to me in the kitchen. Even though Belle witnessed firsthand her mother getting attacked by Kayla, held at gunpoint, and then her scream at me in the craziest of fashions, I don't want her to have to hear any more of this. So I set her on the couch, give her a glass of milk, and I put *Paw Patrol* on for her to watch. She seems fine right now, but I want to hurry up and get this interview over so I can get her back in my arms so she knows everything is going to be all right.

Maybe after that, I can ensure that Bridger is okay, too, because as of right now, I'm sensing that he's not.

A HAND ON my face, pulling my hair back and then stroking my cheek.

I come awake slowly, blinking against the glow of the lamp I'd left on beside Bridger's bed. I knew I was overstepping boundaries when I came in here to lie down and wait for him. I knew he might be pissed to find me here. But damn it… he'd spent most of the day looking at me like I was a fragile glass ornament that could break at any moment and completely avoiding any personal talk.

After the police left, so did Bridger. I know the only reason he felt safe in doing so was because he'd had his chief of security, Cain Bonham, come and stay with Belle and me. All he'd said was, "Gotta go into work," and then he was gone. And I was left staring at Cain, who I didn't know other than what little I'd learned from Sloane on poker night. That consisted of the fact that he'd let Sloane have sex with Bridger, Rand, and Logan, as well as himself, which was still beyond my comprehension.

I cooked dinner, and Cain ate quietly with Belle and me. While he prowled around the living room and kitchen, checking doors and locks, I put Belle to bed and snuggled with her for a while before finally deciding to wait in Bridger's bed.

No clue what Cain did. I felt his presence was unnecessary. Kizner felt pretty confident that Kayla was acting alone in her attack of me, and I felt confident in that as well. I mean, her exact words to me had nothing to do with protecting Zeke from further charges of kidnapping, or even protecting herself from criminal charges.

No, she'd said, and I quote, "Think you could fuck my man all those years, spawn his hell brat, and not think I was going to get some payback?"

Yeah… today was personal, and it was all about Kayla. I didn't think anyone from Mayhem's Mission was coming after me, but Bridger couldn't be talked out of having Cain come stay with me so he could "go to work".

And now he stares down at me, his hand falling away from my face. I sit up in the bed and give a slight yawn as I look at the bedside clock.

Almost one AM. Work must have been hopping.

"What are you doing in here?" Bridger asks gruffly.

"Waiting on you," I tell him testily. "Figured you couldn't avoid me if I was lying in your bed."

"Not avoiding you," he says as he pulls his shirt off and tosses it aside, then brings his hands to his belt buckle to work at it. He removes it swiftly.

Of course, I can't think to argue with him. Not with his glorious chest and abs on full display, not to mention the erection clearly outlined against his jeans.

Turning, he sits on the edge of the bed. Bends over to take his boots and socks off.

Bridger angles toward me, sliding his hand around the back of my neck, and then he's pulling me into him. His mouth meets mine in a kiss that rivals a firestorm, all hot and consuming. He groans in my mouth, pushes me back onto the bed, and brings his big body over mine.

I think about all the things I want to talk about with him. How I need to know where we stand. How I need to reassure him I'm okay and won't break. Most importantly, how I really believe we could have something together if he'd just take the chance on me.

But none of that comes out because my mouth is occupied with his, and then his hands are stripping me bare, and then he's got his jeans open and he's inside of me.

"Oh, Bridger," I moan as I tear my mouth away from his and stare with glassy eyes at the far wall. He's hot and huge and filling me so completely that there is no rational thought to be had. It becomes only about the way he feels inside of me right now and the way he's going to make me feel even better.

He moves his hips in luxurious strokes, taking his time and content to let us both build slowly. His mouth is everywhere... my lips, my earlobes, my throat, my nipples. One hand snakes between us, and he fingers my clit in agonizingly slow circles. My hands snake around his neck, sliding to the base of his scalp where I feel nothing but the prickles of stubble.

"You cut your hair because of me," I whisper.

Not a question.

A statement.

His answer?

His mouth comes back to mine and he's kissing me

again, so he doesn't have to answer me. So he doesn't have to admit that something I did was so awful, he had to ensure I never did it again.

An overwhelming wave of sorrow flows through me, and I know this is the beginning of the end. Any self-respecting woman would push a man such as him off her, knowing he'd never be able to fulfill what she truly needed deep down.

But I've got no respect for myself. Not where Bridger's concerned.

So I accept his slow lovemaking. I let him continue to kiss me and flutter his fingers against my clit while his cock thrusts deep and true. I let him build me up to the ultimate pinnacle, amazed when he bursts apart at the same time I do. He comes inside of me with a long groan right into my mouth, grinding his hips hard and setting me on fire again.

And as I fall back down to earth, I can't say as I'm shocked when he pulls out of me, rolls off the bed, and tucks himself back in his jeans. He bends over, picks his shirt off the floor, and turns to me. "Listen… I'm wiped. I'm going to take a shower and hit the bed. Why don't you head back into your room with Belle, okay?"

"Sure," I say, my voice betraying me as it cracks with emotion.

To give him credit, Bridger actually winces before he turns away and walks into the bathroom.

The minute the door closes, the tears start flowing as I hastily gather my pajamas and underwear, putting them on with jerky movements. I have to bite down on the inside of my cheek to keep from letting out a sob. I'm losing him before I even ever really had him.

As I turn toward his bedroom door, the sound of his voice stops me. He's talking to someone from inside the bathroom.

Without any regard to his privacy, I pad over to the bathroom door and place my ear against it.

"…so if it's okay and you're up for a visit, I'd like to come see you," I hear Bridger say.

A long pause. Then, in a soft, caring voice, he says, "It's been a long time, I know."

Another pause, then, "Thanks, Adrienne. See you soon."

I quickly back away from the door, my heart literally cracking in two. He's leaving. Not sure when, but he's leaving. And his voice was soft and gentle. Her name's Adrienne.

The tears start pouring again, and I have no fight in me. As I said, no self-respect where Bridger's concerned. He just fucked me and kicked me out of his bed, then quite possibly called a woman so he could go and see her.

I spin and run out of his bedroom, then crawl into bed with Belle. I wrap my arms around her and silently let my tears fall as I realize I'm nothing to Bridger at all.

I WAKE UP early, hear Belle breathing deeply, and look at the alarm clock.

5:45 AM.

Slipping out of bed, I change out pajamas for jeans and a t-shirt before heading into the kitchen to make coffee. I slept fitfully last night, sometimes for maybe a half an hour at a time, before I'd dream about Bridger. Or were they nightmares?

As the coffee brews, I start putting things in order.

First, I need to call Aunt Gayle once the sun fully rises. My only choice is to go stay with her. Perhaps if I had a job, or a place to live, I could make a home here, but I have none of those things. I'm sure she could wire me some cash for bus tickets, or maybe she and Randall could come get us.

Second, I need to sit down with Bridger this morning after he gets up and let him know of my plans. While I'm clearly not within his, he needs to know I've decided that he can't be in mine. I'm cutting out before he has the balls to finally tell me to my face that what we have has run its course.

The coffee finishes brewing so I pour myself a cup before heading back to check on Belle. She's still sleeping. I head back into the living room and glance out the front window, do a double take, and then look harder.

Bridger's car is gone.

Setting my coffee cup down on an end table, I pad back to his room. His door is open and the room is dim since the blinds are all shut.

But it's light enough for me to see the note on his bed.

With my chest feeling like there's a cinder block on it, I walk to the bed on shaky legs. I pick up the note and see it's brutally short.

I'm sorry.
Bridger

My fingers curl inward, and the note crumples in my hand. Tears sting my eyes over the unfairness of it all. It's not fair that he left me like this, without an explanation. It's not fair that he's crushed me and that he doesn't even have the balls to sweep the mess left of me out his door.

Most of all, it's not fair that my heart is so tied up with a man who can't give me back what I so desperately desire.

I drop the note to the carpet and head back into the living room. After I grab my coffee cup, I walk to the phone, intent on calling Aunt Gayle and begging her to come get me. I'd talked to her just last night and filled her in on everything that had happened, assured her I was fine, and I know she could hear the hope in my voice that maybe I could have a good life here with Bridger.

Just as I pick the phone up, movement out the window catches my eye. For a split second, I think it might be Bridger coming back to tell me he made a terrible mistake, but then I see it's Woolf walking up the porch steps, his black Range Rover parked in the driveway just behind him.

I walk over, open the door before he can knock, and say flatly, "He's not here."

Woolf surprises me by nodding. "I know. And I need to talk to you."

"Oh," I say with surprise as I step back from the door. He walks past me. "Want some coffee?"

"That would be great," he says softly.

We settle down at the kitchen table after I make him a cup of java and I check one more time on Belle. She's sleeping later than usual, but yesterday was pretty damn traumatic and she had cried so much, she was just exhausted. Of course, I cried a lot last night too after Bridger kicked me out of his room, and there's no denying the zombie-like feeling I've got going on right now.

After he takes a sip of his coffee—he takes it black—Woolf sets the cup down, rests his forearms on the table, and his expression goes troubled. "Bridger went to stay with a friend for a while."

"I know," I cut in bitterly. "I heard him on the phone last night after... Well, last night I heard him talking to a woman named Adrienne. He said it had been a long time and he wanted to visit."

Yeah, I let Woolf in on the fact that Bridger is two-timing me. Well, wait... can he be two-timing me if he's not even one-timing me anymore? Are we officially over? Is that what the note was about?

So fucking confused.

So heartbroken, but I refuse to let it show.

I look at Woolf with my chin held high, and I expect his expression to turn even darker as he knows that I know about this other woman. Instead, his lips peel back and he gives a bark of laughter, followed by more laughter, and then on to dwindling chuckles.

"What's so funny?" I demand.

Woolf looks at me and the chuckles die instantly when he hears the anger in my voice. "I'm sorry," he says, and he does sound truly apologetic. "It's just… Adrian's not a woman. It's a man. He's an Episcopalian priest in Cheyenne that Bridger's close to."

My brows draw inward, knitted in confusion. "I don't understand."

"I didn't mean to laugh at you, but your jealousy got to me. It also confirmed to me that you'll fight for Bridger."

"No, I won't," I proclaim firmly.

"Yes, you will," he says just as staunchly. Before I can open my mouth to argue, he continues on, "Bridger's fucked up in the head. No better way to say it. And while it's not up to me to tell you the root cause of that, I can assure you that his issues run deep and stem from some horrific shit. He left so he can try to get that shit sorted."

While I want to be heartened by this… while I want to have hope… I can't find it within me. "He left me a note that sounded pretty much like a final goodbye."

"Maybe it was," Woolf says with a shrug of his shoulder. "Maybe it was just a temporary goodbye."

"Well, he could have been a little clearer," I snap, the frustration and heartbreak crashing down on me. "He could have told me to my face. He could have given me some indication of what he's feeling. Instead, he fucks me, kicks me out of bed, and then skulks off in the middle of the night. Well, fuck you very much, Bridger. I don't need that shit."

Woolf actually winces, jerking slightly in his seat. "Maggie—"

I can't stand the pity in his voice, so I stand from the table and move to the coffee pot to keep myself busy so I don't shatter. I give a slight cough, clear the shakiness from my voice, and tell Woolf, "I'm going to go live with my Aunt Gayle in Coeur D'Alene. I'm hoping she'll come pick me up, so Belle and I should be cleared out hopefully by tomorrow."

"I think you should stay," Woolf says, and I spin around to look at him. "Bridger wants you to stay."

"What?" I ask in surprise.

Woolf nods. "He called me on his way out of town. Asked me to keep an eye on you and Belle. Told me to extend the invitation to stay here at his house for as long as you wanted, and for me to help get you set up with some type of job. He's having me set up a bank account and transferring some money for you to use for living expenses and stuff until you can get your first paycheck."

"Oh, how magnanimous of him," I mutter as I pour another cup of coffee.

"He's coming back, Maggie," Woolf says confidently. "And then it will be time to figure out shit between you two."

I snort in disbelief because I'm still ruled by anger

and betrayal.

He's coming back.

But when?

And is there even anything left between us that makes me want to try to figure shit out?

I don't know the answer to that, but I have some decisions to make.

Chapter 25
Bridger

One week later…

I PUT A log on the chopping block, raise the ax over my shoulder, and swing it in a perfect arc so the blade hits true. The log splits in two, falls to the ground. I take another and do the same. I do this three more times before tossing the ax to the ground, taking a moment to wipe the sweat from my forehead by rubbing it against my right arm, hiss because I hit right over the grooved, burned flesh from the bullet that's still healing and tender, and then immediately start picking up the firewood and stacking it up along the back wall of the rectory.

"At that rate," Adrian says from behind me, "I'll have enough firewood to last me through to retirement."

"You'll never retire," I mutter without looking at him before picking up another log and placing it on the chopping block.

Adrian watches me silently, sitting on the back stoop and sipping a cup of tea. He's aged a lot since I last saw him almost thirteen ago. His dark hair that he always shaped into a tight, neat cut is liberally streaked

WICKED BOND

with gray now. I know I shouldn't be surprised as he'll turn sixty in March, but I wasn't prepared to see the lines of age across his face and the brown spots starting to appear on the backs of his hands. Or that he gets up a little slower from the kitchen table, or that his voice sounded a bit frailer when he gave his sermon on Sunday.

I haven't seen Father Adrian in thirteen years, but it didn't mean I left him behind. We talked regularly, usually by phone once a week and via email and Facebook even more often. Other than Woolf, he's the only person in the world I trust.

Well, except maybe Maggie, but not going there.

Adrian has never held it against me that I didn't come back to visit. He knows Cheyenne holds all of my bad memories—except the ones with Adrian—and that it's difficult for me to be here. It's not only the city where my stepmom robbed me of my innocence, but it's also where I was kicked out of college when I took the fall for Woolf's slight indiscretion of fucking the dean's daughter in the ass in a three-way.

When I finish the last log and have the split pieces stacked, I cover them with a tarp and secure it with rope. Only then do I wipe the sweat from my face once more—left shoulder this time—and take a seat next to Adrian on the stoop. He reaches behind him, grabs a bottle of water he'd brought out for me, and shoves it my way.

"Thanks for doing all that chopping," he says as he

stares out over the small backyard of the rectory. "I would have done it myself, but…"

I laugh. "Shut up, old man. You can barely lift that teacup."

Adrian snorts. "I could take you over my knee if I wanted to."

I snort too. Because Adrian would never raise a hand to me or even dare think about spanking me. I can still remember with brutal clarity when he found me on the streets. I was barely conscious behind a dumpster after five street kids jumped me for the measly twenty bucks I'd just made sucking some fuckwad's dick in a back alley. Even though I was big for a sixteen-year-old, could pass for eighteen for sure, five against one was not good odds. Father Adrian, who had been handing out meals to the homeless, had tears streaming down his face as he helped me to my feet.

My life was not pretty after I walked out of my step-mom's house. I didn't go to the police because I was too ashamed of what I let her do to me for so long, and I wasn't about to go into foster care, or, worse yet, get sent back to my stepmom.

So I spent almost seven months on the streets, turning from fifteen to sixteen. I learned fast the only way I had to make a quick buck was to sell my body. Unfortunately, there aren't many women—none really—who will prowl the known prostitute streets looking for a young boy. It's all closet gays like Jared, who have unsuspecting wives at home, who are out to get their quick fix.

Mostly it was blow jobs because that could easily be done in a dude's car, but I took some ass fuckings too. Those usually occurred in dark alleys with me bent over the hood of a car. On the lucky occasion I got a bottom, he'd be bent over the car and he'd have the well-used ass when I was done. I'd at least have the benefit of getting off then. Actual sex over blow jobs was how I made my best money, and a sore ass was a small price to pay for the ability to rent a seedy motel room for a night and have a hot meal.

I survived, no doubt. It was awful, also no doubt. But it was a far cry better than submitting to my step-mom's cruelty and abuse. It was better because *I* made the choice to let a man fuck my throat or my ass rather than being forced to have sex.

But even though I survived for seven long months without getting caught by the cops once, I don't think I would have survived it for very long. I was either going to get picked up for prostitution, or I was going to get killed when someone jumped me.

Father Adrian rescued me that night and brought me back to the rectory that sits just beside his church. He let me shower, lent me clean clothes, and fed me. Most importantly, he didn't call the police, a concession he granted me after I threatened to bolt if he did. Instead, he put me to sleep in a guest room with soft sheets and a fluffy pillow, promised again he wouldn't call the police, and left me to sleep better than I ever have in my life.

Even to this day.

That's not where my street story ends though. I couldn't stay at Father Adrian's for long because he'd be forced to turn me over to child protective services. He very reluctantly let me return to the streets as long as I promised to reach out to him if I needed help. We became friends, and I came to visit him often, every once in a while accepting his hospitality to stay the night. I was still acting like a trapped animal at times, and I was terrified of being sent back to my stepmom. Over the course of the next few months, I slowly opened up to him. This was accomplished without him pushing me to do so, but by treating me with respectful distance in a consistent pattern so that I learned to trust him. It also came from listening to his sermons. Although I wasn't then, nor am I now, an overly religious person, Father Adrian always taught from the scripture in such a relatable way that I learned something and took it to heart. Father Adrian's sermons helped develop me into the man I am today, albeit with a shit ton of emotional baggage to screw it all up.

Although there are a million things Father Adrian has done for me and a million ways in which he saved me, the most important thing he ever did for me was help me to get my emancipation from my stepmom. He hired an attorney—a parishioner who gave him a very good price—and a carefully orchestrated plan to convince the courts I was able to take care of myself ensued.

This also came at the price that I had to give up my

stepmom. It meant I had to tell the truth of what happened to me, and the only person in the world who knew about the atrocities was Father Adrian. I told him everything one night over bowls of French onion soup he had made and served with crusty bread he'd baked. I had to choke the story out and to this day, I can't eat French onion soup.

But that started the ball rolling. My attorney got an emergency order giving temporary physical custody to Adrian while legal custody was controlled by the state. I was interviewed by the police, and then they went to have a chat with my stepmom. Only problem was, she'd apparently vacated the house she abused me in right around the time I'd walked out, and she was nowhere to be found. I guess dear stepmom was afraid when I'd left that I'd go straight to the cops, and she hightailed it out of town.

To further the plan to get my emancipation, Adrian got me a job at a local restaurant as a bus boy, although I had to spend a certain amount of hours each day doing homeschooling with him. The one thing he remained staunch about was that I had to graduate high school. I was almost a year behind given my time on the streets, but with Adrian's patience and the fact I was a pretty bright kid, I ended up graduating before my peers did.

Just three days before my seventeenth birthday, the judge ordered my emancipation. Just three months after that, my stepmom was found dead in Illinois from a heroin overdose. That news meant nothing to me. Still means nothing to me.

"How much longer you going to loaf around here?" Adrian asks slyly, mainly to get my goat.

"Loaf?" I ask with mock offense. "I've been busting my ass since the day I got here a week ago."

Adrian laughs softly and nods. "You're the hardest working person I know."

It's true. After I became emancipated and because I graduated high school just a year after starting home-school with Adrian, I took on three jobs. The first was at the restaurant where I moved from bus boy to waiter, which was slightly better pay because of the tips. The second job I obtained was in a bakery where I worked early morning shift and helped to make bread and pastries. The third job was on the weekend, and I did odd jobs for the parishioners of St. Paul's. By the time I turned eighteen and was ready to start college, I'd had a nice-sized nest egg to help me get there.

I met Woolf at University of Wyoming and my life changed yet again for the better. Even though I got kicked out of college when I took the fall for Woolf, I never let it affect my feelings for him. I'd do it all again in hindsight because that's what true friends are for. Of course, Woolf sent me to the Double J where I worked range for his father until Woolf graduated, and then we worked range together while he learned how to take over the entire JennCo company. We were, and still are, the tightest of friends. Have built and opened a sex club together. Hell, he chose me to fuck Callie so she could experience a three-way. He has my absolute trust and I know I have his.

"But seriously," Adrian pushes at me. "How long you going to hide out here?"

"You love having me here," I say evasively, but then affectionately, I add, "It's been thirteen fucking years so I'm figuring you'd kill to have me stay a bit with you."

Adrian doesn't even bother correcting my language. It's something we fought about early on in our relationship, and I ultimately won. I remember the convo like it was yesterday because it showed me true grace and love.

"I wish you'd stop cursing," Adrian had snapped at me one day.

"I wish you'd stop telling me not to curse," I'd retorted, and then slammed my point home. "I think after all the things I've been through, I'm entitled to use foul language."

Adrian had blinked at me in surprise, and then his eyes filled with sorrow. He'd laid a hand on my shoulder and said, "Bridger, after the all the things you've been through, after all the joy you've brought me despite all the bad things, I think you're entitled to live the remainder of your life in peace. Curse all you want if that makes you happy."

I uncap the water bottle and take three huge swallows, wipe the back of my mouth on the flannel sleeve of my shirt, and tell Adrian, "I'm not ready to go back. Need more time."

"You know my door's always open," Adrian says sincerely. "But don't be static in trying to figure things out. Your problems aren't going to go away."

I grunt in acknowledgment. That's true. "When are you going to nose around in my business and ask what my problems are?"

"From the moment I first saw you," Adrian says with quiet reflection, "I knew you were a man who would get to where you're going in your own time. My ears are open when you're ready."

I've never held a single thing back from Adrian. He's the only person in the world who knows everything about me. Even Woolf, who I love more dearly than a brother, doesn't know all the details of what happened to me with my stepmom. But Adrian knows everything. The good and the bad. He knows all the pornographic details of her abuse—and he always prayed for her soul before we found out she was dead—and he's celebrated all of my accomplishments. Adrian even knows about The Silo and while he doesn't approve, he doesn't disapprove either. He understands with absolutely no judgment that I need The Silo and the whip in order to maintain peace with what's happened to me in my life.

But for some reason, my tongue feels glued to the top of my mouth at the thought of sharing Maggie with him. I'm not afraid he'll judge me for my cowardice, shame me for the hurt I put on her, or even chastise me for using her in the way I did. No, I'm terrified he's going to push me to go back and grab hold of all of Maggie's goodness.

God, I miss that fucking goodness.

"Her name's Maggie," I say quietly as I fiddle with the cap of my bottle. "And it's entirely possible I'm in love with her."

Adrian's head snaps sideways and when I dare to look at him, his mouth is hanging open in stunned surprise, which lasts only seconds before his eyes light up with joy.

It pains me to knock the joy out though, for I say, "But I don't think I deserve her and I'm scared I'll hurt her worse than I already have."

Adrian merely nods, lays a comforting hand on my shoulder—a move he's done many times in my life—and says, "Start from the beginning, Bridger. Tell me everything."

And I do.

Chapter 26
Maggie

5 weeks later

I BREEZE INTO the front doors of The Wicked Horse and immediately shrug out of my heavy coat and gloves. We got our first snowfall last night. It was only two inches and the roads are already cleared, but it's cold as fuck outside. It's only 10:30 AM and I'm half an hour early to start my shift, but I wanted to give myself time because I wasn't sure what the roads would be like. Turns out it was fine, but the air is brisk, the ground covered with a sheen of fine powder, and it makes me unbelievably happy for some reason. Maybe it's because I love the freshness of winter.

Woolf stands behind the bar, stocking beer in the coolers as he watches me saunter up to the bar and then hop onto a bar stool, dumping my coat, gloves, and purse on the one beside me.

"What are you smiling about?" Woolf asks with good nature.

"You'll never guess what Belle did last night."

"What's that?" he says with interest although he continues to stock.

"We were cuddling on the couch—watching *Frozen* for like the bazillionth time and I wish she'd just "Let It Go" if you get my meaning—and Barney jumped up and snuggled up on my other side. Belle turns to him, pushes him away, and says, 'Go away, Barney. That's my mommy."

I break out into laughter remembering how affronted Belle was that our rescue dog, Barney, wanted to impede in on her mommy time. I also go warm all over as I remember the feeling of utter joy as she said those words. It's confirmation to me that Belle thinks I'm great, and I sure as fuck need that after all the crap I let her see those first few years of her life.

Woolf chuckles as he shakes his head, his lips curved upward in amusement. "That kid. She's got a personality the size of Wyoming."

"Right? I swear she's going to be a comedian one day. Or a lawyer. That kid is learning how to negotiate. Trying to get her to go to sleep at night is a major pain in my ass. She has to negotiate how many songs I'll sing for her, and trust me... I'm getting a little tired of singing "Twinkle, Twinkle" four times in a row."

Woolf doesn't respond, although he's still smiling. He merely opens another box of beer and starts putting the bottles in the cooler. He's part of a brotherhood of guys who have all stepped up to the plate since Bridger left town almost a month and a half ago. Woolf has been handling the operations of The Wicked Horse, while Cain, Rand, and Logan have been keeping an eye on The

Silo. My face still burns as I remember what Cat told us the other night during our regular girls' poker night we instituted.

What she and Rand did at The Silo.

Apparently, it was his night to sort of watch over things, so, of course, Cat was with him. Apparently, they'd both gotten so horny watching all the action that they joined in on the fun. Camped themselves out in the orgy room and played with another woman.

I know my face was beet red when she was telling the story, although Callie, Sloane, and Auralie all leaned forward and listened with avid interest and what may have been envy on their faces. Cat chatted away as if it was nothing, sipping wine and talking about how Rand and the other woman took turns going down on her.

I was affected by her story for sure. A tiny pang of desire in between my legs, but not for another woman to do the same to me. Not even the thought of the uninhibited freedom of doing something so naughty.

No, the pang was pure desire for a solid, trusting, and reliable relationship with a man who would make me feel like a queen the way I've observed firsthand how Woolf, Cain, Rand, and Logan all do for their women. A man who would put me first, protect Belle and me at all costs, and would give me the world.

Who gets off by me getting off.

Sadly, I don't know anyone like that.

Bridger's been gone almost six weeks. At the one-week mark, I kept waiting with baited breath for him to walk through the door.

At two weeks, I thought, *Well, maybe this is an extended vacation.*

Three weeks, I called it a sabbatical.

At four weeks, I crossed the point of no return because I realized I was a fool for holding out hope and holding up my life. To pine any more for him past that would just be plain pathetic.

So I moved on. These last two weeks, I've concentrated on setting up a stable home for Belle and settling into the Jackson community. And I've settled in marvelously, becoming closer than ever with my poker girls and learning more about their men. It wasn't even awkward in the slightest when we all gathered at Woolf and Callie's place for Thanksgiving, and I didn't feel like odd man out without a man because I had Belle.

Yeah, I wished I had Bridger there, but he wasn't, and it was lovely all the same.

Meaning... I was moving on.

Woolf had told me the morning after Bridger left that Bridger said I could stay in his house. I actually accepted that offer, because yeah... during that first week even though he'd crushed me, I still expected him to come through that door and make it all right.

Woolf put me on to work at The Wicked Horse as a waitress, and I started saving all of the money I earned. It was hard work and my feet ached at the end of the night, but the best part of that was I usually fell into an exhausted sleep each night and couldn't pine over a certain man. I worked mostly night shifts, which meant I could spend my days with Belle. In the evening, Callie, Sloane, Cat, and Auralie all took turns watching her until I could find a reliable babysitter.

When the third week rolled by and Bridger didn't return, I went ahead and used some of the money he left me to put a deposit down on a small apartment for Belle and me. I was still using Bridger's truck for transportation and had no qualms with continuing to do so. I was fronting the gas for it, and from every paycheck, I put a small amount aside to pay Bridger back for the money I'd used for the deposit.

After he'd been gone for a month, I decided to move on. I have no clue if Woolf has heard from Bridger because I didn't ask. I assume so, since he still had a business to run, but I wasn't about to let anyone know how crushed I was. It meant I smiled as I moved on.

I had new friends, a new place to live, and a good, solid job. Kayla and Zeke were both in jail awaiting their trials, although the federal prosecutor did tell me that Kayla's attorney might assert a psych defense. Not sure how that makes me feel. I sort of believe that woman *is* bat shit crazy, but I'm pretty confident she's going away for a long time, so I choose not to worry about it, just as I choose not to worry about Zeke coming after Belle or me. He's history and word on the streets is that Mayhem's Mission has crumbled from the inside out with the arrest of the key players from all the major chapters.

I did take care of one important thing that didn't

give me full closure, but it made me feel somewhat better. Joseph Kizner passed me the contact information for Kyle's sister, Andrea. She lives on the coast of North Carolina, and I reached out to tell her how grateful I was for what her brother did for me. It was an emotionally raw conversation, and I was afraid she'd hate me for putting her brother in jeopardy, but she was really quite proud of his work even though she was grieving deeply.

"Everything going okay with you?" Woolf asks.

I blink my eyes, pulling out of my thoughts. "Yeah," I say brightly. "I found a car I'm thinking about buying. Maybe you could take a look at it. One of the customers here is selling it. It's about six years old, but it has low mileage."

"Sure," he says amiably. He's become almost like a big brother to me. "Where's it located?"

"I guess at his house, but he said he'd drive it up here one night if I wanted to check it out."

"Just let me know when and I'll come by," Woolf says as he empties the last box and sits it on the stack of empties. "And now that I think about it, why are you in so early? I know I saw you on the schedule for tonight."

"I could use the extra money," I say vaguely.

"For what?" Woolf pries… quite nosily too I might add.

"To buy the car," I admit grudgingly because I'm not going to lie to him.

"Bridger left you plenty of money to do that," Woolf points out.

I consider getting into this with Woolf, but something holds me back. He's not said a word about his friend to me since the morning after Bridger left. I also have been quite silent on the matter. I think I want to keep it that way.

"Well, I better get ready to start my shift," I say with complete avoidance of his question as I hop off the stool.

"Sit your ass back down," Woolf growls at me and I freeze in place, looking at him warily. When I don't move, he growls again, "I'm your boss and I could fire you, so sit your ass down."

I hop back up on the stool and try not to pout as he lean his arms on the bar. Woolf stares at me intently for a moment, and then asks gently, "Why aren't you using the money Bridger left you?"

Well, looks like we're going to talk about it. "Oh, you mean his guilt money? That pile of money he left because he didn't have the balls to say goodbye to me and tell me it was over? That pile of money left to soothe his conscience that he wasn't abandoning me? Or maybe it would help him sleep at night since he so royally fucked me over."

Woolf doesn't even flinch once during my tirade, but his eyes do grow soft with understanding. All he says is, "I understand."

His gentle voice and the compassion almost embarrass me because I don't want him to feel sorry for me. Like I said… I've moved on from Bridger and I don't need him giving me those looks of pity.

I flash Woolf a brilliant smile. "Well, it's been nice chatting, but I'm going to get ready for my shift."

I start to hop off the stool again, but the front door of The Wicked Horse opens. I can't lie to myself; I always get a jolt of awareness, wondering if this will be the time Bridger comes walking through. Even though I've moved on, I can't help but still wonder… what if.

It's not Bridger though, just the senior bartender, Ted McKeon.

When the door closes behind him, his eyes slide behind the bar to Woolf, to whom he gives a lift of his chin in greeting, and then to me, where they light up with genuine surprise and delight.

"What are you doing here, sexy girl?" Ted asks.

I give a quick glance to Woolf and see his eyebrows shoot up high. I almost want to laugh with glee because this is exactly what I needed to wipe that look of pity off Woolf's face. I don't want him to think I'm still stuck on Bridger.

Because I'm not.

Much.

I slide off the stool and step up to Ted, giving him a huge smile. "Hey, stud. I'm picking up an extra shift today."

Ted looks upward and holds his hands out. "Thank you, Lord, for answering my prayers. Beautiful Maggie is here for me to stare at all day."

I giggle because it's cute and because Woolf is watching. Ted flirts with me all the time and has been doing so since the day I started working here. I'd engage him in a friendly, fun way, but I always held myself in reserve so he knows I didn't mean anything by it. He's a smart guy. He got it.

But it didn't stop him from repetitively asking me out. I was honest with him the first time I declined, telling him I'd been in a relationship that had ended recently and it was too soon for me. Ted understood, but he also told me straight up he'd keep asking until I said yes.

And I figured there would come a time I would say yes. I mean, why not? He's gorgeous with sandy-blond hair, a ripped physique, and a rumor floating around that his cock is at least eight inches.

Not that I'm interested in that though.

I'm just saying.

Still, maybe I should just bite the bullet and do it. Take the plunge into the dating waters and see what else is out there. Ted's clearly interested in me. He's very nice, knows I have a daughter, and often talks about his nieces in a really sweet way. He could be not only a nice start to my new life, but maybe something real could also develop.

This sounds very good, even though my heart is screaming that Bridger is my soul mate and I shouldn't give up.

I give a quick glance to Woolf, see he's still watching with avid interest, and reach out to hook my index finger through one of Ted's belt loops.

I give a playful tug before I release it and bat my lashes. "Come on, McKeon. Might as well get it over with and ask me out again."

Ted blinks in surprise because I've never initiated flirting or brought up us going on a date. He steps into me, reaches a hand out, and gives a lock of my long hair a playful tug in return. Not going to lie… my heart beats a little faster.

"Going to finally make my day, Maggie, and tell me you'll go out with me?" he murmurs, but I know Woolf heard it.

I lift up on my tiptoes, place a hand on Ted's chest—which is very nice—and tilt my face up to his. "You know, I do believe I will."

"That's fucking awesome," Ted says with a brilliant smile as he kisses my cheek and then pushes past me. But he looks back, points a finger at me, and says, "We'll talk details later."

I wave at him, still smiling. "Can't wait."

I watch until Ted disappears into the staff room, and then turn back to Woolf. I level him with a no-nonsense stare, and he looks back at me with calculating eyes.

Lifting my chin, I tell Woolf, "As I was saying, I don't need anything from Bridger."

"So it appears," Woolf says thoughtfully, and then gives me a nod of respect. "And that makes me very happy indeed."

He turns away from me and walks through the swinging door to the kitchen. I stare after him, not really sure how to take his last words. I made a date with a hot guy right in front of him and then told him I didn't need anything from Bridger. He said that made him very happy and he actually looked like the cat that swallowed the canary.

Not sure how to take that, but I guess it just means he's happy I'm moving on. He's fond of me, I know, and yeah… I'm sure that's it.

Chapter 27
Bridger

I STARE DOWN at the small, plain headstone that says nothing more than "Levi Payne" and the years that encompassed his life. There were thirty in total. It sits five rows back and three plots over from my mom's headstone. It merely says "Abigail Payne – Loving Mother and Wife". She died when I was six, a tragic accident where she apparently slipped trying to get out of the tub, hitting her head on the edge hard enough to crack her skull and damage her brain. She lingered for almost a week before she died. I don't remember much about it… just bits and pieces of the ambulance there and Dad trying to keep me away from it all. Sadly, my memories of my mom are just as dulled, not because I want them to be, but just because I think that's what happens with the passage of time. Still, I hang onto a few memories that are vivid to me—like her helping me with homework or cheering for me at soccer practice. I'll visit her grave when I'm done here with Dad, but I have no clue why they're not buried near each other. I assume *she* had something to do with that.

My dad's death was just as tragic as my mom's, maybe even more so since he left me all alone with a monster, yet he went much quicker than my mom. Head-on collision with a drunk driver.

Instantaneous death.

I stare at his grave impassively. I want to hate him for leaving me with her and trusting her to take care of me. But if I'm being fair, and I know I should be, she didn't show any nastiness while they were together. She was kind and attentive to me. She had me snowed, so I guess it's only fair to assume she had Dad snowed as well.

I wonder if he loved her.

I wonder if she loved him.

I'll never know, but really… how could I? I don't understand the concept of love. Not between a man and a woman, anyway. I've never had any role models by which to learn. I can barely remember my mom and dad together, and my dad and stepmom were only together a few years. I spent many of my formative years where my only familial relationship was my stepmom beating and fucking me, always in that order. After, I spent some time on the streets, and then with an Episcopalian priest who was single and apparently content to be so. While Adrian is kind, loving, and paternal, he could never teach me about the type of love that I'm so fucking confused about right now.

That's not to say I'm without some guidance. I've watched over the past year as each of my friends fell deeply in love. I mean passionately—will die for you, am nothing without you, together to the ends of the earth type of love. I can't say as I know what each of these dudes are feeling, but I see the things they've sacrificed to be with their women, the lengths they go to make them happy. I've seen each of them give up The Silo because whatever was leaving them unfulfilled in life before has been filled and is being continuously replenished by whatever fucking love mojo those women bring to their lives.

Most importantly, I see my buds happier than I've ever known them to be.

Turning from my father's headstone, I cut over five rows and then turn right, walking past two more plots before I look down at Abigail Payne's little concrete stone. It's not fancy marble, but I expect my dad couldn't afford much better. He was a blue-collar man, working for the city water department as a meter reader. My mom worked part time as a cashier at a grocery store, but she was always home in the afternoons when I came home from school. Or so I seem to vaguely remember. At any rate, he couldn't afford fancy marble. I consider now that perhaps I should upgrade both of their stones.

Better yet, maybe I should have them both moved so they can have side-by-side plots.

I squat down, reach out, and pull a few tall weeds from the base of the stone. My fingers brush against the cold surface, and I grimace. I don't have a pair of gloves. I regret not breaking down and buying a pair. It's fucking twenty-seven degrees outside and while I had the foresight to pack a heavier coat when I decided to come "visit" Adrian, I sure as shit forgot my gloves and a hat.

But even as the temperatures continued to drop over the last few weeks, I kept telling myself, *You'll be headed home soon. No sense in buying gloves when you have a perfectly good pair at home.*

Except, I never did go home, and here I am freezing my digits off as I pay my respects to my parents. I look at the grave marker for a few more minutes, and yeah... I think it will be nice to arrange for my parents to rest beside each other. When I'm done, I stand up, feeling my knees crack as they straighten back out again and turn to see Adrian patiently waiting for me in his car.

I trudge across the cemetery, cutting diagonally across the rows until I reach his olive-green Ford sedan and climb into the passenger seat, immediately putting my hands up to the vents to let the heat warm them up.

Adrian puts the car into drive and slowly drives through the cemetery to the exit.

"All good?" he asks after he turns back onto the main road and heads back to the rectory.

"Yeah," I say with a smile. "I think I'll move them so they can be beside each other. Maybe next spring."

"There are some plots available in our parish cemetery if you're interested," Adrian offers.

I smile in appreciation. "I'd like that a lot. You can look over them in my absence."

"Let me guess," Adrian says dryly. "It'll be another thirteen years before you come back to visit."

I laugh. "That sounds an awful lot like whining to

me, and here you've been bitching and moaning at me every day to go back to Jackson. You can't have it both ways, old man."

Adrian snorts at the old-man comment, but then he goes straight for my throat. "But seriously, Bridger, when are you going back? It's past time."

"Can't believe you're sick of me already," I grumble.

"Oh, cut the shit," Adrian snarls.

I jerk in my seat, my head snapping to the left to look at him. I think that may have been the second time I've ever heard Adrian cuss, the other time being when he was trying to drive a nail into a two by four when we were building a garden box one summer, hit his thumb instead, and dropped the unholy of unholies… the dreaded "F" word.

"Damn," I say with a low whistle. "I've pissed you off, haven't I?"

Adrian's lips flatten out in a grimace but when he turns to glance at me before turning back to watch the road, I see a wealth of exasperated affection in his gaze. "Bridger… I love you like a son, but you are wasting your time here. Your life is back in Jackson. You have friends there who are like your family. You have a business to run. You need to go back."

Yeah, but I also have a Maggie there who I'm terrified to confront.

It's been six fucking weeks since I left my "I'm sorry" note—a fact Adrian chastised me severely over—and I'm pretty positive any remaining splinter of a bridge has been burned.

Demolished.

Obliterated.

"Bridger," Adrian says somberly. "What can you possibly be afraid of?"

"Not afraid," I tell him assuredly. "Just unsure."

"You've been unsure for weeks," he reminds me. "Surely, you've gotten some clarity."

Not really.

I mean, I'm as clear as I ever was. From the day I told Adrian everything about Maggie, I've been pretty clear in my head about things.

I love her.

I fucking love her so much.

But I have no clue how to go about accepting that about myself. I have no clue if she feels the same. And let's just say we *are* both on the same page—I am beyond confused about how my life will play out because I don't understand how to be committed. I don't understand how to be monogamous. Well, that's not hard to figure out. Haven't wanted anyone since Maggie, but still… how do I be a good man for her when I am completely and utterly fucked up in the head when it comes to sex and intimacy?

What if I end up hurting her because I can't be what she truly needs?

"Still running through all the self-doubts in your head?" Adrian asks, and it goes to show how well he knows me.

I sigh. We might as well hash this out again and see if I'm ready to really listen. "I don't know that I can be everything Maggie needs."

"Do you even know what she needs?" Adrian asks. "Ever bothered to ask her?"

"No," I say sullenly. Because we hadn't been big on deep conversation.

"Then I suggest you ask her," Adrian says simply.

I push that aside, because yeah... that's easy enough. "Okay, let's say I can give her what she wants. She wants me and accepts me warts and all... what if I end up closing off? What if I decide I just can't hack being in a relationship? What if I hurt her?"

"What if a comet strikes the earth and incinerates us?" Adrian points out. "What if you get hit by a bus tomorrow? What if, what if, what if? Come on, Bridger... don't let the unknown scare you. You're far braver than that."

Am I? Am I really brave enough to do this? I sure as hell have felt like the world's biggest pussy these last few weeks, not even able to make a move one way or the other. I've been content in just knowing Maggie and Belle are safe, well cared for, and seemingly happy. Well, that's at least what Woolf is reporting to me, and I don't hesitate to ask him during every phone call how she's doing. He happily reports with details if he can, but it's not every call. He goes days without seeing her at times, but it seems like she's definitely adjusting nicely to life outside of Mayhem's Mission.

My phone rings, cutting into my thoughts, and I recognize Woolf's ring tone—Ozzy Osbourne's "Bark at the Moon".

Get it?

Woolf. Moon. Bark at the Moon.

I answer the call because Woolf has graciously watched over The Wicked Horse for me, and I need to be available to him in case he needs something. It's been several days since we talked. While I know he'd do it if I asked, he has stayed away from The Silo. I asked the other guys to watch over that instead. With Callie's dad coming into an election year, Woolf has to keep his nose well beyond clean.

It's no worries him helping to oversee a bar.

A sex club, not so much.

"What's up, man?" I answer the phone and look out the driver's window as Adrian navigates his way to the rectory.

"Just checking in," Woolf says.

Every time I hear his voice on the phone, I get a pang of loneliness. It's been hard being away from Maggie for sure, but I also miss the shit out of this dude.

"Want to let you know everything's running smoothly at The Wicked Horse, and Cain says The Silo is fine too."

"Appreciate it," I say in return, a rumble of guilt coursing through me that he's running my business while I'm sitting on my indecisive ass. "Everything else going okay?"

"As in?" Woolf hedges.

"Well… you know. How's Callie?" I stammer.

"She's fine," he says, but offers no more.

"The guys?"

"Fine."

"The girls?"

"Which girls?" Woolf asks.

"Jesus, dude," I grumble into the phone, but I immediately shoot a guilty look at Adrian for taking the Lord's name in vain. He ignores me thankfully. "How are Maggie and Belle?"

"Well, Belle's doing fantastic according to Maggie. I told you they got a rescue dog, right? At any rate, that kid is so damn smart. Not even two and a half and can already say her ABCs and count to ten. Plus, she can sing any song after she's heard it only a few times."

Christ, I miss that little monkey.

"And Mags?" I ask after clearing my throat.

"She's doing great, Bridger," he says gently. "No need to worry about her."

This is usually where our conversation ends. The minute Woolf assures me I have nothing to worry about, I become a fucking pussy and take him at his word. I choose to put her out of my mind as best I can and trust in Woolf that she's doing okay without me.

But for some reason, I decide to push it a little further. "How's she doing at work?"

I did know Woolf put her on at The Wicked Horse, because he told me so. I'd asked him to help her find employment, and I wasn't bent out of shape she's at The Wicked Horse. It might make it awkward if I eventually return, but it's fine for now.

"She's doing fantastic. Works mostly night shifts, but sometimes she'll pick up extra shifts when she can."

"Why's she doing that?" I can't help but ask. I'm too fucking curious about any news about Maggie. Like does she still smell amazing, is her hair any longer, or does she talk about me at all?

"She... um... she rented an apartment and is looking at buying a car, so she needs some extra cash," Woolf says cautiously.

"What the fuck?" I growl into the phone. "I left her plenty of money. She couldn't have blown through it already, and why would she rent an apartment when she can stay at my place?"

Woolf's voice is completely chastising, as it should be. "Come on, man. Did you really think Maggie was going to live on your generosity? Or, as Maggie refers to it, your 'guilt money'."

I wince. "That's harsh, dude."

"It's the truth, Bridger," Woolf says candidly. "You did it to ease your conscience."

"Whatever," I mutter, completely pissed that Maggie is struggling. Well, not really struggling but totally refusing my help.

Woolf is silent, and I'm quite sure he's afraid to poke the bear.

"Is she... has she moved on?" I ask, my words practically clogged in my throat and barely able to get out.

More silence, but then he finally says, "She says she has. She's going on a date soon, so I guess that's moving on, right?"

"A date?" I wheeze out. It feels like someone just took a sledgehammer and hit me smack in the middle of my chest. "With who?"

"Ted," Woolf says quickly. Almost too quickly.

"Are you fucking kidding me?" I practically roar into the phone, and Adrian's head snaps my way again. I ignore him. "He's a fucking Fantasy Maker at The Silo, Woolf. He's got a big fucking dick, and he knows how to use it. You do not let him take her to The Silo, you hear me? Better yet, you do not let him take her on a date. You go and tell him that—"

"You go and tell him yourself," Woolf says softly. Even though it's said softly, his words pack a resounding punch.

"What?"

"If you don't want Maggie to go out with him, stick your hand down the front of your pants, fondle your balls to make sure they still work, then get your ass home and tell him yourself. Better yet, if those balls do still work, drag Maggie off, fuck her, and make her yours again, but do not ask me to do your dirty work for you. Man the fuck up, Bridger."

I blink in surprise over his harsh words and the frustration in his voice. I look sideways at Adrian, feeling slight mortification that Woolf just threw my balls into our conversation, and even though Adrian didn't hear him, I'm sure God did.

But Adrian just sits there, looking out the windshield with a smirk on his face. I figure he knows I just got my ass handed to me.

Taking a deep breath, I let it out. "Woolf…"

"Bridger," Woolf says, now in a gentle voice but no less firm. "Get off your ass and get home. Profess your love to Maggie or let her the fuck go, but get your ass back home. You have a life here, and it's passing you by."

Maggie's going on a date.

With fucking Ted McKeon. I've watched that dude in action, and he seriously knows how to fucking please a woman. If she has sex with him, she'll totally forget all about the asshole who ditched her six weeks ago with an "I'm sorry" note.

Am I going to let that happen?

Am I going to risk losing Maggie forever?

Up until now, I'd been able to rationalize that I'm sort of on a hiatus from life. In my mind, I chose to reason that meant everything else was just staying status quo until I could figure out what I wanted. Even though I know it's ridiculous to even think Maggie wouldn't move on, it was easier to let myself believe she would always be there if I ever got off my ass like Woolf suggested.

But she's moving on, and she's doing it in a bold way.

If I want her, it's time to shit or get off the pot.

"Okay," I tell Woolf impulsively. "I'm heading back. But you do not let her go on a date with him, you hear?"

"Sorry, man," Woolf tells me, and I can hear the laughter in his voice. "Means that much to you, I suggest you get your ass here fast."

"Asshole," I grumble affectionately and disconnect the call, tapping the phone against my chin in thought.

"Your girl forcing your hand?" Adrian asks quizzically, but I can hear the amusement in his voice.

"Something like that," I mutter.

"Well, let's just pretend I didn't hear that part about big… um… appendages and stuff, but the gist of what I got was that Maggie's going on a date with someone and that finally got you motivated to do something?"

"Appears that's the push I needed." This I also mutter because I know Woolf and Adrian are taking perverse joy in how quickly the tables have turned on me.

"Then let me impart one more piece of advice," Adrian says wisely. "Do not give up. She isn't going to make it easy on you, I suspect, and I think I've come to learn a lot about Maggie from you. So if she denies you, don't give up. Keep groveling. Apologize, accept responsibility, be genuine in your feelings, and be kind. Don't hold anything back. Be honest."

It all sounds like fantastic advice, and I'm going to need it. Still, I can't help but give him a little ribbing. "What could you possibly know about this stuff? You're the eternal bachelor."

"Accept responsibility," he repeats. "Be genuine. Be

kind. Be honest. That doesn't just pertain to love, Bridger. That should be how you live your life every day to every person you meet."

Damn... Adrian is still and will always be the wisest person I'll ever know. He amazes me.

Reaching out, I put my hand on his shoulder, just like he's done for me so many times. "Thank you, Adrian. For everything you've ever done for me. I'd be dead without you."

Adrian snorts in a self-depreciating way. "You would have survived just fine."

"That's up for debate." It's all I'm willing to concede to him. "But plan on me coming back soon with Maggie and Belle. I really want them to meet you."

Adrian laughs with delight. "That's the spirit. Don't expect you to come back without them."

Damn right.

I'm going to get my family.

Chapter 28

Maggie

OKAY, I CAN do this.

The restaurant is lovely. Dimly lit with a flickering candle on every table. White linen tablecloths and a menu filled with fancy food and expensive wine. Soft music plays in the background and the waiter is unobtrusive. It's the most romantic setting you could possibly envision, but it's making me slightly uneasy.

Ted is pulling out all the stops, and I'm nervous about what he'll expect after.

This week, he's continued to flirt with me and yeah... I engaged back even flirtier than ever. It was a way to make myself remember I'm moving on with my life. It's an important step that has to be made, not because I'm eager to jump into a relationship and have a man in my life, but because I have to keep pressing down that tiny bit of hope that Bridger will come back.

The waiter appears at our table as if out of thin air, brandishing a bottle of wine Ted ordered. He holds it out for Ted to inspect. After his eyes roam over the label, he gives a nod of acceptance. I watch fascinated—because honestly, I've never been on a date like this—as the waiter deftly opens the cork top and pours a tiny amount in Ted's glass. He picks it up, swirls it, and then takes a small sip, seemingly holding it on his tongue a bit before he swallows.

"That's perfect," Ted tells the waiter, who then pours two glasses, sits the bottle on the table, and disappears just as quickly.

Leaning slightly inward, I have to ask, "What happens if you don't like the way it tastes?"

Ted shrugs with a playful smile. "I don't know, to be honest. Wine tastes like wine to me. Never had one that was bad."

I laugh, because he's funny and cute, and I need to relax and enjoy this. Ted's eyes brighten when I laugh. He picks up his glass of wine and holds it up in front of him. I stare stupidly for a minute, but then his eyes shift down to my glass.

"Oh," I say with embarrassment and take my glass in hand, holding it up just like he does.

Any dates I've ever been on have been in bars where only beer or liquor is served, and you know it's good if it's cold and it's bad if it's warm. Either way, you would never send it back.

Ted gives a little clear of his throat and says, "To you, Maggie… the prettiest girl in these parts. Thank you for finally agreeing to go out with me."

That's sweet and I feel like I should say something back, but the words are stuck in my throat. It shouldn't be this hard to make conversation, but it feels a bit stilted.

So all I do is take a sip of my wine and smile at him over the edge of the glass before I set it back down on the table. I force my mind to find something to talk about, to fill the awkward silence, and then it hits me… music. Ted loves music, and we talk about it all the time when we're at work.

"So, have you heard the newest album by…?"

My words stop in mid-sentence as movement behind Ted catches my attention.

No… it can't be.

I blink my eyes hard, ignoring Ted when he says, "Album by who, Maggie?" and focus in on the large man walking through the restaurant with his eyes pinned on me.

Oh my God, he's so beautiful. He's let his hair grow. It's maybe half an inch in length now and looks darker than it did when it was longer. Again, I marvel at how his shortened hair makes the beauty of his face shine through, including the hard set to his jaw as his gaze flicks down to Ted before coming back to me. He's so classically Bridger in jeans, heavy biker boots, a dark gray shirt, and a black leather jacket, completely inappropriate for this type of restaurant. Ted actually wore khaki pants, a white dress shirt, and navy blazer with a red-and-blue striped tie. It's so boring compared to the man coming up behind him.

And that's when the reality sets in, and I realize the hard set to Bridger's jaw has everything to do with Ted sitting at this table with me.

"Maggie?" Ted asks curiously, and because I'm still looking at Bridger behind him, he finally turns around in his seat to see what has my attention.

"Dude," Ted says affectionately when he sees Bridger, clearly disregarding the menacing look he's getting. Ted stands from his chair, puts his hand out to Bridger, and says, "Welcome back, boss. What are you doing here?"

Bridger ignores Ted's hand, brushes right past him, and comes to stand at the table beside me. I vaguely notice Ted sitting back down in his chair, but it's only from my periphery as my head is tilted way back to look at Bridger towering over me.

"We need to talk," he says gruffly. "Let's go."

I'm absolutely humiliated and pissed off at myself when my first inclination is to bolt out of the chair and follow Bridger out of this restaurant. But I'm redeemed in my own eyes when I just as quickly feel my spine stiffen and a flush of anger go through me that he would dare demand me to do anything. He doesn't own me, nor does he have any say so in my life whatsoever.

"I'll pass," I say politely before turning my attention back to Ted. I give him a reassuring smile as I pick up the menu. "Let's figure out what we're going to eat."

Ted's not falling into line though. His gaze cuts between Bridger and me, with his face awash with confusion.

"Mags," Bridger says in a warning tone. "I need to

talk to you."

I put the menu down and my head snaps up to look at him. "Then you can wait until an appropriate time to do so. As you can see, I'm on a date. It's not the best time to talk."

"Take off, Ted," Bridger growls, and Ted's butt comes off the chair.

I snap my attention to Ted. "You... stay in that seat. We're on a date."

His ass hits the seat.

My eyes cut back up to Bridger and narrow. "Now you're being unbelievably rude. You should leave."

"Not going to leave until we talk, Mags," he says, and fuck... his voice is now all gentle and mellow. Hypnotizing. And my name... I'm still Mags to him.

With a sigh, I give Bridger an understanding look. "Listen... I'm on a date. Ted is not going anywhere—"

I'm stunned when Bridger turns away from me, glances around, and then takes two steps to the nearest table that seats four with only three people sitting there.

"Mind if I borrow this?" Bridger mutters and grabs a chair, sliding it over to our little table for two. He pulls it right up to the edge, him on my left and to the right of Ted, but he angles the chair so it faces me slightly.

"What are you doing?" I hiss as I lean toward him.

"Talking to you," Bridger says simply, and I want to slap him when his lips tilt up in an amused smile. "Ted can listen for all I give a fuck, but I have to talk to you right now."

"Bridger," I say in exasperation.

"I love you," he says at the same time.

My eyebrows shoot sky high, and Ted mumbles, "Okay, that's awkward."

My jaw drops, and I tilt my head. Did I just hear that?

Ted pushes his chair away from the table, and my head snaps his way. "Maggie… I'm going to go…"

"No," I exclaim, reaching a hand out even though I don't really mean it. I want to hear more of what Bridger has to say.

"Yes," Ted says firmly. His eyes cut to Bridger, who hasn't even spared him a glance. He's staring at me expectantly. When Ted looks back to me, he gives me an understanding smile and nods his head. "That dude right there loves you. You need to hear what he has to say."

"But…" I start to say, but my words die off. He's right. I need to hear this.

Not sure what I'll do with it, but I have to listen. Because for him to walk in, bust up a date, and publicly proclaim he loves me after ditching me six weeks ago demands a little of my attention.

Ted gives me a small smile. Before he turns away, he says, "You two enjoy that wine. I'll pay for it on the way out."

I watch him walk out of the restaurant and feel guilty as shit while I do. Finally, I turn my face back to Bridger and give him an admonishing look. "That was seriously rude."

"Do I look like the type of man who gives a fuck?" he asks.

"No," I say primly as I pick back up my wine and take a large swallow. When I set the glass back down, I say, "You look like a ghost from my past—one I really never expected to see again."

"Come on, Mags," he says softly. "You had to know I'd come back."

"Maybe," I admit grudgingly. "But I didn't think our first conversation would go this way."

"Never thought you'd hear me say 'I love you'?"

"Yeah," I admit with my eyes lowered. "It's kind of shocking. And quite possibly a little too late."

"You don't mean that," Bridger says confidently, and my eyes slam into his while flaming with anger.

"Bridger… you left me behind weeks ago. Six fucking weeks ago to be exact, with nothing more than a measly note that said 'I'm sorry'. I've not heard a word from you, but you come waltzing back into my life as if nothing's changed. You don't think you might have missed your opportunity?"

He looks appropriately chastened. "Fuck, I hope not, Mags. I really hope to fuck you give me another shot."

"Why should I?" I grit out and fold my arms over my chest.

Bridger opens his mouth, clearly ready to convince me, but we're interrupted by the waiter. He looks completely confused but graciously says, "Sir… can I get you something to drink?"

"No, I don't want anything to drink," Bridger growls. "Leave us the fuck alone for five minutes, okay?"

The waiter nods stiffly and scurries away. Bridger's eyes follow him for a moment, and then he turns back to me with a frustrated sigh. "Look… can we go somewhere else? My car would be fine, but we should talk in private."

I arch an eyebrow at him. "You had no problem spilling your guts in front of Ted."

"Mags, please," he says.

I'm convinced that's probably the first time Bridger's ever begged for anything in his life. "Okay," I say with a nod and stand up from the table. Bridger stands along with me, his eyes shining with immense relief.

Bridger and I walk out of the restaurant, his hand at my lower back. Just that little touch and I feel my resolve where he's concerned weakening. He gently steers me to his Corvette and opens the door for me. When I settle in, he shuts it gently and walks around to the driver's side. I take a moment to look at him in the glow of the parking lot lights. He's walking with his shoulders hunched and his head hung low.

And fuck me if that doesn't break my heart a little.

But then again, I knew there were a million things about Bridger that could break my heart.

When he situates himself in the driver's seat, he turns and angles himself toward me. I wait patiently as he looks down at his hands, clasped loosely in his lap, and then up to me. "Telling you I love you should have been one of the hardest things I've ever done in my life, but I just found out that it was one of the easiest. Trust me, Maggie… I'm kicking myself about a hundred different ways for not doing this a lot sooner."

I don't know what to say to that. He's twice now said he loves me, and the overwhelming sensation of joy and peace that fills me is surreal. But I'm also hurt, and I don't understand anything.

I need to understand.

"Why now?" I ask hesitantly.

"Honestly?"

I nod.

"Woolf told me you were going on a date," Bridger admits without an ounce of shame in his eyes. "It was the motivator I needed to make the decision to grab a hold of what I really wanted. It was what made me push past the fear."

"Fear?"

Bridger looks slightly uncomfortable, but he leans in a little closer to me. Reaching out, he takes my hand in his and looks down at it, his fingers stroking softly over my skin. With his face lowered, he murmurs in a low voice, "I had a terrible childhood, Maggie. It was so horrible, I'm afraid to tell you about it because I don't want you to be hurt, and I know you'd hurt for me."

The hair at the back of my neck prickles as Bridger raises his face, his eyes locking on mine.

"But I *am* going to tell you," he says softly. "Because you need to know everything about me. Only one other person in the world knows what I'm getting ready to tell you."

"Adrian," I say knowingly.

"Yes, Adrian," he affirms.

Then, he leans in even closer, his hand never letting go of mine. In a pained murmur, he tells me all about his childhood. My stomach rolls as I listen to his words. Tears fill up my eyes. On the first blink, they course down my face. Bridger reaches up with a free hand and wipes them away as soon as they fall. He repeats this four times while he tells me about what his stepmom did to him, how he almost killed her, and how he lived on the streets prostituting himself. I smile when he tells me about Adrian and becoming emancipated, and then smile more when he tells me about meeting Woolf, but then cry again when he tells me about getting kicked out of college.

Bridger tells me about coming to Jackson and working on the Double J for years while Woolf finished college, and about how they hatched the plan to open The Silo. Without any shame or apology, he tells me what The Silo means to him and why it's so important.

"And the BDSM," he says in continuation of his story. "I really got into that in college and found an affinity for that type of kink. I enjoyed being the one to hand out the pain, but it was healing in a way because the other person truly wanted it and got sexual gratification from it."

"It was the opposite of what you'd experienced as a

kid," I whisper.

He nods. "Yeah… the BDSM and the debauchery that goes on in The Silo. I needed that so much. It was affirmation to me every day that sex is good, beautiful, and without shame. That I can fuck, get sucked, whip a woman, or any other manner of kink I wanted, and still hold my head up high at the end of the night because I was in a place where it was accepted. It was what I needed so I could believe I'd survived what *she* did to me and wasn't completely and utterly fucked up."

"Then I'm glad you have just such a place, Bridger," I say with an understanding smile. "I'm glad it helped you heal, and that you have it now so you will always have that affirmation."

Bridger shakes his head. "No, you see… I may have needed that before, but I don't anymore. The minute I said I love you, and realized just how fucking easy it was, I'm pretty fucking sure the only thing I need in my life is you. With you comes Belle, and I love her too."

"What are you saying?" I ask hesitantly.

"I'm saying I'll give up The Silo. Sell it or close it down, as long as I have you. You are what makes my life complete, not the shit that goes on in that building."

"I… I… I don't know what to say," I tell Bridger honestly. He's laid so much on my doorstep, and he had me hook, line, and sinker until he said that last part about giving up The Silo. I know down to the depth of my soul that I can accept everything Bridger just told me about his life. I'll grieve for that little boy and all he's lost, but I would take Bridger with every single piece of dirty baggage that comes with him.

Except... I don't know if giving up The Silo is really the right thing. It's an integral part of his life, and I think he might still need it. I'm also not sure how I feel about it. It's his place of work, but could I really accept that? Could I let him work in that environment day in and day out and not have my doubts?

"Bridger," I say as I gather both of his hands in mine and squeeze them. "Thank you for telling me the truth about your life. The fact you'd share something like that with me... that you'd trust me with that... speaks volumes. But I really need some time to digest all of this. I'd just reconciled myself to give up on you, and now here you are laying an overload of stuff on me."

With a small nod of understanding tempered with slight disappointment in his eyes, he says, "I get it. And I'll give you time, but it doesn't mean I'm not going to keep pestering you about this. I want you, Maggie, and I'm not giving up until you agree to be mine. I want you and Belle to be my family, and I want it more than anything I've ever wanted in my life. I'd even gladly hold onto every shitty memory I have in my life if it means I can have you there to temper it. I can do anything with you by my side, Mags. I need you."

God... my heart fills with so much happiness that it actually compresses my lungs so I can't breathe. He looks at me so earnestly and with such naked devotion in his eyes that I go dizzy from the wealth of emotion coursing through me.

Still, I manage to say, "Give me some time."

He nods again, squeezes my hands. "I will. But you are not going out with Ted, right?"

"Right," I promise him.

"Good," he says with a smile. "Now… let me take you to your place."

He then drives me home, giving me just a kiss on my cheek after he walks me to my apartment door, and then leaves with a soft, "Don't forget, Maggie. I love you."

My heart sighs with abandon, and I'm pretty sure its mind is already made up. I just have to figure out if that's really the best thing for me.

Chapter 29
Bridger

I T'S BEEN THREE days since I drove Maggie home from the restaurant, and I felt it went about as good as it could have gone. I did something that was scarier than anything that's ever happened to me in my entire life.

I bared my soul to Maggie and then I offered it to her.

I offered every bruised and sliced piece of it, as well as the parts that had already healed, and I hope to fuck she accepts it at some point.

As Adrian advised, I'm not giving up. I have indeed pestered her the last few days.

First order of business was to get her cell phone number. That was easy enough by accessing her employment records.

It's good to be the boss.

I sent her a text the day after I told her I love her, and I reminded her in case she forgot. *I love you.*

Smart-ass that she was, she texted back almost immediately. *Ted?*

Going to spank your ass if you give me a second chance, I wrote back.

She only sent me a smiley face, and that was good enough for me because let's face it, she has every right to tell me to go fuck myself.

And yeah, Ted was not going to be a problem going forward. I confronted him the next day when I made my way into The Wicked Horse by jerking my chin at him and then toward my office. He got the hint and followed me straight back.

And when I say confront, I wasn't an ass or anything. In fact, I didn't have to really say anything at all as Ted spoke first and said, "You don't have to say it, Bridger. I'm backing down."

"Good," I said with a smile. "Prevents me from firing you."

"You'd never fire your best Fantasy Maker," he scoffed.

And he's right about that. He's given up on Maggie and keeps plenty of people happy at The Silo, so I'm not firing him.

The second day, I actually called Maggie from my office at the back of The Wicked Horse and was surprised when she answered with, "I can't talk now. I'm at work."

"You work for me," I reminded her as I pushed out of my desk chair and walked to my office door.

"Even more reason why I can't talk because clearly... the boss is onto me," she said impishly.

By this time, I'd made it down the hallway to the main portion of The Wicked Horse, scanning the interior for Maggie. I saw her standing at the end of the bar, phone to her ear and smiling at me.

I smiled back and said, "Just wanted to remind you that I love you."

And fuck… the sigh I heard on the other end and watching her chest heave before relaxing punched straight through to my cock. I disconnected and turned around. Went back to my office and jacked off to the memory of the first time I came in Maggie's pussy without a condom.

Today, I decided to up my game. Clearly, Maggie was not pissed at me, as evidenced by the humor that came through in our communications. But I needed to press harder. Since she hasn't rolled over yet and pro-claimed her love for me, that meant she was still thinking things through and I didn't want her getting stuck in her head.

So I dial her number and wait for her to answer. She's not on duty right now, so no clue where she is when she answers breathlessly, "What's up?"

I then hear her huffing and puffing into the phone.

"What are you doing?" I ask curiously.

"Having sex with Ted," she quips.

"Not fucking funny," I growl, and she bursts out into laughter that's stilted because she's breathing heavily. I can't help the smile that breaks out on my face. "No, seriously… what are you doing?"

"Belle and I just got done rolling the biggest snowball in the history of snowballs," she explains. "It's the base to our snowman, and I'm about to die."

Fuck… the image of Maggie and Belle, dressed in their snow gear, cheeks all rosy from the cold and laughing with delight as they played in the snow… yeah, that causes an ache in the center of my chest. I want to demand she tell me where they are so I can come and play with them too.

But instead, I play it cool and say, "Belle is exactly the reason I'm calling. Was wondering if I can take her horseback riding again?"

"Really?" Maggie asks with surprise.

"Well, yeah, Mags," I say with a touch of exasperation. "I told you I wanted both you and Belle in my life. And because you're being so stubborn, figured I'd work on Belle from here on out. I'd have her like putty in my hands in no time at all."

"You'd bribe her with horseback rides," she accuses with a laugh.

"I could bribe you with something," I say, my voice dropping lower and turning husky. "What would you want me to give you, Mags?"

She groans on the other end, and that sends a punch of lust straight to my dick. I palm it through my jeans, knowing I'm going to need to whack off again at the end of this call.

"Goodbye, Bridger," Maggie taunts me with good nature, and then has me smiling when she adds on, "and of course you can take Belle horseback riding."

I hang up with a satisfied feeling in my heart but not

my dick. I take care of that problem immediately before I get back to work.

A KNOCK ON my office door causes my head to jerk up. I was engrossed in the quarterly profit and loss statement for The Silo, as I continue to think about selling it off. I truly don't need it, and I want Maggie to feel comfortable in her life with me.

"Come in," I call out and speak of the devil, Maggie pops her head in.

"You busy?" she asks.

"Not at all," I say as I push out of my chair but I have to physically restrain myself from grabbing her and kissing that mouth.

The door opens all the way, and she steps in but doesn't close it. She's not working tonight and looks gorgeous in a pair of boot-cut jeans and a dark brown turtleneck. Her hair is pulled up into a ponytail and she has little gold studs in her ears, which is the only adornment she has. She doesn't need anything else though.

"I want to go to The Silo," she says abruptly, and I jerk in place.

"What?"

"I want you to take me to The Silo," she says calmly.

"Why?"

"Because I'm not comfortable with you giving it up, but how can I really know unless I know what it is?" she says simply.

"Maggie… that's not a good idea," I say hesitantly, because fuck… do I want her exposed to the shit that goes on there? Not going to lie—the thought of it both repulses me and turns me on a bit.

Well, that's totally fucking confusing.

"It is a good idea," she argues. "I've been talking to Callie about all this, and she's helped me to get a better understanding of things. I mean… I'm not a prude, Bridger, but I'm also not sure how I feel about it. So I want to go see."

What to do?

Deny her this request and she doesn't get the understanding she needs to make a decision about me, or give into it and possibly turn her off beyond repair if she hates it.

"Bridger, please," she says, her eyes pleading with me to give her this.

Decision made.

"Let's go," I say as I grab her hand and pull her out of my office.

When we enter The Silo, I'm immediately tuned into the sounds of sex all around. It's a Saturday night, it's late, and The Silo is filled. There will be some kinky ass shit going down once we clear the hallway.

I have an overwhelming urge to try to sugarcoat some of the things she's going to see, but then we enter the circular room and Maggie gasps as she takes her first look around.

There's a couple on a low-slung couch ten feet from

where we stand, the man sitting with his legs stretched out and a woman reclined over him, sucking his dick. She turns her head, taking in the various glassed-in rooms. Every one of them is filled with endless fucking. She walks along the exterior of the glass, watching everything from vanilla missionary sex to Angel pegging a man up the ass to one of my Fantasy Makers using an industrial-sized dildo on a woman.

She turns and looks out over the patrons who fill the interior, some chatting while having a cocktail, others kissing and stroking, and one man fingering his date while she spreads her legs lewdly from her perch on a barstool for everyone to see.

Maggie turns to me, her cheeks red but her green eyes brimming with curiosity. "Do you have sex here?"

"What?" I practically choke out, but before she can repeat the question, I tell her, "I have in the past. Not frequently, but I have. I prefer to be more private. And I mostly only do the BDSM stuff here, but then I don't get off on that."

"Would you ever want to experience that with me... here where people can watch us?"

"Sex or the BDSM?" I ask hesitantly.

"Either," she says with a slight shrug of her shoulders.

"I honestly don't know, babe," I tell her truthfully. "We'd have to tread those waters carefully. I definitely wouldn't practice BDSM with you. Not the hardcore stuff anyway. Might take a soft flogger to you, or my hand on your ass, but that's about it."

Fuck if my dick doesn't turn to stone when Maggie shudders over my proclamation.

She steps into me, putting a hand on my chest. "But what if I want to experience it from the prospective of being just a girl with a really gorgeous guy who can engage in some guilt-free passionate sex in a very debauched way? What if I want to feel what it's like to do it and walk out of here without an ounce of shame?"

"Or you could be overwhelmed with shame," I point out.

"Maybe," she says, but then almost destroys me when she says, "but because I love you so much, I think I could give that to you if you wanted it."

My knees almost buckle on me and my heart nearly bursts open at her words, but before I can even think too hard on what that means, I feel the need to clarify to her. "Mags, I honestly don't know if I want this for us. Maybe, but again… we'd have to really talk about it."

"That sounds like a plan," she says with a brilliant smile as she goes up on her tiptoes. I bend down to her, and she gives me a soft, sweet kiss.

"You love me?" I ask when she has her heels back on the ground.

"Yup," she says with a smile, but she doesn't elaborate, merely points to the exit door. "Now, we should head to your house. We have some making up to do."

Gripping her hand tight, I turn and lead her back to the hallway, out the exit door, and back through The Wicked Horse. I pull her through the crowd of dancers.

The loud music doesn't even penetrate because I'm so focused on getting Maggie in my bed that I can't see straight.

I'M ON HER as soon as I have her in my bedroom. Spinning her around, I grab her by the ponytail and force her upward so her mouth meets mine in a fiery crash of lust and love. She groans at the first contact of my tongue against hers, and then our hands are flying at each other, trying to stroke and pinch and pull at clothing.

When we're both naked, I kiss her again, my hand once again finding that ponytail. I slip my free hand down her stomach, to her pussy, and push my middle finger into her. It slides in easily, and she grips me tight as she moans from the sensation. I pull my mouth from hers, look down at her glazed eyes, which stare at me a moment, and then I tell her, "You're never going to regret giving me a second chance, Mags."

She must like that sentiment a lot because her hips buck against my hand.

With my finger still lodged in deep, and my hand gripping her ponytail, I walk Maggie backward to my bed. Every step she takes rocks my finger inside of her, and she whimpers in frustration.

I force her backward until the mattress is at the back of her knees and push her down to the bed, my finger never missing a stroke inside of her. She looks at me, her green eyes dark shades of forest green now, and mewls like a kitten when I pull out to circle her clit.

Fuck, that's sexy, but I want her to get off quickly because she's strung tight as a wire right now. I fall onto her body, scooting back until I'm kneeling on the floor, and I pull her body down to me. Mouth to pussy, I eat her out, spreading her wide with my fingertips and attacking her clit hard. Maggie's fingers graze my temple, and I peek up at her to see her looking down at me.

I freeze, sense her hesitancy, and then reach up in a move so fast that she gasps. I grab her wrist, force her hand to my head, and push her fingers into my short hair. I lift my mouth from her pussy and whisper, "It's short, Maggie, but there's enough to pull."

Her eyes widen at the implication.

"Pull it hard," I growl at her before I latch my mouth back onto her.

Maggie cries out when I hit her clit again, and both hands go into my hair. She strokes the pads of her fingertips over my scalp for a bit, but when I purse my lips around that bundle of nerves and suck on her, she grips my hair in between her fingers as best she can and pulls when she comes.

Fucking beautiful.

I gentle her down with a few flicks of my tongue over her flesh before I crawl my way up the mattress, pulling Maggie up with me with an arm around her waist. I know exactly how this is going to play out, and I flop onto my back, pulling her on top of me until she's straddling my lower abdomen, just out of reach of my aching dick.

My hands go to her thighs, and I look up at her. "Maggie."

Her hands come to rest on my chest. "Yes?"

"I want you to ride my cock," I say thickly, and not just because my throat is clogged with lust. It's also filled to capacity with emotion. She tilts her head to the side with curiosity. "I've never let a woman ride me before… before *she*…"

Maggie's eyes go warm with understanding and she leans over me, pressing her lips to mine. When she pulls back, she looks deeply into my eyes and whispers, "Are you sure?"

"As sure as I am that I love you," I tell her with naked honesty, and I realize… I don't feel one single ounce of fear, disgust, shame, or indecision. In fact, I'm quite decisive in the fact that I want Maggie bouncing on my cock.

Now.

My hands push at her thighs, urging her back a little so she'll get to work. The tip of my dick bumps against her ass, and fuck… can't wait until I have that too.

But first things first.

Maggie rises up, her knees digging down into the mattress, and she takes me in hand, maneuvering until the fat head of my cock presses against her wet folds.

"Christ," I hiss through my teeth, because that feels fucking amazing. I hope I don't fucking shoot my load too quick.

Maggie's eyes flutter closed and she rotates her hips a bit, the motion sucking my dick up into her as she starts to sink down on me. My eyes drop down as I watch my cock disappearing into heaven. My balls are already starting to tingle before she gets fully seated. Her eyebrows furrow inward with concentration as she pulls up a little, and then pushes down again. Another circle of her hips, and I get sucked in deeper.

Maggie moans a little as she rises, and then finally pushes all the way down until I have her fully impaled and her pussy lips are molded around the base of my dick.

My gaze slides up and I find Maggie's eyes now open, staring down at me with pure love mixed with electric desire.

"Feel good?" she asks.

"You have no idea," I tell her, my voice husky and thick.

Her hands come to my stomach, and I feel the pad of one fingertip tracing my skin. I look down and see her touching the wing of one of the blackbirds as her eyes travel up as the others take flight, straight toward the center of my chest, where one explodes in a burst of feathers before it can touch my heart.

She looks back to me and before she can ask, I tell her, "It's just a general symbolism. Many things have come my way, but nothing has ever penetrated my heart before."

She nods.

"Not before you, Mags."

She smiles and nods again. "I love you."

Emotion courses through me. I have to focus on the feeling of my cock in her cunt so I don't cry, and I give her a nudge so she'll move. Maggie complies, rises up, and sinks back down on me again.

"I love you." I groan from the sensation. "So much."

"Then we're agreed," she pants as she starts to move faster on me. "You're keeping The Silo."

I can barely comprehend what she's saying because all the available blood in my body is congregating in my cock, which I'm pretty sure has never been this hard before. "Wait! What?" I groan after she slams down onto me.

Then I go dizzier as she starts riding me up and down harder. I can't concentrate, my eyes now pinned on her tits bouncing and her nipples puckered. My fingers pinch at them, and I go dizzier yet when she adds in some type of gyration on her down strokes.

My balls shrink... harden... and I bite down on my tongue to try to hold my shit together.

But then Maggie goes absolutely still on a hard slam down onto me, her back arching as she cries out, "Oh... Bridger..."

As her pussy spasms all around me, a fiery orgasm bursts and I punch my hips upward as I start to come.

"Fuck," I curse as I practically hold Maggie off the bed as I arch into the pleasure.

My hips fall back to the mattress as my entire body trembles with release. Maggie falls forward, collapses against my chest, and her lips go to my neck where she mutters, "Just… damn."

I chuckle and wrap my arms around her back, squeezing her tight. "So, I'm keeping The Silo, huh?"

She lifts her head, smiles down at me, and nods. "Baby… I just heard and felt how much you love me. So yeah… we're totally keeping The Silo."

"We—as in you and me?" I ask, just to make sure.

"As in a team," she confirms. "Although I'm expecting we'll make that official at some point."

"Are you proposing to me, Mags?" I ask her with a grin.

"I do believe I am," she says with an answering smile of her own.

"Then I accept," I tell her as my hand goes behind her head to pull her mouth down to mine.

Epilogue
Maggie

Five months later…

OH, WOW.

Bridger in a tuxedo.

Just… wow.

In my past life—the one before I fell in love—I would have never had the confidence to envision this moment. A small country church swathed in gardenias and white tulle, only two rows filled with people because my circle of friends is small but fierce, and a gorgeous man who looks at me like I hung the moon and the stars for him.

He stands there waiting for me with Woolf at his side. Both men are impossibly handsome, although Bridger is far sexier to me. His hair has grown out a bit more. It's shaggy and in need of a trim, but it's oh so much fun to pull.

Yes, Bridger has overcome nearly every hang-up he's wilted under in the past. I can pull his hair to my heart's content and ride his cock whenever I want. Doesn't mean that the nightmares are gone forever, but they don't happen often and when they do, I'm there to talk him down.

The biggest change for my soon-to-be husband though is the fact that he's almost like a different man since he declared his love for me. So easygoing and laid back. He smiles and laughs often, my favorite being when he's smiling and laughing with Belle.

About a week ago, he came home from work overly excited as he whipped off his shirt. I stared at the huge bandage across the center of his chest, gasping in horror that he'd been hurt. "What happened?"

He rolled his eyes, peeled the bandage off, and I got a look at his new tattoo.

The blackbirds are still there, still undisturbed in their flight toward his heart. Even the one that almost makes it and bursts apart before it can make contact. But to the left of that spray of black feathers are two new tattoos that converge right over where his heart is in his chest. Two white doves, one larger than the other, rising up with wings spread to hold a hover over his heart. The larger one holds a golden banner in its claws that says "Mags" and the smaller one mimics it with the word "Belle".

"Oh, Bridger," I'd said in wonder, not wanting to touch the irritated skin but wanting some contact. I put my hands on either side of the fresh tat and just stared at it in wonder.

"Didn't change those blackbirds, Mags," he whispered. "Before, they represented ways in which my heart would repel, but now... I choose to think of them as all the bad things that couldn't destroy my heart. And of course… the doves are kind of self-explanatory."

"I love it," I choked out, my voice garbled from emotion as the tears started to flow down my face.

Yes… that tattoo is very special and so representative of just how much Bridger has transformed.

He waits for me at the base of the altar, his dark golden eyes eating me up while he tenderly holds Belle on his hip. The grand plan today was for her to walk me down the aisle, but just as the music started, she had a minor freak out and tore out of my grip. Belle ran down the aisle, dropping her little bouquet of gardenias and wild sage at the midpoint, and hightailed it straight to Bridger while everyone in the pews laughed.

I merely watched with tears stinging my eyes as he squatted down to receive her and she threw herself into his arms. When he lifted her and she laid her head on his shoulder, I almost lost it.

Almost, but not quite.

I blinked furiously and pushed those tears aside. I didn't want anything to mar my vision of Bridger and Belle, my two loves, waiting for me.

Life is very, very good.

At Bridger's insistence, I've "retired" from waitressing at The Wicked Horse. He doesn't want me there on my feet all night. He's offered me the option of staying home with Belle, finding a job more suitable for his woman, or going to school—a prospect I'd never considered before.

I chose school.

Cosmetology school to be precise. Our girls' poker night has turned into girls' mani-pedi night as I practice my newfound skills on my girls. More often than not, Bridger lurks around on girls' night and that's because he lurks around most nights. He's given up keeping a careful watch over The Silo, preferring to let Cain take over, and he has actually been talking about bringing him on as a partner.

But even though Bridger doesn't go there often, it doesn't mean he doesn't go there.

He does.

With me.

We don't go a lot, but we do pop in every once in a while, and let me tell you… the things that man does to me when his imagination is fueled by such a deviant atmosphere is almost too overwhelming to handle. It's why we don't go often, as I just don't know that my heart could take that type of excitement on a frequent basis.

For the most part, Bridger and I have become home-bodies, preferring to spend our time quietly hiking on the ranch with Belle, cooking together, or reading the paper over a lazy breakfast. Every night is when we really come together, just the two of us, and in every touch given and every word spoken, we reaffirm our love for each other.

Just like I'm getting ready to do in front of our family and friends.

I take a step toward Bridger and Belle, measuring my

stride to the tune of the "Wedding March". Bridger and Belle look at me as I walk down the aisle. I watch as he inclines his head to my daughter, whispering something that's meant only for her to hear. She grins from ear to ear. He turns his focus back on me and his eyes are blistering with excitement, love, and pure happiness.

I smile back at him and hold his gaze the entire time I traverse the distance between us.

When I reach him, he switches Belle to his opposite hip, never once thinking about putting her down, and steps in close to me, his arm snaking around my back. He gives my ass a quick squeeze, causing everyone behind us to snicker, and then pulls me tight to his side.

Adrian stands in front of us and gives Bridger a chastising look before he looks past us and says, "Dearly beloved, we are gathered here together…"

Bridger turns his head and looks down at me, the same exact moment I turn and look up at him.

He grins and whispers. "Love you, Mags."

"Love you too."

Bridger

I WATCH AS Maggie tears up the dance floor with her girls—Callie, Sloane, Cat, and Auralie—and Christ, my wife has some moves. I shouldn't be surprised because the things she can do with those hips are beyond astounding.

My wife.

Doesn't seem strange at all to me.

In fact, it feels rather perfect.

Someone moves into my line of sight. I look up to see Aunt Gayle standing there, holding a sleeping Belle. I stand up, lean my head to the side to see her little face, and grin at how peaceful she looks as she slumbers away on Gayle's shoulder.

"Randall and I are going to take Belle back to your house," Gayle says in a whisper, despite the fact that some loud dance pop bullshit is playing right now. "We'll see you there later tonight."

"Okay," I say, putting my hand on Belle's head before I lean in and kiss her cheek. Then I give Gayle a wink. "But don't wait up for us."

Gayle laughs before she turns to the dance floor and heads over to break up the dance party so Maggie can say goodnight to her daughter.

Well, strike that… our daughter.

I've got an attorney working to get Zeke's parental rights terminated so I can adopt her, but regardless if that happens, she's my daughter too. Gayle and Randall volunteered to stay with Belle so Maggie and I can take a real honeymoon. We're heading to Hawaii tomorrow for ten days of sun, surf, and a whole lot of dirty fucking.

I sit back down in my chair and watch as Maggie stops dancing to give Belle a kiss before doing the same to her aunt. Her parents didn't come to the wedding, and that's because they weren't invited. Maggie made overtures to them, but they're being a little unforgiving that she would dare to have done something so stupid as to put them in danger.

Maybe they'll come around, maybe not. Doesn't matter because she has a new family now.

I turn to see Adrian taking a seat beside me. We're silent for a while, watching the girls dancing again, but now they're joined by their men. Cain, Logan, Woolf, and Rand all out there boogying without any dignity or skills. Maggie turns to look at me and waves cheerily, but she doesn't beckon me out there. I told her I'd give her whatever her heart desired for a wedding—turns out she wanted a traditional church service with Adrian marrying us and a small party after—but I told her the one thing I absolutely would not do was dance except for slow songs with her.

She immediately granted that wish, more than happy to get her church service and me stuffed into a tuxedo.

"I'm so proud of you, Bridger," Adrian says beside me.

"I did good, didn't I?" I ask, my eyes drinking in Maggie.

He knows I'm talking about Maggie, and Maggie alone.

"She's your soul mate in every sense of the word," Adrian says, but then in a wise voice that Adrian has perfected on me over the years, which means I straighten up and really put on my listening ears, he says, "But I mean I'm proud of the man you've become. You're caring, generous, and loyal to your friends. You're fair, honest, and protective of what's yours. If I were to have a son, I'd want him to be just like you."

And fuck... that gets me choked up. I turn to look at him, not even abashed by the wet in my eyes. "We may not be related by blood, Adrian, but you're the father who was taken away from me too soon. God gave me a second chance with you."

Adrian's own eyes mist up, and he nods at me.

"I love you," I tell him, and I'm surprised it's the first time I've laid those words on his doorstep. Just like when I told Maggie that for the first time and it was oh so fucking easy, I have to marvel that it's taken me this long to say it to the man who saved me in every sense of the word.

"I love you too, Bridger," he says, and then his eyes cut back to Maggie. "So, how about you two get started on giving me another grandchild?"

He means "another" because he already considers Belle to be his granddaughter.

"Already ahead of you," I say without taking my eyes off Maggie. I'm only forced to tear my gaze away from my wife when Adrian's hand clamps down on my shoulder.

He stares at me with shock and awe on his face. "She's pregnant?"

"Yup," I say, beaming. "Two months."

"No wonder you wanted a fast wedding," Adrian says with a grin.

"Nah…" I wave him off. "I would have married her a hell of a lot sooner, but these things apparently take some planning. The pregnancy wasn't a big surprise because we got rid of her IUD pretty soon after we got back together."

"A baby," Adrian says in wonder. "I hope it's a boy."

"I hope it's like Maggie," I add on, and he laughs.

As if she can sense she's being talked about, Maggie abruptly stops spinning and turns our way. I crook my finger at her, and that's all it takes. She leaves her posse on the dance floor, picks up her dress, and runs barefoot to me. She ditched her high heels an hour ago.

Maggie throws herself onto my lap, swinging her legs toward Adrian so she can look at him. "Thank you again, Adrian. The ceremony was everything I'd hoped it would be."

"My pleasure, Mags," he says, and I love how Adrian has picked up my special nickname for her.

"I told Adrian you're pregnant," I say as I lean in and kiss her neck. It's moist with sweat from dancing, and I flick my tongue against her skin.

She shudders and leans into me, but addresses Adrian. "If it's a boy, we're going to name him Adrian."

I lean my chin on Maggie's shoulder and watch as Adrian's eyes get wet again.

"And," I say, reaching a hand out and gripping his shoulder, "if it's a girl, we're going to name her Adrienne."

With a choked voice, Adrian stammers, "I'm honored."

I start getting choked up myself again and squeeze Maggie harder. As if sensing that the men folk are the ones who wear the panties in this conversation, Maggie jumps off my lap. She spins and gives me a quick kiss before she pulls Adrian out of his seat. "Come on, Adrian. Come dance with us."

Adrian laughs and follows her out on the dance floor, proceeding to show all the young ones just how it's done. Maggie bumps and grinds and twirls around with happiness, her eyes coming to rest on me more than once. I smile back at her, imagine more than once peeling her out of that dress, and not for the first time since Maggie took me back, I utter up a small prayer of thanks to God for seeing fit to give me an amazing life.

If you enjoyed *Wicked Bond* as much as I enjoyed writing it, it would mean a lot for you to give me a review on your favorite retailer's website.

Connect with Sawyer online:

Website: www.sawyerbennett.com

Twitter: www.twitter.com/bennettbooks

Facebook: www.facebook.com/bennettbooks

Other Books
by Sawyer Bennett

The Off Series
Off Sides

Off Limits

Off The Record

Off Course

Off Chance

Off Season

Off Duty

The Last Call Series
On The Rocks

Make It A Double

Sugar On The Edge

With A Twist

Shaken Not Stirred

The Legal Affairs Series
Legal Affairs Sneak Peek (FREE)

Legal Affairs

Confessions of a Litigation God

Clash: A Legal Affairs Story (Book #1 of Cal and Macy's Story)

Grind: A Legal Affairs Story (Book #2 of Cal and Macy's Story)

Yield: A Legal Affairs Story (Book #3 of Cal and Macy's Story)

Friction: A Legal Affairs Novel

Stand Alone Titles

If I Return

Uncivilized

Love: Uncivilized

The Sugar Bowl Series

Sugar Daddy

Sugar Rush

Sugar Free

The Cold Fury Hockey Series
(Random House / Loveswept)

Alex

Garrett

Zack

Ryker

Hawke

Max

Roman

4 Book Bundle – Alex, Garrett, Zack, Ryker

The Wicked Horse Series

Wicked Fall

Wicked Lust

Wicked Need

Wicked Ride

Wicked Bond

About the Author

Since the release of her debut contemporary romance novel, Off Sides, in January 2013, Sawyer Bennett has released more than 30 books and has been featured on both the USA Today and New York Times bestseller lists on multiple occasions.

A reformed trial lawyer from North Carolina, Sawyer uses real life experience to create relatable, sexy stories that appeal to a wide array of readers. From new adult to erotic contemporary romance, Sawyer writes something for just about everyone.

Sawyer likes her Bloody Mary's strong, her martinis dirty, and her heroes a combination of the two. When not bringing fictional romance to life, Sawyer is a chauffeur, stylist, chef, maid, and personal assistant to a very active toddler, as well as full-time servant to two adorably naughty dogs. She believes in the good of others, and that a bad day can be cured with a great work-out, cake, or a combination of the two.

16695502R00220

Printed in Poland
by Amazon Fulfillment
Poland Sp. z o.o., Wrocław